Also by James D. McCallister

KING'S HIGHWAY
FELLOW TRAVELER

Let the Glory
Pass Away

Let The Glory Pass Away

A Novel
James D. McCallister

Mind Harvest Press
COLUMBIA, SC

For more information:

Mind Harvest Press
PO Box 50552
Columbia SC 29250-0552
www.mindharvestpress.com
www.jamesdmccallister.com

First Printing, 2016
Printed in the United States of America
Designed by MarcCardwell.com
"Dixiana" Illustration by Patrick Mahoney/Totally Mundo
Productions

ISBN:(ppbk) 978-1-946052-00-1

Library of Congress Control Number: 2016920281

*Columbia will have bitter cause to remember the visit of
Sherman's army. Even if peace and prosperity soon return
to the land, not in this generation or the next—no, not for
a century—can this city or this state recover from the deadly
blow which has taken its life.*

—Major George Ward Nichols, aide-de-camp to
General William Tecumseh Sherman

Part One:
IMPOSTOR SYNDROME

1.

Who could have guessed that the beautiful sky greeting downtown Columbia, South Carolina as the first annual CityArt Festival began would later unleash with such ferocity? By afternoon, the azure clarity of the springtime morning transformed into a foreboding mass of storm clouds, like mysterious bruises found on alcoholic shins upon awakening from a screaming blue bender.

On one memorably historic occasion, fire had cleansed this fair city of its sins. Now, as I stood beneath a white canvas pop-up tent with several other local authors of note watching the weather deteriorate, I pondered whether the coming deluge of water and wind foretold yet another apocalyptic force of destruction.

This time, however, the whole city would not fall. Only a dear friend. Bad enough that my career felt ready to be interred, but losing my principal advocate and cheerleader to a sudden heart attack tasted of icing on a cake gone stale and sour. Losing Leora's life felt for a time like losing my own. Springtime had never felt so autumnal.

When I first allowed Leora Wood-Cobb to browbeat me into resuming an active part in the arts scene in Columbia, South Carolina, I'd have laughed if someone had revealed that in a little over two months' time she'd be stone dead. That's life for you. There, and then not. I'd lived it on a most personal level. The tragedy of Leora, far from my first roundup at El Rancho de los Muertos. But one that would dig down deep.

Much money and dignity on the line—Leora had had to grovel and scrape to put together the event, which had been attended by only a smattering of interested area art patrons. Around these parts, you need football or pulled pork to draw the mass of multitudes, or maybe a Free Beer sign like in that old Warner Brothers cartoon about the singing frog—hell, even the crowds on Confederate Memorial Day at the State House are smaller in this, one of the few American cities to have been burned to the ground in warfare, and for reasons ranging from accidental to necessarily sacrificial, even symbolic, if you will. A ruinous arts project, of a sort, the burning. Able to be read on a variety of levels that reveal potential dimensions of meaning within meaning.

Like Leora's death, a multilayered, benchmark milestone in my own life.

Good opening for a novel, perhaps. She'd love the idea of me taking notes for one.

Again.

At last.

Poor Leora, plugging away a long time at this advocacy stuff. Forty years. Tornado or not, I suppose she had been at the end of her road.

Stress, a killer.

As well in this case a killer instance of irony: the purpose of expressing ourselves through art exists not only as a primary method of personal fulfillment, but also as relief from the anxieties and banality of our daily struggle to survive. Art exists to celebrate our aliveness, in fact. Certainly not to occasion tragedy.

No amount of art-making, of course, could have prepared me for standing huddled in the towering NetBank lobby with dozens of Columbia's most prominent citizens watching hailstones clatter and wind and rain whipping sideways between the buildings, Leora's blouse torn open and flesh exposed as two EMTs zapped her frail, slight chest with the paddles of an AEG. A final indignity, her nakedness—one no more deserved than any other aspect of the failed arts festival. Her pale body, arching, but with what I grew to understand were death-spasms rather than resurrection.

Another day on the job: I heard one of the EMTs say all too casually, "If we can get her back, let's take her to Providence, not Baptist." The latter only a block or two away, but the former, at two miles distance, represented the more reputable heart center. "Sound good?"

"Yep. Hit her again."

But she didn't come back.

Stillness.

Horror.

An awful groan swept through the assemblage like that of an audience disappointed by Leora's final public performance. I averted my eyes and held onto Marcy, a local singer-songwriter I'd been courting.

My emotions roiling like the storm clouds, I struggled to stem the tide of my grief.

Outside, the actual storm had passed. Sunlight too bright to fathom flooded back into downtown Columbia, the glass faces of the buildings staring upon the grim scene sunstruck with implacable indifference.

Sunbeams to bear Leora Wood-Cobb away from us, perhaps?

To her final reward? An arts angel, borne away. But not too far, I hoped.

That blustery day Columbia lost more than its longtime arts doyenne: the community sang fare-you-well to a decent and well-rounded human being, as well as a dear friend who wanted only to stoke the stove of public recognition for the talent and beauty and creative spark inherent in the citizenry of her home state.

Devoted her life to the idea.

To the end.

On a crisp and cool morning a few weeks before that dark April day, I met Leora for lunch, saw her spirited and spritely, engaging in what she did best: friendly persuasion. For decades, she'd been the chairperson and administrator of the Council on the Performing Arts, a government agency charged with supporting arts-related activities in South Carolina—in fact, to most people in and out of the scene, Leora Wood-Cobb *was* COPA. As such, she knew how to lobby. Here, she pitched the idea of my participation on a committee of some sort. I supposed it regarded the upcoming CityArt Festival, which I'd only heard about through unofficial channels.

I asked what on earth a drudge and dullard like me could possibly offer her. Picking at leaf-lettuce dressed with self pity. Feeling like a fraud. Dreading the question about what I'd been writing. When I'd have something new to say. Pages worth printing. The answer, elusive.

"This city needs you, Cort. It needs your expertise. Your voice." Leora, making one of her characteristic diminutive karate-chops for emphasis. "It hungers for your astute and experienced worldview."

"Nice to be needed. But if I end up abusing someone, don't say I didn't warn you."

"'Abusing someone'? Gracious. Where's that coming from?"

I wasn't sure. For the last couple of years I hadn't done much communicating with the human species on any meaningful level. That I sat lunching with Leora Wood-Cobb that late winter's day seemed novel in itself, a small miracle of social interaction. "Just a writer being melodramatic."

"Save the drama, Cort. Please. Or at least save it for dessert."

"Yes, ma'am."

I'd met my old friend on the main drag in the college ghetto they called the Old Market, once a place of horse barns and the commerce of the antebellum day, as had been Charleston's own City Market: a trade in human souls that had unfortunately defined our economy and culture for so long. Surrounded as we were by students of all races studying and old men playing chess and philosophers adjudicating interpretations of reality at the hippest of several coffee bars serving the sprawling, greater Southeastern University area, the time of bondage and torture seemed far in the past.

As it is.

A relief. South Carolina seemed like America, now. With quirk and personality, of course. Ask Jon Stewart and Stephen Colbert—hell, Colbert is from here. He'd know.

The thought of sitting on an arts advisory committee, or whatever it was she'd called me there to pitch that day, however, caused a rock in the gut. "Haven't a clue what I could bring to such an endeavor, other than eagerness to be released from whatever obligations come with the presumptive honor. My patience with the outside world is as gossamer as the wings of a fairy."

"First the drama, and now the dialogue. Reserve it for your characters, would you?" Leora, surly, gnashed her iceberg lettuce and became choked. "Think of this as a favor to your old friend," wheezing and waving for the server to bring more water. "For your dear old Leora."

"Calling in a debt?" A smile. "You little devil."

"Perhaps. If we must be so blunt." The server topped off her glass. Leora chugged until breathless. "But nobody's keeping score. I hope."

"You'll get no debate from me there. Only gratitude."

She smiled, waiting. Leora, knowing she could call in any number of markers.

Acquiescent. "I live to serve. I draw no line perhaps short of a contract killing—unless it's a political assassination, of course. I might have that in me."

"Don't tempt me, my boy."

"She's quite something, our fearless leader."

"Better change the subject. If you can't say anything nice about someone . . ."

Governor Sandy Three-Rivers, a drown government in the bathtub right-winger, appeared so far in her first term as no friend to lefty partisans like Leora, who happened to be a state government employee. One didn't even joke about such extreme matters as murder, of course, but I'd heard that COPA could be completely cut out of the next state budget. That meant no more Leora to advocate for the arts. No more grants, no more community outreach programs. The idea made me want to retch. I could well imagine how Leora felt about it.

Terrified about a political element, I managed to ask what this arts committee's charge would entail. Her answer left me flabbergasted: not lobbying for arts money, but rather facilitating the installation of a permanent, public tribute to a still-living, famous rock musician who hailed from the city.

"You want me to sit on something called the Duncan Devereaux Committee? To plan the placement of, what? A statue? To a heavy metal guitarist? Surely you jest."

"Hardly. He's the most significant cultural figure to have emerged from the midlands of South Carolina in the late twentieth century."

My turn to choke on the iceberg lettuce.

She explained that the city and the Downtown Business Alliance, a nonprofit advocacy group and neighborhood association serving the Main Street and Old Market commercial districts, had decided to erect a monument to Devereaux, a musician who embodied Columbia's principal contribution to mainstream pop culture history. "Not a statue, but yes, a piece of public art. A sculpture, let's say. In any case, a loving and appreciative tribute to one of our own."

I grunted. Popular music's not my 'thing,' as they say—my aesthetic preferences run less to the Devereaux end of the spectrum than the Dvořák. My mom raised me to have what one might call a refined ear. I'd rather drift along to the ethereal beauty and sadness of Chopin or Schumann than the harsh heavy metal of Duncan Devereaux. To me his métier presented a genre coarse and brutal, one fostering in its adherents a condition less of aesthetic critical approbation than cases of pervasive tinnitus. In my view, the jury would be long out before the rock musicians of the world got the privilege of having their statues. Ah, the precious ego, protecting itself by declaring Mine to be the POV of POVs.

But still: "To be frank? The idea seems fairly ridiculous. The man's band was called 40DD. Doesn't a feminist like you find that terribly gauche?"

"Of course I do. But not only did he grow as an artist, Duncan got his start right here," tapping with a manicured talon of metallic pearl on the tabletop at the Carolina Beanery Café.

"Here? At this coffee shop?"

She shot me a look: silly boy. "You know his story as well as any of us."

"Guilty." While in the throes of my own ascendant literary stardom, relative in scale as it was, I'd interviewed the rocker for an article published in a national magazine. Had helped sell a few of my own books.

In other words: another debt.

Argh.

So, yes, I knew the story as well as anybody: Sure, the midlands of South Carolina had produced such notables as jazzman Dizzy Gillespie, the smooth-voiced soulful romantic throat of Brook Benton, and an authentic and quirky blues legend in Drink Small; but, Duncan Devereaux, who'd been a chart-topping sensation in the late 80s and early 90s, attained true notoriety, if for no other unfortunate reason than a disastrous concert at which a number of his fans were crushed to death. Nothing begets a legend like becoming super–famous only to then disappear in a puff of tragedy. For fifteen years now, few other than his neighbors down on exclusive and wealthy Sedge Island have reported glimpsing him in public.

No new music. No concerts.

No new art.

A pop-culture ghost.

My antennae wiggled. Maybe this would be interesting after all.

As the server cleared the remnants of our salads, Leora could see from my expression, however, that I needed further convincing. "What this city wishes to do is acknowledge his enormous contribution to the arts. His having put Columbia on the map in a manner that most of us can only dream of having accomplished. One of our own—like you."

Catty son of a gun that I can be: "Since when do we build monuments to people who've merely sold a pile of records?"

Matching my snark: "At least be thankful it isn't a committee to put up a statue of a football coach."

True-dat, as the kids say.

"Still . . . Devereaux's catalog isn't exactly considered high art, even by music lovers. Not the music lovers I know."

At Leora's disappointed scowl, I knew I needed to find a more conciliatory spirit within the crusty shell of my cynicism. "World fame's an accomplishment worth acknowledging, one supposes. But still, why me?"

"Cort, don't you understand? You're the one out of all of us who actually knows him. That's why we need you—that's why I need you."

Busted.

Truth: As an emerging writer around the same time Double-D began to hit it big, I'd been hired by the local alt weekly to pen a cover story, complete with interview. Despite having heard not a note of the man's music, I eagerly agreed.

A rising local star. Thought I'd grab hold of his sparkling, luminous trail.

You know what they say about opportunity.

When his tour landed at good old Collegiate Coliseum, the show he put on for his hometown was a mindblower, a triumphal, orgiastic musical experience—for his fans, that is. This chronicler's takeaway had not only been a well-received profile of the rock star, but a case of jangled nerves and distorted hearing. I spent the next three days going around shouting at everyone.

I'd gotten more than a good article out of the aural torture: My interview with Duncan had been rich and interesting enough to rewrite and sell to none other than *Rolling Stone* magazine, which I will admit sold a few of my own books. Evidence of this work may be seen preserved under glass in a permanent Columbia Public Library exhibit of works by local writers and artists next to the cover of the autobiographical novel that kickstarted my career, *Keys to the Rain*, which one waggish reviewer likened to 'Bret Easton Ellis filtered through a genteel, Southern aristocratic lens,' and which another called 'Holden Caulfield transported to a 1970s Southern small town.' Not too shabby.

Leora's principal mistake in choosing me for her Devereaux committee, came not in judging my ability to discern an appropriate tribute to our homegrown music superstar, but rather in the presumptive access I offered, my actual value to her. For all its merits, you see, the finished article constituted a bit of a naughty fraud:

The DD profile had been written in a manner that might lead one toward the impression that I was more than journalist—even, by the end of the four thousand words, an actual friend to the rocker—but it simply wasn't so. We had clicked that weekend, sure: Duncan, a well-read English major who dreamed of one day writing a great novel to match his music industry success—wasn't that enough, for heaven's sake?—turned out to be nothing like his swaggering, hard-rock image. A nice guy, intellectually curious.

The overall experience, however, had been a glimpse into a distasteful world I felt I could never fully understand. Maybe that's why I've never written a rock star novel.

After the piece had run in *Rolling Stone*, I received a lovely, handwritten thank you note from the rock god, but in the years since, I'd heard nothing from him.

So, as I explained to Leora, yes, I would serve, but I wasn't friends with Devereaux, and hadn't spoken with him since long before his retirement from the music business, which had been for devastating reasons that anyone could understand: some of the fans who'd so loved him had paid for their loyalty with their lives, and before his rock-star eyes. An accident, yes, but the responsibility, as he'd said in his final interview regarding the tragedy, had been too much to bear.

I remember well the above-the-fold headline in the *Columbia Record*:

Devereaux Draws Curtain on Two Decades of Music
Homegrown Fans Devastated By Star's Retirement

Tragic and awful. All I had truly felt at the time, however, had been a twinge of annoyance that the reporter hadn't sought me out for a comment—didn't I make for a local expert?

Of course not.

On the sidewalk outside the coffee shop, I continued to insist to Leora that I held no secret of access into Duncan Devereaux's world.

Pleading. "We're desperate for his imprimatur on the idea. Surely there's a way."

Dogged, that Leora—a quality I'd heretofore always admired.

"I suspect Devereaux's happy enough in his relative anonymity without someone building a statue to celebrate a career from which he's lived in hiding. I don't think he's given an interview in years, much less had to deal with the kind of attention this is going to bring."

"We understand that this may be an obstacle."

"There it is, then."

Leora's normally sunny face clouded, a hard crease appearing between her gray, wiggling eyebrows. "Well, whether or not we get his stamp of approval, this project's going forward." Snippy. "And for that matter, without your approval either, Cortland. Respectfully."

"As it should be."

"But look," she confided, lowering her voice, "this is going to be a full-blown piece of public art, one that will do proud not simply

Duncan Devereaux and his great contribution to the arts, but the city itself, and all of South Carolina. In the way that you made us all proud. With your wonderful novels and stories."

I caved. Leora, she knew how to work me. Got to give her that. "I'm duly honored by all this, dear. But I'm not sure I can open doors any easier than you."

She asked that I please try; a carrot, dangled, came in her offer of my participation in an open-air arts bazaar and concert Leora and the other organizers were calling CityArt, the inaugural multidisciplinary gathering of art-makers and concomitant, curious and appreciative art lovers there on Main Street, in the shadow of the capitol and our modest row of skyscrapers.

A new tradition for an old town, as she put it; a greeting to the coming spring, a symbol of both nature's rebirth, as well as the modern incarnation, in her view, of the vibrant city that Columbians of artistic aspiration have always dreamed.

"What do you say?"

Noble; graceful; classy. I hugged her, said I'd do my best. For her, for the committee, and for my home, Columbia.

2.

Wishing I'd found a tactful way to bow out of this obligation, I made the drive back to my secluded home on the northwest side of the city. With the feel of a mountain hollow, Cypress Creek boasts densely forested, undeveloped rolling land. Secluded but convenient, it's always five degrees cooler than anywhere else in this county, even in the summer. A little hideaway from the world, accessible by the highway that's nearer by than the vibe of isolation down in this peaty bottomland would suggest.

Perfect for a writer in search of solitude.

As I thought through the narrative of my relationship with this rock legend and navigated the curves of the county road, I found myself contemplating the idea of mining Duncan Devereaux's story for fiction, what I realized was the first spark I'd had in ages for a new story.

I nearly motored onto the shoulder.

An actual new idea?

Mercy. A watershed moment, at least a drizzle from the sky that might dampen the fallow, barren ground of my writing; a sprinkle from the headwaters of creativity that could grow into a river, a mighty, raging torrent of words flowing to their terminus, a completed manuscript.

A man can dream.

Did I desire to renew my creativity to say I was writing? To make an artistic statement? Heaven forbid—for money? Of course not. Like any artist worth his salt, I write because I love the process. Always have.

A writer, even one who has already tasted success, needs motivation, however. As well as something to say. Not sure that I possessed much of either, but desire, always the first step on the road to success.

Free of student papers and knowing that I'd need a new project to fill the summer months following the end of the school term, I cruised into my office and began typing what would become the crucial and exciting first scene of a novel that I might never experience the pleasure of seeing to its conclusion. Any writing would do for this creative beggar—for the last year or three, fresh pages had appeared about as often as the legendary Lizard Man, South Carolina's rarely glimpsed version of Bigfoot.

I've been dry, a writer bereft of text, since about the time the door-knob to the bathroom broke, back around the time my neighbor's house caught fire and burned, not that any of that makes sense out of context. In any case, I hoped that my fraudulence didn't come off as rankly and pathetically obvious to my students as it did to me.

The morning I met with Leora it'd been spring break at Edgewater Technical College, where I teach American Literature, English composition, and two different writing workshops—if in a given semester the course generates enough interest. At a school like ETC, most of the kids are hoping to learn an actual useful trade, which I can assure that writing stories and novels, at least as a stand-alone career, is most assuredly not.

Having said that, one writes because one must. And, if I were going to prove anything to myself about how I've chosen to mark the days of my life, I had a book to write.

But then, I'd had one cooking before the neighbor's fire, pun intended.

The project? A long-held ambitious historical romance inspired by and intended as homage to the original South Carolina novelist and American giant of letters William Gilmore Simms, author of *The Scout*, *The Cassique of Kiawah*, and numerous other novels, stories, and poems, distinguished later in life as author of a first-hand newspaper series documenting the circumstances of the burning of Columbia; admittedly, a potentially biased document. Watching the fall of a prosperous and beautiful American city must surely have catalyzed high emotions.

We can but only imagine.

Who ought to be a member of the pantheon of giants of American letters, Simms is instead marginalized and all but forgotten. Considering how the corpus of national literature is taught, the average student would be hard pressed to realize the fact that perhaps the first American author to actually make a living from his writing hailed from South Carolina.

My manuscript, which sought to remedy this grave and pernicious omission through the portrayal of Simms as the main character, remains unfinished—in fact, unwritten to any substantive degree at all.

I'll get back to it. Soon. One day, maybe. Simms, a bit unreconstructed regarding the circumstances of the Civil War, slavery, race, and so on. Perhaps reputations were sometimes better left in obscurity.

The research is there, of course, on the hard drive and in the notebooks, most having to do with the burning of the city rather than with Simms's life itself; oh, the afternoons spent reading Emma LeConte's diary of the lead-up and aftermath of Sherman's March, or in deep perusal of additional period minutia in the South Caroliniana Library or the Edgewater County Archives. The comfortable bosom of research, a womblike life to which it's easy to become addicted.

But no novel.

No matter—with all that research, I could revisit UNTITLED SC PERIOD ROMANCE any time I pleased.

If I had the fire in the belly.

Ha ha.

Another problem: Hadn't a book by Margaret Mitchell already covered this milieu quite memorably and indelibly?

Undeniable.

A revelation, this, one morning in the midst of taking notes—I considered that *Gone With the Wind* had likely deterred other scribes from using the burning of Columbia, an afterthought compared to that which had been depicted by Mitchell. As well, E. L. Doctorow—no literary slouch—also set a substantial portion of his award-winning Sherman saga *The March* in Columbia, and had gotten away with it. Why not my own take? As a South Carolinian? Like Simms?

Had I anything to add? Any elucidation to offer?

Eh.

Crickets.

Such hubris, to think I had anything to add to one of the key symbolic episodes of the Civil War. At that point I realized I'd become caught in a creative sinkhole.

The booth at the CityArt Festival was a bone thrown to me by Leora for my service on the Duncan Devereaux Committee. I accepted this fact. When she called the next morning to give me the particulars, she said she could see in my eyes at our lunch that the news I'd gotten from her the month before—that I wouldn't be a featured author at Book Expo this year—had needled me.

A buttery tone, an attempt to assuage my hurt: "But we'd be so terribly overjoyed to have you as part of *this* event, the first annual in what we hope is a *long series* of CityArt festivals. In fact, I *cannot imagine* putting on such an event without the participation of Cortland Beauchamp."

"I'm duly honored," and I meant it. "I'll be there."

"Now, this appearance, how shall we promote it? In support of *The Collapse of Language*, I presume?"

She knew damn well I didn't have a new book out. "I suppose so."

What she didn't know, or anyone else besides my last editor, Josie-Anne Merkowitz, was that this musty, stale story collection, published three long years ago, didn't stand as a fresh exemplar of the current state of my writing career and life, but instead had been cobbled together from material that'd been as much as twenty-five years old, stories produced back in the golden age of daily output that'd resulted in my various successes.

Another fraud.

That I needed to sell.

"Yes, still have a few boxes of *Collapse* in the garage that haven't been pulped yet. And I have the cover poster and my easel at the ready. Dusty, but ready."

"Ha-ha-yes, of course you do." Ringing off with the utmost of grace and gratitude, she said she'd see me tomorrow at my first DDC meeting.

Perhaps my civic obligation had already yielded a benefit—maybe I'd sell some books at this CityArt thingy. That, I told myself, would constitute the upside here.

Or maybe I'd find inspiration for this new book I'd started. Better than sitting around the cabin, alone, reading or sifting through an online cascade of the daily depressing news, ostensibly looking for clipping-file material, but finding only the same political back-and-forth, the same murders, the usual outrages. A big fat bore.

The next morning I tried to re-familiarize myself with the music of Duncan Devereaux, which I attempted by watching YouTube videos of several of his seminal works, the 40DD canon, but only for a very few excruciating minutes before relieving my eardrums of their dissonant, grating burden.

I got it, I got it—heavy, strident rock'n roll with suggestive lyrics and thumping bass lines and howling banshees in the form of endless guitar solos. Yes, yes, yes—I remember the concert I attended, perhaps all too well.

In the car, I got back to my preferred genre with Mendelssohn's *Hebrides* overture and motored south to downtown and the main branch of the county library, where my committee was set to meet. At a succession of red lights I squinted at my iPhone and scanned through the introductory email regarding the mission of our advisory committee.

The location of the public art piece had already been chosen, at least: a prominent downtown corner near the museum. This had been predetermined following what in the email were termed 'private discussions' between Leora, Felicity Belinda ('Feebee') Elmendorf of the influential municipal advocacy organization known as the Downtown Business Alliance, and City Services Coordinator Mandy Polk-Richardson, who will sit representing the concerns and possibilities of how the local government will facilitate, allow, or disavow various details regarding the street art's feasibility. Other members seemed to be involved in the staging of a concert event that I mused would include the performing of the dreadful heavy classic rock music of our honoree. But, again, just what my job would be beyond providing a familiar ambassadorial face to the musician remained a mystery.

I hoped not much—I needed to be writing.

Anyone, I supposed, could be duly proud of Columbia having produced an accomplished and well-known, if troubled and reclusive, rock legend. Skeptical that the vast majority of South Carolina citizens would consider Devereaux's so-called music to be aesthetically pleasing much less worthy of such tribute, I assumed these activities would be underwritten by the city itself. Taxpayer dollars, doled out. Wasn't that how it all worked?

What would penny-pinching Governor Three-Rivers—a would-be Native American politician who looked more like the bottle-blonde former newsreader she was—think of our little scheme? At least we weren't trying to put a statue on the State House grounds next to Pitchfork Ben or Strom Thurmond. Then we'd be wading into the culture wars big-time, wouldn't we. The city itself leaned heavily "blue," however. Hell, City Council wanted this thing. No worries on the political side there.

Except maybe when it came to money.

It always came to money. Didn't it?

Tee-hee.

I arrived only minutes later at the sparkling and award-winning municipal library at which the committee was to meet, and due to the modest downtown traffic I found myself a solid twenty minutes early. The dossier of names comprising my fellow committee members had contained a familiar one or two that I either knew personally or had at least heard of, had seen their names in the *Columbia Record* that I've read every morning for most of my life, now on an iPad. I foolishly and naively bought the first iteration of the tablet device, bulky and cameraless compared to the 2.0 version which came out a year later.

Rick Wragg, a techie and gear-head I know, had chuckled as he saw me stabbing at the tablet with my tentative digit. Told me I had a bad case of what he termed early adoption, one of those who must be the first on their block to own the newest toys. Rick was a DDC member and acquaintance, whose company had provided the A/V support for the SC Book Expo, whom I got to know by hanging around backstage, so to speak, over the years. I told him the device had reminded me so much of the handheld computers that crew members on the TV show *Star Trek: The Next Generation* used while walking around on the bridge in their vibrant spandex uniforms—a series, I further elaborated, that comprised part of my guilty-pleasure penchant for cheesy science fiction—my one sop to what I'd normally consider lowbrow pop culture unworthy of scrutiny or time. When the tablets came out, I simply had to have one.

The future—it had arrived. Almost as though the television had predicted it.

Books, to cover the past.

Moving images, to predict the future.

Music, to put us in the moment.

Talking to Rick Wragg about my little theory at last year's Book Expo, and about my pathetic first-gen iPad, he derided my early adoption, called me an easy lay; I replied that neither advertisement nor a need to be a competitive consumer hadn't swayed my purchase; that I wasn't quite so softheaded.

"Oh, no question," grinning a devilish, bullshitter's smile. "Famous writer and all. Not softheaded. But an easy lay."

And laughing it off, sudden, before I could argue further, grabbing me by the meat of the forearm and saying 'just kidding' over and over and hurtling onto the next subject, which is Rick's style—rapid-fire, mile-a-minute enthusiasm and ideas and what-ifs tumbling out of his mind and mouth, with no apparent distinction between the two realms. Rick, whom I picture running around at the Book Expo making sure sound reinforcement, as he called it, was top notch and clear as a bell. I supposed he knew about music, and how to listen to it; and that's why he sat on the DDC.

I stopped by the Congaree Local History room, and stood staring at my book cover and the *Rolling Stone* feature article beside it, my ear buds jammed in and humming along to the playfully dizzying, darting strings of Henri Vieuxtemps's Violin Concerto No. 3. I considered my work and pondered:

Did I write that? Do I remember doing so?

Do I remember how it felt to see my name in print, on a national magazine?

On a book cover?

Is this me?

One answer I seemed to have at hand: Staring at evidence of past glories had only made the current sense of failure that I felt all the more acute. No escape, except out into the stacks to browse, and a feeble attempt to forget myself.

3.

I stayed downstairs browsing for so long that I missed the beginning of the meeting.

But despite being late, the group barely noticed: I came bustling through the heavy glass doors to a round of uproarious laughter as Rick Wragg, the only one of the committee members on his feet in the plush library conference room, regaled the others with an anecdote from his time as a 'rigger,' show biz parlance for what I thought of as a stagehand, though this appellation underserves such a unionized, specialized trade. Rick, mugging and gesticulating, finished what sounded like a ribald tale of the touring rock'n roll life. Everyone laughed.

Leora, her mouth downturned—*you're late, you bad boy*—pointed to the one remaining seat next to Feebee Elmendorf, who beamed and proffered and looked starstruck, as she had the first time I'd met her back when *Collapse of Language* had been released to its piffle of fanfare. A welcoming, sheltering feeling of safety, this minor cascade of adulation.

A wicked voice whispered: *An impostor, you, greeted with love and respect by the easily duped. Pray that none of them asks what you're currently working on.*

Sitting around the table, the other notables onboard: Feebee, of course, and Mandy and Leora and Rick; a Columbia native named Goodman Champagne, wealthy owner of a chain of regional menswear outlets, a veteran of familiar late night TV commercials and whose wife, Melora, sat on City Council, the both of them ardent arts advocates and patrons; my friend and one-time lover Opal D'Alessandro, president of the Downtown Business Alliance and Feebee's nominal boss, a slightly uncomfortable glance between us; Doug 'Doober

Dougie' Wallace, Columbia's most infamous and beloved longtime local rock jock and car commercial voice talent, more significantly here the DJ who 'broke' Duncan Devereaux 'back in the day'; Elvin Lachicotte, a young arts critic for the *Columbia Record* that I knew, but only in passing, and noted as a good connection to make should I ever again have a new book to sell; and Gendry Lizette, a lovely, wide-eyed woman who seemed a touch shy and awkward, the only one of the players I didn't recognize in some form.

"Our superstar has arrived," Leora called to me from the end of the table. "Ladies and gentleman, I suspect that you all know the author Cortland Beauchamp. Welcome, Cort. We're just getting underway."

As I made my way around the room, murmuring and shaking hands, Feebee Elmendorf held out her arms. So bright and sunny she twinkled; she always wanted a hug.

"Mr. Beauchamp, how wonderfu—*EEEEEE*," she shrieked. Sliding into my seat I had put down a heavy foot, crunching what I came to understand were Feebee's toes, already distressed from their berth inside a pair of narrow stiletto power-heels. This set off a flurry of concern that disrupted the meeting long enough for me to now feel humiliated and self-conscious to the nth degree. Mortified, I found the words to apologize, but Feebee, eyes tearing with pain, still shone with her bright and professional enthusiasm.

"Quite an entrance—are you okay?"

"It's okay," she said with a wince. "Now we can get started."

I deserved that stinger—it meant they'd all been waiting.

Of all the committee members, only Opal seemed unmoved by my bumbling appearance; whenever our eyes met a warm glow rose inside me, as it always did when I saw her: Opal, a love who got away. Not *the* one, mind you. I wouldn't know that person if she came up and stepped on my foot as I had Feebee's. But Opal, how nice she'd been and how lovely it was; I still don't know what happened, but in any case that was that, and it's another story. Our relationship coincided with a time in which many daily hours were spent drinking my life and my mind away, quite a few at her restaurant's bar, and since sobering up, I hadn't been back.

"Hi."

"Hi," she whispered, a reluctant, secret smile sneaking onto her pointed chin. How I remembered the afterglow of our assignations, that chin resting in the hollow of my shoulder, her breath hot and steady against my skin.

Mercy. Sweating, I fanned myself.

Opal broke our gaze and took charge—running a busy, upscale restaurant, the woman knew how to clap her hands and get people moving. "Let me be the first to say thank you for coming, and I do know that we're all busy people, so: may we begin, please? Feebee?"

Feebee, massaging the injured foot, started going down the mission statement and agenda. This committee had been underway for some time, and all sorts of minutia had already been decided—besides the sculpture placement on a strategic downtown corner, a side street in the college neighborhood that's home to Slim Lupo's, still the longest operating rock club in town and first venue of note for 40DD, would undergo an honorary, permanent renaming as Duncan Devereaux Way. All would culminate in a street party and concert held on Main Street, utilizing a similar footprint to the upcoming CityArt Festival. All quite civilized and appropriate, made more so by Feebee's obvious preparation and professionalism.

I didn't even bother to open my Moleskine. "Y'all seem so far along. Not sure how I fit into this little scheme."

"Truthfully, Mr. Beauchamp?" Feebee, massaging her toes. "Our million small details are mostly in place. It's one particular detail we still need squared away."

Leora, grim, a portentous air. "A major detail."

It sank in: they still had zero response from Devereaux.

That damned article—these poor SOBs were trying to make me into some sort of dreadfully important linchpin because of it.

Whoa, whoa, whoa. I had to confess my fraudulence. "If you folks consider me a ringer, I can't deliver. It's not like it seemed in *Rolling Stone*. I'm not really—"

Feebee, her smile dimming. "A ringer?"

"An ace in the hole. In getting through to Mr. Devereaux."

Leora, patting me on the arm. "Cort, you're the one out of all of us who *actually knows him*."

"It's kinda true." Doober Dougie, sounding as though he had post-nasal drip. "Dude was always like standoffish as heck. Shy artist type.

At first? He was like Jim Morrison when The Doors first started—he wouldn't face the audience."

"How sad." Gendry Lizette's eyes had pooled. "It was like he knew what was coming at RFK," shorthand for the football stadium that had been the site of the career-ending tragedy.

Silence. A bit mystical for the room, perhaps.

Elvin cleared his throat. "He certainly hasn't responded to interview requests I've made. It's frustrating. But if it's someone who knows him—look, I read your *RS* piece. I'm in awe of it—you put us right there backstage with Duncan Devereaux."

My heart pounded and my face flamed. Sweat trickled behind an ear that during the long winter of my creative dotage had begun to sprout stiff, gray hairs. "Acquainted is what I am with him, and two decades ago, at that."

Feebee, grabbing hold of my other sleeve. "Your modesty's adorable."

I mumbled that I'd try. The meeting turned to matters of materiel and money.

At this point eyeballs began to drift over in Mandy Polk-Richardson's direction, but her strained smile revealed little about the fiduciary cards she held. Like most cities, and people, for that matter, funding remained tight, especially in a heated political atmosphere surrounding the Governor's continued demagoguery over such divisive issues as public arts funding.

After further prodding: "The situation on the city funding is the same as before—we're still counting on you guys to come up with corporate matching sponsors for the Special Funding grant request that the H-Tax Committee approved. Nobody's budging beyond that." Mandy, shaking her head. "The mayor, now, he's taking a lot of heat for the EPA ruling on the water treatment plant. He's got to tread lightly," making lacquered-nail, fingertip footsteps across the agenda on the table in front of her. "Last thing he said to me today was, Mandy, you're gonna have to work with what you got on this Duncan thing."

Feebee, wrinkling her nose. She squeezed my forearm, some secret signal.

What—I was to get into outside fundraising, too? Not multiple assignments. The ninth circle of Hell. I stayed silent.

Next topic: selecting the actual piece of art from a number of sample sculptures solicited through that arm of Leora's COPA grant work, all interesting renderings in miniature of what would one day be a fifteen-foot installation, all displayed on a long shelf around which we stood gawking and bumping into one another.

"Perhaps a public competition to select the winning artist." Eyeing the *modellos,* as Leora called the pieces, all modernist and abstract to some degree, I swept my hand along the four submissions and spread my arms wide to the expectant, shining faces turning toward me. "Let the people of the city decide."

A wonderful idea, I thought. One immediately shot down by Feebee and Leora and one or two others, all citing the inexpert, inexact nature of holding a vote on art—by the general public, that is.

My egalitarianism found an advocate, however, in Rick, who launched into a motormouthed oration expressing pleasure in opening up the process to the general public who'd made Devereaux a star in the first place—a chance for ordinary folk to contribute to the creation of a permanent piece of sculpture, of street art, that would be seen by many thousands over its lifespan—nay, millions, in the aggregate.

Rick, a jittery, yeah-yeah chipmunk. When reaching to make a point, he contorted his limbs as though spastic. "Yep, yep, yep—think about this crazy idea, people. The American voters are like totally pitching in together on the thing."

"Please, let's not turn our event into one of those dreadful, so-called talent contests on primetime television." Leora, smiling at Rick in that way she did when speaking to some philistine lacking in knowledge of the art world, and How It All Worked. "A public competition would present a wicked, sticky wicket of a bugbear to administrate with any sense of fairness to the artists. I can't support it."

"Agreed, too-too unwieldy. Yikes." Feebee, younger than most at the table, had an energy and a fire in her eyes that I found unnerving. "I cannot get bogged down in managing an art competition—this committee will sleep on it, and we'll vote next time. Moving on," flipping over her agenda to page two, "we have yet to address the most *unknown* unknown-unknown." A smile, toothless and forced.

The grim trifecta of "unknowns" had caused a dramatic pall to settle over the room. Rick, refusing to meet my eyes. "Lay it on us, Feeb."

Every other face had turned not to Feebee, but toward me—yikes, indeed.

Leora, prissy. "Cort, we need more than Mr. Devereaux's sanction—we need him to attend the unveiling of the piece. And if possible, perhaps even play a tune or two."

Gendry Lizette swooned; Doober Dougie's eyes, red-rimmed, flew open as wide as they could; but Rick? Rick snorted and rapped the tabletop with his knuckles. "Fat chance."

"This could be it." Gendry, emphatic. "This could be the thing that gets him to come back out of his shell, Mr. Wragg. That's why it's so important to me, as a fan, that we do this."

A few beats of throat-clearing silence followed.

Leora, breaking the spell. "And that's why *you're* so important." She reached across to put her aging, arthritic hand on mine, as much of a squeeze as she could muster. "You're the person who's going to convince Mr. Devereaux to give us his blessing—and perhaps more. Isn't that so, Cortland?"

Panic. "But how? I don't even know him."

"Not this again—of course you do."

"That well. I mean."

Gulp. I felt like a guilty man on a hostile witness stand.

Oh, 'twas my own fault: In depicting the birth of what seemed like a true friendship, my new-journalistic piece on Devereaux had done its job too well. But that had all been a ruse, a conceit, an angle; what none of them realized, I guessed, was that journalism, however true it might be, could present only a faux-objective version of epistemological truth. This, a philosophical debate to be had with Elvin, should I ever get the chance.

"Speaking of that article—" Gendry, clumsy and shy, produced her own treasured copy, with its four thousand words of you-are-there breathless rock reporting under my byline, an enormous thrill at the time, but now? A vacuous, fraudulent bit of side-trip nonsense from when I was actually hungry enough to whore myself out like this.

She carefully extracted the magazine from its 4 mil heavy plastic archival protective sleeve, along with a fine-point, standard black

Sharpie. As I signed, I experienced a modicum of gut-guilt, or what a psychologist might classify as something like impostor syndrome.

What a production number, one designed to put me on the spot.

"Look, everyone—what I'm trying to say is, I really don't know him like it seems."

Rick: "Yeah? You know the cat better than any of us, ace. From what ya wrote all those years ago—"

"—but Rick—"

"—it's, what's the word, wordsmith? Incontriverti-able or whatever, that you're the only one out of this group who can pull this off."

Now everyone chimed in, heads nodding and faces insistent.

Leora, at her most pleased, purring as though she were my proud grandmother: "Cort's too modest, aren't you, my boy? He's always been that way."

I tried to answer, but found no spit. Instead I nodded, grinning and foolish, hoping they'd be able to find another way.

More than wanting to get out of this meeting, I gave in and pledged my allegiance to the cause over the complexity of trying to explain it all, that I couldn't help not because I didn't want to, but because I simply didn't want to bother the man with all this. How could I tell them no, though? I've always wanted people to like me, and if I refused, what would they think?

I will admit that the stupid crap that happened to me in adolescence has made me a little emotionally stunted. That's what I told Opal anyway, who in the meeting has remained eerily quiet, mostly looking at her phone and avoiding my licentious gaze that keeps wanting to drift over toward her lovely, red lips, the taste of which I'd never again enjoy. We drove each other nuts anyway. Ah, well.

All right. So I'll make a stab at contacting Double-D, and when it doesn't work, I'll say, that's-that and go back to my life of unfulfilled artistic solitude in the leafy woods around my cabin. Duncan Devereaux had experienced the shock of his life seeing his fans crushed to death, and knowing what sudden horrors can do to a body and a mind, the poor bastard had more than my sympathy—I halfway wanted to protect him from all this attention: If he wanted to stay out of the limelight, then by god we ought to let him. Nevertheless, I told them all that I'd try. How much of this constituted a white lie remained to be seen.

4.

As the meeting broke up, I sent a vibration toward Opal that she seemed willing to acknowledge, and she asked for me to wait to exit with her once she managed to drag herself away from Feebee, to whom Opal, as executive officer in the neighborhood association, stood in a supervisory position. The two huddled for an interim at the end of the long conference table, Feebee the possessor of an arm's-length additional agenda of merchant business for Opal to consider.

Meanwhile, I examined the tips of my Weejuns and tried to come up with meaningful small talk with Rick, Elvin, Mandy, and Doober Dougie. We made for an odd, murmuring quintet. Only Lachicotte asked the dreaded question—about what new books I had in the works.

"Your last novel was—really strong." A ginger, he possessed the shining countenance of a drunken Irishman. "I remember it well."

"You probably remember it better than I do."

Doober Dougie busted a gut at that and texted his way downstairs to go back to work for afternoon drive time, or so he called out, his voice deepening and resonant as though already on the air.

Mandy, bless her heart: "I know why you're reluctant. You've probably written so much since then it's all a blur."

Half serious, I told them that I now had an outline for a reticent rock star dramedy, a statement that garnered hearty laughs. I declined to elaborate further, and our cluster of small-talkers broke up.

Rick's area of expertise would be the actual concert event, a much bigger job than mine, though one by which he'd profit—I wondered, briefly, if that represented a conflict of interest. I noted that he seemed focused on the attractive Gendry Lizette, a vision of springtime femininity in her short skirt and sandals and floral top.

"Earth to Cortland." Opal, snapping her fingers and pulling me out of my reverie of watching the body language of the others: absorbing their behavior as much as making note of it—wanting to walk in their shoes, to feel in their skin. All I've ever wanted, in a sense, is to be someone else. "Calling out to the boy with the faraway eyes."

It gave me something of a thrill to be touched by Opal. How could it not? I missed her, but no point in saying that. This, a quasi-professional environment. Still: "How lovely. This is the most I've gotten to see of you in ages."

"Wanting to see more of me, eh?"

"Well." We had clashed, honestly. Clashed well in certain contexts. Not so much in others. "Not sure it's worth the irritation."

"What do you say we change that?"

I demurred. Not feeling it, et cetera.

"Come let me feed you," with a sly glance. "We have live music tonight, too—my pal Marcy. You remember her from when we were hanging out. Rick and a couple of the others are coming."

My gut rumbled through a layer of blue oxford. "Sounds wonderful."

A moment of deep eye contact. Whoa.

"You can come on with me now, if you like."

Why not; wondering what was cooking besides the fine Italiano cuisine.

"Then let's stroll over. It's nice out."

I suppose it must have been written on my face how much I looked forward to her company. But, oh—not Opal. Not again. The affair—as much of an affair as two unmarried people can have, that is—ended under conditions of drama. We were lucky to still be friends.

On the escalator I intended to stand and ride, but Opal, a go-getter, went clomping on down as I tried to keep up without stumbling over my own clumsy feet.

At the bottom: "Remind me never to run for office again. You would never believe how much there is to do being the neighborhood majordomo. I should've known better."

"You carry weight in this town. Draw water, and so on. Enjoy the notoriety." And I meant it. "It's more than a neighborhood. It's people's livelihoods. The business heart of the community. Counting on your leadership."

"Fuck that." Opal, a former teenaged punk rocker, often still spoke like one. Her coarse words came at a lowered volume: "When my term's up, all these C-U-next-Tuesdays can kiss my tattooed ass sayonara. I got a fucking restaurant to run, a legacy family business in a high-rent space with a big overhead to cover. Enough politics."

"An extra obligation." A wry little smirk. "Like I feel about being seated on this committee?"

"I hear ya. But you've gotta help. Obi-Wan, you're our only hope."

"Hey, ho, hold up kids—"

Rick Wragg, always a bundle of energy, bounced his way down the escalator and caught up to us. "And where you two lovebirds sneaking off to?"

Terribly familiar, and not off the mark, but shot down by us both with pink cheeks and head-shakes.

"Only friends," in clarification. "Old friends."

"Are you kidding," tagging along with us as we crossed the street. "This, Americans, is chemistry right here—wait." He snapped his fingers. "Not chemistry—history."

Those eyes of Opal's, finding mine. He had us there.

"Guilty. But not anymore."

"He'll always be my best bud, though." Opal, giving my arm a squeeze. "I got to check 'famous writer' off my list."

My cheeks felt hot.

"Knew it. I knew it the second I laid eyes on the two of you. No question. No question. I got the touch, though. I can always tell—besides, Marcy used to talk about all of Opal's various BFs and their, what ya call it, their little peccadilloes—"

"Hey—" Opal shouted, and not jokingly. Now on the street, the knot of homeless men standing around smoking all turned to look. "Enough, smart-ass."

"Change of subject: Now let me bend your ear about the CityArt Fest stages, Madam President, if I could."

"That's Feebee's job."

"Yeah, but I want to lay some outta-the-box ideas on ya . . ."

And he did, on the entire zigzag walk over to D'Alessandro's, me not so much listening as observing the two of them.

Mostly Rick. Opal I knew, and could mine for character traits and spunky personality tidbits from morning till night. Rick Wragg presented as a freshly compelling, extroverted personality, busy and childlike and with a certain wonder in its eyes—in his eyes, rather— and this seemed like a kind of person I hadn't known. That would be of enormous use to me. Fodder for fiction.

But then, wasn't everyone?

I watched and absorbed the details of Rick's gait, his gesticulations; the way he'd get excited and do a little skip-step alongside Opal. His vocal pitch and cadence as he pitched this idea or that about where and how his stage would be erected; how it'd be stabilized; when he could get the streets blocked off so his riggers could set to work; by what time it all had to be cleared out. Exhausting. Rick.

5.

We were early, a shade before happy hour, which in my sobriety I now thought of as witching hour. Quiet inside the restaurant; the dinner trade hadn't yet begun. Opal's youthful serving staff, in black trousers and crisp linen tuxedo shirts soon to be speckled by the steaming platters of cuisine drenched in marinara or wine sauce, did their prep and side work with good cheer and bonhomie. A pleasant atmosphere.

Except that it made me want a drink.

Not so pressingly. But enough.

I had over a year in, though, and wouldn't be treading any old destructive paths. Meditation and bike rides and writing, once I got back to my trade, would serve instead. And coffee, of course. Decent coffee, but not too decent. My palette remains adjusted to regular grade rather than the high-test everyone guzzles these days.

In the early part of the century, the brick building had been the main downtown firehouse, one made superfluous by the construction of the large headquarters nearer the capitol, a version of which is still in use today. Opal's great-grandfather, an immigrant who'd come south during the Depression in search of construction work, had managed to buy the now-abandoned building to open a pizzeria, Columbia's first, in 1939. Ever since, D'Alessandro's has been part of the social fabric of the city, its modern incarnation under the fourth-generation stewardship of Opal enjoying a stellar reputation with a gourmet menu once featured in a *Southern Living* spread about Columbia fine dining—no higher honor 'round these parts.

But I know the truth, which is that Opal's heart is only halfway in the venture—she'd made a deathbed promise to her father that she'd keep the place going. Would make it hers as it had been his, and the men before him. How he'd wept with gratitude, she said. How that and only that, he'd pleaded, would give his life meaning. Opal had wanted to be a rock star, or at least to get out of Columbia, she'd told me, but *respected local restauranteur and job creator* would have to do. Represented a sound enough legacy to me. Best pesto and shrimp scampi ever, but furthermore, in my drinking days I had heard from her own staff how much respect she engendered, how tough but fair she was; an attitude of admiration, one mirrored by her peers in the business community. Genuine respect is always harder to acquire than lucre, gleaned easily enough through the dark arts of subterfuge and trickery—respect, however, cannot be bought, only earned.

Opal led us into the bar area and suggested we have a drink. Remembering that I'd hung up my spurs: "And of course a Pellegrino for you?" she asked, tentative in that way of people who know alcoholics and their delicate natures and the whole wretched awkwardness of it all. I nodded and saluted, aye-firmative.

"What about you, Ricky Ricardo?"

"Pellegrino for me, too." Rick, licking his lips. "But I prefer Perrier," laughing as though he'd made a joke.

"No beer? Really?"

"Naw. I'm OTW."

"Since when?"

Rick and I, our eyes meeting, giving one another little shrugs. A new connection.

"A while. Ya know."

Shooing aside her bartender, who protested the big boss taking on such a menial task, Opal slipped behind the burnished oak bar. She opened a liter of sparkling water, set out glasses and chunks of lime, and poured herself a half-glass of red wine.

"Excuse me, gents."

In her wake, Rick leaned in, a confidential air. "Friend of Bill?"

Not as such, but I knew what he meant. "Let's just say I don't imbibe anymore."

"Because . . ."

Because I shouldn't, I explained in not-so-few words.

"Same here, same here. Boy. S'tough. I got a few months in. It was rough at first. It was—eh."

I glanced at Rick—I didn't think we should be sitting here at the bar. I had a problem, yes, but when it came to booze, I could take it or leave it. I wasn't suffering enough from my writer's block to have succumbed to true depression, and didn't suffer from a virulent enough form of alcoholism to be too terribly tempted by my presence in an old stomping—and glugging—ground like the bar at D'Alessandro's; didn't feel the tug of the comfort that booze provided. An ordinary Wednesday, with no real issues other than trying to get in contact with a reclusive rock star I supposedly had a close relationship with but in fact did not, and papers to grade once the term resumed next week, and a fading, moribund writing career to kick-start . . .

No, even in the face of all that, I didn't have any problems over which getting drunk, or even having so much as a drink, seemed worth the tradeoff.

My concern was for him—is this a good idea? Is he as stable and steady as Cortland Beauchamp, mostly recovered, mildly dyspeptic wine wastrel? I hoped so.

Thoughts of everyone's drinking problems vanished when the lithesome and graceful beauty Marcy Baumbach arrived to load in her PA and electric piano. I knew her, of course, from all my time spent in the restaurant. During my tenure as Opal's fling of the season, however, Marcy had remained aloof, as had I from her. It was fine. I sensed competitiveness between the two old friends, a potential crossfire out of which I wished to stay.

As happy hour rolled around and got underway in earnest, Mandy Polk-Richardson and the ever-starstruck Gendry Lizette arrived, as did Feebee. We sat chatting and listening as Marcy Baumbach set up her compact PA and flourished her keyboard, which I knew from experience came capable of producing a variety of tones and sounds. Our party, a mini-version of the DDC group, assembled at an eight-top Opal had had her staff prepare in the main dining room. On a slow night with few reservations on deck, Opal seemed happy to allow us to stay, listen, and drink-slash-eat as long as we wished.

The songstress had set up her gear on the riser in the back of the dining area, looking down on us and smiling as she assembled her instrument and sound reinforcement. By the time the appetizers came, though, and with her starting time still a few minutes away, Marcy joined us, and she and Opal, friends from adolescence, regaled the group with stories from their girlhood.

All the while, I convinced myself, Marcy kept stealing glances. At me.

With me.

Marcy. She'd never looked so attractive, in her striking eye makeup and with shoulder-length hair colored a deep metallic auburn that, depending on which way she turned her head, caught different shimmering highlights; the eyes that kept sneaking and catching my own watching her right back.

Whoa. Thrilling, yet somehow naughty.

Opal, who'd been coming and going from the table to make sure the restaurant was ready, finally settled in with a fresh glass of wine and told us about her first attempt at an all-girl rock band, one that'd included Marcy, in the springtime of a mid-80s tenth grade that I calculated to have occurred at about the time I'd been completing my MFA and getting my first book written.

The name of the group she described as her first stab at artistic merit and riches and fame confused a number of us at the table. "'The Sisters'?" Rick asked. "I picture five black chicks with big afros."

Opal, spelling it out, quite different from everyone's expectations: "C-y-s-t. The Cysters. Get it?"

Rick, a spit-take of the iced tea he switched to from the sparkling water. "Excuse me? For real? That is hardcore, man. That is—gross."

"Yeah, no shit." Marcy, a gleam in her eye. "Tried to talk her out of it."

"That was the point. Badass—and kinda gross. Whatevah—we only played a few gigs. First one was a house party over at Kevin Marquand's. You remember, Marce."

"Sure, I remember—how could I forget?"

"After about three songs they made us quit and put on a Michael Jackson album." The table groaned and commiserated at such an insult. "Guess we weren't enough of a 'thriller' for them."

Opal related the entire hilarious saga of their high school rock act, influenced, she said, by hardcore punk bands with a list of names that made my sphincter clinch and quiver: Black Flag, The Meatmen, Suicidal Tendencies, The Crucifucks, and an all-girl ensemble of musicians Opal took great delight in telling the table had been called Pussy.

"Pussy was big." Guffaws and knee-slapping and shrieking from Feebee; a busboy refilling water glasses reddened and scurried off. "The Cysters were going to be the East Coast version of Pussy, only more hardcore, more feminist, whole bit. That was our plan."

"A plan that didn't quite come together."

"Nope." A look of longing, almost, between Opal and Marcy. "A mere—wait for it—thirty years ago, now."

Marcy, livid at such a temporal disclosure: *"Shut the fuck up."*

Despite having heard versions of all this badinage before, I got caught up in the merriment—I found myself giggling at Opal's well-worn schtick, Rick and me both with tears streaming down our faces. Marcy, however, seemed chagrined, covering her face. I wondered if I wasn't catching from all the red wine guzzling what marijuana smokers call a contact high. Rick himself seemed to do lots of lip-licking, his gaze flickering across all the hands raising glasses.

As did my own slightly envious peepers. I called for another fizzy-water.

At Rick's breathless insistence, Opal next launched into the epic tale of her adolescent rock band in detail that I'd never heard, with a ridiculous central event so amusing and vivid that I broke out in a rash of goose pimples, and wanted desperately to take notes, a practice about which I'd become terribly self-conscious—death for the writer and observer of his environment, to be self-conscious about scribbling things down. Notes are the seedlings.

Maybe I felt afraid that if someone saw me taking notes, they'd ask what I was writing, a question I didn't wish to address. I preferred to hold such matters for the gala press conference announcing my return to publication notoriety, sure to occur any year now.

Ahem. As soon as I write another book, that is.

Opal began by noting that her father, like her, had done a stint in neighborhood politics, including as an officer of the Columbia Chamber of Commerce, an extracurricular task that kept him neck deep in political hoodoo and the folderol of meetings and breakfasts and cocktail hours and endless schmoozing. By then, the 70s, the family had moved into a sprawling, renovated farmhouse on a tract of rolling Edgewater County land about fifteen minutes away from my childhood home, but closer to the Pisgette National Forest that occupies the eastern, poorer half of the county—yes, there is provincialism even within a South Carolina county like Edgewater. Her father stayed so busy and committed to the restaurant that he often slept on a cot in the back, in a room where she said the occasional immigrant cousin would also bunk until finding permanence here on these bountiful and freedom-loving shores.

As she spoke, my mind raced with potential story ideas. All of a sudden I didn't care about her high-school rock band—I wanted to hear about immigrant kitchen help fresh off the boat in the New World and sleeping on a cot in the back of the restaurant, struggling, assimilating, and maybe even triumphing. Now *that* sounded romantic and interesting and down to earth.

Besides, I already knew the punchline to Opal's story:

Among Basil D'Alessandro's many municipal activities outside the restaurant, all in service of the promotion of the family business— as he so often asserted whenever criticized by his wife and business partner for all the time the extracurricular dealie-wheeling ate up— had been the obligations that came with seats on yet other boards and civic organizations, including that of the St. Patrick's Day festival committee, a bacchanal held in the Old Market on the other side of the university campus from downtown, a neighborhood of taverns well suited to the occasion.

"His status on the committee afforded him an honor—a float in the St. Paddy's parade that kicks off the festival, one that we used to promote the restaurant. But once we had the band, see, I needed him to get something else out of that influence he wielded, other than a rolling billboard for an Italian joint everybody in town's already heard of." Opal sipped her wine and dabbed daintily at her full red lips, the heavy cloth napkin now acquiring a variety of stains. "I needed him to get my fucking band booked into that fest."

"Tough to pull that off, even nowadays." Rick, knowledgeable about such matters. "Gotta be a top-shelf act to play Paddy's day."

"Right. I didn't have any illusions—sure, I was a teenage girl who didn't know shit. But I wasn't asking for the moon. I didn't think we deserved, nor did I want, a headlining spot. I mean, yo, I thought we were awesome, and some guys from a hardcore band at Southeastern called Choking Hazard—they were on the way up, selling out Lupo's and yadda yadda—told us we sounded tight. That was one afternoon after they heard us at the warehouse where all the bands used to practice. You remember that, Marcy, yeah? Sure you do."

"Of course—that bass player?"

Opal thrust a pointed tongue into her cheek. "Choking hazard indeed."

All the women at the table laughed with a low, conspiratorial tone, exchanged knowing glances. Rick worked his eyebrows. I felt my face redden.

Rick leaned forward with his chin resting upon clasped hands. He seemed to be trying to make eye contact with Marcy. For reasons I'd soon find out, she avoided his gaze.

"All I wanted was for Daddy to get us on the bill somewhere," Opal continued. "A side stage, maybe opening the festival at noon, when nobody's even in the fucking thing yet. It was going to be awesome— I'd decided that we were going to arrive, like, in that moment. Turn all these people on to hardcore—Pussy-style," she added to chuckles from her rapt audience. "Next big thing."

"Cyster-style," Marcy, with a rueful air.

"You got it."

I broke down and finally pulled out my notebook out and started scribbling.

"Cort." Opal, leaning over and trying to see what I was writing. "You mean you didn't get this down the first dozen times you heard me tell it? Back when we were hooking up?"

Throats cleared. Feebee's eyes bulged. I shrugged and smiled. "This is a particularly vivid rendering."

The joke was on Opal, though, and all of them: I wasn't truly listening. The notes I took had to do with my historical novel. They need not know this, of course. Let them think the writer sits taking dictation about their interesting lives. More interesting than mine, anyway.

"So I asked Daddy," a pleased look on her face as she dragged her eyes from the dancing cap of my pen. "I begged. I pleaded. He sat me down, explained that it wasn't as it seemed, that the live music part of the festival had its own pressures and experts and obligations beyond his modest influence and task on the committee—a liaison to the Chamber and to the interweaving of other committees and boards, with no real power. Short version: he couldn't possibly wrangle a spot for his teenage daughter's garage band. All due respect, I think was how he put it."

Rick, with a snicker. "What'd he think about the pussy-power sound?"

"Not. Impressed. Didn't fill him with the 'fullness of the soul,' like real music does, or some such shit. Old fart—he loved opera. We heard so much Caruso in my house I wanted to puke at the very thought of classical music."

As I'd told Opal before, her dad sounded like my kinda guy.

"So: I cried and begged some more, but like I said, I was halfway realistic. I understood, when the emerging rational adult side of my brain was able to interject itself. But then I got this idea, see. The parade float, it—"

"I think I see where this is going." Rick, butting in. "You asked him if—what? I don't want to spoil it."

"I asked him if The Cysters could play, not on a festival stage, but—"

"But on the D'Alessandro's float. In the effing parade." Rick, delighted. "I freaking love it."

"Right. If there was no way to get into the festival itself, and since other floats had music and there were the marching bands from high schools and the army band from Fort Jackson, et cetera, why not The Cysters? Boy—he resisted this idea, too. Said, yeah, he thought he could make it happen—he could put whatever he wanted on the restaurant's float. But there was no way in heaven's name, young lady, that her grandfather's pizzeria was going to be associated with what he kept calling 'screaming and noise.' All due respect."

"'All due respect.'" Rick, nodding. "I like it. I'm gonna use that. 'All due respect, but we're gonna need more money for the Duncan Devereaux Committee, Mr. Mayor'."

Grunting, I scribbled down the phrase.

All Due Respect: title of short story?

Opal went on to describe how she'd made a bargain: that on the thirty-minute parade ride her band would play a set of music that wouldn't embarrass the restaurant. That they would learn songs that she knew her father and mother liked. "Billy Joel. Fleetwood Mac. I even started pretending to practice that shit, to throw them off the scent of what we had in mind: The plan, of course, was for The Cysters to get on that float and instead cut loose with our own awesome shit. What could anybody do? The parade would be underway, Daddy would be nowhere near us—he always ran in the Pot O'Green 5K associated with the festival—so we'd get to make our statement untroubled by his concerns about our 'scream rock,' as he called it."

Marcy, her eyes wide: "For the record? I was scared as shit of your dad."

"Okay, sure: maybe Daddy was going to be mad. But it was worth it: no one would ever forget our big debut. I pictured kids running alongside the float, pogoing up and down and slam-dancing and it being this big pied-piper deal where I was leading them to the essence of Hardcore. So, I did succumb to some teenage girl nonsense, but, fuck, I was sixteen, you got to cut me some slack," despite no one having said a word.

Marcy, Opal's bandmate and probably oldest friend, remarked in her soft Southern voice that lapped at my ears like golden, aural honey, "We had the same dreams, girlfriend. It wasn't so crazy."

"Didn't say it was." She turned in my direction. "Get a load of this guy. Cort?"

Busily jotting down phrases like *scream rock* and *pussy power*, I didn't hear her.

"Planet Earth to Cort." Opal, calling me out of my trance for the second time that day, and in an unamused cadence. "Asshole. This," her eyes going around the table, "is why me and this suspiciously quiet writer-type didn't work. Always scribbling away, never listening to a fucking word."

A hush fell over the table. I closed my Moleskine, snapped the elastic band. "Sorry—I suppose I just had anecdote fatigue, dear. Like you said: I've heard all your stories."

She softened. "I shouldn't begrudge a writer his notebook. That's ego, isn't it? Wanting everyone to pay rapt attention to my little stories of failing at my silly childhood dream?"

Marcy, sudden, shoved back from the table. "It's time for me to play."

"Damn straight." Opal, pounding the table, making the wine glasses and heavy, polished flatware—D'Alessandro's represents fine dining, after all—dance with a clatter. "Here's someone who's living the dream."

Marcy seemed humiliated. She whirled round and strode up onto the riser to play to the assorted tables back there, which had filled party-by-party during Opal's story.

The tone left in Marcy's wake? At best, awkward.

"I didn't mean that sarcastically," Opal explained. "She's a professional musician."

Rick: "I don't think it came out that way. You know how she is. Still a little hungry."

A faint smattering of applause greeted Marcy as she plopped down and greeted the diners, a captive audience, her microphone feeding back a tiny bit; she made an adjustment on the PA controls and said *check-check* into the mic, which then sounded fine.

She began to play a song I knew from time spent as a kid sitting on the floor in an aunt's house and listening to her pop albums of the day, including the one that'd featured among its hit singles a vocal and piano composition entitled "Songbird."

"Oh—I know this one."

"Fleetwood Mac," Rick confirmed for me. "Guess that's a reference to Opal's story."

"Got it."

"Ain't you gonna write it down?"

I shook my head. "Like I said, it's familiar."

Opal finished her tale with far less steam, talking about how the parade got underway and her drummer broke a stick on the first downbeat and her guitar amp blew and how halfway through, the D'Alessandro's float got a flat tire and had to pull out of the parade with The Cysters not having played a note, not one blessed effing note, of their genre– and gender-bending music. Not a tragedy, nor nearly as wacky and amusing as I'd half-remembered. I was struck only by the sense of melancholy that Opal was unable to hide from me and the others, a tinge of regret that I'd not heard in prior tellings.

I looked down at the black notebook sitting beside my sweating glass of watered-down Pellegrino. I put my notes away.

Rick stood up and stretched. "Do you guys mind? I'd like to hear her." He motioned over to an empty four-top against the brick wall closer to Marcy's rig.

Mandy nodded to Gendry and Feebee, and the trio got up to follow Rick.

"Well, that was kinda-sorta passive aggressive," in that sardonic growl of Opal's.

"How so?"

"She fucking wants me to get her on the bill for the CityArt Fest. And I'm sorry for calling you an asshole."

"Marcy wants to play in the festival? Solo?" I shrugged. "So, let her play. She sounds wonderful."

"See, that's the thing: she's got a band going. She's doing music full time. She's—she's having an 'it's never too late' moment, and I think it's—silly. A little bit."

"Good for her—it's her dream."

"Like my dad all those years ago, I feel odd throwing my weight around. Cort, I've heard them, and they're fine, they're perfectly good enough." She lowers her voice. "But it'd be better for her to do a solo set—that band's not ready. They've only been playing for three months. And, being president of the association doesn't mean I can just dictate what fucking bands get booked. Besides, it feels like cheating . . ." She adopted a pained wince, as though a mechanic had said she needed brakes on top of the four new tires already costing a fortune. "Especially since I'm doing it for my brother's band already."

"Ah-ha, nepotism rears its ugly snout." I withered her with narrowed, judgmental peepers. "Like insisting on your father allowing your coarse noise-rock act to ruin the St. Patrick's Day parade?"

"He should never have done that—we were lucky we didn't really get to play, because—"

"Because you weren't ready."

"See?" She diddles her long nails on the white tablecloth. "I'd be doing her a favor."

As much as I missed the feel of those nails on my skin, I put the idea out of my mind. "By—?"

"By saying no."

"This is like going into business with a friend," I mused. "Sticky."

"Tricky."

"Fraught with peril."

"I fucking gotta say 'no.' Right?"

I refused to fully concur. "In theory, but she's your friend. When she sees your brother's band on the bill . . . oy."

Opal chewed her lip, ran a finger around the rim of her glass. "You want friends to tell you the truth. Don't you?"

Again noncommittal, I opened my notebook and flipped back through the small lined pages covered by inky print, smeared and sloppy, writing often done under difficult conditions. Surreptitiously, even. A thief in the night.

I thought through Opal's story. The elements of it. The synchronicities with my own life. My own connections.

"Here's what I'll do: I'll strong-arm Leora into giving Marcy a singer-songwriter slot, maybe to open the day's festivities. That ought to make her happy, right?"

"Leora?"

"The songbird, silly." Marcy's voice, drifting down the hall. Exquisite. I couldn't imagine Opal not wanting to pull strings and get Marcy booked. "She—sings like an angel."

Opal regarded me with suspicion. Went *hmmmmmm.*

I ask about the *hmmmmmm.*

"Nothing—it's a wonderful idea." Opal, smiling and devilish in a manner on which I couldn't put my finger. "She's all yours. Why so kind to her, though?"

I grunted. Opal could see the attraction, I guessed, on my warm face.

"Oh, holy-shit. I get it."

"You get what?"

"You really like her, don't you."

All I could manage was a shrug, tiny and insubstantial.

"My best friend . . .? Hoo-boy. Okay."

I protested, but Opal patted me on the forearm. "She's awesome. But I'm done playing matchmaker. Like I'm trying to say: you like

Marcy? Go for it, Ace." Opal, waving over the busboy to get started on the brutal task of clearing our messy table. "Thought you might have been hanging around tonight waiting for someone else."

"As though you haven't moved on."

"Of course I have. No way—we already tried it. Remember?"

"Mostly."

"*Mostly?*"

"Yes—I mostly remember it." Our fling had been at the height of my drinking. "Not that it wasn't lovely."

Opal, her eyes shining with hurt. "Fine."

She left me at the table. I conversed with the busboy in my pidgin Spanish, apologizing for our profligacy. Untroubled, he whistled while he worked. I downed the last of my soda-water and pondered my relationship with Opal, the minefield that could result in dating Marcy. My head swam with songs and music and singers and lyrics, and as I considered Marcy's almond eyes and lilting contralto, I grew warm and gooey inside.

I jotted down one more note, in large block letters that I underlined three times, and that would, in late summer, become a short story, the first in ages I found myself motivated to complete, none of which would have happened without the three most important women at this moment in my life: Leora, Opal, and Marcy Baumbach:

SONGBIRD

<h1 style="text-align:center">6.</h1>

Rick Wragg, unshakable, indefatigable: Small talk and stories and jokes and voices and trivia and this'n that. In other words, Rick, a perfect foil for the studied and quiet writer content to observe and absorb; Rick, doing all the social butterfly work, leaving me to coast along, nodding and noting. A solid partnership.

I joined him in the back room to listen as Marcy finished her set and the restaurant's last few diners sipped coffee and clinked forks against Opal's dessert china.

Marcy, luminous—how glorious she looked when singing. Her joy. Her life. At the dinner table and in our few prior conversations while I'd been dating Opal, music had clearly been Marcy's principal calling and interest; I'd always noted how alight became her face and eyes as she sang. Ethereal. Fulfilled.

And sexy. I found myself getting an arts-bliss chubby.

"Now there's a musician who knows her place." Rick and I both sipped our coffee. "Knows the room."

I shifted in my chair, which'd begun to hurt my bony, aging posterior. "Pardon?"

"Her song choices, the volume, the dynamic range, which there ain't much of. You don't want to startle diners while they're sipping wine and choking down crusty Italian bread hot outta Opal's oven—Opal's oven, oh boy, you know all about all that, dontcha, Bo-champ, eh, eh, hey hey?—and scaring the shit outta everybody by suddenly belting out some big screechy note or building up like a goddamn Jimmy Page guitar solo . . . nah." He lowered the volume of his voice. "At this gig, you're not a superstar, you're background. That's all you are."

"That makes it all sound so—inconsequential."

"Marcy knows this. I mean, lookit, that girl can belt it out. But she ain't doing that here tonight. *It ain't about her.* It's about the meal, and the ambience, and the vibe. She's background. She'll endure some dipsy-doodle with too many under the belt wanting to sing one with her. Or asking her to play some crap she either hates, or is sick of. She'll get some tips. Opal, she'll slide her two bills, more on a busy weekend night. And you know what, Bo-champ? All that makes her a fucking pro—she does this all over town. A pro, a fucking pro. I tell ya, though. She don't even know it."

Rick's words seem cannily observant: we are not in a concert hall to hear Vladimir Horowitz. We are here to eat and drink and socialize—oh, you say there's a lovely woman up in the corner softly playing rock ballads and standards? I hadn't noticed. Wonderful. But Marcy seems no less happy and enthusiastic by the fact that what few diners remain pay her scant attention.

Marcy's set ended at 9, and the restaurant had all but emptied. The workers came and went again in their silent duty, a more languid sort of bustle. Marcy and Opal stood on the riser talking, Marcy's body stiff as Opal gesticulated. The songstress finally nodded, her eyes downcast, and the women turned away from one another, their faces tense.

Rick stretched and watched Marcy coil cables, asking me about what-next. Told him, back to the car, and home for beddie-bye.

"Jesus—where'd the day go. You parked back over by the library, too?"

Indeed, I was parked back over on the big avenue.

"We walk together, then, Kemosabe."

Annoyed that I wouldn't be able to shake Rick and go talk to Marcy while she broke down her gear, I settled for telling him to go please ask Opal to prepare our checks, as we'd both ended up starting a new tab by getting coffees and slices of the homemade cheesecake for which the restaurant was known: I'd savored Key Lime and Rick had chosen Oreo, both of us noting our post–alcohol cessation's cravings for sugar.

"And I got yours, brotherman," shooting me with a thumb and forefinger. "No worries. Right on."

"Right. On." I gave him a power-fist like those young black men at the Olympics that time. My version, anyway. "Very generous."

"S'nothing. Money? Forget it. What is it, anyway?"

"Money?"

"No, yeah," pausing in mid-step and turning back to me, his face frowning and serious. "What is it? Who decides what it's worth?"

I told him I hadn't a clue.

"All numbers up in the air. Pieces of paper. All a buncha bullshit." He took out a dollar bill. "See this?" He tore the bill in half, then again, and again, and again, tearing until he could tear no more. He sprinkled the tiny pieces of paper into the dirt of a large potted fern. "Paper. Meaningless. Abstractions—money, it's all abstractions. Forget it. But, hey, you can get the tip, all right?"

I agreed, did so. Thought: mercy, but Rick Wragg did not seem to be the kind of person who needed to drink any late-night coffee.

The distracted songbird seemed faraway before engaging this writer's probing and appreciative eyes. "Mr. Beauchamp, it's been good to see you again. I was so sorry to hear that you and Opal—that you didn't work out. Y'all were so cute together."

"Me, too." I'm not sure about what part I mean—about seeing Marcy, or breaking up with Opal. "I loved your voice tonight. You sing like a proverbial angel."

Marcy, scoffing and winding a snaky black microphone cable. "Please. But, thank you. Cort?"

"Cort." I thought about Marcy and the festival and what I'd discussed with Opal. "And, really, you should be singing to bigger audiences than this."

Another mild scoff, and a shadow of disappointment flittered across her face. "That—old friend of mine," through an acidic fake-smile, "won't help me get the chance. Did you know that?"

Coy, I asked what she meant.

"You're part of the CityArt thing, right? I saw a mock-up of the poster."

I nodded and said that I was, leaving out the 'barely' part of the equation, the skin-of-my-teeth nature of my inclusion on the crowded literary bill. I leaned over and intimated as though sharing a closely held secret. "I'm quite close with Leora Wood-Cobb, you see. Would you . . . like me to put in a good word for you? About playing the festival?"

"O-M-G—are you fucking serious?"

I didn't quite know what she was trying to spell, but I confirmed that my intentions were genuine, mainly because they were: I wanted to help.

Marcy put down her microphone cable and stepped around her electric piano, made by Kurzweil, a solid instrument. "I hope this doesn't seem too weird."

I asked what she meant.

Without replying, she gave me a hug befitting a wrestler like the ones I used to sit and watch on a small black and white television with my grandfather, that period when he lived with us near the end of his life, and the beginning of mine. A squeeze so tight, in fact, that it caused my upper back to pop, a not entirely unwelcome event. She apologized, explained that it meant a lot for someone of my artistic station to offer someone of her vastly lower stature this sort of favor, this generous boosterism.

"That's the way these things go, don't you know—by friendship. Some of the most talented people in the world never get the chance to sing their songs, or publish their stories, or make their movies, what have you, simply because they don't ever get the right break. I've had my own good fortune mainly through knowing Leora and from a break she once gave me; so, I tend to feel an obligation to help out my fellow creatives in any way I can. The way she helped me. Have to give something back, right?"

Marcy, fetching, tilted her head. Said she thought she understood.

"Let me do some legwork on this." We exchanged cards with email addresses.

"L-M-K." Flashing a mysterious dark glance, eyes somehow demure yet probing. "About the fest."

"Excuse me?"

"Let me know," with a sweet smile. "You sweet man."

I pledged to let her know. "Do you need a hand?"

She considered my offer. "Sure."

Rick and I made our goodbyes to the servers, bartender, and Opal, who prevented our sincere efforts to pay for the cheesecake now bloating my not-insubstantial, fifty year-old Southern man's gut. In the end Rick and I ended up making generous disbursements of quasi-meaningless folding money to the staffers who'd served us with diligence, faith, and smiles that always seemed genuine.

Marcy. The longer I'd spent listening to her, the more I felt drawn to her. The glow she had as she sang. Her mind, her soul, seeming to shine.

I felt so lonely, perhaps nudged by the proximity to lovely and sexy Opal. We'd been close, as physically close as people could get, and I still ached for her in that way. I had to remind myself that on other levels, however, we had not enjoyed a similar level of intimacy—that's why we broke up. Duh.

Rick and I lingered with Marcy in the back, him talking to her about her PA and other gear, and among the three of us we loaded her out the side door to the parking lot, Rick making sure I knew the term for the activity: load-out. After shoving her gear into Marcy's aging Passat wagon, an angular, gray vehicle that appeared in the light of the street lamps decidedly sharklike, we bid our adieus, both receiving quick hugs, mine held longer than his by a few milliseconds.

Rick watched her go back inside to get paid by her best friend. "Dude. You haven't even heard what she can do. She's got some pipes. No question. Marcy B. What a gal."

"She's terribly attractive."

"Oh—you like Marcy? I thought you and Opal were a thing."

Thought about how a younger person might put it. "We were a thing for, like, five minutes."

Rick burst into staccato laughter that echoed among the building facades. We started over to the library, hanging a left onto Main Street. "Go easy, bro. Take it from me."

I asked what he meant.

"Marcy . . . dude." Rick, saluting. "Major Marcy Baumbach is a Section 8, Colonel Bo-champ."

Again: I asked by what he meant, exactly.

In response he whistled the theme to the *Twilight Zone*, which seemed terribly derogatory—Rick also spun his index finger around by his right temple. "You'll find out—first hand info."

I asked yet again for clarification as to meaning. And then I got it, finally. Rick. Marcy. First hand. "Oh."

"Full disclosure: first-hand-info, bro. Can you dig it, brother?"

I dug. It didn't matter—so Rick and Marcy had dated. "I'm sure she's fine. And besides, what are you suggesting? I got a few words in there about getting her into the festival. That's not exactly a simmering romance."

"Sure it ain't. And sure, she's fine. A fine handful. As you'll find out."

We began to cross the six lanes of Convocation Avenue, the cube of the library awaiting us, and I blurted out the whole mess—Marcy's desire to play, Opal's reticence, my willingness to help, blah blah.

Rick nodded, quiet for what seemed like the first time all night. As the stoplight silently cycled through and we went to cross: "That there's a sticky wicket. Let me think about this. Yeah yeah yeah. Let me chew on this sitch. Marcy in the festy, eh? We might could do this. We'll work Leora from both angles. Ooh, a three-way with Wood-Cobb. Yeesh. Forget it."

I began to truly feel annoyed by Rick's crudities. Wanted to be released.

We rounded the corner, stepping over a homeless man sprawled and snoring, his brown-bagged beverage lying as prone and empty as its owner.

"Poor devil."

Rick said in his off-color manner: eh, eff the guy. "We all got probs."

Standing by our vehicles, sedan for me and SUV for Rick, he seemed incapable of ceasing his jabbering.

But at least complimentary in nature: "Dude—can I say something? I can't believe I'm hanging out with a writer like you."

"You're too kind, sir. Embarrassingly so."

"When I was a rigger I worked some big rock tours, couple of Broadway road shows, met some celebs and all? But a writer like you. That's—ah, shit. Writer. That's the stuff, yo. Fucking books, and all. Under your name. Now that's having done something with your life. Ain't it?"

"One supposes."

"Damn if it ain't."

I thanked him again, but insisted that for a writer of my modest stature such enthusiasm wasn't terribly warranted, and thus unnecessary and overboard, though duly flattering.

"But I was thinking, see. I was thinking about new directions. And I always wanted to write. So . . . wonder if sometime I could pick that authorial brain of yours."

Alarm bells—a would-be scribe. Hopeful for advice, for direction. For encouragement.

I braced myself—despite instructing writing students, I hated to hear from anyone that they wish to write. So much pain involved. Time. Sweat equity beyond measure. A modicum of joy and fun and seasons in the sun, yes, but only a modicum. And, waiting at every turn loomed abject failure in the form of rejection. Until the rejection turns to acceptance and validation. At last.

If it ever does.

But such a long road to that moment, I always want to insist, one fraught with emotional and spiritual and sometimes physical peril—the problems I'd had with my back, partially from stress and partially from sitting stooped over in a chair cranking out ten pages a day, day-in and day-out, for years—with rare chance of true success that I'm not sure I'd wish this life on anyone. If I hadn't had other family resources and ways and means back when it counted, I wouldn't be here as a writer at all, maybe. Not if I'd had to make a real living. Still fortunate to be a published author, even after having had those advantages. Statistically speaking, anyway.

An author. Back when I still wrote. Eh.

I couldn't say all that, of course—all I could do was indulge Rick. "What do you want to write?"

"Dude, when I was a kid I was reading Stephen King and Clive Cussler and those cats, and all I wanted to do was tell stories, bro. Stories."

"Story is everything."

"Man—stories. Those I got. I'm talking real stories," he intimates, lowering his voice. "I got show business shit that will make you hair stand on end. And that's funny as hell, course. Funny as shit. I just got to get it all written down. Put into story-form. Whatever."

Everybody has stories, but life does not equal fiction. The hour, too late to get into this discussion. But he persisted:

"Anyways . . . I feel like an idiot for asking, but: so, could I? Pick your brain sometime? About the whole book writing game? Man, I'd be so grateful. I would be like, best friends with you forever. Can we do this? Can we?"

"Talk about writing? Of course." I tried to sound soothing and reassuring and open to it all. Inside, though? Cringing. Rick already seemed like too much for me. So sincere and bright-eyed, dancing from foot to foot like a kid enthusing over the idea of building a tree fort. I chirped the car doors to let him know that the time had come to wind it up.

"No—I don't mean just talk about writing, man: I mean be best friends. Is that weird? I can't believe I said that. Shit."

Surprised and touched. "Best pals? Certainly, Mr. Rick. Best friends it is."

Rick told me he has a kid, but that Cadence is with his mother all week, and despite it being almost ten, he remains antsy.

"You wanna get coffee somewheres? Shoot the shit?"

"After we just had coffee?" Even I have limits. "I'm turning into a pumpkin."

"What—there a curfew? C'mon, dude. Let's hang."

I didn't so much mind Rick's company, only that I wished to get on home. The passionate note-taking had gotten my blood percolating, my juices stirring. Maybe I'd stay up for a while, get some work done— real work. Stare at the bright blinking cursor. Twinkle twinkle.

As intimidating as that alternative sounded, I attempted to decline Rick's invitation.

His chagrin and disappointment, palpable. "Crap. You think I'm a flake."

"Not at all. I find you—you perfectly—fine."

"S'not what I meant, about getting coffee. Not to pick your brain. Not tonight. I only wanted to see if you'd hang for a bit. Or, just go over to my place. I live right across the river. You could follow me. Not to talk about writing." He walks in a tight circle on the sidewalk and waves away the idea as preposterous. "Forget about that. Let's listen to music. Talk about whatever—talk about the chicks. You can tell me all about Opal." He chuckled, leaned in. "And I'll tell you what I got on that Marcy. Hoo-mama. She's a hot box of chocolates, that little golden-throated sparrow. But a handful, brotherman. You'll see."

Every fiber, screaming to hard-about, feint and jab, or high-step my way out of this cornered and desperate situation. But instead? I said all-right, Rick. "Lead the way."

A grin warm as the orange sunset had been earlier. "You're the man, Bo-champ. I only live five minutes away, right across the bridge."

I had to admit that it wasn't only Opal's story, or Marcy's beauty and charm, or the DD committee, that'd inspired all my note-taking—it'd been Rick, too, with his distinctive and childlike cheer, style, and energy. He toiled in worlds in which I'd never dwelled; as he said, he's got characters, and stories, and history. He adds fuel to my simmering creative fire—and like me, dry as dust these days, a couple of boozers who'd gone OTW, a support group of two. I piled into my sensible sedan and followed my freshly-minted new best pal over the bridge into West Columbia.

Part Two:
WALL OF MASKS

1.

Rick lived in an old mill house he'd bought, gutted, and renovated—at a cost he whispered, with a headshaking sense that he'd gotten a raw deal, none of which I wanted to know about. Here in the South, we simply don't talk about money. It isn't proper.

Such houses as Rick's had once housed hourly, working class wage earners, folks like those that had populated Edgewater County in the textile boom decades. Back home we have our own, smaller and more dilapidated version of this neighborhood next to the enormous, abandoned, red-brick electric mill, once the heart of industry there near our lovely and charming Sugeree River, but the one-time heart of the local economy had been sitting shuttered and decaying since the 1980s. Many South Carolina towns and counties were the same. The times, and good working class jobs, apparently, march on.

Once inside I marveled at how Rick had remodeled what he described as a ramshackle, clapboard duplex into a terrific one-family home, complete with a head-spinning and nicely appointed array of modern touches like: a stainless steel chef's kitchen created from what'd originally been two separate kitchens on either side of the wall, a huge upstairs master suite again made from what'd been two bedrooms, a media room, an office, a guest bedroom, a screened-in back porch with a hot tub and inlaid stone patio with a partially covered outdoor kitchen and privacy fencing and a bubbling kidney-shaped Zen garden tucked in the corner, which he pointed out, glowing and encircled by recessed landscape lighting, a mysterious oasis amidst the darkened and sloping saltboxes, as he informed me the architectural style of the old mill house was called.

The exterior had remained unassuming but for a fresh paint job on its repaired wooden exterior, the style no different from the others in the surrounding, lower income pockets that permeated the gradually gentrifying old millworkers' community.

On the inside, though? Rick Wragg, apparently sparing no expense, lived in a domicile to satisfy the most discerning of McMansion hunters.

I considered the house. For what it had likely cost him to renovate the drafty duplex, he could have had one of those suburban behemoths out at the lake; but, I supposed that living in a perceivably 'hip' neighborhood as this made it all worthwhile to a certified scenester like Rick.

I guessed. Who knows with people? Why they do what they do? Want what they want? It isn't always obvious.

Along the wall of the stairwell that bisected the house—at one time there'd been two, but the matching one on the other side of the wall had been removed—Rick showed me his wall of masks: a collection of over forty genuine tribal artifacts he'd amassed through the years.

Sounding as though a cousin of Indiana Jones, he listed off this or that exotic style of mask-carving from Mexico or Indochina or Peru or the Congo.

"Not that I went all these places to get 'em, and some might be fakes, but it's really for the overall, whatcha call it? Aesthetic effect. Rather than some . . . some . . ."

"Curated museum exhibit? A most decent docent you needn't be tonight, Rick, not at this hour. But I do admire and enjoy the collection on its own aesthetic terms."

"*Exactly*. You always got the words. Man. A de-do-what, now?"

"It's not important."

Rick next ushered me into his media cave, as he called it, a place of speakers and couches and recessed lighting, stereo gear, and a massive glass-paneled plasma screen set like a gaping gray mouth in the middle of the wall, hung at a slight angle and glowing backlit by cool neon blue, futuristic elliptical floor lamps at either end of a cushioned sofa. The artwork on the walls consisted of what appeared to be signed and framed album covers, elegantly and mysteriously psychedelic and vintage concert posters.

Built-in shelves of a variety of specificities held the media: CDs, DVDs, and older forms too, like reel-to-reel tapes and an entire wall of

LPs, thousands in total—but also what looked like a shelf of computer hard drives lined up like book volumes.

"Make yourself at home." Rick left and came back carrying two glasses of lemonade. "For the Friends of Bill, one last hit of sugar for the day."

Delicious and brisk. It was just past eleven, now. I hadn't been up this late in ages. What was this? Hanging out and playing records deep into the night as though a pair of pimpled teenaged boys? What next, burning a reefer?

Rick directed me to one end of the sofa and adjusted the lighting via a panel with dimmers and glowing switches. He next wielded a brick-sized remote at the wall of gear. Twinkly LED lights began glowing like the nighttime stars on various components and devices.

"What ya wanna like listen to? What's your poison? If you don't mind compression, I got it all on mp3," cocking an elbow at the row of hard drives. "And I mean, all."

"All?"

"All."

Not to seem like some refined aesthete, I pled, but classical was and remains my first love, and I'd love to hear some. "But not from a computer." I turned to the wall of record albums. "What about those?"

He grinned. "I'm a serious collector and lover of all music. You don't think a collection like that," gesturing to the wall of LPs, "would lack in the basics, do you, Bo-champ? Take a peek in the far right section, nearest the corner."

I flipped through the forty or fifty classical LPs, most of which I had familiarity with from my own family's collection, which of course was now my own. I felt yet more kinship with Rick.

After toying with Stravinsky's *Firebird Suite*, I instead chose a noted recording of Prokofiev, the Piano Concerto No. 3 in C major—in other words, an assessment of the stereo's dynamic range.

I considered the hour, and the mood. Russian drama and bombast? No.

Instead, I slipped out a familiar recording of the *Gymnopédies*, avant-gardist Erik Satie's simple and glorious piano compositions—studied, quiet, and suitable either for full attention, or else as background to a late night conversation with a monologist like my new best bud.

Rick frowned at the selection, put the LP on the turntable. The sound system, glorious—the delicate piano, played by Pascal Rogé, felt present and alive in the room with us, the sustain of the notes ebbing shadowlike.

"Just piano?"

"Satie's a minimalist pioneer," goose pimples sprouting along my legs and arms like time-lapse wildflowers blooming. "And, it suits the mood and space—it's late."

"Sounds effin' classy. Just piano. Yeah, I dig it. Late night. Awesome."

I sank back into the plush and accepting sofa. "I would go to sleep on this trying to watch television."

"Oh, hell yeah. I've missed the ends of more movies than I can effin' count. Course, it's not so bad now."

"How so?"

He held out his hands. "No liquid um analgesics."

"Oh." I felt thickheaded. Of course not. Had I already forgotten how I used to pass out in my recliner or on the porch, sitting and looking in the direction of my neighbors and their house several hundred yards down the winding road from mine? Two empty bottles of wine? Perhaps a sherry or brandy or three?

And smelling the woodsmoke? Catching whiffs of it?

And drinking more?

I pushed such thoughts out of my mind and turned my attention to Rick, who'd begun digressing autobiographical.

"I'm a workaholic, you know. Not just an alcoholic. I got one of those addictive personalities, sure. My dad, he was a teetotaler, never touched a drop or smoked or nothing, but still a workaholic. That's who I get it from."

"I did not know this." I crossed my legs, wondering if I were about to play amateur therapist, if this were about to be a group talk session for two. My name is Cortland, and I'm a pickled Pete.

He gestured around. "And so, when I get home, finally, from a gig—it's not usually this late, not when I have my kid here, of course—I'm all amped up, I can't sleep. Can't sleep for shit. So, in here watching movies. Or old concert vids on YouTube." He leaned over, put down his lemonade glass onto the immaculate glass coffee table and dug through a satchel to pull out a spiral bound notebook. "I got streaming setup from the PC, I can control it with the iPad Mini over there. We can watch some shit, if you want. Search around for cool stuff. I spend hours doin' that sometimes. Half the effing night."

"Oh. I'm good on TV watching."

"Figures—a writer." He cleared his throat, paused—the longest such pause I'd seen from Rick Wragg. "Well, look: in that spirit, let's talk about something real. About writing."

The devious little con man: he'd gotten me cornered and lemon-aded and unable to escape his brain-picking about the craft. I sighed. I sipped. Listened to the music. Gave in.

Shame response pulsed in my stomach like gas bloat. "Truth be told, I haven't been doing much of that so-called writing myself. Not sure I have much advice to give to anyone anymore."

"Yeah, *right*. Sure, sure. Look, I want to talk to you about this thing I been working on," in a voice that shook ever so slightly. "It's a story about—well, it ain't about him, but it's inspired by—that's how I should say it, right?—it's inspired by my uncle. Who got me into all this music stuff, into going to concerts, into wanting to work in the business. It's called 'Superfan'," holding up his fingers like a director framing a shot. "I'm not asking you to read it."

"No?"

"Nah. I just wanna tell you about it."

I settled in, gestured in silence to the notebook he held in his shaking hands, and gave Rick Wragg the warmest smile I could muster. "Tell me your short story . . . start at the beginning."

2.

The next morning, late, I rolled out of bed and went through the log home to my office, looking out a bay window onto the sloping back yard and the creek and the deep woods beyond. So thankful not to have to teach at ETC today.

I puttered, made coffee, mild and weak and lousy, I'm sure, to everyone in the world but little old simple-tasted me. The Folgers did its job, and my eyelids began to droop less. Somewhat.

Rick, and all of them, had worn me out.

But from my experience all day and night, I felt I had a surfeit of fertile seed-material at hand: the women at dinner, particularly the luscious and captivating Marcy Baumbach, about whom I'd dreamed, and Rick's story, which I'd awakened wanting to write my own version called COLLECTOR, which would be a terrible thing to do, since that's what Rick's story was about—an uncle obsessed with chasing rock stars, with 'nailing them' as he put it, which was his way of saying having a moment with them, getting an autograph, or getting a dozen autographs, if possible, on albums and posters and T-shirts.

To what end, I'd asked?

Because a guy—a collector—like Rick's uncle didn't just love all that stuff, Rick explained, he traded in it. Literally made his living at conventions and shows and through mail order in the backs of fanzines and magazines. As such, the rock stars weren't quite so gracious to Rick's uncle as they might be to the ordinary starry-eyed fan waiting outside a stage door or a hotel lobby, much like how paparazzi are often welcomed, which was, not at all.

The details came in a breathless recounting of an adventure Rick had had with his uncle chasing a busload of rock singers around the Washington, DC, metro area in search of autographs, a telling that despite the hour had filled me with excitement, but hesitation. Far from being feasible (even if it wasn't so morally wrong), I couldn't run creatively with Rick Wragg's idea the way I'd at first thought, like one of Prokofiev's bold and dizzying piano concertos running up and down the scales in an exultant rush—I didn't have a grasp of Rick's unique voice, and that'd been the element, I realized, that had most grabbed me, rather than the details of the collecting or the rock stars.

As for writing my own version, the story he'd told was too personal and set in a milieu about which I knew little; and, on another level, how would such a theft of material make me look?

As pathetic and dried up as I was?

As I always tell my budding writing students, however, inspiration's where you find it, and all experience, even someone else's, should be recognized as fodder for fiction. Here in my own life, now, to take my own advice offering an ethical dilemma: a juicy story idea that a fellow writer was working on, so juicy you just ached to steal it and make it your own.

I spent an hour castigating myself for even entertaining such dele-terious thoughts, scribbling in the journal and chugging Folgers until my valve protested and I belched hot and stinging into the back of my throat. Pull thyself together, scribe. You shouldn't rip off Rick's idea. Don't you have enough of your own?

Of course I did. I was simply afraid to work on them.

I weaseled out of a detailed critique of what Rick had shown me, instead focusing on the story elements as he described them, which I found immensely interesting and intriguing: an action sequence; a chase scene:

If I'd been impressed with Rick's media cave and its artifacts, he said his uncle's place in Silver Spring on the edge of the DC beltway, a 70s split level in a wooded, dense subdivision not far from the national archives, would have seemed a veritable shrine.

"Basement, den, living room, spare bedrooms, laundry room, mud room, closets . . . nothing but framed memorabilia and T-shirts and posters, every fucking thing you could imagine. He had gold records he'd bought at auction. Signed this, signed that, everything from ticket stubs to backstage passes to head shots to frickin' underwear—I shit you not. Had two of those dick molds that famous groupie chick made, but it wasn't for nobody too particularly famous, one of the Doors guys—a sideman—and Jimmy Greenspoon. Not too impressive."

I hadn't a clue what the hell he was talking about—'dick molds'? I wasn't given time to ask.

Rick described how his uncle had gotten such a collection, and to what lengths he'd gone, including taking a teenaged Rick, all of fourteen and 98 pounds soaking wet, on a chase of the bus carrying members of Jefferson Airplane, who by then had transmogrified into Jefferson Starship.

"He had come into this box of hippie crap, as he called it, bunch of assorted stuff from the old Haight-Ashbury era, most of which had to do with the Airplane, usual crap—posters, handbills, this and that. So, he explains to me, you take Grace Slick, Marty Balin, whoever the fuck was in the band then, you go and get yourself some of these handbills signed by them, and you've got real money at these collector shows he used to go and set up at, like, every weekend somewhere—I remember he would come all the way down South sometimes, maybe even to Columbia. I don't know. And by 'money' he meant currency at the show—maybe somebody would have some cool crap he wanted, and he could trade Marty Balin or Grace Slick for it. He wasn't no big San Francisco sound fan anyway—more of a Springsteen guy, right? In any case, it wasn't all about the money for him, but that was a big part of it.

"Anyway: So on this night he takes me with him we're chasing the Starship, who used to be the Airplane, they're playing this joint there in DC, not the arena 'cause they ain't that big anymore, but like the Warner Theatre or someplace like that, few thousand people. And my Uncle Ritchie, he's got this whole network he's patched into, all these 'superfans' as I like to call them—get it? Like the title?—and so he finds out shit like where the band is staying. Turns out they got a gig the next night in Baltimore, only a half hour from the last gig, and so of course they are being put in a hotel instead of hitting the road. Typically, a working band gets onto the buses after the show and gets driven to the next town overnight, when it's cool and it's dark and there's no traffic and everybody who can gets some shut-eye and you wake up in the next version of Anytown, USA, which is how I lived for a couple years. Life on tour. Brother, and let me tell you, it ain't pretty . . . nah."

"So," getting him back on track. "The Starship is heading to the next gig, sure, but to crash in the hotel instead of on the bus."

"Cornered, as Uncle Ritchie puts it."

His digressions continued, including side-trips and hints about any number of interesting tangents, but as I watched the time go by and the Satie LP get flipped over, I pleaded for him to stick with the story at hand, which went on to describe the crazed chase from the concert hall to the hotel as the bus driver tried to evade Uncle Ritchie, who had tipped his hand and gotten recognized by too much hanging around outside the stage door—Ritchie Wragg, well known to local promoters as an autograph hound and dealer, an annoyance to be shunned. A not-insider.

"A dividing line."

"'The backstage door is one helluva dividing line.' I should write that down."

I told him yes; that's what writers did.

Uncle Ritchie wanted to take a second try at the hotel, how he would let the bus driver think he had shaken the two of them in the classic two-tone GTO, a car the maintenance of which, and nostalgia for, manifested as another of Rick's detailed digressions.

"But then we took off across freaking side streets and hotel parking lots, me catching glimpses of the band zooming down the main road, while us, we're hurtling through on access lanes and alleys, and a shortcut he knew that allowed us to come squealing into the back entrance of the hotel parking lot, right in front of the band busses. It was like some car chase in a movie. Most exciting thing I ever been mixed up in. No question."

The fortuitous timing allowed them to get into the lobby where Uncle Ritchie had positioned the cute, young Rick to ask Grace Slick for autographs on his 'late father's 1960s Bay Area handbills and stuff,' as Uncle Ritchie had prompted his nephew to recite. "Grace fucking Slick like, not only tousled my hair and went 'aw' and gave me a wet, boozy kiss, but stood for pictures with my Uncle and me and Marty Balin and the bus driver. She asked him to come into the bar for drinks.

We were golden . . . until the promoter guy came through the door and saw Uncle Ritchie, totally dropped dime. We got hustled outta there then. Party over, oops, out of time."

"Busted. At least you got in the door, albeit briefly."

"It didn't matter—Uncle Ritchie, he was giddy. I had gotten every piece signed, but more than that, he had *hung out and partied with Grace fucking Slick*. It was a big score. He went home a happy boy that night. Yes, he did."

Exhausted, I told him I thought it'd make a hell of a story.

At that moment he presented me with the pages that he had written, which, in skimming, I found to be a reasonably written recitation of the above sequence of events, and in a facsimile of Rick's distinctive and entertaining voice. Out of politeness I offered to take the material home and give the story the once-over, as Rick called my reading of it. The once-over, he asked with hungry eyes, and go easy on me.

Now, the next morning and while savoring my sixteenth enjoyable and mild cup of Folgers, I perused the pages. Went *hrm*. Said, let's see: If Rick were one of my students, I'd gently advise that the characters aren't quite 'there' in the sense of being distinct from one another (they all sound like Rick), and we do not exactly have a story in the sense of a protagonist having learned or changed or otherwise been changed in some significant fashion. It's an anecdote, not unlike his telling of it to me, full of action and color, but with little underlying meaning or metaphor.

I would explain all this to him.

In writing, of course:

The red pen came out: Tumbles and jumbles of words struck through, admonitions on too much exclamatory dialogue, and finer points of narrative fiction like establishing a consistent POV. His was undisciplined work, a shade shy of amateurish; but, faced with this bracing assessment, I'm a shader shy of actually writing that as a critique note. At least he had the basics of grammar and punctuation down, if a touch gracelessly; it was more than could be said for many of my students, even ones who ostensibly wished to be thought of as writers—or when it came to early drafts, even for the estimable word-wright you see typing before you today.

I rinsed my coffee cup, walked outside, and took in the glory of the sunlit Carolina woodlands, the gurgling creek down the back slope, the chittering birds and flickering, bushy tails of the army of squirrels who already this early spring had descended like a gray plague upon my sieged and battered bird feeders. I drank in the rich and peaty forest-smell that's quite different from the pine barrens of the part of Edgewater County in which my family home sits, and to which I ought to pay a visit to see my Uncle who still lives there.

Hate even driving over that way, however. Lot of bad memories—but then, so, too, holds this neighborhood now, a recent fire in the area that turned tragic, and it's then that the scent of charred wood, ephemeral, wafts across my nose, sending a sudden chill down my spine and making me want to put my mind elsewhere.

Anywhere.

I shook off the phantoms of someone else's tragedy and fetched myself a trusty, fresh legal pad. I went out to the picnic table at which I sometimes sit in the spring and fall to work or read, and instead of marking up Rick's pages and treating them like a student's assignment, I decided to simply hurtle ahead and make my own assignment out of his work: with no thought of publication or letting the work be seen by anyone's eyes (other than Rick's, perhaps) I'd adapt not so much his 'story,' such as it was, but instead remember the way he'd described the experience, and try to write a fresh piece from that perspective, that of the adolescent Rick and not the adult-looking-back Rick who seems to be the nominal narrator of his 'Superfan,' and to perhaps layer in enough backstory to give the uncle's actions more weight to the adolescent protagonist and narrator—a lesson to be learned, perhaps. Ideas would come to me, but not from consciously trying to think them into existence, only in the alchemical, esoteric process that is the composition phase of writing. The process is difficult to teach.

With all this grandiose and hubristic ambition in mind, I carefully wrote out a single word at the top of the page—COLLECTOR—and immediately set to scratching ink onto paper, which I'd end up doing until my back and neck ached, and the sun had long crossed over into slanted afternoon light. Fast as the pen would pull. Pages, a stack creased and wrinkled and bled blue into by my aching, shaking fingers. Glory. The fun part of writing.

After going inside for lunch and a fresh cup of coffee, I set to typing up what I'd written. By nightfall, glory of glories but I found I'd produced the first finished short story I'd written in ages; in longer than I cared, or dared, to admit. It may have been someone else's story, but I'd used Rick's inspiration to shake off the dust.

I felt two inches taller; I made a large meal and went through my instructor's bible for the second half of the semester, feeling, for once, like a writer instead of an impostor.

Taking a stroll after dinner along the road in the pitch black of the country where I live, I recalled the last exchange between us as Rick walked me out to my car the night before, at close to one in the morning.

"So—this Marcy," I probed. "Did I detect some tension between the two of you?"

Rick snorted. "Look. It's history. Besides—there's tension between me and every woman alive, Bo-champ. Trust me. Marcy's . . . special, all right. Good luck with all that."

"Are you serious?" Opal on the phone, furious. "You want my permission to go and screw my best friend? Beauchamp, you're a piece-a work. *Gah*," a gag-me sound. "Men. You're such dogs. All of you."

"Now, now."

"Do what you have to do, why don't you?"

"Not asking your permission, but I suppose your blessing, dear. If it's a problem, I . . . won't."

"Don't 'dear' me, boy, I'll rip out your—wait." Her tone softened, thank god. "I love you both dearly, is all. I would just hate to see it all get weird. The friendships. It's already strained with me and her, as you know."

"I'm taking care of that."

"Sounds like you're in the mood to take care of quite a few things." She purred in a seductive quaver that never failed to get my blood racing, even when discussing the likelihood of potential romance with another woman. "You naughty, naughty little satyr, you."

In a flash, I saw how this could all go so wrong. Maybe Opal was right: I'm just a horny man trying to get laid a few more times before this Southern heart of mine goes for good. Who ought to know better? Who ought to have settled down with the one that had seemed an opposite on so many levels, and yet compatible, too? With her? I tried not to parse the subtext. "She has such magnetism—those eyes. That voice."

"She's a beautiful woman, Marcy. Inside and out."

We both sat there in digital silence.

"*Hrm,*" I finally managed. "Well?"

"She's terribly lonely these days, you know—I think that's why she started the band. So look, you like her? Do her a favor."

"Anything."

"Get Leora to put her on the bill as a solo act, like in the restaurant. To do her own songs, of course. But just Marcy and her piano. That's her at her best rather than trying to ape Chrissie Hynde. Not at her age. It's—unseemly."

"Oh, come on."

"No, really. That band is not ready."

I agreed to attend to this cronyism and subterfuge. I knew they already had bands booked, but perhaps, I suggested, Marcy could do a mini-set in between the main acts. "Surely Leora would agree to that. She'll do anything I want."

"Then you're all set. Have fun. You and Marcy."

Ominous.

Before I rang off with Opal, she asked me what I had planned for the rest of my spring break, besides trying to get both Marcy Baumbach and Duncan Devereaux on the hook. I told her that besides the inordinate amount of time I planned to put toward those crucial and pressing endeavors I had much writing to do, and on a variety of new projects.

Goody for you, she said, but you better get me Duncan Devereaux, and then a flatline for a dial tone left me alone, again, in my cabin. Lonely, like Marcy Baumbach. Perhaps we had common ground. A foundation. A beginning.

3.

Instead of two more full days of good writing work during my spring break, however, only one: the next morning I found myself neither on the way to Columbia for a DDC meeting, nor over to the ETC to teach my classes, nor down into my office to take in the morning and take the blue pencil to the work of yesterday, but as I'd been considering, taking a drive north into Edgewater County to the family home in which my uncle, Clete, lived as the last link in the familial chain.

Well, besides me, of course. All the others who could lay claim or title to the Beauchamp plantation land had died, my own parents longest ago of all, it seemed.

Was it thirty-seven years, now? Something like that.

Mercy.

Cletus Beauchamp, my father's brother, had hung on into his late 80s, in decent health and with his full faculties. He occupied the far reaches of the house, which was large and stuffed from top to bottom with books, family heirlooms, antique furniture, cobwebs, paintings, and memories I'd just as soon leave behind. Not so much childhood memories, but anything after thirteen, boy, those memories you could keep.

After my parents had died, nothing had been the same—understatement, this—and so living there with my aunt and uncle had been like a different life. Someone else's. My father's brother wasted no time in getting their bedroom stripped to the wood and refinished, and then all of us settled in together into the house he'd said he'd never be caught dead living in, and so far he seemed prescient: despite his advancing age, indeed, he hadn't yet been caught in a condition of acute mortality.

I couldn't wait to get out of there. Before I died inside. Soon as I could I swore I would be the one who'd decamp from that creaking and now haunted-for-real Southern mansion on a hill:

Hillsborough, the old plantation land.

And so I had. Not far. But far enough.

Today, it seems, my presence would be a boon: when I called to see if my uncle would favor a visit, I find that he's suffered a fall. Nothing serious, but still requiring my—or somebody's—help running errands.

"I need to go into town to sign a number of papers." Uncle Clete, shouting, me holding the phone away from my ear. "And I simply don't got no one else to turn to, Cort. Arthur, he's gone off up into the mountains for a few days. It makes me sick, I tell you, to hafta call you like this. Sick. But I'm asking for a ride, m'boy."

"It's not a problem."

"I know how you hate to come here."

"Nonsense."

He said the hell it was.

As though some shoe-gazing, inarticulate teenager—and I hadn't been that way even when I *was* a teenager—I mumbled 'whatever' and said that I'd see him later.

Following the interstate leg of the brief trip, I took the long two-lane of Old Seventy-Nine past subdivisions near the Tillman Falls exit and the modern commercial corridor, then through the hilly part of the county skirting the ridge that paralleled the Sugeree River toward downtown. Sandwiched between the modern motorway and the old Southern town ten miles to the west, here the county wore its poverty on its sleeve: trailer parks and ramshackle hovels and skinny dogs and downtrodden people of all colors and creeds. Closer to town the road widened to four lanes, followed by a choice of business district or bypass, which I ought to have taken, but I haven't been to the old town in quite some time, now. Surely my hometown warranted a quick peek at its current condition.

During the drive I'd enjoyed Schubert's No. 8, the forbidding strings and woodwinds of the scherzo's first movement, the *Allegro Moderato in B minor* resolving into a stately and elegant melody that carried me along and into the hinterland that was my one and true home. Why the composer never finished this piece, and despite living another six years after the completion of the first two movements, no one can say. But as I approached downtown proper, my iPod shuffled not to the second movement of the Schubert but rather to the Bach Partita No. 6 in E minor. This, a problem encountered when on shuffle and when movements within a given piece are individually track-marked, or as explained to me by one of my ETC students.

Despite the incongruity of shifting orchestral works midstream, I found that the Bach provided an atmospheric piano accompaniment for my drive through the other section of antebellum homes known as the historic district. Yes, there are a couple of bed and breakfasts, antique shops, a well known restaurant called the Southern Sideboard, the county archives, the library, and the old town cemetery all lined up along Common Street. The wealth on display along what locals call Whaley Way remained a sign that Tillman Falls was somehow still a place of Old South money, and this despite the expanse of time since the "glory" days of wealth and plenty produced by the brutal hard labor of the plantation era, and later the twentieth century postwar boom in which the textile mills had chugged and churned out industrial fibers and tennis shoes and pantyhose, another monied epoch having deteriorated into the far more impoverished Now. But I supposed that it was like any number of other places in contemporary South Carolina, that Edgewater County still held both pockets of wealth alongside extensive swaths of some of the most impecuniously poor souls in the whole country.

Just who still owned all the old mansions on Whaley Way—besides legacy inheritors, of course—stood as a mystery to me.

But then, I don't spend much time ruminating about Edgewater County history. Dangerous for me to do so. On a basic and essential level, I could give a poop who owns these ostentatious bastions of unearned prosperity, or less who did in their original incarnations, such wealth 'earned' on the backs of suffering, brutalized human beings bought and sold as cattle. Long time ago now, sure, but the wounds, lingering and exacerbated by the occasional sight of a Confederate flag drooping from some weathered flagpole.

Passing by Forest Knoll Garden cemetery one is welcomed to downtown by The Dixiana, a venerable legacy honkytonk that stays in business I know not how. I shook my head at the iconic Southeastern Redtails mural painted on the side of the building: a half-block long rendering of the Southeastern University's old mascot and logo, a fighting cock wearing the old grey and trailing behind him the stars and bars of the proudly waving Confederate battle flag. Fading and peeling, the mural, but General Reb, long retired by SEU in favor of Big Red, an anthropomorphized redtail hawk of considerable bulk, stature, and charisma, still stalked the honkytonk; still ushered motorists from this direction into the heart of the town like a redneck version of the Welcome to Tillman Falls sign affixed with the emblems of the various lodges and civic organizations. In fact, the condition of the mural was so degraded that it clearly ought to be removed or updated in some fashion. Vanishing, like the Old South ways that its controversial imagery suggested.

Rounding the corner, the quaint heart of downtown came into view—the town green with its monuments and mature oaks, the second-story newspaper office of another local institution, the *Edgewater Advocate*, and the bank and attorney's office to which I'd bring my uncle; down the block the restored marquee of the Palmetto Grande movie theater caught my eye, now the Edgewater County Fine Arts Center. I noted that most of the storefronts seemed to be active; antiques, a tattoo and piecing parlor, cash advances and title loans. I suppose in these challenging times, good business was where one found it. Many South Carolina towns hosted few, if any viable retail businesses outside of the local Wally-mart, and now even some of them were closing.

Quite a change from my childhood. Here's hoping they can keep those big boxes going—if not them, what then?

The Old Charlotte Highway out of town led me through several neighborhoods of ranch houses built in the 60s and 70s, the last decades before the textile mills had all closed, after which any legitimate hope that a place like Edgewater County would ever again enjoy much of a stable economic engine faded like that nasty old mural. Done and done, never again like it'd prospered in the age when textiles ruled. A huge hydroelectric mill had once operated on the river, but it'd been shut down in the 80s, this after being bought by an enormous international conglomerate called Gray-Peele.

At least someone had had the sense to build the Sugeree Nuclear Station, two reactors that provided power for nearly half a million South Carolinians, so there remained that core employer. So long as nobody was unduly worried about radiation or meltdowns or cancer, everyone could continue to enjoy fresh brewed coffees and teas along with their "hot & now" Krispy Kremes.

Our family land lay five or six miles outside of town to the north, a crumbling and ancient house sitting on what once had been the vast track of a King's Grant working plantation. The house, called Hillsborough, indeed sat on a hill high enough so that one could see the shimmering snake of the river, at least in the wintertime, when the trees were for the most part bare. Along the rural highway and regardless of a reciprocal greeting, I made sure to wave to everyone I saw. Waving to friend and foe alike, it's in a Southerner's blood.

Maybe I wanted them to know that a true-blue son of the county, not a stranger, had returned. Why this mattered, I knew not.

From Hillsborough's listing on the webpage of the Edgewater County Archives devoted to the surviving antebellum houses on Whaley Way and elsewhere in the county may be read a description of my family's historical structure, first built in 1835 and later renovated in the Classical Revival style:

> *A central projecting portico, supported by four colossal Ionic columns, embellishes the façade, which is surmounted by a flat roof with a turned balustrade above a molded entablature. Small Ionic columns support the first story porch, which extends beyond the façade and repeats the portico balustrade. The same balustrade occurs across the width of the second story uncovered porch. Private. No tours available.*

I made the last turn and rumbled down the incongruously named Snowbank Lane, then right onto a gravel drive that went up a gradual, overgrown slope through a dozen enormous magnolias. Beyond lay the crumbling stone gate and walls, and there loomed the house:

The upper porches, sagging.

The portico, blocked by stacks of old appliances and junk.

The grounds, weedy, overgrown, untended.

A rotting shadow of its one-time glorious self; its spiritual scars on display.

Ugly.

Home.

As one pulls around back, the house takes on a more hodgepodge air, with a modern, modular addition stuck onto the back where a cooling porch had once been, and where I could recall sleeping on hot summer nights when the air inside lay heavy upon a body like a woolen blanket. I suspected Clete spent most of his time in this new addition, which allowed him to enjoy easy, first-level access to the modern kitchen and a bathroom. An old man had no need to go upstairs and sleep in cluttered and dusty rooms in which troubled ghosts, melancholy and hollow of spirit, most certainly dwelled.

How I went on sleeping in my room after what happened to my parents, I cannot say. But I did.

Clete awaited me in a rocker on a screened porch that had also been added onto the back. Hanging baskets of dead ferns framed cinder-block steps. Wildly overgrown shrubs and holly and weeds and trees in need of pruning filled the back yard, an encroachment of the natural world. If it had been later in the summer, the grasses would be over-grown with weeds and dandelions—it didn't look like it'd been mowed very many times last year. I wondered what Clete's son, my cousin Arthur, had been doing with his time. Traditionally, he had taken care of all this nettlesome landscaping for his father.

Buried under kudzu and chokeweed vines, the fig tree, gnarled and ancient. I wondered if it still bore fruit. As I switched off the car and got out, my eyes misted.

"Will you hurry your ass up?" Clete yelled as a greeting. He shuffled down the steps from the porch in his old-guy golf pants pulled halfway up over a beach ball of a belly. When I saw that he'd taken to using a cane, that one of his legs seemed inordinately stiff, I leapt out of the car and rushed over to assist him.

Cursing and sputtering, he rebuffed my offer of a helping hand. "Cortland, I been sitting here cussing you up and down—it's Wednesday, boy, and if we don't get on down yonder the bank'll be closed."

"Uncle Clete, don't you bank at Wells Fargo? They don't keep banker's hours like that anymore, not even in Tillman Falls."

"Wells Fargo? What in the *hale* you talking about, boy, taking a goddamn stagecoach line out west? I bank at Carolina Federal, like I always have."

"Of course. Carolina Federal. I should know these things," a teensy bit snide and sarcastic.

"Look here, I don't care how many damn books you done wrote: I know when the banks's open and when they ain't. I tell you what, boy—you remind me of your mother's side more than the Beauchamp side. It makes me sick, sick to my soul to say that to you. But you always did, son. Course, that ain't all bad."

I cleared my throat and opened the door to my car. He struggled to get in, wincing and moaning himself into position. My uncle didn't smell that pleasant, a little old man redolent of camphor and mildew. I began to grow angry with Arthur.

"Are you sure you're okay from this fall?"

"Shit yes—my back's not worth a durn toot on a good day. Used to it. By now." He futzed around trying to find a place to shove his cane. "Good as gold," and yet exclaiming with hot pain when he twisted too far to toss the cane into the back seat full of books and papers and assorted crud that for some reason I refuse to clean out.

I buckled up and drove back around the circular drive and through the stone gate—HILLSBOROUGH, carved in weathered and nearly illegible letters—back down toward Snowbank Lane and the highway beyond.

"When was the last time Arthur had a crew work on the yard?"

"Couldn't say." He sucked his teeth. "A crew? You must think I'm made out of money. He come and do it himself nowadays. Every now and then."

"So I see. Tell you what—let's get somebody over here. I'll pay for it."

"The hell you will. Arthur keeps the yard up."

"I owe you . . . don't I?"

"Shit, no." He gaped at a cluster of trailers stuck on a vacant lot not two hundred yards from our front gate, shook his head and made a sound like 'feh.' Both my father, and later, his brother sitting next to me, sold off various lots through the years. Not to mention all that my grandfather had sold; we still owned maybe ten acres total. Luckily the land behind us almost all the way to the river had remained untouched—there were no roads to get back in there, all of it too far from the main road to be of any use. Hilly, rocky land.

Nearby ran the old rail lines—this part of the county had once had a train intersection and depot with several general stores, and felt, for a time, like it'd grow into another commercial center of the county to rival Tillman Falls. That'd been over a hundred years ago, though, and with the modern rail line far on the other side of the river and the entropic economic dynamic continuing, Hillsborough, my very own personally historic and relevant symbol of antebellum wealth and plenty, now sat amidst one of those impoverished and dusty swaths of poor South Carolina earlier mentioned, a relic of a forgotten time.

For many, myself included, a time best forgotten, really.

I mean—really. The thought of what went on here during the time of slavery makes me want to vomit with revulsion.

Most of the people who still bother remaining in this part of the county are still African-American, in fact, and while certainly free as any other citizen, still living in a kind of modern-day plastic grocery sack and greasy fast-food squalor that is in its own way a different but perhaps similarly oppressive sort of forced indentureship. I know about these lives not from living them—for heaven's sake, I went to Mendenhall Academy; I grew up a Beauchamp living at Hillsborough, with a brilliant but mad father and a beautiful piano playing mother, and mostly in the time when the prosperity had all but leached away from everyone around us here in northeastern Edgewater County. My students at the ETC are the ones who tell me how it is among the poor people. I don't have much money, certainly, not compared to some; I don't know, and have never known, what it is to be as poor as the majority of neighbors living near my haunted, boyhood mansion.

Probably as much as reading had, growing up against that deep, dense river forest behind the house instilled in me the desire for quiet and solitude that's led me to being a writer. As a child I spent countless hours wandering those woods making up stories in my head, hiding from the violence that'd gone on in that big Southern plantation house between my parents. This ongoing fever dream culminated when I was thirteen, in a moment worthy of any Southern gothic potboiler you could imagine, right down to the hot summer night when my parent's lives ended in an explosion of death that'd missed me only, I supposed, because their beef had been with one another, and not with their son on the other side of the echoing, ramshackle mansion.

My uncle always told me that no one in the family had ever believed that my father, smart and urbane and poised as he seemed, was truly right in the head; but, as the sheriff and the coroner and the boy who found their bodies could attest—that's me, the boy—there'd been no doubt that it'd been him, drunker than a skunk, who'd pulled the trigger on her in their bedroom.

Then turned the gun on himself.

Leaving a bloody mess for me to find.

Or it could have been the other way around, at least in the order of the shots. My mother had been exasperated, exhausted. Drinking, too, as she'd confessed, as though I couldn't tell, or smell. Said she'd rather die than put up with his hateful shaming of her, his hectoring, his mental abuse. I didn't see much of that—it stayed on the other side of the house. Or maybe I was able somehow to ignore their muffled, heated arguments.

Until I couldn't ignore what was happening. How father started drinking earlier in the day. How, after a while, they both had.

The irony? My father had been a mental health counselor in the South Carolina Department of Corrections. He went around and listened to murderers and thieves and rapists talk about their problems. No wonder he'd gone mad.

And not the only one in the house.

"I swear, I'll kill him and I'll kill myself," my mother had slurred to her thirteen year-old son through piteous tears. "Don't you tell anybody I said that, though. Don't you ever tell."

At this I wept alongside her. Mewled and begged to know how to help.

"Oh, baby—mama doesn't mean to scare her angel. It's all just grown-up talk. A buncha dumbass foolishness. Forget everything I told you. Let's never talk about it again . . ."

Of course, she didn't fathom that I knew about her lover, or lovers, whom she took to provide the tenderness and succor father either couldn't or wouldn't—and that there were other layers to their lives no young boy should know. That they both had made drunken confessions to me about this and that—and how my tears at her ridiculous and melodramatic blather were born more of frustration than of sorrow. Grown-up talk indeed.

My tears dried up. I told her to shut her filthy, recalcitrant mouth— to go and change her torn slip spotted with Bordeaux like the splattered blood that was to come. To stop drinking so much wine—that father should, too. That I would have a word with him. That I'd had enough with their childish behavior. That I had reading on which to catch up for my schooling. Thirteen years young, yet the oldest in the house.

The most grown-up, anyway.

Someone had to be.

A week or two later, it no longer mattered whether I could help.

I'd heard the first shot, and thought it thunder; I'd been under my covers with a flashlight, reading *The Moviegoer* and fixating on the description of the pink cube of the Gentilly movie theater out by the water as though a living entity, a pulsing, fleshy artifact of the Gulf of Mexico washed up on the shore of Walker Percy's imaginary New Orleans suburb. The second roar, which came after my father's anguished wail—"Cordelia, oh, *Cordelia*"—sounded like what it was: the howl of death taking away the second of my parents from their bedroom, with its access to the upper veranda, a promontory that even then had begun to sag with age, making the house appear as though it was smiling at the thought of an eventual and blessed collapse upon itself.

The room was later gutted and rebuilt with new plaster, and the floors had been stripped and the paint redone and all traces removed, and I'm pointing this out for the second time so it will be clear how important all this is, at least on the level of symbolism: Despite the refurbishment, you see, as far as I know no one's ever used the room for anything again. I certainly never did, not while I lived there. Did not so much as darken the door. Thankful the house was as large then as it remains now. Decrepit pile of lumber that it is.

How I hated it, then as now.

And yet, for the rest of my teen years I stayed there at Hillsborough with my aunt and uncle, who decided after the tragedy to move into the family house. Every night I suffered the psychological depredation that came with hearing the ghosts of my parents creaking and stepping around, and shook and secretly cried as the gun blasts rang out both in dreams as well as waking moments, phantom bursts of what I now understand is called PTSD.

I wonder, then as now, whether my uncle hears them. Feels their presence the way that I did. I hope not.

That's right—following the tragedy, I spent the rest of my adolescence in my old room, yes: where else was I to go? But I didn't succumb to the horror of my parents. Instead, I became strong—I wrote the fear out of me. I had read Frank Herbert's *Dune* the year before, and *Fear is the Mind Killer* became my mantra. Wrote away their haunting presence until they could do me no further harm.

I'd gotten over it all, long ago, but not to hear my ex Lori-Kaye tell it. She always said that since I'd seen how quickly and terribly life could end, and the only real loss I had known was sudden and swift and brutal and bloody, I'd never again let anyone get truly close to me. Maybe she'd been right. Maybe she still was.

In any case, Uncle Clete and I didn't discuss any of that during our time in the car on the way to the bank; I didn't know what business he had to conduct, but while he did, first at the Carolina Federal, which indeed remained open until 5pm as in the rest of the nation, then at his lawyer's office, Glasscock & Associates, I planned to sit on a bench and make a few notes in the comforting sun, as far away from the small statue of Ben Tillman on its ostentatious pedestal of red granite as I could get.

Jasper Glasscock, a ruddy ginger of a town father, had been a private investigator and attorney by trade, but more well known as a local musician and, at one time, a fellow published author, a fairly notorious one, at least in South Carolina: he been asked to interview, and write up, a semi-famous serial killer's quote-unquote last and final confession. This individual happened to be a psychopathic, itinerant murderer, Coy Wando, whose last place of residence, and source of his only verified victims, had been our own Edgewater County. His reign of terror had been during a season of fear in 1980, after I'd gone away to college.

He'd told me the story first hand, at a book signing I'd done at the Edgewater Fine Arts Center after *Keys to the Rain* made its little kerfuffle of literary noise. Jasper, who'd known Coy Wando from hanging around in The Dixiana, had been chosen, he explained, because Coy remembered him shooting the shit with the boys at the honkytonk about wanting to be a famous writer, but not having "the first durn clue" what he ought to write about. If Coy Wando, the killer said, couldn't give a motherfucker something to write a book about, then nobody could. This had been Jasper's opening line. One hell of a hook.

But a hook that came with a cautionary stinger: *As right as Wando turned out to be, once I was done with that book, that you now hold in your hands? I'd never want to write another.* And so, as intrusive narrators are wont to say, he had not.

I'd told Jasper that it was all downright Capote-esque, and asked if he'd send me a signed copy of *Wando: A Final Confession,* which had indeed been so gruesome and extreme in the details that many readers and observers took Wando to be a fabulist; that maybe he'd never killed any other girls but the ones here. Those had been the only murders truly attributed to him, after all; but, after his confession, every jurisdiction in which he'd ever lived 'liked' him for this or that disappeared child or young adult. Coy, a lover of attention, had been only too happy to oblige by insisting he'd killed more than he could remember. Dozens.

True or not, a sick individual. I still toyed with the idea of working a psycho like Coy Wando into a future story. But really, I've had enough killing in my life.

But murder and torture, that was the kind of thing that sold books—ask any agent. I would—insert drumroll—but I haven't had one in ten years. Failed author drops mic. Crowd goes ape.

Daytime Tillman Falls lay quiet while I sat and sketched out characters for an idea, a series of stories inspired by my pre-tragedy, All-American childhood memories, not the terrible ones vying to occupy my head. A thousand visions flashed through my mind—of seeing movies at the Palmetto Grande; meals at Lucinda's Kountry Kitchen, now a restaurant and nightclub called Manny's on the Green; enjoying sandwiches and cherry Cokes and hamburgers after school at the Congress Street Grille; and last but not least, youthful speculation about the redneck goings-on inside a tavern of ill repute like The Dixiana, which wore its PBR-drinking, countrified shitkicker sensibilities on its sleeve.

Not my scene, "man." Never was.

I remain ever curious how a honkytonk ended up occupying such a high profile corner at the heart of Tillman Falls. Surely the town fathers—and mothers in the form of the ELMS, who many claimed were the real power behind the throne—would hold no truck with a true dive sitting catty-corner on the green from the courthouse and the newspaper and all the other legitimate businesses.

I craned my neck to see that the wig shop and the beauty salon and all the small town essentials had fallen by the wayside and been replaced by the cash advance joint, a cellphone store, and the combination tattoo parlor, piercing studio, and hair salon called Head Trauma, as counterintuitive a business name as my imagination could conjure.

At least The Dixiana offered a quasi-famous music hall, where pickers like Ralph Stanley and Earl Scruggs and innumerable other bluegrass and country notables had appeared; legend had it that in 1969 Johnny Cash, with Bob Dylan onboard, had diverted his tour bus all the way to Edgewater County just to see the place. The Dixiana had character, sass, history, and mystery, but was it truly more than a honkytonk? I doubted I'd ever set foot in there to find out if it could be more than what it appeared, like a mass market paperback with a lurid, unappealing cover one passes over without so much as a second look. Country music? Forget about it. Here, let me put on some hip-hop, or one of Duncan Devereaux's rock operas; or maybe stab knitting needles into my ears.

"Jasper asked after you in there."

Lost in a writer's trance, I flinched and cried out—Uncle Clete had appeared on the sidewalk by the bench. I'd been furiously scribbling notes, though not about Tillman Falls and honkytonks and the death of small town America, rather my story 'Songbird' and its central character inspired by Marcy Baumbach. Despite the suddenness, I felt energized coming out of this hazy, meditative headspace, an unfamiliar sensation of late.

Clete sat down. Seemed winded, stiff. "Sends his regards."

"Maybe I should've gone in after all." I'd made up an excuse about not wanting to intrude on my uncle's personal business, but the truth is that I didn't want to see a fellow author. Coward that I am, avoiding the answer to the question of what I had going—when the next book would be published—had become an instinctive self-defense mechanism. "But then, you had business."

He nodded, wouldn't meet my eyes. "Well, in any case he said you ought to come up and see him sometime. He'd love to hear what you're working on."

"That'd be wonderful." What a liar.

After we got back to Hillsborough, my uncle, less irascible than before he'd gotten his appointments squared away, insisted that I stay on at the house for a spell. I agreed only when he offered to make me a fresh cup of Folgers, except that it would be Eight O'Clock instead of Folgers. I didn't mind. To me, coffee is coffee.

With Clete's modern addition on the back of the house, Hillsborough didn't feel the way it used to, for which I felt thankful. Sitting with my back to the hallway leading through the original kitchen to the front rooms, which Clete's wife had turned into a sitting area, I could almost forget where I really was. That part of the house had always enjoyed a Southern facing, receiving the track of the morning sun in its graceful and inexorable arc across the Carolina sky.

A board creaked from overhead—one of the old ghosts. My chest felt tight. Now I knew exactly where I was.

We sat sipping and attempted further small talk. His eyes, which continued to avoid my own, suggested to me that all this had a deeper meaning.

I asked what was new.

"It's not good," he confessed. "You know."

"'It'? As in—"

Nodding, grim. "Yep."

Gently, I plied for further information.

"Use your imagination."

In doing so, I noted the sallow, sagging complexion of an old man—a sick man. "How not-good?"

Mouth downturned and jowls quivering, anger and frustration flashed across his soft face. He reached for the cup of coffee, his hand trembling.

I didn't press him for the details. "That's why you wanted me to come today. Not for a ride."

"I needed to run some shit by you," in a pent-up rush. "Can't leave you hanging."

The disposition of the family property.

A stab of icy terror in my gut like I hadn't known since being a child forced to stand for the first time in front of classmates to make a speech . . . or, perhaps, more akin that hollow sensation of easing over the top of a roller coaster's big hill. This, a moment I'd filed away:

that I'd one day be responsible for this place, a role I've never wished nor desired in any way, even when Lori-Kaye had so pushed for us to live here, to renovate and turn it into a showplace like houses over on Whaley Way. "There's time to figure all that out. Let's just sit and catch up for a while."

We did. We talked about that old codger of a car dealer, Hill Hampton, who'd been mayor for two terms, and two terms too long for Clete's taste. How the Reverend Roosevelt Nixon kept stirring the pot over the old mural on The Dixiana, and threatening to run for town council on a platform of removing it, and righting other cultural and social wrongs, for which he'd have my vote if only I still lived in the county. How the *Edgewater Advocate* hadn't been the same since it'd gone from a three times–weekly to a twice-weekly, and that its longtime editor and publisher Gaston Bundrick had been threatening retirement. How Rabbit Pettus, the owner of The Dixiana and a contemporary of Clete's, kept threatening to retire and close the joint; how it seemed, however, that the aging Rabbit's grandson and only heir, Roy Earl, had no interest in inheriting an old Tillman Falls honkytonk, and how Rabbit couldn't stand seeing it just flat-out gone. Not after all this time, and with all that history.

Gone, gone, gone. The upstairs floorboards creaked again.

"The boy made good," my uncle said of Roy Pettus, who'd been Gen X to my last-of-the-boomers status, and thus a few years behind me in the Edgewater County school system. "He lives down yonder on the coast."

"Sedge Island?"

Clete went *mmmmmyep*. "Or maybe it's Kiawah. Hell—it don't matter." His voice broke. "Why we beating around the bush?"

"Because you said you wanted to; and, because that's what Southern families do."

He laughed, hearty and genuine. "Lord knows but that's the truth."

I needed to say something, so I did: I thanked him for the years in which he'd raised me in the stead of my troubled, deceased parents. How he'd kept me afloat in lean times, those first years out of college. Before the first book, before I began to teach. When the trust had run dry.

"What was I supposed to do? You became my boy, then. After that durned mess. Lord have mercy," he choked off. The most anyone had spoken aloud in the family about the tragedy. "What else could an uncle do for his nephew."

Staggered, I maintained composure by sipping quietly on my mug of steaming Eight O'Clock. I'd never thought of Clete as my parent, only the uncle who had stepped in and done his duty, a fraternal requirement. Of his wife, Eldora, I thought even less so—she'd been a taciturn, unhappy woman who'd died at 62 from a cancer I'd always been convinced had been borne of her seeming antipathy to life in general. Clete, however, had been kind to me. They both had, I supposed, Eldora in the warmest manner that she could, which wasn't very.

Before the family tragedy, my aunt and uncle already had a couple of their own kids, my cousins Arthur and Lizzie, both a few years older. I always got along well with my Beauchamp cousins, two young adults who also helped me through the tragedy of my parents in their own way. I missed them both, but had to admit that nothing was keeping me from seeing Arthur—he had lived here all his life working as a cabinet maker and general carpenter; Lizzie, more of a wild child, had taken off for California, where she lives still, keeping her own brand of physical distance between her and whatever it was she wanted to forget about her hometown—most people have something.

A pang of guilt. My whole time here I'd barely given Arthur a thought, other than my annoyance over the condition of the grounds. We've nothing in common but our blood, which apparently isn't enough for me.

The sound of the upstairs floorboard creaking. A glance up at the corner of the ceiling. In the direction of the bedroom. Where it happened. A shudder.

I found my throat closing up with emotion. "You did right by me, Uncle Clete. You all did, even before—the tragedy."

"That's what family does." He picked up a napkin and wiped his eyes, then his mouth. "But what I reckon I really need to say to you is this, and I might as well just say it. I don't cotton to none of that sneaking around shit: I want to leave this place to Arthur. How's— how's that gonna sit with you?"

Uncle Clete's bluntness had often gotten him in trouble, and as established, Southern families don't communicate that way. If one did, one risked censure and ridicule and estrangement. Even when someone was dying before your eyes, as Eldora had been for several years, you didn't acknowledge it or talk about it. For two holiday seasons running we'd sat around the big table in the front room and spoken of her chemotherapy as 'medicine.' About the trips they wanted to take the following summer after Clete retired. Not, how do we feel about this terminal illness as a family, or is there anything we can do to make your life easier? Not our way.

He'd gotten me with the announcement of his mortal illness, caught me off guard: I had figured the next news would be the opposite: that he hoped I was prepared to reclaim this house and land as my own.

I sat in silence. I didn't know how to feel about Hillsborough, or this news.

Cutting me loose. But in a flash I realized this was in the best way: For my own good.

I didn't have a connection to the place, as I needed to remind myself, except steeped in tragedy I had tried with enormous vigor to forget.

Right—I wanted no part of the dump.

Brilliant. Bloody brilliant.

I told him I was taken aback . . . but also that his plan made enormous and demonstrable sense. Was a decision I felt that I could stomach. "I have my house in the woods already, don't I?"

"Couldn't say, Cortland—ain't never been invited over to see it."

As in an old Warner Brothers cartoon, my head turned into the heel of a shoe. "We need to fix that."

"I wouldn't hold the invite too long, my boy. S'all I can tell you." Three taps of his cane accompanied his following words: "Not. Too. Long."

I pledged to have him come one night, Arthur and his wife, too, all of us over for dinner. We'd grill steaks out on the patio like Granddaddy once had, with the family—or in this case what remains—arrayed along the back porch hearing the whippoorwill calling through the rolling hills to the river.

"You know what this is?" he asked me on the front porch, following a handshake that'd turned into an initially reluctant embrace—reluctant on his part, not mine. Men of his generation didn't hug.

"Tell me, Uncle Clete," not truly being sure what 'this' meant.

"This's a real gut check, this dying bullcrud. This is when you find out what character's all about, son. But you already know that, don't you. You know all about characters. And endings." He managed a wry wink, and even a smile. "And death."

"A writer has to keep his eye on the ending." Tears stung my eyes; I closed them to see the lights of the ambulances and Sheriff Truluck's prowler the night of the tragedy from inside that front bedroom.

The booming of the shots.

The smell of woodsmoke—wait, that's a different drama, from much later in life. Another story.

"I could tell by the way them people in your books talk about dying all the time. I didn't right catch on when I read them, not at first. But I can hear what they're saying, now. What you were saying."

I asked if he could tell me, truthfully, what he thought about the themes and subtext of my novels and stories.

He shook his head and held out his arms—*what more do you want me to say?* "You writing a new one?"

I shook my head. "Not for a long time, now. If I may confide that in my uncle."

"Then you better get to doing so, don't you think?"

"Confiding?"

"Writing."

A more suitable and apropos farewell I have not enjoyed in some time.

With these filial marching orders close in my mind, I took his advice and raced home to journal for an hour, and then to work on 'Songbird' and its protagonist 'Ruby Mendenhall,' a character name that'd come to me as I passed my old private academy.

I thought about the novel I'd attempted to write about my parents—it's my only 'trunk novel,' which is a manuscript that a writer managed to knock off but maybe didn't nail, that lies in a drawer somewhere like a musty literary gravesite. I couldn't tell their story because I didn't truly know all the circumstances behind the violence, only the broad strokes—infidelity, alcoholism, unhappiness. So trite and familiar that the very idea of trying to see it published inspires enervation rather than anticipatory glee.

Why through this fiction should I reveal the reasons for my father's act of murder-suicide? Sure, all the other factors were in play, but the truth, my mother's betrayal with another lover, quotidian as that reason might sound, had driven him over the edge into an aggrieved, out-of-control expulsion of human emotion that had manifested in murder. *Ack.* Who wanted to relive such horrors? Not I, said he. I hadn't even finished the damned manuscript, and now hoped I never would. Even if it were the last book I ever tried to write.

4.

Arriving the morning after Easter, I parked under the shade of the youngish oaks lining the ETC drive and around the faculty parking area, situated in the shinier and newer part of campus that'd been built in the late 80s. I fumbled with the phone buzz-buzz-buzzing in my pocket, an annoyance beyond measure, like suffering a squirming field mouse in one's sport coat.

Lori-Kaye. My ex-wife. Gah.

I didn't answer. While we didn't suffer a surfeit of lingering conflict, but nor did I have time to stomach one of her emotional dumps. The part about we're-still-great-friends is welcome enough, one supposes, except when the mind is racing at the speed of light, and wishing you had another week off from teaching to keep cranking out pages. The story kernels and seeds I'd collected were swirling around in my mind like leaves in a mini-whirlwind racing across an empty parking lot at dusk . . . rock stars and memorabilia collectors and songbirds all right; oh, all right, all right. I needed to get my feet on the ground, at least for the duration of the work day, so I answered.

Mistake. Doing so only reminded me of another failure, a most personal one.

But no drama or tension here. As I strolled through the busy parking lot bustling with student traffic, my chatty ex and I got caught up; she sounded happy but hesitant. Lori-Kaye, owner of a stationery and greeting card shop in Tillman Falls, quaint and nestled within the row of antiques purveyors, and as such, forever facing the trials, travails, and economic vicissitudes inherent with small business owner-ship. The best news? Now a member of the ELMS, the Edgewater Ladies Munificence Society—the century-old civic organization that

I'd always heard described in my house as a coven of vile and wicked meddlers rather than do-gooders, but in reality one that behaved little different from Opal's big city business association—my ex-wife felt as though she'd finally found her place in the community.

This, my opportunity to veer into my own new adventures, which I described after taking off my coat and sitting down on a bench in the shade of the classroom building, how I was helping Columbia, as much my home as Edgewater County, honor one of its own, he who had made us all so proud with all the rock music and such. How despite my mild cynicism, I felt no less inspired enough to be creative myself, again.

"Oh gracious, how marvelous, hon. How marvelous for you."

"Marvelous? I'm not so sure, not yet. But at least I'm writing again."

"You've always been a part of the arts scene in the capitol city, CB," her old nickname for me. "You've always identified yourself as an author from South Carolina, and more specifically, from the Midlands. And unreservedly so, if memory serves. Mm-yes, you do have a stake in your community there in Columbia," sounding like the politician it seemed she was becoming, "and they in you. So, good for you, you crotchety old writer. Something to get you out of that cabin sounds like a win–win to me. What else have you been doing with yourself lately?"

"Teaching these kids. Trying to persuade them of an actual point in the act of reading—and perhaps even becoming writers themselves."

"Marvelous. Marvelous, dear."

"And yet . . . I wonder on some days what I have to offer."

"There's the Cort Beauchamp I know. Him, and his self esteem issues . . ."

"Withdrawn."

I waved to one of my students, a young woman of Asian descent who'd shown the most promise out of this semester's edition of workshop students, the ones who'd had the guts to make a commitment to actually producing pages for the class instead of merely reading and thinking about the act of writing in an academic sense. A writer writes, I taught them through my fraudulent old fart's lips. A fifty year-old dried up prune insisting he had something to offer these fecund flowers, their lives in bloom; whereas, mine degrades into senescent uselessness—into suckitude, as one of these beautiful children might put it.

I changed the subject back to the Duncan Devereaux celebration of special-ness, as I had taken to privately thinking of the efforts to pester a man who didn't want any attention, whose stony silence had thus far served as rebuff to the attempts at persuasion. "I personally think we should leave him alone. Despite his former profile, it's obvious he now abhors such attention. As would I."

As I entered the classroom building, nodding to students familiar and otherwise, Lori-Kaye's voice, amused, broke up into jagged, digital noise. "Oh, please—you love attention. You know you dream that somewhere down the line, one of the old men," meaning the stately mature oaks of the town green, "will be dedicated to you." It was a verbal wink; there existed no higher Edgewater County honor.

A concession. "At one time? Sure. Now I suspect bigger royalty checks would be a greater honor."

"I know the feeling. I must confess that for the last year or two, business has been falling off."

"Oh, drat. That's terrible." And I meant it. "How bad?"

Catastrophic, as it happened—she planned to throw in the towel. I felt kicked in the stomach for her. "I'm so sorry—Lori." I had to check myself to keep from calling her 'honey,' an old habit.

"Besides my manager, you're the only one who knows."

The plans to shutter the biz would be kept under my hat. I knew that a business owner never admitted to customers when things were going south, because such verbalizations tended to create a psychological sense of failure both in the minds of customers, and the community at large. People wanted to be a part of successes, not failures. They wanted to hand over their money to a good cause, not a lost one.

"Maybe it isn't irrevocable," she said. "Hoping for a good summer of tourists. And the horse races," which happened in the spring and fall, and brought in tens of thousands of visitors to eastern Edgewater County, the wealthier half—the Whaley Way half. "But I'll be fine."

I knew she would. Lori-Kaye, like me, from dusty, old Southern money. Not a truckload, but something like a small pile; like brown, brittle oak leaves raked into a modest mound in the yard during football season, when the high school stadium would be lit up at night and glowing from the other side of the ridge, a sports complex that held no meaning for me other than being the place where I had kissed my Lori-Kaye for the first time—or to be truthful, when she had kissed me.

My bones, creaking at the passing of the years. We married too young. Hadn't served either of us very well, but at the time? It felt right, and so we'd done it. An eon ago now.

Melancholy and loss threatened to take hold, but I detached myself from the feelings. Grew analytic. I didn't pine for Lori-Kaye per se, only for what she represented. A metaphor for lost . . . no, wait. Fading youth. Not lost. Only fading.

Metaphor? More like stark reality, staring back out of the morning mirror.

We said goodbye and pledged to do better about keeping up. As I put it away and entered my classroom the phone felt hot in my pocket, oven-baked by wistful memories of young love gone wrong. What I needed to make were new memories.

"Good morning, campers. Nice long weekend?" Whole class, even my star pupil, seemed a little groggy rather than fresh, all mumbling and nodding in relative unison.

"I want to throw you all a curve ball this morning."

A rustling; mumbling became grumbling.

"Everyone relax. Let's have some fun by starting with a reading today, from one of you. I know that everyone's making good progress on their stories. Right . . .?"

At last, a hand, tentative.

"Excellent." Taking a notebook and pen, I took a seat in the front row.

While my student, a young woman of Lebanese extraction named Layla who'd shown considerable promise, read her five-page story in a voice that quavered and with hands that visibly trembled, I scribbled notes like a madman, hearing not a single word that poor dear had to say. What a selfish shit I can be.

The class, on the other hand, laughed and gasped; at the end, they erupted with a hubbub of approbation: she had a winner. She had a hit. She'd written a piece that, whatever it said, had spoken to her peers.

More than I could say about anything I'd written and published in ages.

Maybe ever—a chilling notion.

"Bravo, bravo," applauding and replacing her at the lectern. "Did you hear that reaction? Your courage paid off."

"Dat shit rocked, girl." Walid, bumping fists with Layla, whose skin seemed to glisten with gratification and accomplishment. "Word."

"Shouldn't I revise it?" she asked with eyes of dew. "Y'all thought it was okay?"

"Don't change a word. Not a word." I stood considering their faces, half of which were scrunched in contemplation, of what I suspected—hoped—were fertile minds trying to make sense of what was so compelling about her piece. "Did you young people realize that one of the most significant writers in American history came from right here in South Carolina?"

Silence.

"William Gilmore Simms. Anyone heard of him?"

Nothing.

"He was the first American writer, a famous one, in fact, to make enough money from his work for him and his family to live on. But because he was unrepentant about who should have won the Civil War, he's been ostracized and mostly forgotten."

Walid frowned at this. "Did he own slaves?"

"Oh, my, yes. Unfortunately so."

"Then maybe his ass shoulda been forgot."

The class, many of them possible descendants of people once enslaved by the Simmses of the antebellum world, tittered in either mild discomfort, or perhaps assent.

Time to let this go. "Maybe so. But this isn't history class."

Walid raised his hand. "Thought you told us that folks who didn't keep they own history in mind was doomed to do it all over again."

"When did I say that?"

"On the first day." He flipped to the first page of his notebook and showed me.

"All very true. As for Simms, I thought y'all would like to know that South Carolina has a long history of producing important artists and writers, including one of the first major voices in our country's literature. But let's worry about our own work—let's talk about point of view. Who is the voice of the story that you want to tell? Besides the author who stood reading to you all, *who* was telling the story that Layla read to us? Anyone? Anyone . . . ?" I certainly didn't know. "Layla, let me see your pages, please."

I covered my personal notebook with Layla's story, and focused on my students and their needs. I had all the time in the world for my little notes and stories and novels—hell, I'd be back home by lunchtime. This time belonged to them.

<h1 align="center">5.</h1>

Once back home at the cabin after classes, I put down my brief-case and remembered to turn my phone back on. In doing so, I cringed at a number of missed calls: from Opal, from Feebee, two from Rick Wragg, and: none of them leaving messages more substantive than to return calls forthwith, ASAP, with all speed, et cetera.

Groan.

Out of the three I figured Rick could wait, so I began by ringing Opal, who picked up and began barking at me.

"No," I responded to her first query, which was about securing Marcy a spot in the CityArt festival; everyone in such a hurry, always. Tiresome. "I haven't spoken to Leora about it. Yet."

"Dude: you gotta fucking move on this. Marcy's got ambition, don't you know."

Mercy—these people didn't want much, did they? "I thought reaching out to Devereaux posed the most urgency."

"True; but, I got another problem. Another layer, now. This kid, young singer fresh out of music school at Southeastern, she dropped her press kit off this morning. Perfect for the restaurant: all jazz and blues standards. Total class act lounge singer type-deal."

"Which has what to do with what, exactly."

Her voice came small and chastened. "I wanna replace Marcy."

Yikes. "My word. Are you out to destroy her self-esteem?"

"Maybe. I did give my blessing to her dating you."

"Amusing. But I'm being serious."

Opal cursed a typically colorful string of invective. "I don't know why I called you. Never good for a damn goddamn thing. Just get her on that festival stage. Do you understand me, boy?"

My face blazed. During our prior courtship, Opal and I had rubbed each other the wrong way as much as we had the *ahem* right way, which of course portended its own particular brand of body heat. "I never took you for such a Machiavellian shrew."

"Hah—just get cracking. Or I swear I'll cut off your dick, scribe."

I thanked her for the kind words, said I'd get back in touch, and rang off in a huff.

If all this hadn't been regarding Marcy, whom I'd thought about nonstop for days, I never would have called Leora Wood-Cobb about this request in a thousand centuries. Galaxies would live and die in the time I wouldn't pull my tenuous strings to yank Opal's narrow Sicilian bum out of the oven, browning and basting there next to her flat-bread pizzas and multigrain dinner rolls perfect with slathered butter; I didn't owe her anything. Besides: I barely knew Marcy. Was attracted to her, yes; certainly and without question. But enough to go through this hell? I detest asking people for favors. The kind of man who wants to be a solitary writer out in the woods fixes life for himself so that he doesn't need favors, or friends, or people. Grumble–grumble, said the hermit.

Wait. Did I plan to like, 'hook up' with my songbird . . . or not?

Now who was scheming?

I ignored the other messages from Rick and Feebee. Instead, I took my time preparing an early dinner of baked tilapia and steamed veggies, which I ate on the back deck while reading Dostoyevsky on the iPad and listening to the late afternoon sounds of the forested hollow. Around happy hour I went inside and made a pot of green tea, after which I began writing—thousands of words tumbled out, a massive output of material that lasted until almost eleven, an hour past my bedtime. Journaling and free-writing, most of it, until finally I settled in and revised 'Collector'—once for style and technical issues, and again, but for story, dialogue, and to see if any subtext or grand metaphor seemed to have emerged:

What did the collecting of the autographs and memorabilia repre-sent? On a deeper level?

'Magic,' the uncle tells the kid. 'These rock stars are like magic pixies who come around only once a year, and if you get to talk to one, a wish of yours will come true.'

Or some such sentimental tripe. Getting my sea-legs back, all right? It wasn't even my story. More fraudulent behavior. But for a beggar like me, writing was writing, and I'd take it where, and how, it came.

I got Leora on the first bounce, but at the first mention of the booking of the CityArt musical acts she sent me straight to Feebee, from whom I already had two unreturned and politely strained messages as well as an email, the existence of said messages making me feel as though I stood charged and in trouble, hence even less enthusiastic about calling her on this vexatious issue. Feebee's command and her facility of organization on the DDC had intimidated me. A part of me wanted to please a figure of such accomplishment, but another part—a big one—wanted to abjure my responsibilities and go take a walk in the woods.

"Mr. Beauchamp? Thank *god* you got back to me. Finally."

Pointed. Ouch. "Please, now—it's Cort. Mr. Beauchamp was my father."

"'Cort'—oh, I love it. I just love it. What an honor. Thank you so much." She sighed. "Are you free for lunch? I realize it's last minute."

"Lunch . . . today?"

"There's no other time but right now, as they say."

By design I didn't have any classes on Tuesday and Thursday, which at one time had been designated as all-writing days, and in recent times more often spent catching matinees with senior citizens and sitting in parks on benches reading better novels and stories than I'd ever manage to scratch out. "Well. I suppose."

She gave me a time and the address of a restaurant in the Old Market. Sounded duly grateful.

I gathered an attaché with various accoutrements of my trade—a notebook and a couple of pens—as well as the iPad for when I invariably turned to reading instead of writing, and set out yet again, south to the capital city. At the last minute I went to shave and trim my nostril hairs. Feebee, much younger—too much so—but terribly attractive.

✦

And who nearly pulled an attractive spit-take when I asked her about Marcy and the festival's booking availability. "All due respect, but, are you nuts?"

"CityArt's still a month away. Surely there's room for her."

She fixed me with a pitying look. "Oh, Mr. Beau—Cort, I mean. Mr. Cort. My famous novelist." She fluttered her eyes, glanced at the screen of a buzzing iPhone, and in the time it would take me to turn the damn thing on, both read and replied to what seemed to be no fewer than three text messages—*bloop, bloop, bloop.*

"You know, gosh," coming back to the subject at hand. "The music's been set since, golly, the end of January. Since before you were added to the author's circle tent, I think. Way before. Set. Done."

Zing. In an instant I knew that, for all Feebee's wonder and delight at being in the company of such a literary god as yours truly that she'd put me in my true place, riven and reduced to fit onto a small postage stamp-sized patch of dirt underneath the point of her high heel. Definitive. I admired her fortitude.

But I had to try. I fought to keep the whine out of my words. "Marcy's so darned talented, though. She could use a break. Rick suggested a brief acoustic set in between the um other musical um acts." I felt a fool trying to speak lingo with which I held little understanding. "Or I mean, solo with piano. Like at the restaurant."

"Marcy Baumbach? From the other night? A break? Acts? Piano? Rick?" She fought to process it all, took a deep breath. "C'mon, Cort—she must play in this city three or four nights out of the week." She counted off her examples with fingers that trembled. "Wednesdays at the Mudcreek Grill. Fridays at Opal's. Another gig during Wednesday happy hour in the lobby bar at the Marriott. During the season, Saturdays out at the lake—I have a condo out there by the Westside Marina. Jesus, I can hear Marcy Baumbach from the dockside stage."

She paused as the server appeared with our enormous platters burdened by sandwiches and fried potatoes and leafy green lettuces and sauces and a thimble-sized serving of sautéed mushrooms and onions. I gained five pounds merely by looking at the food.

"Thank-*you.*" Feebee, squeezing her eyes and wrinkling her nose at the young college student working for tips, who responded in kind. "But we're gonna need more ketchup. Thanks."

"Marcy's got some fine original songs, though. CityArt exposure, it could—"

"Cort. Please." Eyebrows arched, she chowed into a burger half as big as her head and continued speaking, thick, through vigorous, wet mastication. "*No.* Let us weep not for the Marcy Baumbachs of the live music trade. Did you hear what I just said? Four gigs a week—regular gigs, now—and in a market the size of metro Columbia? Tell me another one—she needs a break like I need another meeting this week." She took a swig of water and licked her lips, which had become frosted by a delicate, subtle shading of mustard and mayo. Impish: "If I could just lay it out there all blunt on ya like that."

I didn't know Feebee well enough to feel comfortable saying what was on my mind, which was, who the H are you to decide who needs a break and who doesn't? But Feebee had earned her place, had shown me and lots of other folks of consequence that her judgment and knowledge were up to snuff. You had to respect that.

"I just know she's had her eye on playing the fest, and said that Opal hadn't been able to help, so . . . I thought I'd try to throw my weight around. Insubstantial as it might be." Time to turn over a winning card. I folded my hands on the table in front of my own barely nibbled shank of charred, ground meat-flesh. "I do represent your link to Mr. Devereaux, after all."

She paused in mid-chomp, a shred of lettuce dangling off her chin. "That you are. But wait, aren't they like, best friends? Marcy and Opal?"

I confirmed that to my knowledge they were.

"Opal didn't say anything to me. About Marcy. About any of this." Her forehead scrunched and eyes darted around, calculating and confused. "Why are *you* coming to me with this? What is this all about? Some kind of end run?" The notion seemed to grip her with terror—a nefarious plot, unfolding. "I'm—confused."

I explained that I had no agenda or subterfuge in mind other than seeing a talented local musician featured at the arts fest, get a rightfully earned place at the table, so to speak. "Opal simply felt she'd used up her capital in getting you to take on her brother's band. Surely you can understand." That all sounded right. "That's really all it is."

"The Green Hole Six? Oh, Mr. Cort—Opal wouldn't have had to pull any strings for *Tony*. The GHS, they've been around this town forever! His band's already at the top of my list."

My turn to be confused by Opal's motivations. I chewed and tried to smile, nodding. Asking through a mouthful of charred beef I shouldn't have been eating, "So what about Marcy? What do ya say?"

"Oh, Mr. Cort . . . oh, my. I don't know."

"Don't make me beg, Feebee."

"Beg? Oh, wait." A sly smile. Her cheeks colored. "I get it. *You like her.*"

"Now, now, nothing of the sort."

"O-kay. Sure." Now she seemed amused and touched. "Her songs. They're that good."

"That's really all it is," my own cheeks heated by the duplicity. "I swear."

"Sure sure sure," her glance piercing. Saying, you horny little devil. "I'll work it out with Rick. We'll have Marcy come on and do a mini-set before the Green Hole Six." She slugged back iced tea I knew to be sweet as maple syrup. "So tell me: Are you writing anything new?"

The curveball caused me to gag on my pickle slice. I sipped my bland unsweetened tea and recovered. "I am. Mainly short stories. But, are you familiar with the history of the city? The burning?"

"Sorta-kinda. The Civil War thing?"

"Right."

"Oh, yeah, sure—I know a little."

"I'm thinking about a historical . . . romance," I managed to say, "set against the backdrop of the burning of Columbia and the aftermath. The story's centered on the *Phoenix*, which was the newspaper William Gilmore Simms helped publish after the—"

"Wow, sounds awesome," chewing her last bite and calling for the check and apologizing about needing to skedaddle to another appointment. "Get dessert—I'll go ahead and pay for a dessert for you, but right now I have to scoot. But your romance, wow, that's just great. Oh, wait. You know what your new book makes me think of?"

"No." But I did. I began counting down from five. Four. Three. Two—

"*Gone with the Wind.* That's my grandmother's favorite movie. So, like, that sounds like it will be really amazing, Mr. Cort. My writer.

My novelist," squeezing eyes and leaving me to order my choice of cheesecake, apple tart with ice cream, or fudge brownie mountain with whipped cream. "T-T-Y-S."

Whatever that meant.

Sigh. I wasn't really writing that historical romance. Her novelist seemed more an inveterate liar than a working artist. But before I could order a sugary sweet treat that I didn't need in any nutritional sense, Feebee, stricken, came racing back from the sunlit sidewalk, a silhouette charging in my direction.

"Oh, what an idiot," her face the color of her red skirt. "You made me forget the whole reason I wanted to take you to lunch. Have you made any progress getting in touch with Duncan Devereaux? Please tell me you have."

If I thought spinning a yarn about working on a big new novel was a white lie, what would a similar approach here constitute? "Waiting on a reply to an email and a voicemail," cheery and nonchalant. "And keeping fingers crossed. We all know what we're up against. A man like him wanting privacy has considerable resources to achieve said isolation. Layers, in fact, that I'm working through."

She let out a sigh, put a hand on her chest. "Thank you, Cort Beauchamp. You are my hero. My real American hero. *Mwah,*" blowing a kiss and dashing back out, clip-clop-clip-clop. "I got you covered on Marcy. This time," she called over her shoulder ominously.

I had used up a favor—a big one.

My apple tart à la mode arrived; I sat for a while carving the sides of the mound of ice cream like Richard Dreyfuss dreaming of UFOs and other bright twinkly lights in the sky. I realized that, in some part of my life, whether creatively or with these civic duties, I would need to reach out to Duncan.

And, to service Marcy's desires as well, whom I was now determined to woo, regardless of helping her secure a performance slot in the festival. A festival, celebrating the creative class.

Creative Class.

CREATIVE CLASS.

I got chicken skin. Legs, arms, wings, back of my neck.

Now, if I were going to write a new novel, that, my friends, could well be a title—a working one, at the very least. If—IF—I were at last working on a new novel. I wrote the two words in my pocket Moleskine and dug into my dessert, relishing every bite.

Rick phoned a third time, happening to catch me strolling around the college neighborhood while staring at my phone and listening to the busy, bouncing notes of Telemann's Suite in G minor. I had been trying to figure out how to program a meeting onto the iCalendar with an alarm that would alert me to my presence being required at the next, rapidly approaching DDC conclave.

Sheepish, I felt I had no choice but to take the call, the ringtone of which had so rudely interrupted the dizzying strings and woodwinds I'd put on to cheer me up. I greeted him apologetically, wondering if after our lunch Feebee hadn't prompted him to call and hector me.

"So, so, so," he says, he says, he says. "I been rapping with that Lizette gal from the DDC, and man, her and my uncle, they should like, I dunno, get together. Peas in a pod. No question. But her thing ain't music in general, only Devereaux. All 40DD, all the time. This is whose brain you want to pick. She's part of this whole network that tracks the dude. Waiting for him to, you know. Come back."

"Sounds positively biblical."

"Exactly. So this DD network, they got the rundown on pretty much his every move. But they keep their distance. They show respect."

"I suppose he should be flattered. Until they show up with a cross and some nails."

Rick barked his staccato laugh. "No question. He's got pads in LA and NYC, but did you know he lives downstate? Like, all-but right here?"

"Indeed—Sedge Island," though a hundred-fifty miles wasn't quite right here. A rich man's resort I'd first visited as a child, back when most of it had been owned by a northern industrialist, the sea island, near the Port Royal sound, had long since been semi-developed into a resort destination for the upper-middle-class set. Parts of the island remained reserved for the extremely wealthy like Duncan Devereaux, an international star—big here and on the continent, huge in South America, revered in Japan; indeed, planet-wide notoriety, yet living isolated on a tiny jut of Carolina sea and sand, far from the limelight as possible. "Among the sawgrass and the sea pines, our reclusive guitar virtuoso awaits. Proximity isn't the issue, though; it's access. A person's privacy is at stake."

"You been trying to get in touch with him? At all, yet?"

"It's only been a few days since our meeting!"

"It's been almost a freaking week, duder."

"I have other obligations, too. Like everyone."

"Cort, a writer like you? And a college professor? I can only imagine." He blew out his lips, a wet raspberry sound. "Bro, you are the linchpin, here. The fulcrum. The crux. The crucial—"

"You're making me sound like the rogue's gallery of super-villains in a comic book. I'm not crucial to anything. I'm merely a writer, a lonely writer, who's being pestered."

"Lonely, you are?" Rick, offering this fractured syntax in a bizarre tone that reminded me of a raspy Miss Piggy. "A Jedi like you must embrace loneliness. Must grapple with the dark side."

"Loneliness," I intoned, unbidden, "happens to be a writer's stock in trade."

"Ah. That shit's like, poetic."

"You really think so?"

"That's why you're the writer."

"The point is, my interview with Duncan was twenty years ago, and furthermore, our friendship, such as it was, wasn't much of one. It was only for a weekend. That's the truth." I mumbled an excuse about "new journalism," about putting the reader in the dramatic narrative of a rock star's daily routine by pretending to be his hometown pal.

It struck me that it had been less journalism than another one of my short stories. I wished I could go to the library and take the print of the article off the wall of fame.

"You know him well enough to have called him Duncan just now, right?"

Morose. "I suppose so."

"Then you got a leg up on the rest of us, pal."

I couldn't deny it. Rick told me I should quit downplaying. That I could instead try, oh, he didn't know. Embracing the challenge.

Which as it happened, he could facilitate: "So here's the dealio: As it turns out I'm heading down to Sedge Island in a couple of weeks, for a reunion with the band I used to manage back in the early 90s—the Steaming Dashikis, you probably heard of 'em. Played the whole southeastern circuit, got big regionally. Course, I was out of the band, er, off the crew by then. Before, though, I *was* the freaking crew. Yanking cable. Rolling in cabinets. Front of house sound. And the manager, of course. Everything. A tough gig—no question. But I loved those guys. Love love love those guys. Love love love 'em still, every one, bless their pointed little heads. The act didn't last much longer anyway. Not without old Rick around to make them sound good as heck."

I begged Rick to get to the point of what all this had to do with Duncan Devereaux, other than the Sedge Island and musician connection . . . when an ah-ha moment occurred like a dimmer switch turning, a warm glowing light appearing in the hallway of my mind like the sunrise at the beginning of the Dawn of Man sequence in *2001: A Space Odyssey*. "So we'll just, what? Show up down there? On Duncan's doorstep?"

"Can you dig it? Check this out: The Dashikis, they're getting a big ass place for everybody, a weekend house party type-deal. Not the best environment for me, I know. Don't say it cause I already know it, but I'm not gonna backslide. But the house, turns out it's right freaking up the beach from our man's estate; and now that we know from Gendry that the dude's got a regular schedule, as in, he's on the beach out on the point near the sound every morning, which is only like a mile down from us..."

"I'm supposed to interrupt his sunbathing, I take it."

"Check. You're gonna just walk your ass right up to him on his own damn beach. It's beautiful, I tell ya."

"This sounds monstrous." During my stroll I'd found my way to the Carolina Beanery Café, where this whole terrible situation had begun over salads with Leora. Shaking with anxiety, I couldn't stomach the thought of that strong coffee they served in there. "I won't do it."

"What? It's beautiful, Cort. Here's how it'll go: You'll break the ice. You'll say how great it is to run into him like this—a freaking freaky coincidence—and how crazy awesome that interview was all those years ago. You'll be slappin' each other on the backs, bro. After you're done waxing each other's wangs over the wonder and synchronicity of it all? That, my friend, is when you'll pitch the whole DDC deal to him."

"Which you expect to work?"

"Shit yes. He's gonna say one little word, and that one word is gonna be spelled Y-E-S. Presto. Like magic."

I didn't take to this idea any more than I had harassing this troubled musician via the phone or email or carrier pigeon, but on one point Rick was right enough: to the committee I presented as the sole life-line to this enigmatic multimillionaire, a man who didn't have to do a blessed thing he didn't want to do.

Perhaps DD would remember me on sight. We'd spent our weekend of interviews doing a great deal of staring at one another, him especially at me, and especially when our talk had gotten deep, and maybe dangerous—there'd been things that Duncan had confided in me that I'd agreed to elide and redact from my narrative. Nothing sexual, as Rick had suggested, or untoward by the standards of typical rock-star proclivities. Personal matters. Feelings. Despite the heavy metal thunder, a sensitive soul. No wonder he'd been so destroyed later by the deaths of those kids in the audience, fans who gave their lives to be near him.

My resistance crumbled into chalky limestone at my feet. "Your plan's not the worst notion anyone's come up with. Me emailing the record company or his manager or his mother here in town won't get us anywhere." One needed extreme good fortune or rhetorical bunker-busters to get through to agents or editors or personal managers. A person like Rick, who'd never attempted to wrench payment for amorphous creative work like songs or stories or novels, would never know how difficult, and frustratingly necessary, the role of the gatekeeper.

"Dude. Bro. This'll work. Believe me, I get ideas all the time—I know the diff between a lemon and a foolproof, surefire winner, and this is that. This is that, bro. Cort, I mean. Bo-champ."

He informed me of the details, this beach trip to somebody's kid's wedding, a thought that sounded dreadful. "When are these nuptials, exactly?"

"Memorial Day. Ha-ha, but not Confederate Memorial Day. The real one."

"I assumed you meant as much."

"You guys are touchy about that stuff."

"Excuse me?"

"You Southerners."

"About Confederate Memorial Day? Some of us. Not me."

"Not even Edgewater County old-South money like yourself, Cortland Beauregard Beauchamp?"

I explained that I wasn't one of those Southerners, that I didn't dress in gray and reenact lost causes and fool's errands, that I wasn't particularly invested in getting my dander up over whatever had occurred between my ancestors and their American brothers from the North. Indeed, I took no umbrage whatsoever, even though the merest mention of such a topic makes my mind want to leap into hyperdrive on both CREATIVE CLASS and what I'd begun thinking of as REVIVAL, a story of survival and redemption set amidst the charred ruins of post-Sherman Columbia, when the days ground on and the city lay in wreckage, ruined and hungry and without guidance. For a month they languished with no word of the outside world, of the war, of whom else Sherman might have vanquished. Not until the newspaper came back. Not until Simms wrote the account, serialized in the *Phoenix,* and later as a pamphlet called *The Capture, Sack and Burning of Columbia.* Not until—

"Yo, yo, yo. Bo-champ, you have a stroke over there? You ain't answered a single question out of the last three."

"Oh—I'm fine. I have these spells. It's a writer thing."

"Gotcha. But what I asked was, what's the deal with the novel."

"Pardon?"

"You just said," and here he started mimicking me to a T, my deep, syrupy Edgewater County blue-blood cadence, lazy and long on the vowels, "that 'this novel about the burning of Columbia is my true life's work, and so I ought'n to get to it.' So I was asking, what's it about? Something that happened to you? Or what?"

"You heard those words? *Aloud?*"

"A version of that. Kinda soft and all, but—yeah."

My head, spinning. "If I said it's about the burning of Columbia, then—"

"Hold on hold on hold on. The other night, you told me it's about something, yes, but it's also about something else, on that other level—

what'd you call it. The sub-texture of the piece. The story. The dealio. That's what I was asking, man. One writer to another."

I had to get out of this. My mouth was producing words of its own volition to this, this Rick person, of all people. Intimate words. Innermost thoughts. "Rick, pains me to run off, but I'm feeling—I should go."

"You were saying, 'the burning, the burning.' That you had to write about the burning. You had to write something meaningful."

I felt pinned to the sidewalk, the smell of coffee from inside the Beanery replaced by horridly acrid, phantom woodsmoke. "Then I suppose I should get to it."

"Which one? The book? Or trying to get DD onboard?"

"Both." Another of my little lies. Actually I planned to crawl into a hole somewhere and read for the rest of the day. Take a bike ride. A walk by the river here in town. Anything but all this drama.

"Final thought, buddy."

Staring down the barrel of one-last-thing, I waited.

"We're all expecting great things."

"The bar is high. By all means. 'We got this'—right?"

"Right. *Ciao,* baby."

Rick, finally letting me go. When I went back to my music, I inadvertently touch-screened the Shuffle function and found the lightness of Telemann replaced by the ominous woodwinds and deep-voiced strings of Bartók's *Two Pictures*, which in any case better suited the darkness of my mood.

Which darkened.

When, after only a moment, the music stopped.

For another phone call.

This one, however, I would find I wanted to take. In the worst way. Marcy.

6.

As I recovered from a case of the flutters, Marcy asked what I was up to, like, right that minute. Despite sloshing with tea and apple tart I agreed with unconcealed, cheerily zealous agreement to meet her for coffee, at a café in the West Vista not far from Rick's house. I found a parallel parking spot and saw that she stood waiting, with an expectant and pleasant smile on her gorgeous face, a flattering tunic that exposed a freckled thoracic region accented by the sexiest clavicles allowed by law. The woman's shoulders were hot. Inwardly, at least, I panted like the horndog I was.

"Look, I've been thinking about you a lot." Sparing me the trouble of hitting on her, she said this in a blunt rush after we shared a brief but electric hug. "Since the other night."

"You *have?* Do tell."

"Well . . . since Opal told me how you felt, anyway."

Frozen, a grinning idiot, a rictus of uncertainty like lockjaw—I suddenly felt the specter of note-comparing between the two women hanging over this attraction. Discomfort. "I admit to thinking you quite lovely."

"That's what came over the wires." A demure, lidded glance. "She said you had something specific you might want to talk to me about, though . . . ?"

Since Feebee's tacit agreement about Marcy's set, I supposed that I did have news. We went into the cafe and ordered coffees to go. Marcy'd suggested strolling down the hill closer to the river and sitting in the shade near the bridge across the Congaree to downtown, its arches and construction a strong and sturdy and aesthetically pleasing reminder of a more elegant time. In the warming spring afternoon, a lovely idea.

On the five-minute stroll Marcy noted the saltboxes, pointing out that Rick lived only about five blocks away.

Not news. "I went over to his house. After our meal at Opal's last week."

Another coy, mischievous glance. "He said y'all played records and talked all night like a couple of schoolgirls. Like best friends."

"A slight case of hyperbole. But we got on well."

Once we entered the riverwalk park area, Marcy pulled herself into a silent lip-chewing space, slowing down, seeming to drift away in a pensive daydream. The sun beat down, warm. We found an unoccupied picnic table in the shade of a huge old river birch. I watched as the rippling quicksilver surface of the water ate microscopically away at a stone that'd been worn to its smooth shape by unfathomable gallons of cascading Carolina river. College kids walked around ankle-deep near the shore, or floated in groups on colorful tubes farther out, one in the middle reserved for a cooler of beer. Bikers, joggers, pregnant women pushing strollers, with two and three stair-step children already toddling along behind Mommy. I'd noted the scene many times; back when I had held the writing workshops at the library, I would often come here beforehand to enjoy an outdoor lunch, get my notes and lesson plan together. More peaceful, back then; the park had been new, and many had yet to discover it.

Columbia had done right by its rivers, but only after a fashion: until the initiative to build the river walks, part of a larger effort to eventually link up what was to be called the Riverwalk Greenway, the riverbanks had sat in private hands, undeveloped and surrounded on both shores by scrubby trees and underbrush full of flotsam and other trash. At last, someone had realized the assets at hand. I wondered if it had to do with the war. And Reconstruction. One would have thought that in 150 years the city footprint might have grown and migrated the half mile from the campus of Southeastern to the shore across from which we sat. But it hadn't, not until the twenty-first century. The citizenry and leaders had to rebuild the old city before a new could arise. Maybe in another century, we'd finally catch up with our own history.

"I feel so bad. I haven't read any of your books." From her handbag emerged a trade paperback edition of *Keys to the Rain* with a faded and peeling barcode sticker on the spine. "I'm starting with the first one. Isn't that what you should do with a new writer? Start with their first book?"

"Depends. If you want to track an artist's progress from piece to piece, chart their growth, then, sure." I reached over and took the copy from her hand, pulled out a ballpoint pen, clicked it open. "Shall I inscribe it to you, my dear?"

"NO," she yelled, startling a flock of geese who'd been floating by us. Aghast, she snatched my novel back. "It's from the library."

I burst out laughing. "I see."

Stricken, her face softened. "Phew. I—I didn't want to have to pay for it. That must sound awful."

"Heavens, no." I slipped the pen back into my blazer and arched an eyebrow. "We couldn't have anyone paying for one of my smelly old books."

Her laugh, itself a gooselike honking, echoed across the water and up into the concrete arches of the bridge. "So I looked you up on Wikipedia—that's why I wanted to talk to you today."

"Oh, how thrilling. Wait—since when do I have a Wikipedia entry?"

She nodded. "And when I got to the part about your parents—"

"*Excuse me?*" My half-sipped Styrofoam cup of coffee fell out of my hand onto the ground and spattering the loafers I'd shined only this morning. I howled in protest at such a profane breach of privacy, that my childhood tragedies were online for all to read. "Who's done such a thing to me?"

"Probably your publisher, or your PR firm."

I explained that I possessed neither, currently; she said, well, somebody put it up there. Stricken and confused and violated, I slumped and sat down on a bench. Pondered what to do.

Marcy sat beside me, her hands clasped. "It's not the end of the world. You can log in and edit what it says. You can do that, you know."

"No, I can't—I'm not very computer savvy."

"I'll help. I made my own page myself. Not like I had any fans to do it for me."

Hm, I thought. "Meaning what?"

"That, if someone put up a Wiki for you, then they must really admire you, and your work. Don't you think?"

I said that however misguided, I supposed that this enigmatic entity must indeed have cared enough to have done so, duly flattered, et cetera.

But then, officious and impatient, I asked Marcy to go back to the parents issue, and asked why it mattered to her. It'd been thirty-seven years. I held no truck with diving into that wretched snake pit of memories, except long enough to deal with this breach of damn internet privacy. I wanted to wiki someone's little presumptuous online ass. Drop some serious, oh, what did they call it, flamebait on the party who had done this. "I'd just as soon talk about anything else, if you don't mind."

She apologized. "It's just that—I'm losing my mom. Well, we've been saying that for so long now that it sounds like a joke you've heard from a comedian you used to think was funny, but through repetition, it's no longer got the same pizzazz. Ya dig?"

Told her I didn't get the metaphor, not regarding the illness of a family member.

"Okay: a song you love and is catchy, until it gets stuck in your head, when you begin to hate it."

"Exactly—wait. I'm confused."

Chagrined. "Her prognosis, it's been bad from day one. She's hung in there. It didn't spread any further for a long time. She's held her own. But it's getting worse, and I don't know how much longer—or how to feel—they didn't give her long. And that was almost three years ago."

"What about your father?"

"Split when I was still a little squirt. I saw him off and on, but Ma remarried a guy for about ten years, then they broke up. Not an evil stepfather or anything, just a doofus she got sick of fast. She's been single ever since." Marcy, beautiful in the afternoon light despite looking aggrieved. She sipped her coffee and seemed disgusted by it. "Single, and a pain in my ass."

"You're weary. It's a natural reaction. You want her to live, but at the same time, she's suffering, you're suffering with each passing day . . . it's natural, this guilt."

"That's the thing—I don't feel guilt. When I think what I'd like to do about her."

"Which is what?"

"Smother her with a pillow. In the night. That if she didn't have dogs that'd bark . . . ha." Her chin now aquiver. Trying to avert the tears. "Killing. I mean—kidding. About killing her."

I wasn't sure how to swing at this emotional curveball, which a part of me instantly grokked was the crux of this visit rather than a romantic outreach. "Dear, you're so tired. You're both so weary."

"Her quality of life, it's not as bad as it could be, but it's not as good as she lets on. She hides the pain well. But in your case, see, you lost both your folks all at once, boom."

Dry. "That's an apropos way of putting it."

"Is one of your books about what happened to them?"

"Sure." Feeling violated, I got up to put my ruined coffee into the waste can, already full to the top with a variety of fast food containers—the picnic table, a popular lunch destination. The river smoothed its rocks. The geese floated. The polystyrene sat in the trash not-decomposing. "They all are, in a way. But no, not directly. As I began this conversation, I don't have much more to say about them, or what happened."

Marcy, pained. "I'm an idiot. Forgive me."

Alarm bells went off: I didn't want to blow it with this frosty attitude of mine. "Let's start over with this. May we?"

She slapped her thighs and got up; Marcy, almost as tall as me, beautiful eyes, a face getting some lines on it, but forty had dawned graceful and handsome on her features. The hair dyed, obviously, but naturally so. Marcy. "I have to play tonight at the Mudcreek Grill— why don't you come?"

"I shouldn't. I haven't gotten a lick of writing done today."

"Work? Bag it, come on out in the suburbs and keep me company."

With all this parents talk I hadn't even gotten to the good news. "Marcy: a little birdie told me how you were trying to get your band into CityArt next weekend—"

"—oh, really now—"

"—and I wanted you to know that I don't wield much influence, but as Leora's favorite scribe I was able to arrange a set for you. How does that sound?"

Her eyes, dewy. "I know you did. I was waiting all this time for you to tell me. You got me on the bill. My angel man."

She threw her arms around me. Our hearts beat together for a long moment, her soft breath against my ear. "Thank you," she breathed. "Thank you so much."

The phone, buzzing in my jacket. A sort of demonic curse, this device.

"Is that an Apple product," she asked, pulling away, "or are you just happy to see me?"

"Damn it all—I was just getting into that hug."

"Me, too." A sigh, lusty. "So—about tonight?"

After that glorious instance of full-body warmth and contact, that breath tickling my lobe, what could I say but, "See you then."

After Marcy's set in the Mudcreek Grill's low-lit dining room, an enormous mural of a blue marlin breaking the surface of the sea behind her head the whole evening, I helped load out the gear, stowed again into the rear of her Passat wagon.

"You sounded lovely again tonight."

"And you're sweet for staying out with me at work."

"It's not really work, though—is it?"

"Pardon?" Her entire countenance soured and stiffened. "Do what, mister?"

I walked back what I now understood to be a craven and grave insult. "I meant, for *me* it's not work to sit and listen to your lovely voice."

Suspicious, now. I'd blown it. Stammering around. Going uh-huh.

I couldn't have this. "Marcy, I have to tell you, I'd like to forget about the music and the writing and the CityArt festival and all of it for a few seconds. If we could."

"Hm. Very well."

"So that I can say—how attracted I am to you," in a strangled and awkward gargle of an admission. "How lovely the rest of you. Besides the voice. I'm trying to say. In such fractured syntax. For a writer. Like me. That I really and truly feel—"

"Hey!"

I stopped cold my risible logorrhea. "Yes, ma'am?"

"I got a better approach for you."

She held her arms out. Her face, softening again, hands outstretched to me. "Come here and kiss me like you meant all that you just—tried to say."

My heart and stomach aflutter—fifty going on fifteen—I came to her, did as she asked. By the time we parted, both breathless, I wondered anew about next steps: to call, to exchange emails, or simply a handshake, now, in parting?

How did this work?

"You want to follow me?"

"Into battle? Not sure."

"No, silly. Physical, though."

Gulp.

I got it; I motored, following, to her little house in Rosedale Heights, a neighborhood of reconditioned pre-war bungalow designs that had been gentrified not unlike Rick's territory across the river. I would report the details of the rest of the night, but suffice to say we exchanged a few relevant bits of information, and it was neither email addresses nor plans about the future, only the moment at hand: explosive, searing, cathartic.

Marcy.

Me.

Birdie, in hand. Maybe my luck was turning. At last.

7.

The weekend of CityArt arrived, with Rick telling me to come watch him and his partner Darren work on Friday night setting up the two music stages, one near Opal's restaurant, and the other around the corner closer to the Art Museum and across from the Main Street Bijou, the film society art cinema that I'd discovered was managed by none other than Marcy's brother Freddie. Columbia's a city, sure, and a capital one, but also a small town; Freddie, a familiar face from various arts events, had only recently taken the position after being in New York for grad school, then in LA for a few years grinding out screenplays, even trying his hand at standup comedy and acting, but with no success.

A minor crisis—Marcy's name had been misspelled in the newspaper article listing all the musical acts featured at the festival, though, and at the dinner Opal threw last night for many of us working the event, she'd complained. Said that it had happened to Freddie, too, almost every time he'd been interviewed in the paper about the film society. "It's 'bach' like the composer, but half the time they print it as 'b-a-c-k.' Dumbasses."

She complained all the while with her hand under the table on my thigh. Squeezing.

Marcy and I, hot and heavy. As for the deets, use your filthy imaginations.

She further confided, while begging my utmost confidence, that her brother had come home to South Carolina and become a drunk, but after bottoming out—he lost consciousness and soiled his pants during a late-evening screening of *There Will Be Blood*, with the multiplex ushers unable to revive him until someone dumped a small tub of ice water over his head—Freddie had pulled himself together. How once awake he had fought the ushers over his car keys, and that the police were called and he spent the night puking in the tank. A low point; rehab the very next day, driven there by Marcy and her mother.

I didn't judge Freddie; rather, classified him as another brother in sobriety. Bonus points for that wild anecdote, which I tucked away in my mind and notebook. I'd have to change it a bit, of course, when using such a personal detail of Marcy's for fiction. You always do.

It occurred to me: "He'd profaned his church. A symbolic moment."

"How's that?"

"The movies—he humiliated himself before the altar of the movies. For your brother, that was as low as he could bottom."

"I never thought of it that way. Would you write it that way in a book?"

"Maybe. Somewhere Walker Percy must be smiling."

She smiled in that tight way when somebody doesn't get it. "Ha ha."

A tight circle, this community. Like I said, a small town, this capital city. Appealing, in many ways, our inbreeding. You knew where you stood. There weren't that many more award-winning authors; not many Cortlands. Special me.

At the festival a few weeks later, however, I found myself sharing the quote-unquote stage with three younger and hotter and hungrier writers, including one using the event as her book release party. A brilliant strategy—a captive audience numbering, I anticipated, in the thousands. Heck, at that rate, maybe I'd even sell some of those *Keys to the Rain* trade paperbacks or *Collapse of Language* hardcovers that had sat languishing in the climate-controlled storage shed, trucked from my parking place on a flimsy, collapsable hand truck.

The fellow writers, all impressive: an MFA with a first novel and an award-winning poet with a latest chapbook, with the bill filled out by a self-made superstar, Leticia, a diminutive African-American woman with an impressive CV of nonfiction work to her credit—life-guides, cookbooks, a gospel CD or two, and a memoir—now promoting her first foray into novel writing, and considered the headliner of this group. In her caftan and handcrafted jewelry, with a sage, sassy, and confident attitude, she presented herself like the real deal, and one who knew it. An actual book tour? I couldn't recall what that felt like.

"Leticia, I'm certain you're going to have a big response." We took our places under a ten-foot white canvas tent, each of us sharing a signing table with cards bearing our names. "Great piece in the *Columbia Record* yesterday. They ran a spread like that for me when my second book came out."

"Honey, we're hitting it harder than ever on social and traditional media. My people better represent."

I dug, told her so. Gazed into the distance at clouds building. Said: it won't rain.

The poet among us, a gamine and impish sprite named Amelia St. Littlejohn, had been shepherded and mentored by a colleague, Brenda LaRose, up at Foothills State; Amelia, a bright, chipper, youthful presence who appeared to be about fifteen and had a million questions for me about a novel she had been working on; I quelled my impostor syndrome long enough to dole out a few nuggets of wisdom, all of which felt hoary and useless and dreadfully twentieth-century. She hung on every word. Her attention gave me a fit of stomach distress.

The last of the slate, a novelist of only twenty-three who'd written his first novel by the age of sixteen, or so he claimed, and who, when I'd taught him briefly in a writing workshop, had displayed undeniable chops and an affinity for character and detail: Ned Allen Parkridge's *Looking for a Place to Happen* had struck contest gold in the prestigious Carson McCullers Prize competition sponsored by Western Appalachian University. Not only that, but his tale of Myrtle Beach in the early 90s—as Ned Allen explained to me, he wrote about characters he'd observed on summertime family trips, older teens who'd seemed so hip, so mature, but whom his narrator eventually finds are anything but—had been picked up by prestigious Algonquin. Parkridge, too, had made this festival part of a regular book tour. He was on his way.

The little shit.

The festival, not terribly well attended.

I wandered off from my lonely table. I hadn't sold any books. Looking for Marcy, I drifted over to the festival base camp in the lobby of the corporate bank acting as primary sponsor of the event.

"The mussels are bad?" Opal shrieked into her cell. "And so, what? You want me to decide what exactly, you fucking nitwits?" A beat. Another. "Here's a clue. Try erasing 'New Zealand green-lipped mussels' off the goddamn specials menu, and then take a fucking Sharpie—one of those thick black pens? Uh-huh?—and striking it off the goddamn fucking goddamned nightly specials insert." A beat. "Oh—that does sound good? Like a good idea? Super. Meanwhile, I'm over here with my dick hanging out trying to help run this festival. Now leave me the fuck alone!" She hung up. "Jesus."

"The price of your natural leadership abilities." The bank lobby area, buzzing with activity and city officials and other VIPs affording themselves of finger foods and comp beverages.

Opal asked, politely but with a slight edge, what I meant.

"After you've shown leadership, people start to expect you to lead."

"Too much, though." Opal, getting it. "They start wanting you to do all the thinking for them."

I nodded. "Wonder why?"

"Because when it's you making the decision, they don't have anything at stake. That's what people really want from their leaders— to make decisions not because they don't want a say, but so they don't have to take any of the risk."

"That's—brilliant." Thinking: my old lover ought to be writing the books instead of me. "Maybe it's that they're afraid of making the wrong decision—you have um a bit of a temper. Maybe they're simply afraid of making a decision because they'll displease you . . ."

"Maybe that's the spoils of leadership, this fucking wisdom and power, eh? Emphasis on the 'spoil'—when I'm done with this term as neighborhood politician, I'm never doing it again. As for the restaurant, they ought to know by now that I trust them. Maybe I'll work on that fear thing, babycakes," an old term of endearment that made me a little wistful and uncomfortable knowing Marcy to be standing just outside, waiting for the first band to finish so she could set up and play her mini-set.

Opal and I, we hadn't worked out. And yet, I still liked her so much. Complicated; how much like a small town this city often seemed.

The breeze along Main Street picked up. Gray clouds streamed overhead. Didn't feel like rain, however.

Or so I kept insisting.

"It doesn't feel like rain. It's just overcast."

"Could this day get any worse?" Leora seemed in physical pain. Wringing her hands, she paced around in the command-center lobby of Netbank, across the street from the museum plaza with its sculptures and gurgling fountain. Netbank had been good to the festival, had sponsored the music stage. Leora hadn't wanted to have any sponsors, she told me, but once Feebee and Opal and the Business Alliance got involved, they had explained to her that without corporate money, this festival wouldn't likely see its second annual appearance, much less have a successful first one. "Look at this attendance. I'm crushed."

"What more could anybody have done? Don't beat yourself up."

"Maybe we should have cheerleaders. A cannon going off every time we score . . ."

I'd heard Leora's disdain for sports more times than I could count. I was right there with her. Literally obscene, the money thrown at such endeavors.

I gobbled a complimentary doughnut—blueberry cake with creme icing, what the food experts call a super-palatable—and drank thin, brackish coffee, which made me pine for my most decent home brew back in the cabin. As Leora went around kvetching to others and peering out the huge glass windows at the darkening sky, I busied myself by watching the body language of a fire marshal going down the line of the various pop-up tents along the blocked-off street. He examined the moorings of the tents. He pointed and scribbled and shook his head. Artists, many of them middle-aged women, held out their hands and gestured and pled their case.

"What about this weather," a police captain named Westinberger asked Leora. "What is the contingency?"

"We'll just have to weather what comes," seemingly unaware of her pun. "Won't we."

"Meaning—what?" Capt. Westinberger, a rangy, leathery man's man sporting a scaly, psoriasis plagued proboscis, folded his arms. "My guys over at Shaw AFB tell me that they think we could have some severe weather later."

Dejected. "Captain, the festival will be over soon anyway."

"I hope so. Let's just hope that all we get is a little rain."

The weather held. Gray, breezy, moist air, but no water falling.

I went to watch Marcy play, which sounded like the Marcy I was accustomed to hearing—solo keyboard and vocals, but here featuring her original songs rather than the standard retinue of familiar cover songs her restaurant gigs demanded. Having little call or expertise to judge, I found her tunes serviceable, if unchallenging pop music. Applauded with much gusto. Made eye contact.

But afterwards, I found I could barely get her attention from behind the stage where all the other musicians congregated. Once I caught her eye she waved, beamed a happy smile, went back to her conversation with a hirsute man holding a stringed instrument.

As the Green Hole Six took the stage, Marcy made no move to join me out front, continuing to schmooze with the other minstrels. I wandered over to the soundboard area twenty yards back. Rick Wragg and the enormous Darren Woczinski, an incongruous pair of Glimmer Twins running the sound & light show, stood admiring their stagecraft. Rick ordered last-minute adjustments, and their crew of union stage wreckers scurried around with tools and rolls of tape and all manner of accoutrements about which I wanted to know more. As I'd gotten to know him, I was already considering working on a narrative with a Rick-like character as its center of gravity, so I'd need to absorb some detail and nomenclature if I wanted to bring a veneer of verisimilitude to the enterprise. No writer alive had a good enough imagination to get by without tons of research, observation, notes, and most of all, living.

Living. Maybe that's what I'd lacked.

Maybe that's why I wanted a family, or thought I did.

But it's true. My midlife crisis isn't only one of romantic travail—or maybe it is—it's more that I don't have anyone to whom I may leave anything. What had I made of myself, except exploring the interior landscape of a white, Southern gentleman of means? Hadn't the world heard enough from my particular sub-species?

The thought wasn't all bad—white men had made a wreck of things. Past time to pass the baton, generationally and otherwise.

But such thinking filled me with the notion that I still had a duty and obligation to set down the feelings and thoughts of someone like me, here in the perceived senescence of a culture and way of life, the era of the postwar affluence we've so enjoyed, having artificially extended it for decades through the questionable and arcane financial instruments of big banking, it now approaching an apparent and precipitous end.

To wit: It's a miracle Leora was able to cobble together the funding for this festival. These days COPA can't fund much of anything other than its established grants, and those have come under fire as well: Governor Three-Rivers has gone on record as threatening to veto the line-items in the budget pertaining to the arts. All election-year posturing, I hoped, but still a chilling notion that, one day, the government, having ceded to unregulated private industry the means of education and the funding of activities related to the common good and mental health of the people, would be expected to restrict its conduct to the business of policing and procuring armaments and prosecuting various levels and iteration of international warfare. As she understood it, the sole role of the gub-mint, as the honorable and duly elected Sandy Three-Rivers exhorted her rallies, was to provide for the common defense, and to create an environment that big business—the job-creators—would find hospitable and profitable.

"The government has no business educating people," I heard the Governor say on TV. "You cannot trust the government—we need to make it this little old bitty thing we can strangle, like a stray cat that's been messing in your flower garden. And as for the arts, that's a nonessential use of the taxpayer's funds. Have you people even *seen* the kind of art that your dollars have gone to fund? Your government—Democrats, anyway—once funded an exhibit of a glass of pee-pee," she lowered her voice, "with a picture of our lord Jesus stuck down in it. What's next? Don't ask that question. Now if we don't got to put an end to mess like that, I don't know what we're here for, y'all."

At that point I wanted to ask, have you seen the kind of governors your educational system is producing? Thoughtless, vapid, and shallow as a puddle? With no sense of difference between simple bad taste and true obscenity? An onerous airhead, her twaddle made me want not to urinate in a beaker full of Jesus, rather to vomit. Oh, how I despised Three-Rivers, as did everyone in the arts community.

CityArt had been a bust, anyway, but now the city officials were ordering that it be shut down early: The weather had worsened. Winds rippled the banners, whipped the special commemorative programs up and down the streets in a forlorn blizzard of colorful newsprint.

"What if we tried again tomorrow?" Leora pleaded to the Fire Chief and the local head of Homeland Security. "So much has gone into this that we can't simply allow a little weather—"

"Ma'am?" The Chief's exasperation, like a visible aura. "There's a strong possibility of a tornado. I can assure you that as of right now this festival is over, the musicians must stop, and the public must leave. I understand everyone's heart has gone into this thing," saying 'thing' as one does when unable to fully comprehend the nature of a given object or situation, "but it ain't worth no one losing nobody's life over. Now make the call to your people out there, or I'll have Capt. Westinberger's boys do it for you."

An editor from the *Columbia Record* and a friend with whom I'd been gabbing there in the command post inside Netbank, Ward Bentham quickly tweeted and texted and posted, which popped up in the newsfeed on my own phone, making it vibrate in my pocket:

CITY OFFICIALS SHUTTER ARTS FEST
OVER WEATHER THREAT

"This is just too bad," waving one of the paper's photographers out the door. "Go get a shot of the threatening sky over the music stage," he yelled to the confused shooter. Ward gestured and pointed. "The sky," he repeated. "The clouds. The stage."

The metaphorical flashbulb went off. The photographer, an Asian woman half my age, offered Ward a small salute and trotted away toward the block-long assembly of art exhibits.

I watched with horror as a gust of wind threatened artworks hanging from the white pop-up tents. Nettie Nabors-Willowbrook, a sculptor working in found-objects and on a scale far beyond anyone else's displays, had already begun breaking down her pieces, some of which had been constructed out of materials like sheet metal, which in a flash could be turned by high winds into deadly projectiles.

I'd long ago pulled my books back around the corner to my car. I hadn't sold a one.

Leora, quivering and wan with disappointment. "Oh, I feel so defeated."

"Be that as it may, I'm with the Chief. Let's call it a day." I stopped myself from adding that we'd already experienced the peak of the crowd anyway, such as it was. If a few hundred people milling around could be called a crowd.

"Whoa," someone yelled, one of the EMTs who'd been hanging around on standby all day. We all turned to see that a stronger gust had snapped loose the giant Netbank Presents CityArt 2012 banner. The canvas flapped in a graceful, slow-motion arc until a heavy grommet collided with the glass window. A forceful sharp *CRACK* precipitated a mass flinching punctuated by gasps, no one more than Leora, who deplored loud noises—she'd been in here all day not so much as the director of the festival, but to get away from the music blaring from the Glimmer Twins PA.

A moment of quiet. Ward and I looked at one another, then began a scramble, the Fire Chief and the Police Chief and the Homeland Security honcho all barking orders.

"All those tents need to be dropped to the ground, and right now," the Fire Chief shouted. "Artworks or not, they got to come down."

I suggested to Leora, Opal, and Feebee standing there in a huddle that they do with all haste everything and anything the officials asked of them. Meanwhile, rushing out into the street I felt shocked to find the air almost twenty degrees cooler.

The music had already stopped, the fire marshal and beat cops rushing around and exhorting the artists to tear down their displays. The other writers, ignored as we'd been all morning and afternoon, had already long gone, even the young, hungry one, who'd seemed the most disturbed at the lack of interest based on how few people attended the festival.

Around the corner, the Green Hole Six scrambled to thrust gear into a step van pulled right up to the side of the stage. Rick, like a crazed monkey, darted in and out of my field of vision in a mad whirl, directing stage wreckers to hurriedly pull down the PA stacks, coil the cables, and collapse the stage with its solid white scrim overhead, which he had worried could turn into a sail should the weather become unsettled.

As it had.

The stage itself had been bolted into the two buildings on either side of the street, both of which had concrete foundations into which I'd watched Darren hammer two large eyebolts early this morning while the rest of us stood around in the early light sipping coffee. I'd stayed over at Marcy's again, and had come in early to support Leora and watch Rick work.

"You okay?" I called out as he rushed by me. "Anything I can do?"

He didn't answer, yelling instead to one of the union guys to 'quit effing around' and drop a speaker cabinet on down to the ground. "We got to get this stage canopy down, guys, or the fire marshal's gonna set *me* on fire."

Darren trotted over to help with the stage. He'd been pulling large sheets of 4 mil plastic over all the mixing boards. Like Rick, Darren knew that securing the stage trumped the safety of the gear, but that had to be done as well.

Lightning flashed, bright and sudden. A hush seemed to fall. A crash of heavy thunder. The air fell still. What light was left in the sky seemed to diminish like a fade-out in a movie.

After a pause and a gasp, new urgency took hold among the stage wreckers and remaining audience.

Marcy. I gestured to her across on the opposite sidewalk, near the various bands and their vehicles parked along the side street near Opal's restaurant. She called out to me; I shook my head for her to stay put, and I started toward her.

An icy gust blew through with a vengeance, accompanied by a fresh crash of lightning and instantaneous thunder. Marcy screamed as the wind, which had been flowing in from the north, seemed to reverse, pushing against the white scrim of the stage cover. The entire structure groaned and shifted.

SNAP!

At first I thought the sound came from more lightning, but soon saw that a security cable sheared loose from its eyebolt, whipsawing around in a deadly arc.

Voices, screaming; bodies leaping off and away from the stage. Rick scrambled over and tackled Marcy, pushing her out of the way of the collapsing structure. What had been a sturdy stage crumbled before my eyes, and heavy sheets of rain fell seemingly out of nowhere.

Frozen in place, I finally snapped to and ran over toward the wreck of the stage. A male voice, screaming—one of the crew was trapped underneath. I went to him, but Darren beat me to it.

"Is she okay?" I called to Rick, who held onto Marcy, his face buried in her hair, not looking at the stage.

"It's him you need to worry about." Marcy, gesturing toward Rick.

Rick seemed catatonic. Whispering, "How bad is it. How bad is it."

As I was about to respond, Opal, mascara running, rushed over to me, hollering over wind that sounded like an approaching freight train. "Cort, it's Leora!"

"*What about her?*"

"Hurry—I think she's having a fucking heart attack."

As we hustled back to the bank, the swirling storm all but lifted me off my feet, praying the entire time that Leora was just having an overreaction to all this stress. I was wrong.

8.

Another loved one gone. There, and then not.

Leora's absence brought with it a yawning emptiness, an unwelcome ghost of past tragedies and losses. Of booming thunder of a different sort. Of acrid woodsmoke. Of loss and failure and loneliness. Guilt—how could I have let her have a heart attack in the middle of her ruined arts festival?

How could I have allowed that weather to happen?

Helplessness, manifest. If only this tragedy had been part of one of the manuscripts instead.

Before the survivor guilt, of course, had been garden variety shock.

In some ways I couldn't yet bring myself to admit that she was dead, that the CityArt disaster had been capped by no less than the loss of the woman who'd singlehandedly overseen and inspired an entire arts community for more than three decades, and who'd meant so much to me on a personal and professional level.

When they weren't taking statements from Feebee and Opal, in the aftermath the news media turned to me for comments on the whole sorry CityArt affair, and I did the best I could to face up to this tragedy and not crumble in a public fashion. Feebee, who'd told me that we were in what she called 'PR Crisis Mode,' explained that we had to be very careful about what we said, which we went over before I'd ever been allowed to speak to the press. The storm, long over, the evening clear and cool, the air scrubbed and mild like after a rain shower. The radar showed that a tornado had been swirling over our heads, but hadn't quite touched down.

How much worse would that have been?

We lost Leora less to weather than sclerotic arteries, but otherwise, only one of Rick's day-laborer crew had been injured in the destabilization of the stage. Later that night Marcy had shown me a bump on her head, lying in bed where I allowed myself the indignity of weeping and shuddering with a delayed and extreme reaction. Marcy, cooing and reassuring and saying it would be all right. Inside I wasn't merely grieving; I was already composing what I'd say about sweet, departed Leora once the request came that I eulogize her, of course. I'd known her for decades. Had met her family numerous times.

My relationship with Leora Wood-Cobb began in 1981 when I won the COPA fiction competition, and at quite a young age. The story had been entitled 'The Figs of July,' inspired by an event from the summer of my tenth year, in which an enormous fig tree tucked behind Hillsborough had put out a veritable bounty of fruit. My mother explained the reason for the fecundity had to do with the wet winter we'd had. A country girl herself, she came equipped with quite the surfeit of folk knowledge and wisdom, most of which would never get passed down to me, or anyone.

An annual tradition, my father, standing far up on a six-foot aluminum stepladder; twisting limbs, reaching far above, groping for fruit, ever higher. Mother, seeing in May and June the volume of figs to come, had pledged pints to so many people that if we didn't pick the high limbs this year, too—and I do mean high, and despite the ostensible bounty at hand from the heavy lower limbs—she might, she forewarned, be forced to disappoint those near the bottom of the comprehensive list, which included friends, family, and certain esteemed members of local society like members of the ELMS. And she couldn't fail at her commitments, as I had her character announcing with vigor and forced Southern dialect. She'd be damned if the Great Hillsborough Fig Bounty of 1970 wouldn't delight as many palettes and hungry bellies full of biscuit dough and butter and preserves as possible.

The inexpensive, flimsy aluminum perch he'd chosen, though, resulted in disaster: in Father's contorted postures and through his own foolhardy attempt to stand one-step-too-high, the ladder began to give under his weight. I could see it happening, almost before he realized—he'd been leaning and reaching to pull down the highest of high limbs that hung heavy with figs. Plump and glimmering fruit that'd been reared close to the sun. The source.

The sunlight *streaked across the father's eyes, blinding him,* as I later wrote.

As his balance went, Father cried out and sprang off to the side, flinging his arms and twisting his gangly body like a championship diver doing a jackknife; the aluminum bucket of figs went flying in a magnificent and gracefully spraying tableaux that rained down all around me.

Rather than breaking his neck, somehow father got his feet back underneath him before hitting the ground, and landed like an Olympic gymnast, his knees buckling but not giving. He steadied himself, stood erect.

The moment hung there. We both started laughing.

"Well," taking a step toward me, "let's collect these figs before the fire ants—oh."

When he bent over to get the bucket, he collapsed shrieking and grabbing at his lower back. He rolled over with squished figs sticking to his face and his short-sleeved cotton summer shirt. He wept in pain, his strained and fig-stained face the color of a stop sign. Before this, I'd only seen him weep when he'd been in the worst of his weekend drunks, which hadn't yet become the all-week drunks they later would.

"Get your mother," he hissed, aggrieved and whispery and urgent. "Hurry. I've—I've knocked out my breath."

Far from his breath being the issue, after the figs of July, Father's back was never again right and pain-free, or so he said. Not only did he drink worse than he had before, but he began taking painkillers, too, and in another three years, his back would still hurt but his mind would be going—or if not mind, then at least spirit.

We didn't know it, really. He hid his pain well, my Father. An amazing actor. Hid the face of madness from us. Until he couldn't anymore. It'd been his training in psychology, his master's degree in how people's minds functioned: We'd stopped having conversations when my mother wasn't around, not talks like we used to have, anyway, like two human beings. He had started treating me like a stranger. That told me something had gone wrong inside my father.

How terribly wrong, though, I had no clue.

Remembering the heat of the day and father's cotton shirt and the aluminum ladder, I blazed through the writing of the piece in one fevered evening, the character's pain worsening as he argues with his wife in front of the child, until the parents forgive one another and his back suddenly gets better and the mother prepares fig preserves—get it? They had preserved their marriage. Leora had gotten it.

So, I turned the beginnings of tragedy into a gentle comedy, with no hint of the alcoholism or the impending nightmare to come, only a life-lesson sprinkled with portent of the young narrator's impending transition into adolescence and eventual manhood.

A few among us are lucky; we've have an outlet: we're able to write or paint or sing or otherwise create away our pain—sometimes literally, sometimes metaphorically. *Keys to the Rain,* for instance, is about my parents and their discomposed marital life and how it all ended, but I told the story in metaphor rather than as a journalist, in a code that probably only one or two people alive besides me would even come close to recognizing. But I never told anyone that. Not even Leora Wood-Cobb.

I suppose now, though, that anyone bored enough to read my Wikipedia page, which I decided to leave as is—any halfway sharp literary adjudicator could already figure all this out.

On another level, making the decision to leave the biography page untouched felt right, as though through this courage I might be exposing myself anew to a potential readership. Doing so made me feel raw and open of spirit, like when you've laid bare your self and your soul in the words of your novels for all to see.

Naked.

I needed to feel naked more often. Especially when Marcy B is around . . .

Or, wait—is that TMI, as the kids would text to one another? Too bad.

The day of the memorial I parked down the street from the old Episcopalian Church on Sumter, which from the cars and the people filing inside appeared to be packed. Leora had touched many lives, from schoolchildren on up to the Governor, whose men-in-black security detail, I noted, were standing around under the shade of a century-old magnolia that seemed a hundred feet tall and half as wide. The ancient and gnarled arms of live oaks loomed protectively over the grave sites of various Wade Hamptons and other luminaries.

I sat in my car listening to Tchaikovsky's Symphony No. 2, which I'd chosen after spinning around the wheel on my iPod until finally just picking it at random; the mournful mellophone of the opening, the building to sublimity of the whole orchestral piece. That's what Leora had done—taken individual artistic voices and magnified them into trumpeting signifiers of the latent, inherent worthiness of their singular and unique visions. That's what COPA's various programs did for the citizens of South Carolina. That's what my friend Leora Wood-Cobb did. And so on and so on, as I kept rehearsing in my head.

I hid behind a tree from the passing entourage of fellow funeral attendee Sandy Three-Rivers, her frighteningly fake bottle-blond, Aryan-appearing 'Native American' phoniness and mendacity trailing behind her like a fog of cheap ideological perfume. I couldn't believe the woman had the temerity to attend the service, to show her recalcitrant and insulting face in this sacred space, honoring a giant of the arts.

Unmitigated gall. I flushed with simmering rage.

Yes—I'd use this wall of anger to keep the grief at bay. Get through the eulogy. Lemons into lemonade.

Three-Rivers knew how to stay on-message, you had to give her that: she had been steadfast and relentless in towing the party line all year about money for the arts being slashed from the coming fiscal year's budgetary appropriations, and whether the good old fellas in the legislature agreed or not—in fact, such monies and promises of funding had in fact had been all used up forever and ever. That the arts themselves had been declared superfluous to the lifeblood of the community of humankind represented by the city and the state. Or so her rhetoric sounded to my ears.

As I saw the sheer number of attendees streaming in from all directions, I began to sweat and strain under the pressure. The notecards in my coat pocket felt leaden and useless. I hoped my voice would carry in the large church, until remembering that cloistered and sacred spaces like this were designed with such orations in mind. The faux-eloquence over which I'd scratched and slaved with the metaphorical nubbin of what seemed a dreadfully dull intellectual and emotional pencil felt terribly inadequate.

As I glanced through my words my bulwark of political indignation crumbled. I wept, sudden and shocking, for the one person, besides the author himself, who had made this writing career, this wonderful life, a possibility rather than a dream. Who was I to summarize such a precious human life? I had to try.

Inside the church I found myself on the dais in the crown of the cross-shaped apse, the red, trompe l'oeil squares of the half-dome arching overhead, daylight streaming through the clerestory windows high above a nave whose centuries-old pews had filled to capacity; indeed, the fine acoustics carried every small detail from the shuffling and murmuring assemblage to me on the pulpit where I sat along with Leora's daughter Belinda. The thirty-something had become a noted research scientist rather than pursue the arts path that made her mother's soul sing; and another writer, renowned novelist and poet F. Gordon Blake, who, despite the early hour, smelled redolent of what I hoped had been a bracer of top-shelf scotch. From the anteroom off the sanctuary, the pastor or preacher or priest or padre—whatever the hell the Episcopalians called their patriarchal soothsayers and sages—stood speaking with another high-collared individual of the cloth.

Blake, from whom I'd once taken classes at Southeastern, breathed fiery fumes in my ear. "I'm going to bolt after I say my bit."

"In the middle of the service?"

Vapors drifted. Belches punctuated his words. "No way I can stomach sitting through too much of this crud."

"I won't be far behind you."

He crunched into a couple of white Tic Tacs he produced, tossing them into his mouth like circus peanuts. "Not a religious man?"

"Not as such."

"Good for you. You just went up two places in my book, Beauchamp." Blake bumped my kneecap with an approving fist. "After reading your stuff, I wasn't so sure."

"I had no idea you'd read my books. I'm honored."

"I wouldn't feel that honored." He chuckled. "Oh—just yanking your rope. You've a helluva voice. I'd say you still have it, except I haven't read anything new by you in a long time."

I drew in a breath to explain, but then the organist began playing, and the service began. We stood for anthems and prayers and lessons and hymns, including numbers 522 ("Glorious things of thee are spoken") and 657 ("Love divine, all loves excelling"); a sacred reading, the familiar funerary passage from John 14 about mansions and houses and were it not so. I had no faith to lose, and I knew it, as Dylan sang in one of the few rock-era compositions I had bothered to notice.

But this service wasn't for me:

Leora, a regular churchgoer, maintained a faith held over from a childhood brought up in the rural South. To its credit, at least the Episcopal church had come out strong in favor of civil unions and even gay marriage, which was in line with the church's long history of socially conscious action and equality. I supposed such progressive attitudes had gone a long way toward keeping a person like Leora satisfied that her church wasn't mired in some prior century.

In the front row sat Governor Three-Rivers, dabbing at her eyes with ostentatious self-awareness while speaking to an aide-de-camp who sat thumbing a Blackberry. I projected a strained, flat-lipped smile toward the governor. How she could show up here was beyond me. The arrogance made me seethe.

My eulogy would be about much more than Leora, I realized—the pulpit would be mine for a brief period, all eyes and ears, including the governor's, sitting upon me. Absorbing my words.

Ah-ha.

At the instant the padre turned and gestured toward us, I felt Blake's bony old-man's elbow collide with the tender meat of my upper arm.

Leora's daughter, a puffy-eyed Belinda, nodded with an encouraging smile.

No choice.

I rose, keeping the hazy, indistinct outline of the governor's blond mane in my peripheral vision. I pushed out of my mind the images of Leora on the floor of the Netbank lobby, her blouse torn away, the EMTs working on her—injecting drugs, pressing on her fragile chest, her face I'd once thought beautiful pulled back into a grim, hard grin of abject and irrefutable mortality. At the time, in shock, I'd felt nothing.

"Oh, Leora," I began. "These faces out here, they miss you so! As do I. You worked so hard; you did so much for us all. For me." I cleared my throat. "But your work isn't done, because the game of making art is never done. 'It's what we're here for on this planet,' as you so often said, my dear friend, my mentor." I went off script; I didn't care. "And my first love, too—is it all right to admit that to you all, now? Or is that TMI?"

A ripple of chuckling, not altogether comfortable.

"Oh, not romantically. Rather, as that beacon of joy and commitment to the artistic process, to the celebration of art, and of the human spirits who animate these creations of ours. How could I not have been in love with one so committed, dear Leora? A love undying, too. A love like a piece of marble sculpture—it will last. It will go on. Not forever. But the carved stone fades away so slowly that you can't see it. Might as well be forever—we're here so damn short a time," and not caring about cursing in this house of the Lord, who'd invented cursing and everything else—right?—and so could hold no grudges against the liberal usage of these glorious and infamous gifts. "And we want to do so much with the precious time we have. Leora Wood-Cobb certainly did. The rest she now enjoys has been well earned. That much I know."

And here, at last, I returned to the structure of my prepared cards, with notations of significant milestones related to Leora's professional career as an artist working in mixed media back in the 60s, to her transition after a decade of poverty into the familiar role we'd all known: as cheerleader and doyenne to a region's worth of artists and aspiring writers, musicians, sculptors, actors, directors, dancers, choreographers, cinematographers, and performance artists, which is how, I noted, she lived her life until its very last, blessed, calamitous minutes.

"For all the other, far less consequential tragedies that befell us that dreadful afternoon, that a celebration of interdisciplinary creativity like the First Annual CityArt Festival came together at all," making skimming eye contact along the row on which sat Feebee Elmendorf, the mayor, and two city council members, "represented a true pinnacle of Leora's contributions to the city of Columbia; the state of South Carolina; and, indeed, the larger world beyond our borders, a contribution that I hope continues on into the future—her influence, and her festival of the arts—growing and changing into one of our community's signature events. We all know that South Carolinians excel at watching sporting competitions such as those conducted by the fighting Southeastern Redtails, as well as at the 'raising of the wrist' as celebrated in city-sponsored events like the St. Patrick's Day festival. What if we were also known for our taste in, and promotion of, the fine arts? What if we were known for our appreciation of the finest of paintings and music and the literary arts? What if? What if? What if? I know that Leora kept that question close to her heart, until the very end: what if we continued the CityArt Festival the next day, she asked the authorities. Her dying words. I don't know about the rest of you, but if I never did before—and as a writer, I've made it my business to ask such questions—in the wake of this tremendous loss to our community, I've taken what-if to heart. I take it with my coffee in the morning like a cube of sugar; I graciously lead what-if into my bedroom at night to rest alongside me like a lover. What if. What if Leora Wood-Cobb's death wasn't in vain. What if it wasn't an ending, but rather a beginning. What if, indeed."

I let out a breath, as did the assembly of mourners. A stirring and rustling. The church had gotten warm.

I'd done my duty: Leora wouldn't have given a rat's tushie how she'd be remembered personally, only in terms of her work and contribution, as well as whether it would go on in her absence. I'd certainly gotten into the writing game, in a sense, so that I'd leave a piece behind representing what my life had meant, something other than a chunk of granite in a grassy field.

Far from finished, I continued with my politicized eulogy for which I'd later learn I was fiercely criticized behind my back, this time making no small sport of letting my peepers find those of the governor, who sat in pursed-lip, head-nodding acknowledgment that I was giving her a thorough and public rhetorical shellacking, right here in front of God and her and everyone, and there wasn't a person in the room who could do anything about it; everyone, sitting there and taking it. I had the bully pulpit. I'd use it. Not for me. And not against anyone, whether the governor or a face or two I recognized as generally antagonistic to Leora and what she represented—no, for Leora herself. To bid her farewell on the journey to commingle with the great and somewhere centrally located Source of It All, to swirl back into the eternal well upon wings of surety and certitude that it'd all meant something, all her days and weeks and years, the sum of a beautiful and productive human being's life. My voice quavered and boomed. I defended the idea of art not only as a shared commodity, but a shared expression of the community's life, mind, and heart. I minced no words; I declared with gusto and words that sliced through the dolorous air in the sanctuary that the arts were a mutual responsibility of all citizens and duly-burdened taxpayers—a term I emphasized and let hang for a few seconds before continuing—and that this investment in the community was indisputably for the greater good of all.

"If the fine arts could fill stadiums the way the Redtails do on a fall Saturday, maybe we'd be having a different conversation. But it doesn't, and we aren't; and as such, I exhort our leaders to do one thing and one thing only when it comes to the future of arts funding: show us the money. We know you have it. Now enough whining, as Leora Wood-Cobb would put it, and come off the dime. Your children, and their children, will thank you one day." I thumped my notes. "And not a blessed one of them is likely to remember who won some ridiculous football game," sounding as bitter as I often heard Leora when she went on such a rant. "And you all know it, as surely as you all recognize a Mozart theme, or a Shakespearian plot."

"Christ in a sidecar." Blake, belching from behind me. "Enough already."

More rustling and throat clearing. The governor's eyes had narrowed, her mouth downturned. All polite nodding had ceased. A stone statue, staring me down.

I relented. As I bade my mentor a final and personal farewell from the pulpit, damn if I didn't crumble. Said in a broken voice for the Great Spirit to bless her heart, and not in the underhanded way the phrase was most often intended. I re-invoked my deep and abiding and eternal love for Leora Wood-Cobb, blathering until I felt a hand on my elbow.

F. Gordon Blake had finally risen and placed a comforting arm around me, leading us both away from the pulpit. "Seriously, now," close in my ear while peeking balefully back at the restless mourners. "Enough, already. Enough."

The padre caught Blake's eye. His face said *well?*

Blake waved him off and boomed out loud enough to rattle the stained-glass windows. "I cede my time to the young lady and the gentleman from Edgewater County!"

The tension in the sanctuary broke with a surprised roar of laughter that erupted from the audience, and from me. I wiped my eyes, letting them drift for a second or two over toward the lovely if reactionary governor of the state, who stared daggers back through me. Through the remainder of the service I bowed my head in quiet reverence as F. Gordon Blake stared at the face of his watch.

Forced mingling out on the street in front of the pale stucco twin towers of the Gothic Revival church, a structure possessing such historicity that it bore a listing on the National Register. I broke into a complete and thorough full-body sweat.

The governor, surrounded by her entourage, schmoozed and pressed the flesh, all the while cutting her eyes through the crowd in my direction. So I glimpsed, anyway, through the throng of heads and shoulders and suit jackets lingering farther up the block, and through which we had to make our way.

"I went too far."

"Horseshit. You did good." An unsteady Blake, inhaling with vigor on his e-cig and leaning upon me for support. "You even sounded like her. Mystical, I tell you."

"What can I say?" A siren screamed off in the distance, echoing from the downtown corridor of towers where the festival had been held. "I owe her everything."

"Right. Let's go get a drink, m'boy."

We made our way down the uneven sidewalk troubled by the roots of the ancient trees in the church courtyard, along the wrought iron fencing and the ancient graveyard of tilting and weathered monuments dating back to the eighteenth century. The faces and voices and handshakes, acquaintances and strangers alike all wishing to steal a moment with the two men who'd sat upon the elder's stage, to tell me what a good job I'd done, how they didn't know how we were going to get by without Leora's wisdom and leadership, how they had admired our recent books, which felt to me like a jab with a knife. I wondered if it were that way for Blake—he hadn't published anything meaningful, truly, in over fifteen years. Another dry bones.

"Excuse us, *please.*" Blake, brusque, impatient, and a little too loud. "I'm *very ill myself you know,* and must be on my merry way. Thank you, thank you all." The throng parted and bade us on through on the crest of a wave of well-wishing and good tidings.

At his car, an aged and sun-bleached Jaguar—Blake had a place on Edisto Island where he lived most of the time now—he asked, "Got a favorite watering hole, Beauchamp? My treat."

I shook my head, explained my situation re: the booze.

"Oh, for fuck's sake. You weren't a drunk, Cortland. I've known tippling drunks my whole life, whose behavior would turn your hair white. Vile monsters. Eh. I'm one—I'm a goddamn cliché walking around in my own bad novel." He pounded the dusty hood of his once-pristine luxury sports car, his face rosy with self-consciousness. "The rages. The need. The morning after. Indeed: a pitiable wretch. Now come drink with me. Ah, that's it. Need. I need someone to pity me—don't you see that?"

"I see someone writing dialogue," meaning this in the best way. "I see someone playing out a scene."

"Fuck your mother, you goddamned accomplished little smartass son of a biscuit eater," he grumbled. Fumbling with his car keys, dropping them and picking them back up. "Go forth and sin no more, Cortland Beauchamp."

"Wait. Let me—" He slammed the door and cranked the car.

I came around and knocked on the window. "For heaven's sake."

He wouldn't look at me, ground the car into gear and roared out of the space. I jumped back, managing to avoid being run asunder by his rear tire. He had no business driving. No condition.

I went to my own car, aghast at the thought of the writer who'd been so influential and helpful to me—the other part of the equation, along with Leora, that'd made my career possible—driving around in a state of near-inebriation. He lived only blocks away, on University Hill. Unless he was hauling ass back to Edisto, of course. Ack. It was out of my hands.

Feeling crushed under the weight of perceived irresponsibility—over Blake, over Leora; as though I could have prevented her heart attack, or the storm that blew through—I took the long way back around to the church and to my car, all to avoid any lingering funeral attendees, in particular the governor, that phony, that soulless, avaricious troll of a politician.

In my own car, alone, I wept hard and long into my hands—not for Leora, or for myself, or my writer's block, but at the passage of time. At my own fifty year-old, sagging bag of bones and meat. I needed to step out of that shell more, get into the cosmic headspace in which the writing had once come.

Maybe I'd work more on meditation. Maybe using that mantra I mentioned, the one about fear killing the mind. I'd been told that with meditation, time no longer mattered. That your comfy armchair became a time machine; that time turned elastic. Then maybe I could get back to that place from whence the words had once flowed. I'd toyed with the practice last summer after breaking up with Opal, who meditated twice a day and had encouraged me to try it. I'd developed no discipline, however.

The other choice would be to say yes to F. Gordon Blake's idea and go to a bar, start drinking again.

Maybe that'd been the problem.

Maybe I'd simply been constipated, in a sense, since I got dry.

Temptation: Bukowski's maxim about a drunk never having to

worry about constipation extended, I now pondered, to the creative end of things as much as the literal and physiological sense.

But to try to unblock myself that way, through alcohol, was the path of failure. I reminded myself that I'd been unable to write before I quit drinking, as well.

The drive home set to Beethoven's *Eroica*, Symphony No. 3. I felt crisp and alive, the cry in the car having done me some good.

By the time I got inside the cabin and made myself tea I felt anything but blocked. Changing into gym clothes and doing a few stretches, I skipped the workout to begin crafting a new short story, this one inspired by Feebee Elmendorf's go-go personality and youth and sparkle and big, beautiful eyes. I called the character 'Busbee Muckenfuss' and began writing in Feebee's rat-a-tat voice, which I did for the rest of the day and night until I'd created not so much a story as an extended character biography.

Eh. Not that impressive. You couldn't send this out to a journal. Work was work, though.

But all my half-finished, recent efforts felt that way—sketches, backstory, prewriting.

Then it hit me: I wasn't writing stories; more assembling an Altman-esque and burgeoning dramatis personae of puppets, which is how I think of characters in my novels—marionettes who eventually develop a modicum of free will—not so much in the sense that I'm their puppet master, no; but, instead to be as entertained by them as an audience watching, and reading, along with their seemingly uncontrollable and unpredictable behavior. Busbee, I reasoned, would be one of the leads in CREATIVE CLASS. I started sketching out what I imagined the life of this imaginary human being to have been like leading up to her present condition, the time frame in which her story would be related. One had to think through these elements in a meticulous way. Enough revelation of the method.

By the end of that night and nearly thirty pages into her evolving, young woman's voice 'Busbee' almost felt alive, as did this novel I understood was now simmering, and would need to be led by a character I hadn't yet created, who'd be the Leora of the piece. On an intuitive level, all felt right with the work so far.

Magic, percolating like the glorious first cup o' the day.

But to do this right, I'd need to work on it, and for a good while. These things took time. You had to become each of the characters. It's like sitting in front of Rick Wragg's wall of masks, in a sense, picking them out one by one and trying them on for size. It was how you managed to write real people. You wore their faces, and thoughts, atop your own.

When I woke up the next morning and remembered all the fresh work I'd managed—in skimming through I discovered much I couldn't even remember having written, which meant I'd been good and snuggled down tight into the writing trance, the eternal well of inspiration—I realized that for the first time in ages I again felt like a writer.

I felt like myself.

Coffee in hand, I strolled outside and headed a few yards down toward the deep woods, where I found the crabapple tree taken over by chickadees: busy little birds wearing black masks like tiny bandits.

Banditry.

Stealing time.

That's what a writer did in order to get pages done. To meet the deadline called completion, which for me had seemed unreachable for several years. To beat time at its own game. I hightailed it back inside and got down to work.

Part Three:
THE RETREAT

1.

The drive from Rick's place in the West Vista to Sedge Island should have taken only a couple of hours, but instead consumed half a day: Rick, needing to pull over a couple times so as to safely finish his telling of a particular story or anecdote, which gave him the freedom to gesticulate and make eye contact with everyone in the car. A whirlwind of character and bits of business, Rick. But exhausting.

Wasn't so bad, not in the back seat next to my new gal-pal.

Who happened to be Rick's old gal-pal.

But no biggie. Everybody friends. Grown-ups.

Even the kid, Cadence, all of ten, seemed to be in charge as much as his father did—as we approached the exit to a state road that would take us onto the island, Rick's son explained that he had updated the iOS on his iPad. Wanted to test the mettle of the Apple Maps upgrade. Told his dad what was what, instead of asking. Cadence, one of those little techno-geniuses that we seem to have these days.

And yet Cadence, I had been told, had tested on the low side of the autism spectrum. That he had suffered a number of socialization issues, the idea of which sounded to this recluse less like a manifestation of disease than a desirable lifestyle choice. But autism, no joke, and I found myself watching Cade and Rick's interactions quite closely. Like always, gathering material. I rarely wrote kid-characters. I hadn't had my own, so what did I know about how kids acted.

Rick told his son to put away the tablet. "I don't need no steenkin' GPS—your dad spent two years living on this rock. That's what people call it who live there, you know—The Rock. If you call it that, folks won't think you're a tourist. You'll be hip. You'll be one-of-us, one-of-us."

"The Rock—like Alcatraz?" Marcy asked.

"Wait, what what what's 'Alcatraz'?"

But Cadence didn't wait for an answer—he began sliding his finger around on the iPad screen to find out for himself. The facts, however, only seemed to further confuse him. "A movie about a prison. No—wait. A prison? *A real prison, too?* Oh-kay," seeming to try to digest the real versus unreal aspects of it all. "Oh-kay," he repeated a few times.

A little sponge for knowledge. Heartening. Marcy, putting in her earbuds, flipping through a magazine. She'd said she had a headache. Seemed uncomfortable with this plan. She hadn't needed to come, I'd told her. Nothing good would come of this attempt to bother a man who'd constructed his life so that he needed be bothered. The thought of what Rick had talked me into doing made me almost literally sick. Too late now.

Earlier, heading toward the freeway from Rick's neighborhood of salt-boxes and while I still squirmed and tried to get comfortable with the "um" shared situation among the adults in the car, we passed a giant recycling/metal reclamation facility on the outskirts of town that, in the cool light of the hazy sky of morning, looked like the set of a dystopian wasteland science fiction film. I could see inside the bay doors of one of the huge buildings, peering down from the expressway at harsh, florescent-lit pallets filled with shimmering steel tubes; a forklift parked at an angle, two guys leaning against it with their arms folded; and last, some poor devil shuffling along in the warehouse in his heavy, steel-toed boots . . . the warehouse, a hard, ugly, loud place where no one wanted to hang out, not unless they had to. Maybe that guy faced a long day ahead, or else paced wearily as the end of the night shift approached. Graveyard. The place probably never stopped recycling. God knows the need won't go away anytime soon.

This sort of life constituted real work, I thought. A real and measurable day's endeavor, both from the standpoint of meaningful physical activity, as well as energetic exchange in the form of wages.

Trudging through the warehouse at daybreak. This simple note would bring all the images and feelings back later. Boiling it down. Maybe it was the first line of a story. Maybe it meant nothing.

And yet, scribbling it all down with my pink, soft hands. No wonder my palms were so pale and soft—an underbelly, the hands of the writer. Exposed, occasionally.

We endeavor to remember how good we have it, thinks the privileged writer and descendant of slaveholders. I thought of Bukowski, working at the post office. Perhaps at 50 it was time to find out how the real world got by—after the trip to Sedge Island and the sneak attack on Duncan Devereaux, I'd get a job, a real job. Maybe in the new Amazon shipping hub that we next passed on our way out of town. Shipping out boxes of books by other writers.

Nah.

Rick, when not gulping coffee and talking the time this happened or the rock tour on which he'd been a rigger where thus and such occurred, pummeled us with a concert by a strident and silly sounding avant-garde rock band called Fish, which Rick's son informed me was spelled Ph- rather than F-, a fact that cast little edifying glare upon the lenses of the polarized Ray-Bans I'd purchased, nor offered relief to my offended eardrums. How they'd all chuckled at me—Rick, Cadence, and Marcy looking like a little family ready for their beach vacation, but stuck with the weird uncle still dressed in his doofus suit of khakis and loafers and sport coat.

"Why. Why. Why don't you have on shorts and and and a T-shirt?" Rick's son asked with what I soon came to recognize as a signature vocal tic.

"Uncle Bo-champ's got this religious thing—he's taken a vow of discomfort." Rick, cracking himself up. "He's gonna sit on the beach all day like that."

"Are you? Are you really? Really? *Really?*"

"Of course not."

Cadence, nodding and satisfied he understood. "It's a joke. The vow of discomfort."

"Yes."

"You—you actually took no such vow."

Well spoken little tyke. Autism? Hell, this is my kinda kid. "Correct."

Cadence made an uh-huh sound and scribbled down a cryptic note in a small spiral notebook.

"Notes, eh?"

"It's how I keep. Keep up. Keep up with stuff."

Again: a boy after my own heart.

Marcy, playful, squeezing my knee. "Uncle Cort thinks it's still the nineteenth century, when people waited to change into their bathing costumes in little tents on the beach."

I fumed and fretted at all this needling. Said that in due time I'd be in swimwear and sandals, though heavy leather ones offering protection to approximately eighty percent of my tender white feet accustomed neither to the sight of the sun nor the sensation of direct contact with grass or sand.

Cadence shrugged. "I'm really like, comfortable already."

"I see that."

"I should make a meme. About all this."

"A *meme*?" I searched my mind for the meaning of the term.

"About this conversation." Cadence, overcome with giggles. "A meme about the Vow of Discomfort."

Chagrined that I didn't understand, I asked for clarification. From a child.

Cadence twisted around. "A meme, Uncle Bo-champ. Here—"

Against Rick's objections Cadence fired up what he called his 'hotspot,' a credit-card sized device which, he explained, gave him more stable internet access than the 3g signal of his iPad.

"But, but, but—a meme's a little picture with a saying like, that's funny. Or it's maybe a question? Or something silly," sounding exhausted at trying to nail it down. Insistent: "*Just wait a minute and I'll show you.*"

Rick, nodding at me in the rearview. "A meme, it's a pithy little— what d'ya call it? An observation. To put it in Uncle Cort's terms."

Cadence, distressed. "Dad: I thought we weren't supposed to curse."

After a moment I guessed which word had thrown him. "Pithy, Cadence. The word is 'p-i-t-h-y.' Pithy means concise, but expressive."

"Or all that white stuff on the inside of an orange," Marcy added.

"Yeth." Rick, further amused by it all. "Pith."

"What's 'concise'?"

I told him. Cadence nodded.

Squinting at the screen, he held up his iPad in my direction, snapped a photo, and began typing and tapping.

"Now listen—"

"Finished and posted!" Another comedian in love with his own material, Cadence convulsed in *haw-haw-haw* kid-laughter. "It's online already in my, my, my social media feed."

Rick, and Marcy, too, had prepared me for Cadence and his level of autism, which amounted to freaking out over otherwise small issues, mild socialization problems—you could have fooled me—and inquisitiveness perhaps complemented by a touch of OCD. When Cadence needed to know something, he needed to know it.

I felt certain with a mind like that, he'd get by fine in life. But what did I know, either about autism, kids, or anything else.

When he was younger, the ten year-old Cadence suffered an interesting problem called 'elopement'—far from a romantic and impetuous dash by youngsters aiming to wed, in Cadence's case it had meant a propensity for decamping from classrooms and school buildings and going on compulsively inquisitive adventures far too dangerous for a four-to-seven year old, after which he'd outgrown the issue. When the problem had been at its height and before his cognitive abilities settled into a pattern of understanding, as Rick put it, about where he was supposed to be (school) and for how long (until Rick came back to pick him up), Cadence would decide to take strolls around busy city streets and other unsafe places.

In telling me all this before the trip, Rick had chalked up the elopement to Cadence's quality of intellectual inquisitiveness more than the autism. After hanging out in a car for three hours with the young man, such a notion made sense to me.

"Here, Uncle Cort—check it out."

Cadence displayed his meme full-screen on the tablet: the snapshot he'd taken of me in my slacks and loafers, a terrible angle that both managed to age me and add weight, also with an unappealing expression of nonplussed impatience; Marcy's shoulder, a ghostly, out-of-focus lump along the right side of the image.

Across my forehead were plastered the bright yellow words

GOES TO BEACH

and across my khaki'd lower legs, in much bigger type, equally garish cartoon colors:

TAKES VOW OF DISCOMFORT

"That's gone all around the world already, Uncle Cort."

"How terribly clever, apt, and—and—"

Marcy cut me off. "Cute. That's so—cute."

"Uncle Bo-champ's cute. In his khakis." Cadence, giggling. "He's cute. *He's cute.*"

Rick, giving me a thumb's-up. "With his freakin' Vow of Discomfort."

The three of them, heaving and gasping with laughter.

Rick, agitated, begged to get a glimpse at the meme but his son refused, saying it simply wasn't safe for his dad to take his eyes off the freeway to look at the tablet screen.

As for me, I didn't get the big effing deal. Only later when I saw it online and better understood the concept of the meme would I realize that Cadence Wragg hadn't simply made a joke at my expense; more importantly, he'd concocted a minuscule piece of digital instant-art and sent it out into the universe, and hadn't needed anyone's help, or funding, to pull it off. He alone possessed the tools, the talent, and the intent, when in the past you'd have been lucky to have anything beyond the latter, that desire to create.

Who knew how many thousands of people had seen the meme by now?

The world was changing.

Fast.

A blizzard of data. Information—the underpinning of the entire universe. Alan Moore, a writer of intense and influential graphic novels, has suggested that we're all dissolving into discrete packets of information, an impending singularity of mankind transforming itself into living clouds of data—into what he calls steam.

Mind; blown.

I wondered how long such materialist matters as Governor Three-Rivers's war on funding for the arts would matter. Soon, we'll all have iPads, all start making memes and movies and write e-books, posting them into the rising cloud of steam with no middlemen, no gatekeepers.

Farm-to-table; artist-to-viewer. Or in my case, reader.

Warmth flooded into me, and not from being overdressed—I'd learned something about the modern world that I didn't know before, and thanks to an autistic boy forty years my junior. As I'd always tried to teach my writing students, inspiration often happened to be lying right where you found it.

Since the disastrous festival Rick had suffered a mini-breakdown; had already moved to sell his half of the company to Darren, get into another trade altogether. I thought it seemed rash. One should never make such decisions under emotional duress.

In the month since the tornado I'd been doing yeoman's work as confidant and hangout buddy to my quote-unquote new best friend, an obligation and a duty that impinged only so much on my budding relationship with Marcy—on many nights, she had gigs anyway.

But coming out in support of quite a number of her normal appearances around town, already I'd tired of hanging out in restaurants I couldn't afford, being tempted by wine and beer that'd surely be my downfall, and basically being forced to make endless chit-chat with strangers when I ought to be home writing. Add in pressure from Feebee, Opal and the rest of the DDC, all the unreturned emails and calls from Duncan Devereaux's people—told ya—and my nerves felt honed to a razor-fine edge indeed.

When it came time for the mission on the beach, it was clear I could use a day or two away from home. Rick, not the only alkie who could use a snort—Leora's death weighed on my mind and soul. Maybe helping keep Rick dry—I could see he needed a sponsor—helped me just as much.

Rick, recounting the stage collapse over and over. Running his tongue over perpetually dry lips. More fidgety than ever.

We discussed how that particular voice, the one you shouldn't trust, kept saying: *Go-go-go. Get yourself a bracer. You'll feel better.*

I knew the voice, that of the beast-brain.

Mine doesn't sound like his, of course. More like: *My boy, don't you realize how wondrous life will be with a bellyful of ale or port or delicious red wine? Why, you run along and get yourself a tankard or three! Be off with thee, posthaste!*

"How do you deal?"

I told him I simply did—I muddled through. I learned this mainly from my grandparents, the ones I'd known. A different generation. They'd been through more. Had known adversity, but suffered in silence, made the best of it. Didn't complain. Did what was necessary. "But, in my case, the truth was that the drinking had begun to interfere with my work."

Rick had gone mmmm. "Hear ya. That's getting close to bottoming out. Isn't it."

I told him, yes, probably so.

As for the Duncan Devereaux conundrum, as I'd expected all the legitimate entreaties I'd finally gotten around to making had been ignored—not one of his representatives cared to write me back or otherwise return messages.

At last Gendry Lizette informed me that all sorts legal restraints as well as unspoken agreements among the fanbase—codified standing orders—existed to discourage approaching Mr. Devereaux, and this would include responses to entreaties from citizens private or otherwise to gain access.

Even with Gendry's report to back up my lack of results, the last DDC meeting had descended into acrimony and frustration, with Opal and Feebee at each other's throats, and me caught in the middle. As in the arts community as a whole, perhaps in losing Leora, the DDC had lost its center of gravity.

Which I realized had existed in the form of their hope that I was a ringer.

That I could bring home the bacon.

That I could complete the process.

Rick, far from the only failure in the Jeep Liberty hurtling toward Sedge Island. Here on our way to try Rick's plan B, I wanted to cry out from my deep well of inadequacy that it might as well be called Plan A.

Marcy told me not to feel bad; that I had been vocal enough in my assurances about my prior relationship with Devereaux meaning little regarding the chance of getting his attention. Duncan Devereaux, done with the world. Or so it seemed.

Upon our arrival on Sedge Island, Rick announced that he was starving for lunch at one of his old favorite haunts, so he took us to a beachfront restaurant. "When we get to the party house, we'll already be 'fooded' and can get on with the relaxation and hoopla and that type-deal."

Inside the restaurant, a nautical theme of weathered wood and sea shells and netting on the walls. Rick made a big deal with the hostess about pushing two two-tops together by the front window so we could have the best view, all while shouting in an exaggerated voice about how this place had the best 'clamanari' he'd ever had, how he hoped the 'clamanari' was on special because he wanted not one not two but THREE orders for the table, and on and on. Rick Wragg, an exuberant little kid, happy to be on vacation at the beach.

The clams came. The writer, scribbling in his notebook. Marcy, pushing her knee against mine under the table. Cadence, lost in his iPad.

But Rick, gregarious and grinning and pink in the face, insisted on toasting the table with his sweet ice tea.

"Here's to it."

We held our glasses aloft.

He made eye contact. "This feel like family? Or what?"

Smiling but fraudulent to the core, I raised my glass and agreed with hearty good cheer. But what did I know about how family felt? If this was it, I supposed I'd better make a note of it. Maybe I'd be able to describe it one day in fiction, at least.

2.

From the moment we pulled into the driveway of a castle of a beach mansion—enormous, turreted, opulent—I suspected I'd made a mistake.

The headache I suffered from Rick's raucous, pummeling, rock & roll 'travel music' hadn't helped, but when I saw the sheer number of vehicles parked in the bottom floor garage-area of the massive beach house, the circular drive, and along the sandy road, I found myself gripped by claustrophobia and near-panic—it was the weekend, and beautiful weather, and the South Carolina seashore of Sedge Island: of course it was busy; of course all the other houses were booked. The writer who craved privacy was about to bunk with two dozen complete strangers.

What a fool.

"You guys are gonna love this Dashikis crew—best guys ever. You too, Cade. There'll be a couple more house apes for you to pal around with."

Rick had referenced many personalities and names of people I'd be meeting—the members of the Steaming Dashikis; their spouses; the aforementioned house apes in the form of children; the inner circle like Rick; and probably Anzi, he said, who'd been the go-to guitar and drum tech, and who, alongside Rick, had done the grunt work on the road.

Out of obligation, Rick had explained, had their labors been born.

But also: for love.

For love of the music.

For love of the adventure.

I couldn't relate to any of it to save my life.

We piled out of the Liberty and were greeted by a Dashiki spouse, a redheaded and freckled earth mother in a sarong and pink, sunburned bare feet named Madge—"Marcy, Madge; Madge, Marcy; Marcy, Madge, wait wait, I lost my place," one of Rick's impromptu comedy routines—who came out and embraced us all, with Cadence receiving a big swing-around hug that seemed to both humiliate and overexcite him. Couldn't believe how wonderful Rick looked after all this time. Hadn't heard of me or my work. Eyed Marcy sidelong the way women sometimes do.

"You people are in for the party of your lives—my little *girlzz* getting married!" Madge shouted this, a declaration. It seemed to me that she'd already had a few.

"Is there, is there, is there wi-fi," Cadence chanted, already squinting at his tablet. Panic crept into his voice. *"I'm not seeing any nearby networks."*

Rick's eyes bugged. He held out his hands in a state of readiness. I was about to find out why. "We're still out in the driveway, sport—chill out."

Madge, dismissive of the impending crisis. "Oh, sugar, there ain't no internet here—it's one of the house rules. No cable TV, either. We're on Dashiki time now."

Cadence began shrieking.

And shrieking.

And shrieking.

Marcy's look said, *oh-shit,* while Madge actually said, "Oh, shit," and as for me? I nearly shat myself.

I asked if Cadence couldn't continue to use his hotspot. Rick shushed me. "The data charges, dude. Only for a couple minutes at a time. In the car."

"OR SOMEWHERE WHERE THERE'S THERE'S THERE'S NO WI-FI," Cadence shouted through gritted teeth. His countenance, indeed, the child's entire being, had stiffened statue-like. "That's the RULE."

"Dude, c'mon. Please don't. Not here."

Rick, stopping his son from flinging the iPad onto the ground. Hustling the boy away from us, walking him around the circular driveway and speaking in a low and calming tone, to which Cadence responded with more of his febrile shrieking and shouting. Now I could see the manifestation of the autism in a more harmful mode than merely repeating words and phrases, avoiding eye contact, et cetera. Poor kid.

Poor Rick.

As Marcy and I unloaded, Rick would spend the first hour of his beach trip comforting and calming his son, who after a fashion agreed to controlled bursts of internet access via the hotspot. How complex to raise any child these days, much less a challenged one like Cadence. But not so challenged—his intelligence burned bright. His condition, manageable.

This was going to be a party, all right; but starting like this made me unsure how much fun Rick Wragg and I were going to have, not unless we both fell off the wagon.

Strength, I commanded myself. *Concentrate on Marcy.*

No. Well—as time permitted.

But in any case, all remained secondary. A mission awaited.

After a whirlwind of a beach afternoon complete with good cheer, getting-to-know-you, questions about my books, cold beer and icy frozen drinks and chilled wine and (for me) iced tea—enormous quantities of iced tea, unsweetened—followed a lavish and presumptively expensive catered rehearsal dinner at somebody's family restaurant.

Marcy and I called for a delivery pizza. Ate on the deck. Got in the hot tub.

Got into other stuff. While we had some privacy.

The hard-partying crew rolled home en masse in their car service vans about eleven, right as Marcy and I returned from a nighttime beach stroll, the sliver of moon making for wondrous stargazing.

The Dashiki wedding crew, roaring and filled with joy. If the rehearsal had provoked such a bacchanal, I could only imagine what this crew would do with the actual wedding between the lovely young people, whom I had met for all of thirty seconds. They didn't know me—I had no relevant connection. They didn't care who I was. The start of a new chapter in their adult lives.

As for my feelings? Somebody else's children getting married at the beach. I couldn't relate.

At about five, with Marcy's nose whistling in time with her slumbering breath, I pulled on a sweatshirt and jeans and soft-soled sneakers. At the seashore and unable to rest, the taskmaster in me commanded:

Get up and write, boy.

I snatched up my current hot-hand notebook, the one I'd been filling all spring with the lives of Rick and Marcy and Opal and Feebee and Leora, the whole complicated and tragic mess about the festival, all manner of tangents and threads, and crept downstairs to go outside. At the last second, I went back into the bedroom and dug in my satchel until I found the flexible book light I'd started carrying back when I was spending so much time hunched over the corner of Opal's bar, reading or working on student papers, or occasionally my own sad attempt at scratching out a new story. How else would I see to take notes on the wide deck facing the ocean—with dawn an hour away, still deep-dark outside.

Sneaking out past Cadence and Rick, both snoozing in the two single beds next door—we'd been assigned what was clearly a children's wing of bedrooms in the beach castle, including bunk beds for Marcy and me, which is how I'd been able to slip out unnoticed (Marcy, literally on top in more ways than one—hubba hubba).

I crept down a staircase I'd discovered, a private egress to the downstairs outdoor area and the relative peace of the beach beyond. Polished hardwood steps going down, down, down three long floors to the garage level and the pool area out front; beyond, the wooden walkway through the dunes to the white sands and salty surf. Plenty of time—and solitude—to clear my head, meditate, and allow my mind to consider anew the big ideas that kept coming, inspired by all my friends and their art.

Coffee. Wish I had coffee. In the short time there I'd already made friends with a Kuerig machine and its several boxes of single-serve coffees.

Notebook in hand, I took off my sandals and shuffled barefoot up a flight of steps to the expansive front porch, and a sliding glass door to gain access to the main level.

I hesitated—inside, a glimpse of bodies strewn about the living room on the large sofas, overflow guests of the housemates proper who'd imbibed too much and couldn't risk driving on the winding, well-monitored island roads. Nor should they have, of course.

I withdrew and proceeded out to the observation deck out amidst the dunes and sea grass. A band of lavender had begun to appear along the distant horizon.

A figure, waiting for me out there.

Super. Small talk with a stranger at 5:30 in the AM? Sure.

But not a stranger: none other than a bare-chested Rick Wragg in pajama bottoms and flip-flops, smoking and gazing into the depthless black of the horizon. The lump I'd seen in his bed obviously only the covers; smoking, a habit I knew him to be trying to hide from his son. Or else Rick, like me, seeking the privacy the deep night afforded the nondrinkers, the rest of the house littered by prone and supine bodies lying in their medically induced comas.

Whispering, trying to hide my mild irritation. "Do you ever sleep, sir?"

"Holy crap," his feet leaving the weathered decking. "Bo-champ, baby, you took a fortnight off my life, there. Maybe a whole month."

"Apologies. I'm—*astonished* to see you awake."

"Eh—I sleep four hours, tops. Sometimes a power-nap during the day. You learn to do that when you're out on the road rigging, going from town to town. Ask any of those guys," hooking a thumb at the dark and silent second floor of the house, where the Dashikis all had their bedrooms. "You grab it when you can. On the bus. While the band's playing. Whenever you can."

The peaceful dawning hour seemed good for Rick—he'd acquired a quality of stillness that I hadn't yet seen in him, a reflective countenance wherein, for once, he seemed to listen more than he talked as we sat and watched the sky lighten.

All afternoon yesterday, however, melancholy and wistfulness seemed to permeate the normally exuberant Rickness that had persisted despite the CityArt disaster and his decision to completely upend and rethink his professional life. Being among old friends, I supposed.

I asked about the prior evening's dinner revelry. He described how the rest of the wedding party got drunker and drunker. "As a dry guy, I ended up giving a few rides here and there."

"Yeoman's service, there."

"Nothing changes—get the band where they need to be. That was my gig, man. On top of everything else, too. Like our interpersonal relationships have DNA-memory, some shit like that."

I thought the idea profound, told him so.

"Gotta talk to you, Cort. Gotta say something."

"By all means."

"Cadence, he thinks you hung the moon. Told me earlier he wants to be a writer like 'Uncle Cort'—man, I thought I was gonna cry. A writer? Even if I don't ever make it as an author, if my kid does instead? That'd be—that'd be like my own dream had come true, too. It's like . . . I understood the value in having a kid, like I never did before."

"I may have missed the boat on that opportunity."

"What—to have a kid?"

I confirmed this.

"Naw, c'mon. That's a problem the ladies got, not us. Charlie Chaplin, he had a kid or two when he was like eighty. Tony Randall, too. And I think Sammy Davis."

"I didn't mean in the physiological sense."

"Oh, yeah, yeah, I get it," as though he didn't. "That Marcy's something else, man. She's—she's a hot box of chocolates. Hoo-mama."

"Yes, we'd both know," thinking with a degree of discomfort over our mutual provenance regarding her. "Wouldn't we."

"No weirdness over all that, right?"

"None here," a gentle fib.

"From her? About me and her? And you? All hanging out?"

"No anomalous behavior. She's wonderful and relaxed. I'm feeling rather lucky."

"Mm. I bet."

"And your son? Despite his medical condition, he's obviously quite intelligent. You're fortunate in that regard, I must say."

"It's nuts. My kid, running around with that iPad, putting stuff on the internet . . . little dude makes me feel like a nincompoop." He chucked me on the bicep. "Both of ya do."

I asked if he were feeling better about the festival, about selling out to his partner and trying to find a new path in life, asked how the exit from the business partnership with Darren was proceeding.

"All good; all right."

"It's quite a decision." Leaving off, *and you with a child for whom to care.*

"I got big ideas for the future. Don't worry."

Darren Woczinski, on the other hand, seemed bewildered and brokenhearted that one bad gig—an act of God type situation, no less—would sap Rick's spine and taste for the rigging trade. He'd even taken Rick's place on the DDC, a shifting of energy at the last meeting.

"We miss you on the committee."

Rick chewed on the side of this thumb, spat a tiny piece of his callused flesh against the seaside salt-wind picking up with the rising light. Over forty now, he explained, "and if that ain't the right time to make a change, when? I need to build something bigger anyway. Something I can leave to the little kidlet up there. Glimmer Twins? It's as big as it's going to get, and for a single guy like Darren, who can hire a crew of stage monkeys and keep the big bucks for himself, it's perfect. But me, I got Cadence to think about."

"So what's the big plan?"

He told me in brief, a broad sketch. Ownership of a different sort of business: a nightclub. "A music room, mainly. A real listening room. That's what Soda City needs."

I shook my head at the scheme. I know he could see in my eyes a reflection, that of the elephant in the room: alcohol.

"I know what you're thinking."

"And I know that you know."

"It's an issue. Sure. I'll deal with all that."

"All I can say is, be careful."

He declined to debate further, not at this hour, and not out here, the designated area where I'd observed clusters of Dashikis smoking tobaccos domestic as well as sharply sweet and exotic smelling.

"But forget all that crud. The club, it's in the future; and the wedding, it's important to the band, and to me—but snagging the big fish down the beach, that's the reason you're here. Everybody goes home a winner from this trip." He yawned, expansive. "Agreed?"

"Agreed, good sir. Now off to bed with you, and let me scribble my nonsense for a bit before the rest of the house begins roiling with activity . . ."

Rick, holding up a palm like a beachfront prophet. After a brief hesitation, more than the sunlight dawned on me, and I responded to the high-five he desired before going whistling along the weathered gray decking toward the mansion.

I pushed out of my mind Rick's scheme to open a music venue in Columbia. How terribly foolhardy that idea sounded compared to owning and running a stable business like Glimmer Twins.

How I hoped I wouldn't need to find a way to say this to him.

To pop his balloon.

But what did a writer and educator know?

Enough to know better. But Rick's train, leaving the station.

Furthermore, I hoped I wouldn't let everyone down re: my dutiful mission to snag Double-D. But knowing Duncan Devereaux at least a smidgen, what small morsel he'd let me get to know that weekend on tour with his band, I already felt terrible for the gross imposition I'm to force-slash-foist upon the poor lad. Duncan had carried the crippling weight of a dozen lost lives on his marker for fifteen years now. If that didn't warrant being left alone, nothing did.

But then, as Gendry Lizette had said when I'd called to get the skinny on DD's habits and schedule and movements here on the island: "Maybe this will make him feel better, Mr. Beauchamp. Maybe after all this time, our little statue will make him feel better."

I didn't see how it could, but I agreed to try—if not for her, Feebee, Opal, or Devereaux himself, certainly for Leora, who had been the most invested in seeing the process through to completion. Had so loved her community that she sought to enrich it at a cost of much more than mere money.

And so speaking of markers I now carried one for her, and thus remained bound to attend to her various loose ends. Spiritual stakes, presenting sufficient motivation.

I stayed on the deck scribbling and scratching my hieroglyphics until the sun came up. Not just any old notes: these comprised a rough, crude outline for a new novel, CREATIVE CLASS. Whole bit—a potentially complete plot, soup to nuts, the details of which would only detract from the narrative at hand.

In any case, I felt off to the races.

Except for this Duncan Devereaux business.

I searched my memory about his life, what I'd learned back when I wrote the article that's gotten me into so much trouble. A piano prodigy from an early age in his family home a mile or so from the street corner where the presumptive piece of art commemorating DD would stand, he'd been, like myself, the offspring of two intelligent parents, in his case the coupling of a language arts professor at Columbia College with a Southern historian at SEU.

The Devereauxs, the rock god had informed me during our weekend-long 1992 interview, hosted what he described as a supper club, a longstanding Southern tradition wherein people of education and means attended dinner parties with likeminded peer-couples. At each gathering, one attendee would provide a formalized seed from which to cultivate that evening's further learned and erudite conversation in the form of a salon.

I was familiar with the tradition, which represented a more casual version of the Columbia Anatheum—an antebellum club enacted, as its constitution read, for 'the encouragement of the amenities and virtues which spring from social intercourse, and the promotion of useful knowledge by the collection of books and periodicals, and by public lectures.'

My own childhood had held similar scenes and rituals, though in not nearly as formal a manner as occurred in the Devereaux household: The Jessamine Society, he explained, gathered on Friday evenings twice a month for cocktails and dinner, with the young Duncan often playing music for the adults until they were ready for that evening's salon and conversation, at least until his adolescence and a predictable period of rebellion that'd persisted well past his teen years. He'd had his punk period in high school, and had gravitated to heavy metal in the years in which he should have gone to college, which he'd told me had nearly killed his parents, a turn of phrase I found to be extreme and unpleasant. This path resulted, as it happened, in a multiplatinum rock career satisfying the metrics by which the record industry, or anyone else, measured success.

Since his parents and their friends never chose popular music for the subject of their gatherings, the youth would learn about these matters on his own: His band, before becoming the more salacious and marketable 40DD, had been called Devereaux. They got their start playing on-campus parties, at a memorable Halloween concert in the Southeastern ballroom at which their rising local popularity resulted in an overflowing, raucously inebriated crowd of exuberant "thrash" fans that'd trashed the student union.

Such enthusiasts followed them off campus and into bars and clubs like the iconic Slim Lupo's in the Old Market near campus. The Devereaux circuit widened to include the other college towns, but their act played better at places like the Sandflea here on Sedge Island, where our own Steaming Dashikis also played so many of their storied gigs.

But greater heights, yet to be scaled.

A record deal. A new name, 40DD; 'as naughty a double entendre as it gets,' is how I characterized the moniker, making me seem like the biggest fuddy-duddy alive.

Bigger rooms. Supporting the headliners, including a breakout run fronting for KISS after they decided to put the makeup back on. An iconic video or two on MTV; an archetypical "hair band," born. And then headlining tours of their own.

Deal, sealed.

I wondered how the big time felt. The glory of adoration on that scale.

No mystery: Duncan had the right sidemen, the right management, a work ethic, a creative spirit, but maybe most of all, he once confided, asking that I leave it out of the article, a drive born of determination to show his parents that his music could also be high art. Could contrive complexity and subtext and meaning. That culture could also mean pop culture. And that he could be well compensated for it.

He built it; they came.

Millions of times over.

Not mainstream pop success, mind you, but a specialized and growing following that Rick has likened to that of the Grateful Dead, whose leader famously analogized his own rabid fan base generated by their refusal to adhere to heterodox attitudes about what constituted success in the music business. "Our fans," Jerry Garcia explained, "are like people who like licorice. When somebody likes licorice, they really like it, and if they don't, they usually really, really don't like it."

A fine analogy—rock music on the whole indeed represented my licorice, the thought of which has always turned my stomach, a candied snack to avoid.

By the time of Duncan's withdrawal following the tragedy, according to Gendry her hero had been ready to make a true artistic breakthrough, one that showed promise far beyond all he'd managed as a heavy metal guitarist and bandleader. Before the destruction and death at RFK Stadium, he appeared poised on the precipice of some greater achievement than mere record sales, one yet to be realized.

As he'd taken the stage, poised to unleash an entire set of his latest, more complex music, the crowd had convulsed, and the kids had been crushed to death.

Before he'd sung a note.

Since that terrible moment, the poor lad hadn't once played guitar in public or released a new song or album, and this state of grievous artistic stasis had held fifteen long years now, an eternity to the fans. Legend had it, Gendry had told me with widened eyes, that he'd amassed enough new material for a dozen albums—songs and rock operas he'd composed and performed with well-compensated and tight-lipped session players, that would one day all be released and fry everybody's mind and expectations. Sweet, starry-eyed Gendry, divulging all this with her cheeks aglow at the thought.

"How did you get so interested in this kind of music?" I had asked her this on the street after our last DDC meeting.

She shrugged. "He was from here. He went to my same high school. He's somebody that's done something—*from right here in Columbia.* How could I not be interested? If some kid from Herndon Hill like me can make it that big, anybody can."

Was it possible, as Gendry and Rick both seemed to think, that I'd be able to simply walk down the beach later and encounter this enigmatic hometown figure, here on this rich man's spit of land jutting out in the briny, green Atlantic?

I had to try.

The sun would be up in another hour or so, and that's when I'd need to get ready: at low tide, when with dedication and regularity Duncan Devereaux apparently went down to the exposed, flat beach at the inlet of the island near his property, a patch of earth that appears twice a day, otherwise hidden from sight beneath the lapping low waves of the becalmed sea.

If the plan worked, it'd all seem like a mad coincidence. Fancy meeting you here! That sort of thing.

And if DD played ball? It's back to Columbia as a hero, fulfilling my debt to Leora, at least insofar as the DD committee was concerned, and again left to my own devices. Free to write. I hadn't had any inspiration in ages. I worried if I didn't get down to business, it'd all go away again.

My back aching, I finally got up out of the camp chair in which I'd been writing to psych myself up for the mission ahead, and the long day afterwards—the Dashiki wedding would be later tonight.

"Look at the early riser."

Marcy, in a short robe. Elegant, alabaster bare feet and lovely legs and tousled hair. A beautiful vision in the golden, early light.

"Same to you."

"Truth be told, I didn't really go to sleep at all."

"Maybe . . . I should've stayed in bed."

Marcy, stroking my face and running her hands through my hair. I put my arm around her; we watched the sun sneak out from behind a gauzy spray of cirrus clouds.

"So you're really going through with this ambush plan?"

I told her yes, but that if she had a better idea—parachuting naked onto the estate, for instance, or hiring one of those beach planes trailing big banners—I'd be all for it.

"What's the worst that can happen?"

"He can only say no—and to be honest, I wouldn't blame the guy."

"So why bother him?"

For Leora, I explained. To finish what she started.

Marcy, understanding fully, fell quiet. "For Leora," she repeated, her voice faraway. "That's the most romantic thing I've ever heard. You like doing things for people, don't you?"

"For the ones I love."

At the L word, Marcy's body stiffened. Maybe another person wouldn't have noticed this slight change of muscle tension. But I'm a writer—nothing escapes my notice. Nothing. A blessing; a curse.

To Cade's great relief, I emerged a few minutes later looking every bit the part of an anonymous middle-aged ordinary beachcomber—I sported shorts, a Strand bookstore T-shirt, sneakers and a visor and sunglasses.

Avoiding eye contact, he sat curled up in his PJs, tucked into the crook of an enormous L-shaped couch in the two-story great room. In the kitchen, Rick, Marcy, and one of the Dashiki wives seemed elbow deep in an industrial-sized breakfast project.

With many still sleeping, we whispered.

"We gonna have a—um—have a beach day, Uncle Cort?"

"Certainly—but after I jiggle my way down to the turnaround. A brisk little jaunt."

Cadence, already deep into his iPad. "Have fun. When the rest get up, we're all having—um—waffles."

"So I smell. Save me one."

Quite serious. "I'll try—but I don't know."

"Worry not. I'll have a granola bar. Not a big breakfast person."

He seemed gobsmacked. "Breakfast is my favorite."

After finishing my last swallow of tepid coffee, I ground spearmint antacid tablets into paste that I allowed to trickle down the back of my throat the way Duncan Devereaux had once experienced with cocaine, which he had described as 'the drip.' My nostrils had not come close to any of that, though quite a bit had been bandied about during my fabled weekend with the rock star all those years ago.

As a pair of the other children appeared and sat chatting with Cadence, I smiled that he had made friends with some of the Dashiki youth. After we arrived yesterday and Rick had gotten Cadence to calm down, the boy had taken to the atmosphere of high spirits among the other kids running around in the sand.

We watched him with the others. Cadence, asking in a steady and loud voice, "Would you all like to play?"

Rick's eyes had moistened. He held a hand up to his chest.

I asked him what was wrong.

"You got no idea, Bo-champ—we had such trouble with socialization. To hear him greet a group of strangers like that . . .? It does a daddy good," his voice crumbling. "He's come so far. Look how he's been with you. It's just awesome."

Rick, needing good news in his life. I beamed inside for him.

Adjusting my sunglasses I hit the beach, heading left toward the northern tip of the island.

The light, falling brilliant along the strand. As predicted by the chart I'd googled, the tide had long begun to creep back out. White, loose sand, rolling across like cloudscapes photographed in fast-motion, the sight of which prompted a note in the pocket-sized Moleskine. Sandpipers, running with their impossibly fast little gait along lapping tendrils of foam that bubbled up white, but with a brownish tint I'd been told could be traced to freighter traffic from Savannah's busy harbor a few sea islands further south. On the earbuds, the martial snares and portentous A-minor crescendoes of Mahler's 6th Symphony, a rousing orchestral accompaniment to this bit of altruistic derring-do on my part.

Immenseness.

Solitude.

Relatively so, anyway. The wide, flat beach held only a few other early birds, dog-walkers, and one spindly legged elderly man—to be fair, probably only ten years older than me—deploying a metal detector with deliberate and consistent side-to-side sweeps.

At the discovery of an object, he froze.

Produced a small trowel from his belt.

Squatted and dug.

Examining his find, a tiny piece of metal. Discarding it. Moving on.

Who knew what treasures and mysteries he uncovered?

A hobby—I should consider getting one of those.

As I drew closer to the point of the island, and the enormous estates thereon, the beach, already quiet and near-empty, became mine. I considered the violation of this man's privacy: DD hadn't been the first rock star to know that his own fans had died in the attempt to see him play, before and after the 1997 horror at RFK Stadium—The Who in Cincinnati in 1979, Pearl Jam at Roskilde in 2000, with body counts of eleven and nine, respectively—but he'd been the one to hang up his guitars. To say, this is all too much: Duncan Devereaux, he'd been the star who'd said, enough. Who'd said, I cannot face them again; I cannot risk another life for my art, nor for the sake of commerce.

I paused, watching the waves lap at the sand. Thought hard about all this.

No wonder he hadn't responded to my emails. If he didn't want to play for people, to perform his music, in no way would he sanction such a tribute as the DDC had planned. Wouldn't it seem but a desperate reminder of a career forever forestalled?

Suffering a bout of shame over what amounted to consideration for Double-D's feelings masquerading as my own putrid cowardice, I plowed ahead, picked up the pace, spewed sand from my heels in little sprays that made my footprints look like little comets chasing me, forever falling behind. I felt the wind, cool before the heat of afternoon sets in, tickling my face and neck. The waves, the spray, the smell. Shells, crunching under my feet. The beach curved around, and I could see the first of several groins, rocky protrusions on either side of the inlet designed to aid in the constant erosion, the pummeling of the mighty forces of the sea from which we all sprang. I was close.

I climbed onto the first of the jagged, slippery rocks. Now I could see the spit, emerged from the ocean as had been foretold: a piece of ground ephemeral as the striking of a particular hour, which happens twice a day no matter what.

My heart leapt into my throat: I could see a figure poised out on the flat, round semicircle of beach surrounded by the lapping, shallow shelf of the Atlantic Ocean. The man, tall and slender, contorting himself by pulling a leg up by his ear, a smooth and practiced motion. Other arm, extended. A finger, a single digit, held aloft. A gesture, it struck me, like one of his devotees might have made at a concert.

Duncan Devereaux, right where Gendry said he would be.

Perhaps this would be easier than I thought.

3.

But as I clambered down the other side of the mossy, slick groin and headed for the spit, somehow I didn't hear the heavy footsteps running across the beach toward me—perhaps the pounding of Mahler's timpani and the wind cutting across my ears had something to do with it. With my prey so close, now only twenty yards away and striking his yoga poses, I had myopia like a camera lens irising to a small round circle amidst an endless field of black.

DD.

In my sights.

"Duncan! Duncan Devereaux—it's me, it's Cort Beauchamp, it's—"

Oof—a massive force from behind, a blackout, my wind knocked out; my face, slamming into the rough hard sand and sliding a foot or so to a stop. I tried to cry out, but my words had no wind beneath their wings, only a mouthful of gritty, salty sand.

A pressure in the small of my back—a knee. A voice belonging to the knee, sonorous, a vibration traveling down the length of my aching body. "Sir—I'm going to release you, now, real slow and easy and we all real cool. No sudden movements. Me and sudden movements don't get along."

Upon the lifting of the knee, my back, cracking in a fine and thorough manner the likes of which I've not enjoyed since I last hit the chiropractor, now over a year ago.

"Gah," I managed to say. "*Blargh.*"

"Mister, you're trespassing on private beachfront right now—"

Another edgy voice from behind me, urgent and upset. "*What the hell are you doing, Reynaldo?*"

The pressure on my back eased.

"Let him up."

And disappeared.

Relief.

I took a tentative, deep breath; much additional crackling ensued, and a modest but sharp flurry of shooting pains.

My nose and cheeks mudded with gray Sedge Island sand, I rolled over to see a looming security goon as substantial as a small mountain. Alongside the olive-skinned man with forearms like Popeye and backlit by the blazing light of the morning sun over the Atlantic crouched a middle-aged man into whom a once chubby, longhaired rock star had transformed: now reed-thin, gray-faced and wrinkled, but still a version of none other than my old interview subject. The eyes never lie, and his intense, probing marbles shone with recognition.

Duncan's expression of concern turned to chagrin. "It's—you."

"It's me."

DD and his bodyguard offered hands that helped me to my feet. I squinted around for the sunglasses that the security guard knocked off my head. I suspected I'd hurt for weeks—the last time I took a spill from the mountain bike I ride around the hilly, rural roads of Cypress Creek, I limped for three months with a sore knee that didn't want to heal.

I glared at the thug that'd put my dingus into the wet sandy earth. "What is the meaning of this violence? You almost broke me in half."

"You're trespassing, sir—this—this is—"

"Enough." Duncan, grabbing me by the arm. "This man, he's a friend. One who's been trying to get in touch with me for over a month now. Haven't you, Cort?"

My face, hot as an oven. I could barely meet his eyes.

"So I guess you finally got me." His smile, genuine. "Might as well join us for breakfast, eh?"

Relieved, I could but agree. And so, for the second time in as many decades, Duncan Devereaux allowed me a glimpse, however brief, into the private life of a rock legend.

We stood watching the spit again consumed by the tide now turning, the view from the veranda into the sound stretching before us in gloriously natural beauty and magnificence. Duncan, who'd served tea and a slice of lemon cake that he also helped himself to—an indulgence, he explained, and a reward for an otherwise abstemious and yoga-driven fitness regime he pursued—had been so mortified, but ultimately happy, to see that his bodyguard had tackled none other than Cortland Beauchamp that he didn't know how to feel, exactly.

Once the apologies and explanations were done, he seemed to want to put off the question of the DDC and honors and monuments, of which he of course knew all about from my unanswered e-inquiries. Instead, he asked me something that both flattered and stung, the one that came from F. Gordon Blake at Leora's funeral, and from Leora herself so often throughout the last decade:

"I loved your books—I read them, you know, after our interview." The rock star's breathy, affected voice hadn't changed. "Anything new in the hopper?"

A gull swooping overhead, screeching, making Duncan's face light up. His hair-band locks shaved to a fine dusting of gray, and so skinny that his Adam's apple seemed as protrudent as his nose, he did not exude the glowing well-being of a yogi like Marcy so much as someone ill. It was clear that health and 'clean eating,' as he described his diet, unbidden, seemed important, especially in Duncan's fit of self-consciousness over enjoying a slice of cake so early in the day— for breakfast, essentially.

A confession? I eat cake for breakfast all the time. Lori-Kaye might not have approved, but damn if a slice of cake doesn't sit pretty as you please on the pallet along with the Folgers, accompanied by, say, a bright, cheery Mozart like I'd listened to the morning before I came on the beach trip, the delightful Piano Concerto No. 22.

Mornings . . .

Cake. Coffee. The Moleskine notebook open. My favorite pen. And Mozart.

Heaven.

"So—this is a wonderful honor that's been proposed. Cosmic, in fact. But—"

I saw an opening. "You know, Duncan, you may be right. Back home in Columbia, there's such a movement to honor the arts, and this acknowledgment we've planned of your accomplishments—it fits in so well."

"Let me finish, let me finish." His demeanor changed for the first time since seeing me being tackled on the beach: frustration, an emotion I'd later find out he wanted, desperately, to keep in check. "You don't understand. I meant cosmic in that it's you who've come here to pitch me on the thing—shit. I'm sorry."

Duncan Devereaux twisted his sinewy, lean body around in the patio chair, gripped the beveled edge of the heavy etched glass tabletop, an outdoor set that probably cost as much as my whole cabin back in Cypress Creek. He couldn't get out what he had to say.

"Look—we don't have to do this. I can go. I can—"

"I don't want you to go. But this, it's so difficult."

I waited. I considered sipping my tea. Instead, I held my hands open, a gentle gesture of go-ahead. I suspected a heartfelt speech coming about his fans who'd died. The tragedy. I prepared to listen, to be empathetic.

But no.

"I've written a novel. I've only just finished the first revision this morning," his voice breaking. "The only real writer I've ever known, besides my father, just happens to show up on my little piece of beach? Today? Of all days?"

His words came as a morass of garbled syllables. Did he just say he'd written a novel? *Oh, god—no.* "Stranger coincidences . . . I'm sure they've happened."

"Cort. There are no accidents. Don't you know that? This was all supposed to happen this way. I've never been able to accept that about what happened to my kids," referring, I understood, to the casualties at RFK Stadium. "In some cases, it's just undeniable. Unassailable. Cosmic. I could never ask for such a gift from the universe—I don't have the courage. Never in a thousand years. But you showing up here—how do we know? *How do we know?*" He bashed the tabletop with a closed fist, making our teacups jump.

"How do we know what?"

He gave me a pitiful smile. "How do we know that you weren't sent here?"

"By whom—God?"

"By the universe," nodding. "Same difference."

Perhaps this was the opening, an opening of honesty and truth. But not yet. Not until I'd put in some sweat equity. Not until I'd acquired some chips to cash in—if my insect antennae were right, I already had Duncan Devereaux in the palm of my devious, writerly hand. He'd be agreeing to the DDC honor. Oh yes, he would.

If he wanted me to read this novel, that is.

So: I told him I felt the same way, that I followed the tenets of hippy-dippy mysticism and the magic of coincidence and confluence, but that before I let myself fully agree with him, I wanted more empirical evidence. That I wanted to hear about this novel of his. I wanted him to pitch me, and tell me the story. To see if it resonated, I said, with my own work, which felt as though it'd become a new novel, and not a series of stories, a book I had thought of calling CREATIVE CLASS. To see if the cosmos had indeed brought us together for a reason.

Rather than feeling devious, however, I felt confessional. "Duncan, you're the first person on Earth I've told about this novel, which is the first one I've really gotten going in many years now, I'm ashamed to admit—that's why you haven't seen any books from me in so long. But I hope you realize that, as hard as it seemed for you to reveal yourself to me, to let your creativity out of its cage and into the light of another's regard, I tell you this to open the door a little wider. To put some skin in the game."

"I get it. I'm down with this."

I sipped my tea, contemplated the ocean and the sun, which was creeping upwards but still playfully lurking behind a scrim of wispy high clouds, far over the placid and lapping springtime Atlantic. I told him my logline, then, which he seemed to dig—romantic travails amidst a small city's arts revival, with political stakes and a death or two for the sake of emotional impact and drama.

"Gotta have the deaths. Don't we," he asked in a small voice. The wind died down, and the heat of the coming Carolina summer fell across both our faces. "Life and death drama."

"Afraid so."

And next I waited to hear his pitch, which despite being a little long for someone in an elevator or in the hallway at a writer's workshop still made me stop in my tracks and say, Bill and Ted-like, "Whoa—now that sounds like a decent read."

Duncan's own logline, a grabber—a recovering rock star doing penance at a rich person's mountaintop rehab facility must fend off a marauding suicide cult, their leader proclaiming that the Retreat, as the facility is known, has been chosen for the arrival of extraterrestrials who'll take the chosen people of the cult 'back home again,' and which turns into a desperate battle for survival with the damaged, recovering addicts desperate to live again pitted against an end-times cult desperate to die, but only in their particular way and time. Title: *The Retreat.*

Duncan Devereaux, who'd performed before festival crowds of nearly a hundred thousand, seemed as shy and self-effacing as a schoolboy presenting a first book report. "A thriller, admittedly. Not terribly literary."

"Show me a reader who doesn't enjoy a solid, ripping yarn."

His voice, tiny: "Really?"

"It's quite something. All I've ever been able to come up with are variations on my own life . . ."

He pressed his lips together. Could barely get out the words. "And you think that isn't?"

I got it. "Not so fast—suddenly I think you've got the literary part covered as well."

He glowed.

I glowed as well, mainly with envy. That logline, and his famous name, would get him a deal in a heartbeat. "So is it—"

"Finished? Yeah, through ten drafts."

I relaxed—Duncan, serious about the craft. He'd learned that you must not only write these things, but write them again and again to get them right.

I masked my jealousy at his hot logline and pretended to be curious to hear more details, which Duncan supplied over the course of a tour of his impressive, modernist home, a showing on which I'd insisted, but undertaken only after much cajoling.

First, however, he presented me with a mug of coffee I'd been embarrassed to request. The tea he'd served was non-caffeinated and floral and lovely, but the Keurig hazelnut I'd slurped at the Dashiki house seemed a long time ago.

Duncan went to shower off his yoga-dew, as he called his sweat. I sipped and waited and made idle chatter with the bodyguard, Reynaldo, who upon learning of my identity and relationship to his boss had lapsed into a state of visible mortification.

His eyes wet with contrition, we stood, awkward, watching shrimp boats dragging their nets along the horizon line. Despite it being a holiday weekend, the beach for nearly as far as I could see remained deserted and quiet. Duncan's exclusive estate, one of several occupying the tip of Sedge Island and protected at the roadway by a stone, gated entrance, lay at the opposite end from the State Park, where the common folk put up their umbrellas and played in the sandy, tepid surf of late spring.

"Mr. Beauchamp," Reynaldo all but exclaimed, penitent hands folded in front of his windbreaker, "I can't apologize enough. You got to know that I was only doing my job. I've been working for Mr. Dev for ages, and it's more than a job, it's kinda my calling. I'm responsible for him, and—and—he's like family. So—"

"A job well done indeed," turning my stiffening neck until it popped, satisfying and sharp. I extended my hand for the third or fourth time. "All very understandable. And, I'm not made of balsa wood. I don't break too terribly easily."

He hung his head. "Still. When Mr. Dev told me you were his favorite writer, and I'd gone and tackled you like that—? Lord have mercy."

"Favorite writer?" waving away such nonsense. "Please. In any case, you're taking excellent care of him. No harm, no foul."

"You understand why I'm here. Right? How bad RFK was for him? And why all this time he's been—keeping to himself. Keeping the world pushed out."

"I do understand."

But of course I couldn't—well, thanks to the tragedy of my parents, maybe a smidgen. Or more than a smidgen, honestly; I've always suffered my panic and horror and nightmares in relative silence. Not even Lori-Kaye ever knew how bad it's been for me since I heard the gunshots. Found their dying bodies sprawled in the bedroom. Why trouble anyone else, that's always been my motto. Why burden them.

"Do many people try to come here like I did?"

Shrugging, nonchalant. "Nah. But at first? He got death threats. From family members of the victims, even from people who couldn't understand why he wanted to quit. Yeah—he got 'em from his own fans. You believe that? Dude didn't stick his head out for years. Except to get driven to an airport to pick up some guys he wants to produce in the studio downstairs, which happens every now and then with younger cats. Says, he can help people make their own records, but he can't make his own. Can't sing those old songs no more, neither. I always tell him, you can sing new songs. He's got a bunch, too, a whole bunch. Cat'll sit down there all night—he'll lay down all the tracks himself, see, cause Mr. Dev, there's nothing he can't play, no instrument he can't jam on. People who only know his metal stuff don't got a clue. He's got this one song he played for me, it sounds as good as anything I ever heard outta Elton John. You like Elton John?"

"Rey-rey, baby." Duncan, wet-headed and looking relaxed in a solid T-shirt and khakis, came back out onto the veranda. "You're telling secrets to a writer. Maybe one who's only here to get those kind of secrets out of us. Or am I just paranoid, Cort?"

"You have a right to be paranoid."

Duncan, looking pink and scrubbed and much healthier than he had at first, arched an eyebrow. "I suppose we should talk about this statue of me they want to put up back home."

I begged off. "Tell me more about your novel, first. Tell me your writing process. And then we'll talk about that whole deal, which isn't nearly as dramatic as you might think."

"Oh," somehow looking both relieved and terrified. "Sure."

Underselling; underplaying; trying to make him receptive, as well as psych him out, which I supposed in my case were roughly the same goal. After everything Reynaldo had told me, I wanted more than Duncan's approval. I wanted him to agree to come and sing to us all.

Sing us his new songs. That, I'd decided, was the real cosmic part of all this. I let him dangle for a bit, though. We'd get to all that.

DD's studio, a complex on a lower, windowless floor that stretched the length of the house would have made a gearhead like Rick Wragg wet himself. Gold and platinum albums, lining a hallway with a series of doors and reinforced glass windows—the studio, the engineer's booth (or whatever they called it—I'd have to ask-slash-look it up), rehearsal rooms, a rec room with a bar, a pool table, pinball, classic arcade games like Galaga and Donkey Kong and air hockey, a chill-out room with low lighting, plush couches, ottomans for tired feet, and small tables ready to receive what I had come to know from my time with musicians as a wide variety of possible accoutrements.

"Impressive—this must've cost a mint."

"It did. But what is money?"

I nodded. Chuckled.

"No, seriously."

Duncan, taking us into the control booth and directing me to a captain's chair next to him in front of a mixing board, a machine that looked vastly and infinitely more complicated than any such piece of equipment I'd ever seen. Again, how I wished Rick could see this. I thought of his Glimmer Twins soundboard, how it and all the other equipment had gotten soaked in the aftermath of the stage collapse. How Rick had been so shaken by what'd occurred that he didn't seem to care about that part.

After asking me to remind him about my musical tastes—he apologized, saying he could remember as clear as day our weekend of interviews twenty years ago, but not the substance of what we'd discussed, and what I'd told him about myself—Duncan played for me a recording he'd been working on with a young band that he'd discovered.

"I do that a lot, but always without credit."

"Oh—seriously?"

"Sometimes even the bands themselves don't know who it was doing the final mix they sign off on—they just think it's their producer the company assigned. But nah. It's me. I do it for free, sometimes. Like with this band."

That sounded awfully noble.

I reminded him about my classical proclivities. How it was difficult for me to judge this kind of music, though the jangling guitars and shuffling rhythms seemed inoffensive enough, and nothing like the bombastic aural assault that'd defined the earliest recordings I'd endured of my host and his first band.

Duncan's body language became self-conscious, his sallow cheeks pinking. "Look at me. Look at this ego-driven crap. What do you want to listen to? Besides, I need to tell you my novel. Right? That's the ego-driven crap you came down here for. So what do you want to listen to? What would put you at ease?" He pushed back and wheeled over to the wide screen of a huge Apple computer and began clicking around. "Classical? I grew up studying the masters, you know. Majored in composition."

"I remember."

"Name almost anything. Or—or I can guess your favorite. Want me to guess?"

I'd already formulated a response. "Smetana. *Ma Vlast.*"

"Really? *Really?* Smetana?"

I told him not-really, the Smetana had simply been the last selection to come up on my iPod before I'd come on the trip, right as I'd turned off my car outside Rick's house. "I don't play favorites. But I'm a sucker for Berlioz. Saint-Saens. A sonata, like the No. 1 in D minor … if we had time, the complete 'Rite of Spring' suite."

"Stravinsky? Bold—we don't want to cause a riot. Saint-Saens sounds good." His fingers clattered; "And there we have it."

The music, filling the space and my soul. Glorious, as I'd suspected, coming out of those studio monitors.

As the sonorous and soothing vibrations caressed our ears, Duncan further explained his novel, and like the promise shown by the logline, it sounded a doozy, complete with subtext that I now saw tying into the tragedy that'd ended his public music career—the 'clean' rock star assaulted by the suicide cultists as he climbed toward an inner peak of attainment that would never be fully realized. Reaching for the stars. Not unlike a surging crowd trying to get as close to their rock star idol as possible, even though the final barriers could never be crossed and full contact achieved.

I got it; I told him so.

He couldn't have been more pleased.

He asked me what I'd been waiting to hear, which offered the opening I needed. "If you want to take a look ... I'm not asking ... but I have an epub file I could put in the Dropbox for you ... or send in an old-fashioned email, even."

"Of course. I'd be honored."

He visibly relaxed. "The honor would be mine."

"Ah ... honor. And emails." Dry, like the 007-style martinis I got into for awhile, when my drinking had been at its peak. "I've sent a few. In my day."

As sheepish as Reynaldo had been contrite. "I'm flattered. But let me understand what it is y'all really want out of me on this."

At last. "They want you to play, Duncan. They want you to play for them again."

All conviviality exhausted in as abrupt a fashion as I'd feared, Duncan Devereaux thanked me for checking with him, pledged to send his manuscript ... and sent me and the entire DDC packing with a word:

"No."

As I'd suspected, we should leave the poor man be. They'd all have to understand.

I tried to tell 'em.

At least Duncan offered a defensible excuse: he had become a writer. Of course he wanted to be left alone. Now here, a rationale I'd be able to not only explain, but justify.

Hey, I tried. At least I'd accomplished that much. So what that my story, so to speak, was rejected? It's happened more times for this published author than most of you would believe. It still happens.

4.

Driven back out of the gated community and down to the Steaming Dashiki party house by Reynaldo, in what seemed to be the gold-plated limousine of golf carts, he appeared troubled anew.

"Never saw him have anybody downstairs like that—nobody who wasn't working on no record. Or anybody in the house at all, actually. Kind of a big day around the old haunted mansion. Having you around."

"Glad I could liven it up." I mumbled, depressed by my lunkheaded, overreaching sudden failure with DD. "For my next act, juggling."

"Seemed to all wrap up pretty fast. Wasn't a half-hour ago he told me to expect you to stay for dinner."

I took a moment to explain what'd happened, mainly on the off chance that Reynaldo could cajole Duncan into participating in the tribute to his life and career that his hometown hoped for. "Anything you could do to grease the wheels . . . would mean a lot. Not to me so much, but to the whole darn city back home, don't you know."

"Ah." Reynaldo waved me off. "Don't get your hopes up. Mr. Dev's fragile, like brittle glass, if I can put things in a way that a writer like you could understand. I don't know he could stand up to all that whatcha call it—scrutiny."

I told him I did indeed understand. And that if Duncan Devereaux wanted to stay hidden, Feebee and the rest of them would have to let him stay hidden—it was the least we could do for a man who otherwise seemed in complete control of his life. An empty life in many ways, or so it sounded.

But how different from my own?

Not much, except in terms of the gold records lining the walls. A little lonely.

Before Marcy, anyway. Back in the saddle.

"I'll say this, though." Reynaldo, signaling and waving to an island cop riding around in his old purring electric golf cart. "That book he wrote sounds real good to me. A lot of action. I read those kinda things—usually grab one offa the rack at the grocery store bout every week. I like Brad Thor. You like Brad Thor?"

"Not exactly." I asked what he meant by 'those kinda things.'

"Thrillers, spy stuff, badass has to go and rescue the president, Dirk Pitt, Tom Clancy, all that crud. I don't much care for TV, truth be told. We didn't have one when I was a kid, and I reckon the habit never took."

I didn't care what sort of reading Reynaldo did, whether he'd read a word of mine, or of Shakespeare's, or the Holy Bible, though I'm betting that he had—the fact that anyone at all made such a statement to me in 2012 did my heart good. The only bumper sticker I'd ever purchased, that sat on my bumper back in the Midlands, had this to say:

KILL YOUR TV

I asked Reynaldo what he thought about e-books, and reading them on a device instead of one of his beloved paperbacks—my mother had been the same way, so I knew the look and feel and language of those potboilers.

"Never tried one. But I'm thinking about asking Santa this year for a Kindle. When you got a new book coming?"

I began to formulate a lie, realized it wasn't a lie that I had one in the oven, sorta, kinda, and told him all about CREATIVE CLASS, which he said sounded . . . all right. Not his cup of tea. Too literary.

Inside the mammoth great room, I sat on the giant L-shaped sofa in shafts of warm, golden light. I tried scribbling in my notebook, but Duncan's "no" continued to needle. Nobody likes hearing "no," even when one expects it.

Dang it—I could see Leora's disappointed face. But the news had come from the horse's mouth. No second chances.

Some of the Dashiki guests began coming back up from their beach time. Rick, Marcy and Cadence were all down there, I'd been told, but most needed to start getting ready for the wedding.

A parade of folks came through. The last group included a mommy with her two little boys of, who knows, I'm terrible at this: maybe four and seven? I watched them approach on the huge deck through the large, open balcony doors. She showered off the sand, pulling their swimsuits down and toweling them both pink as newborn mice, then rushing them inside the great room where I sat.

Startled by my presence, the mom apologized and hurried her sons along. The little boys, naked, innocent, and beautiful, dashed giggling and bouncing off each other through the living room until disappearing up the stairs.

How did it feel to be that innocent?

No clue. Not at this late date, if I'd ever known such a feeling.

I supposed that I had. I wondered if the line of demarcation hadn't been the Figs of July incident? A mutual infidelity too far?

A dashed dream—father, a writer. Mother, a concert pianist.

Neither realized.

A yearning chasm threatened to open inside me. But as I learned to do long ago, turned the feeling around—remembering my parents and their unrealized hopes, not to mention their tragic, early demise, had always fueled my fervor to persevere. To write another story. To start another novel. To try to help another human learn how to write their own story.

To keep on.

The mother, wrapped in a robe and barefoot, followed carrying an armload of their beach clothing. Apologetic. "I shouldn't've told them to run through like that."

"They were fine. Good boys, having fun. No worries."

"They are good. I love my little fellas so much."

"That's wonderful. A wonderful feeling."

Not that this childless man could possibly know. Come to think of it, my stories rarely feature children, or people with children. I should get to know more of them.

The wedding came off without a hitch—a lovely young couple, both of whom looked about fourteen but were actually college seniors: Aimee and Brian, the bride being the daughter of the Dashiki who'd hosted us all weekend, the real estate mogul and hometown boy who'd rented the beach mansion for the occasion. Love, laughter, and life ahead of them.

The reception, an enormous affair and a concert at a marshfront golf and country club around the horn of the island, so to speak, to the other side of Bayport, the nominal town center; I'd been cajoled into going to the reception by Marcy, who'd been wide-eyed ever since I reappeared at the front door, as though my return from the inner sanctum of Duncan Devereaux equalled traversing the rubicon of death and coming back to tell the tale.

"And he seemed—what? Like a normal dude?"

"A little twitchy. A little . . . nervous. About me being there." I didn't feel I should say that Double D planned to reinvent himself as a novelist. I couldn't divulge such a private and personal goal. Not until I'd been asked to do so. "A touch testy. I'd say that his participation in any sort of ceremony back home is unlikely."

"That's too bad."

"Maybe I'm wrong. In any case, not a whisper to motormouth—I mean, Rick—until I can say for certain."

"Check."

The ballroom floor, open to the marsh and cooled by lazily turning Bermuda fans hanging from the salt-weathered, exposed beams, creaked beneath the feet of the assembled dancers, the old polished hardwoods carrying the vibrations of the band across the room and up my spinal column; I had to continually reinsert the wads of toilet tissue I tried stuffing into my eardrums to muffle the bombast. The marsh smell, so rich and different from the clean and pure salt air of the seashore so close by—local bards like Pat Conroy have described it all so much better than I could ever do justice, but safe to say it's a unique olfactory stew that's not altogether displeasing while at the same time not especially pleasant to these upcountry nostrils.

Rick, his tie askew, hung around the tiny mixing board, yelling into the ears of the wedding band's sound guy, a young man in a shirt and tie but who had those big, dark plugs in his ears making the lobes stretched out, and tattoos snaking around his neck and peeking out of the white cuffs of his dress shirt. He sported a sour expression, and his arms wrapped around themselves in a tightly held body language of the person who feels uncomfortable, or defensive.

I didn't need to hear the words: Rick, busting the kid's chops over the sound mix.

Did it matter? The band was playing standards, the sort of lounge singer material one always hears at these events, familiar and inoffensive and with an occasional rave-up about mysterious and vivacious women with names like "Mustang Sally" and "Polk Salad Annie," or a Chuck Berry proto-rocker, or songs from later in the pop culture pantheon of the familiar and safe—tunes from the 70s and 80s, melodies and words that feel familiar to me, but to which I never enjoyed any primary exposure. Not in my household. I doubt any music composed after 1900 was ever played at Hillsborough, not in my youth, anyway.

When I looked back over, Rick had disappeared into the non-dancing throng of wedding revelers clustered at the back of the hall among the tables of half-eaten dinners and dirty glasses and crepe paper and flowers and disposable cameras, crude 20th century artifacts we were expected to use to capture candid moments for later scrapbooking and treasuring, but archaic objects that had been barely touched: in the era of our mobile devices and integrated smartphones, actual film seemed a ridiculous anachronism. The information didn't even have to be dumped onto the hard drive anymore, not when in a bare technological instant it could be promulgated and propagated into the digital ether.

Live.

Here and now.

We could make a meme, send it around the globe in an instant. If a nine year-old autistic boy can do it, who couldn't?

I scanned the gathering. Cadence and the other children were off in a huddle of their own that seemed distanced and secreted in more ways than age from the adults dancing and drinking and socializing. The children, dancing gaily in a circle, pogoing around and laughing with gusto, including Cadence.

Another vision of innocence. I smiled, yet at the same time ached.

At Rick's direction, the front-of-house guy gave the musicians the twirling index fingers understood throughout the known universe as the wrap-it-up signal.

"What a crowd this is! And what a beautiful bride and groom," the buxom, dark-haired female songbird at the heart of the wedding band called into her microphone. Cheers greeted her, hooting, catcalls—the reception had been going on for some time, and the drinkers were getting into their cups.

A dolled-up beauty in a sequined red dress, late thirties and vivacious of figure, the vocalist smiled, beamed and glowed with a professional sheen; she and Marcy had chatted it up while they were taking a break. Marcy had related to me that the band was local, but in demand all over the Southeast—during the prime wedding season, they played as many Saturday-Sunday road shows as they could book.

A real, thriving enterprise, as Marcy put it. "'That allows them to keep the day jobs, too. Not that I would want a day job . . .'"

I asked what was wrong with that. "Who knows what obligations they all have."

Marcy chewed her lip. Singing for her supper; singing during supper. "Yeah, but . . . you get locked into that life, you'll miss your chance."

"The path is different for everyone—hey, look at me. I still managed to miss the big time without all that career and family bother. Don't forget how fortunate you are to be making a living at what you love."

Gurgling a flute of champagne, Marcy seemed unconvinced.

I got it; I knew she burned for more. In bed together, whispering to me that she still held close Opal's teenage dream—of being a recording artist, a real one with a label deal. That it'd been her own childhood dream, and that ever since she'd turned forty—Marcy could barely get the word out—she couldn't shake the sense that it wasn't too late.

I had quoted some Taoist koan about the master, or mistress, freeing herself of desire and letting matters flow like water and this'n that. She'd rolled over, tucked in her knees. Sighed.

The backing band, composed of older cats and one prodigy on keyboards, a kid who looked young enough to be in high school (and who I'd later find out was exactly that, all of 17), vamped and crescendoed and came crashing to a thunderous conclusion.

I breathed my own sigh, one of relief. Removed the wads of tissue from my ears.

"We're gonna take a break, maybe cut a steak, and eat some cake with you awesome *legacy* Sedge Island originals," the ginger-haired singer announced, smiling radiant and happy as the bride herself. "I remember being a little girl, and being driven to school over at Stapledon Academy," a name met with cheers, what I reasoned must be a school many of the people in attendance at the wedding had attended as children, and with a name like that and on a place like Sedge Island, was probably a private school, "and clear as day I can recall seeing on the marquee of that mysterious rock and roll club they called Harvey's Hideaway, and then later the world-famous Sandflea," more hooting and cheering and outright foot stomping, "and the name I saw was the name of a band I regarded as one the biggest acts around. And that they were, to all of us here—they were OUR VERY OWN SEDGE ISLAND ROCK STARS! Ladies and gentlemen, put your hands together for the Steaming Dashikis—guys, get on up here and show us how it's done!"

Thunderous. A seismic reaction. Heads on swivels, looking for the legends. My own heart pounded with involuntary excitement. All very vivid.

The five guys came from five different directions in the ballroom. As if on cue, a cool marsh breeze blew across our heated faces. Now onstage, the thickened middle-aged men with tuxes askew and unsteady gaits and shiny red faces were hugging and slapping five and gearing up to play, taking instruments from the hands of the wedding band. The crowd began singing the chorus of a song, one I would be later told was the band's signature tune from its heyday there on the island.

They "rocked," as it is said. Tears on faces; out-of-practice voices cracked and strove to make harmony; clams were laid by guitarists not only rusty but half-lit.

None of it mattered. The gathering exalted in their presence as though the Steaming Dashikis were living legends. Gods among mortals.

I shoved in the tissue.

After a dreadfully loud modern rock song, the father of the bride, with whom I'd spent some time out on the deck the previous night—which I'm sure he didn't remember—flourished his guitar and brought the band to a crashing halt and called out into the microphone over the cheering: "Cool it, cool it. Let's cool it down. There's a sixth member of this band here tonight, and I want to tell you all that I'm not playing another note until he's onstage, too. Rick Wragg—getcher ass over here, boy." A more muted cheer, and then I spied Rick—and Marcy, her face not happy and gay and relaxed, but troubled. Frowning, she whipped her head around and made hard eye contact with me:

Only then did I realize a detail that I suspected might be the source of her consternation—Rick, smiling and triumphant, strode toward the stage. In one hand he held a fluted, half-consumed glass of what appeared to be champagne.

Before I could address my own concerns over this development—not to be a busybody, but rather as confidant and fellow alkie to someone who'd confided that his life would prosper again, he was sure, if only he never again took a drink—the band, with Rick on tambourine, rocked into an even more supercharged number, an order of magnitude louder, now, than the wedding band had played.

Wads or not I made straight for the large open deck area, with views across the marsh and to the golf links and upscale housing developments beyond.

First, however, I grabbed Marcy Baumbach and dragged her along, and instead of Rick himself, I asked her what in the hell our friend thought he was doing with that sodding drink in his hand.

Once the Dashikis began playing in earnest, what Rick called "jamming," described to me through the baby-vomit stench of champagne on his breath, I was finished. Got a ride back to the house with one of the wives and her kid, an adolescent boy who'd made friends with Cadence, and who sat in the back seat communicating in a kind of many-layered code that seemed impenetrable to me, except for the parts about iPads and apps, with which I'd developed a particular facility. They giggled. Knowing what Rick had said about Cadence's socialization difficulties, I felt glad that his son had made a friend.

And that I had made a friend in him.

About eleven, the wedding party returned—rather, the old people portion of the wedding party; the younger set had planned further adventures at various island watering holes—and a raucous cacophony fell upon the house, but Marcy and I had retired. Considering the events and time that'd passed since my last good night's sleep, the single day felt as though it'd been two spins around the blue ball.

We snuggled; we snoozed.

But voices boomed and a radio got turned on and a blender began whirring. I jammed in the foam earplugs, tightened my sleep mask. I could feel more than hear the thumping music and boisterous chatter and clinking glassware. I had traveled a universe away from the solitude and quiet of my Cypress Creek home, my circadian cycles disrupted.

To center myself I breathed with measured rhythm, deep and yogic in a manner that Marcy had taught me, less a true meditation than a pure relaxation technique. Soon after, I found myself skittering off the cliff into fitful sleep with her arm thrown across my midsection and head tucked over close to mine. As I drifted off, I lay hoping that Rick hadn't had more to drink. That tonight was an aberration—for Rick's sake, and for that of his son.

Over our coffee outside on the beachfront deck, this time at a more civilized hour than the prior day, Marcy mused aloud that she wished we could stay—not with all the Dashikis and Rick and Cadence with his constant questions, just me and the sea. "I need down time, Cort. And being caught up in someone else's wedding bullshit wasn't it. Fuck—back to the grind. The Mudcreek Grill tomorrow night."

"We should have looked into getting you a gig down here."

"If it were only so easy. Besides, like I said, down time, Cort. That's work, those gigs. I need time to write."

I considered the possibilities: Nothing more I'd enjoy than being with Marcy here at the beach. As her lover, yes, but also friend, helping her through what I would discover as a complex family situation, and the music dreams and all of her other various issues I'd heard about, either from her, or filtered through Rick's memory of how she'd put it all to him when they had dated.

Rick dished of his own regard, though. I hadn't asked for any stories. If this was love, I wanted to find out about Marcy on my own, in my own way, and in hers, too.

Oh, pish posh. It wasn't love. That I swooned and felt breathless and tight in the gut, still, whenever she came near me hardly translated into an emotion as complicated as romantic love—we were screwing like rabbits, but that wasn't love per se.

What did I even mean? Poetic love? Who knew if all that messy emotion wasn't simply biological lust in the first place.

Love.

Chemicals.

Who could really tell the difference?

"I always felt wistful that way at the end of my childhood beach trips, which weren't that many—the wilds of Edgewater County seemed a long way from the seashore, and I longed to stay, to be a beach bum, a surfer, a lifeguard with all the lovely girls hanging around. It's why I set my first book here on the Carolina coast. Being here on the shore—we didn't really come here to Sedge, usually Isle of Palms, because my parents always wanted to be close to downtown Charleston—always made me feel cleansed in a way that I could never feel back home. Not with all that humidity."

"'Famously Hot.'" Marcy, quoting a witlessly ironic PR line that had been created to use in tourism advertising regarding Columbia and the midlands of South Carolina. "They got that right."

I snorted with derision. A more dunderheaded and insensitive tag line for a city that'd once been burned to the ground in warfare I could not imagine—a city of beauty and culture and history that'd been destroyed despite being a surrendered territory, with a literal white flag waved by its mayor. The burning of Columbia had been one of the more famous incidents of early 1865, certainly one of the most memorably destructive and (allegedly) drunkenly vindictive property crimes of the war. So, accurate enough a tag line, one supposed. I wondered what Simms what think.

I felt awash not in the nearby sea of saltwater, but in thickheaded literalism. I wanted to go back and write—not CREATIVE CLASS, rather my long-planned historical romance. I wanted to disappear into research for a year or two—a comfortable, amber womb, research.

"So—are you writing a book? You never stop scribbling in that little notebook."

"You noticed."

"How could I not?"

I explained that I wasn't, not really. And, as I'd already told her, that I hadn't in some time. I didn't use the term 'writer's block,' because it's never that reductive or simple. But if I didn't reduce it to such a cliché, then I'd have to place the blame on the real incident that'd precipitated my creatively stymied logjam of a psychic obstacle.

With woodsmoke and smoldering pine needles in my nostrils, I shook inside and begged off by discussing my difficulties in the driest of clinical terms—the mechanics of formulating plots and characters and situations that hadn't gelled, being lost in the morass of the burning of Columbia research that'd gone nowhere: burning, burning bright, my idea for that book, but alas, another fire would come along and squelch my momentum. The teaching; Leora's insistence that I take some sort of place as an elder of the arts community; the festival; the DDC, and all its attendant foolishness.

All in the way.

Even Marcy, I realized with a start. I had to be careful—I had to be up to mastering roles as midlife lover as well as unblocked writer.

"Flattering, all this attention, but I feel like neither elder nor expert. I've always had impostor syndrome anyway," I mumbled. "But especially without a real project in the pipeline. Maybe I'm finished."

Marcy went *mm-hm* and squinted out toward the horizon. She waved to a man power-walking down the beach from the north.

"Look at that skinny dude—he must walk like that every day. Jesus, I need to get back to the gym. My fun layer's getting poochy."

"Horse hockey. You're about as perfect a woman as I've ever seen."

A slow burn that broke into a smile across her face like the easterly sun peeking from behind clouds. "Cort . . . that's the sweetest thing anyone's ever said to me."

We kissed, long and deep. A welling in me—affection, warmth, lust, what have you. A special feeling.

"Marcy, I—oh."

Before I got the chance to take matters any further, I heard footsteps on the boardwalk across the sea-oat covered dunes coming up from the wide, low-tide beach. We both looked to see that the power-walking man, his hoody zipped tight down around his face like a street thug, had mounted the steps and came striding straight toward us.

"You . . . know this person?" Marcy whispered.

Recognition: I did. But I couldn't believe he'd decided to pay us a visit.

"I'd say that we both do."

The voice came thin and penitent. "May I join you both? If I'm not intruding?"

"Of course, Double D. By all means."

Marcy, drawing in her breath, gripped my arm. "Ex-cuse me?"

The rock star came to us on the decking, the Atlantic breeze whipping and shifting direction and making the sea oats to either side of us dance. As he spoke, his eyes never quite left the tips of his shuffling New Balances. "I was hoping, um, you'd be out here—I remembered how much you said you loved the beach in the morning. How's—how was the wedding gig?"

Marcy tugged my sleeve.

I smiled. "First things first: Marcy Baumbach, I'd like you to meet a friend—Columbia's own Duncan Devereaux."

"Hi," extending a hand to her. "Folks call me Dev."

"Hi!" Marcy nearly shouted. "Wow!"

"Where's our friend Reynaldo this morning—did he give you a hall pass?"

A naughty smile played on Duncan's lips. The hoody withdrawn, he revealed himself fully. Impish: "I kind of ran away from home. But I left a note."

We ended up staying at the beach after all, but only for an extra night, and not at the beach house but at Dev's estate, our wealthy friend offering to ferry us back home to Columbia in a day or two by car service, what I pooh-poohed as a needless but appreciated extravagance. Marcy, on the other hand, loved the idea.

We'd broken the news to Rick, who freaked out and said that he just had to come with us. To get Cadence in there to meet the man.

I refused. Said, if you want me to be able to talk him into showing up back home for the big shindig and unveiling, I couldn't descend on him with Marcy and an entire entourage.

"Cadence'll be crushed."

"I'll make it up to him. If this works out, Cadence can meet Duncan when he comes to Columbia."

Rick looked misty. "He loves ya, Uncle Bo-champ. You know that?"

I expressed my own affection. How I wished I'd had a son. But Rick, he only smiled. He had heard all of that out of me already.

We hugged, went to pack up our stuff, slipped out while Cadence was playing with the kids one last time down at the beach. Better that way, Rick said. If I'm already gone, he can't lobby for me not to go, which could turn into a big emotional scene. As though I didn't remember the wi-fi debacle.

"He's good, not like when he was little, but still—he's autistic. He has little fits sometimes, still, when he gets surprised or disappointed."

I understood, and we quietly made our way out front to wait for Reynaldo and his gold-plated golf cart.

Part Four:
SODA CITY SABOTEUR

1.

June, a blur of DDC meetings and Marcy hangouts, as she'd taken to calling our time together—a clue she was slipping away from me already, though at the time I'd been too obtuse, and busy, to notice. Not with spritely and triumphal music like Rossini's overture to "The Thieving Magpie" fueling the flying of the fingers.

Writing again. How good it felt.

Over that month Cadence and I grew ever more comfortable and close with one another, and by the third week of my visits, listening to classical music from Rick's LP collection on the magnificent gear in the media cave. One evening Cadence blurted out, "I'm think I'm going to be a writer. Writers are smart."

I was terribly moved and complimented by this statement, which as we sat on the couch listening to the stately, sweetly delicate strings of Corelli's *Concerto Grosso in F Major No. 9*, seemed to him a matter of record rather than sentiment. Maybe Cade didn't even consciously realize why he wanted to be a writer, which I thought was safe to assume came from his association with Uncle Bo-champ. The best writing was like that—unconscious, flowing out of your mind and fingertips like water from a sluice. The more you thought about the writing, the less it would come.

Rather than to make a reader and fan happy with a couple of inscriptions, the day I met Marcy's mother, Meredith Baumbach, had been to receive maternal approval. Or so I suspected, all couched in some business about wanting copies of my books signed.

A likely story, the skeptical investigator mused.

Apprehension: Marcy had informed me that her mother play-acted constantly in order to lull everyone into complacency about her illness, which remained dire despite a long period of relative stability. "So that when she does die, it'll hit us all really hard again. It's how she rolls. High drama. Oh, boy. You have no clue."

I noted that Marcy's used that phrase a number of times—'hit me really hard.' I asked if she'd suffered physical abuse as a child.

Taken aback. "You writers. Not everybody's working with subtext and hidden meanings, ya know. I'm only being a smart-ass."

"Withdrawn."

"They said she wouldn't last a year." Marcy seemed aghast and confused. "And here she is eighteen months later—ill, yeah sure. But with hardly no sign of further decline. WTF?"

"Now who seems to want 'high drama'?"

Chastened.

On a less shrill level we discussed her mother's illness, and Marcy said the oncologist calls Meredith's prognosis 'stable.' "It's not the kind of cancer from which you go into remission. But she's stable. Whatever that means."

"Means she's lucky to be here."

Sounding cruel and mean-spirited. "Dunno how much 'luck' has to do with it."

"One way or another, you sound like a sick woman's playing a trick on everyone."

Catching herself, she flipped raven locks out of her eyes, a metallic new color for the week—Marcy's hair changed almost as often as her moods. "Of course she's lucky to be here among the living."

"And you're a lucky daughter to still have a mother."

"It goes both ways."

"No, really—trust me on this one. You only get one mother . . ."

Marcy and I had started the day of the visit by hiking down the steep, rocky hill of the Botanical Gardens to go inspect the old ruins by the river, which was my idea: I'd planned to write about the Sugeree

Factory location there, burned, of course, as an act of war in the general 1865 conflagration. It was rebuilt, but through accident or misadventure some thirty years later burned again for good. Twin fires—I thought, here, a nicely resonant and poetic framing device. In any case, voluminous new notes on my once-moribund historical novel seemed to be nurturing the narrative into a multigenerational tale covering several decades of life in postwar Columbia.

Yes: instead of CREATIVE CLASS, which over the last few weeks had begun feeling like a linked collection of short stories, I found myself spending an hour or two a day revisiting my fabled burning-of-Columbia novel. This happens. The attention, it wanders.

Other big ideas that came with the clarity and frequency of fresh energy were a pair of new characters I'd created based on composites, on one side anchored by the teenaged diarist Emma LeConte, on the other with a variation on the aging old bard of Southern American letters, William Gilmore Simms, whom I needed to fictionalize and de-age by several decades in order to exploit the romantic angle in a non-icky fashion. I researched during the day on that project, while at night composing scenes and characters and stories for CREATIVE CLASS.

I called the Simms character, in this case an aspiring rather than established author, 'Benjamin Pomeroy Schulein,' chosen merely for the sound of the syllables and to have a thread of Norwegian blood in the story—I'd been observing and writing about drunken Scots-Irish nitwits the whole of my career, and I longed to include any sort of exotic bloodline I could, anything to be able to explore a backstory that came from somewhere, anywhere, but here—and I'd heard tell that somewhere along the way we had a Scandinavian thread in our Beauchamp bloodline, somehow running from Sweden through Ellis Island and down to South Carolina. And, this was a way to have a character who was not in fact a blood-born Southerner, one who could claim a legitimately alien point of view of the proceedings and provide a lens through which the reader could view the South and its travails.

As for Emma LeConte, I'd already fallen in love with her character, whom I'd named Pansy Meredith Vandegrift … but, alas, as with Simms himself, she's much much too young for me.

It hit me—I had a handle on not one new book project, but two. My worm had turned. Spring had sprung prosperous for this struggling scribbler.

In real life, I needed no literary romantic avatar—feeling as enamored as I was with Marcy had informed the romantic angle of REVIVAL to no small end. Plus, when Marcy told me her mother's name was Meredith, which I hadn't known before naming my character, I thought some cosmic nonsense might be going on; and so, it had delighted me to hear of the request to meet the daughter's writer-slash-boyfriend.

To sign some books.

Visit.

Commune.

Who knew, maybe Marcy and I would become serious. I wanted to meet her mother while I still could.

But as I'd soon find out, such thoughts of seriousness were chimeric in nature, that in fact I'd already lost Marcy Baumbach, and that it'd happened before my eyes back on Sedge Island. A less self-absorbed person might surely have noticed what had occurred between Marcy and Duncan. Not I, said he . . .

About that extra day spent at Dev's mansion: I sat for several hours in Dev's 'writing studio,' as he called it, with its curved windows and magnificent view of the ocean and sky, reading through the first half of his manuscript. A small price to pay, I thought, for him entertaining the idea of some modest level of participation in the DDC event, a reconsidered answer that'd make me a hero to Opal and Feebee and Gendry and the rest.

Meanwhile, once DD had discovered that Marcy was herself a musician, he'd ushered her hurriedly downstairs to the music studio complex for the tour, and they'd stayed there for the next seven hours working together and laying down what they told me were called 'scratch tracks' of four of Marcy's original songs, the recording of one of which I got to witness firsthand: her solo on piano like I'd been used to seeing at the restaurant gigs, her voice shaky and cracking over difficult notes, along with her palpable embarrassment and frustration.

As I watched the recording, Dev punched up the intercom from in the booth where we both sat. "Marcy, Marcy—they're scratch tracks. Who gives a rip. Let it out. It's just me and Cort Beauchamp sitting here."

"Like, I know! Argh."

"Again, please. From the top."

"*Argh.*"

By that point I'd been in the booth ten minutes, but Dev hadn't yet deigned to make eye contact. At last he turned to me. "Okay. I think Crabby Patty out there's having a case of nerves." He peeked out of the corners of two squeezed and pained eyes. "Speaking of which: What are you waiting for? I'm dying over here."

"Oh—the manuscript?" I grinned with a devilish and teasing air. I mentioned that we were all dying, really, if one wished to think about it that way.

Dev didn't find my stalling amusing. Said so.

I relented. "It's good. You write well—it has real pull. It's a real novel. Is it literary? I'm not sure about that, but in its initial chapters it certainly acts like a solid genre exercise in the undertaking, maybe with something more on its mind."

He cracked a modest, tentative half-smile. "Really."

"Does it need some work? You know the answer to that is yes, but not much on a technical level that I can see—like I said, you write well. As it goes along, will it have problems at the conceptional level? The highest compliment I can give you right now is that I want to know what happens. You've given your protagonist, a flawed one ripe for transformation by his experience, one hell of a challenge. Impressive. Most impressive, sir."

"What the hell are y'all talking about in there." Marcy, hollering and pegging the meters. "My ears are burning."

Duncan Devereaux seemed to collapse in his captain's chair. He potted down Marcy's mic and looked at me with wet eyes, made a sound of relief like huh-huh-huh.

"Are you all right?"

He confirmed his wellbeing. "Whether it's true or not, I needed to hear it."

I assured him that I wasn't simply buttering him up. Which I wasn't. Boy could write, told him so.

He went back to Marcy. "Look: I want you to sell me your soul in that song, Marcy Baumbach. Let go of all pretenses and expectations. Remember, you're not in some record company studio. You're in somebody's basement. We're a couple of guys about to burn one and chill out to your music. Groove to it. Nothing at stake. Nowhere to be."

On the last song, 'I Didn't Know Your Name,' which I'd heard Marcy sing once or twice at D'Alessandro's, Dev potted down the speaker while we discussed his story and I agreed to take the rest of the pages back with me.

Next he showed me how to do a couple of adjustments on the massive sound board, as well how to click RECORD on the computer program capturing the session, simple enough. I observed how his hands shook. All the yoga and green tea in the world couldn't quite undo all the damage.

I examined the moons of my own nails. A couple of calcium deposits. And maybe a tremor that's never quite gone away. Maybe when I was drinking, I was drinking more than I've let on—even to myself.

Duncan went into the studio, grabbed an acoustic guitar, a look of astonishment on Marcy's face as he sat down on a stool next to the grand piano. Her body language tight, Marcy seemed to physically withdrew from the energy of his presence.

Alone in the control room, I watched the backlit digital meters dance along with their words, dashes of laser-green occasionally hinting at red near the peaks.

"May I sit in?"

Marcy, shooting me an open-mouthed look like, O-M-G.

To Duncan. In that little girl voice of hers. "How could I say no?"

Duncan, a warmth in his smile. A relaxation like I hadn't yet seen. "I'd never force a sit-in on anyone. But I think I have the chords."

"Okay."

He nodded twice—once to me, and once to her. I clicked the round, red record icon and signaled Marcy to begin to playing her song again, and Dev indeed followed the chord progression, strumming along with her lovely melody. At that moment she glowed, her eyes closed and hitting every note pitch perfect, an aching quaver in her voice, the ringing of his gentle guitar shimmering, tasteful, and providing a perfect and apropos accompaniment—so unlike the ridiculous heavy metal on which he'd made his name and fortune!

At the end of their performance, the last notes faded into silence. I clicked the cursor, stopped the recording.

Marcy's reaction: "Wow."

"Beautiful," Dev agreed. "Nailed it."

I chimed in: "Very nice." But they couldn't hear me through the studio glass. Not that they would have noticed anyway.

That was the moment, wasn't it. Of course it was. Spoiler alert.

Later that evening we went up to what Dev called the crow's nest in time to enjoy a spectacular, early summer sunset from the other side of the island. Marcy, still high from her recording experience, sipped white wine and Reynaldo a light beer while Dev and I savored one of his flavorful floral teas, this one over ice and sweetened only just so with agave nectar—I told him I would have been satisfied with Lipton's or a cup of good old brewed Folger's or whatever was in the cabinet, but he insisted on his tea routine.

Routines are important to someone who suffers PTSD like Dev. All sorts of horrors underlie the condition, but the more I thought about it, the brand of survivor guilt carried by a still-worshipped human being like a rock star had to be a unique and stupendous one. I sympathized and understood Duncan Devereaux's reticence to engage with the public—after all, I have PTSD myself. Smoky, burning, bloody layers of it.

But we didn't talk about that on the roof, the sky turning from mango at the horizon to bruised plum over our heads, Venus winking out crystalline and glimmering amidst its field of darkening indigo:

"Marcy, soon as I process those tracks I'll email them to you. Here—" He handed her a USB drive. "But go ahead and take the raw WAVs. You should try to sell those songs. They're solid. I know all sorts of people."

"Um." Marcy's jaw dropped anew, her eyes dancing and distant.

"Are you freaking serious? I feel like I'm—dreaming."

"Let me know. You know. If I can help. Your voice is just beautiful." He raised his tea cup to the two of us. "Cort, you are a lucky man, my friend. Here's to you both."

He'd fed us, then, an elaborate sushi affair prepared by a private chef who, assisted by Reynaldo, had wheeled in the meal served in a small ceramic dinghy that he parked beside Dev's kidney-shaped dining room table, set in an alcove with a spectacular starlit view of the sound, the lights of freighters chugging in and out of the port of Savannah to the south of us.

"Better enjoy this. I'm done with sushi, I think. After the tsunami."

We discussed for a few minutes the terrible situation with the reactors in Japan, how in truth they still didn't have the situation under control, and if the mercury alone wasn't enough to put you off tuna, then maybe radiation would be. I'd barely heard a word of the tsunami coverage, but Marcy, who not only followed mainstream news but also consumed a steady diet of internet conspiracy and 'truth' websites, confirmed to Dev that her fears were largely the same.

The conversation cast a pall over the candlelit meal, at which Reynaldo joined us to eat a small mountain of tempura fried shrimp and vegetables, and to ask if, now that I'd started reading he might also be allowed to take a peek at Mr. Dev's book, a request that Duncan said would have to remain under consideration.

Ashen and with a jaw set as though he ground his teeth, Dev came back into the dining room. "Wow. That call—my mind is blown. I need to get to Columbia tonight, guys. I wanted you all to stay, and you may if you wish. But as for me, my mom's had a fall and broken her damn hip."

"Of course, of course." Marcy, her eyes widening in recognition at the thought of infirm parents. "We should get going."

A ripple of frustration seemed to cross Dev's tight features. He squeezed eyes and fists, like a toddler on the verge of a tantrum. "We haven't finished talking about the book."

"Ease your mind—THE RETREAT is imminently publishable.

Time enough for that when your mother's feeling better."

He apologized about being flummoxed regarding her. "A bedroom's been prepared for you both here. Reynaldo's coming with me, but Nigel will be close at hand."

We all turned to see a wide-shouldered, inky black man in his twenties whom we hadn't encountered. He beamed a smile and introduced himself as our 'footman' for the duration of our stay with them there. "Anything you need, I will provide."

"Cort and Marcy, take this." Duncan handed us both simple business cards with a phone number. "No one—and I mean no one—has this number. Please respect that."

"Sure." Marcy, nodding and looking to me. "No prob."

"It's in the vault."

I wouldn't see Dev for some time after that, but for the moment—and indeed, with thoughts of the interesting story he'd written dancing across my mind—I cared little for being in this rich person's palace of a home, only about securing a commitment to showing up at his own party. My own reputation back home required it.

No: Leora's memory required it. Right. That was the reason it was so important.

"Duncan—wait. There's some other things to discuss, too."

"I know." A sly smile. "Tell your committee I approve of their plans."

"All their plans?"

"Hrm. Maybe not all. But most."

Exhilarating. Good enough, I thought, to get me through the next DDC meeting.

After Nigel showed us to our equally spectacular guest bedroom—was there a bad view in this place?—Marcy and I hadn't had too terribly much to say to one another. I draped my sport coat on a chair, opened the vertical blinds on a massive, curving window to the beach and the ocean beyond. I went over and put a hand on her face, gentle, cupping it there. She tilted her head into my palm, and I experienced, then, a kiss that over the course of the long night turned into a thousand, a night in which we'd barely slept: Marcy, having recorded with one of the most famous musicians alive, seemed to be swept along by a tide of carnality that bordered on the febrile; the scratches on my back, deep—but I didn't realize, then, how indelible.

As dawn broke, I stood naked looking out those blinds at the spit of land on which Dev did his morning yoga and meditation, and I felt for him: his routine had been disrupted by his mother's injury. In the coming weeks Marcy's behavior would disrupt me as well, but once back home I slipped back into my own new writing routine, so much so that by the day we went to visit Marcy's mom, I felt relieved to get out of the cabin for the afternoon, but only so long as I had my pages done for the day, of course. Which I did.

2.

We pulled to the curb in front of the Baumbach bungalow in the desirable Herndon Hill neighborhood to find Marcy's mother working outside in her gardening clothes, hunched over in the front yard digging in a flower bed beside the concrete steps leading up to the side porch adorned with lush hanging baskets.

Marcy, shoving the Shark, as I couldn't help calling her gray station wagon, into park. "Look at that."

"What?"

"I have never gotten the gardening thing."

"Everyone needs a hobby."

Marcy, at her most sardonic and cutting. "She's fucking dying, and out there on her knees in the dirt? You'd think she'd realize she'll be in there herself soon enough."

"If she can still do the things she enjoys, I suppose she should. Don't you think?"

"She might live longer if she took it a little easier. If I were croaking, I know I would. Wouldn't you?"

"Never thought about it."

"About what you'd do if you knew you only had so much longer? Bullshit."

I shrugged. "The only death I've really known with any intimacy was sudden, surprising, and tragic. I never considered the alternative."

Her tone softened. "Your parents."

"This is about your living parent, not my dead ones. Now let's go visit."

Inside the house, we sat around a dining-room table in the morning sun enjoying delicious, glorious kitchen-pot coffee—Maxwell House, not quite in the same league as Folgers, but good enough. The soft babble of AM talk radio provided a murmuring, strident background to the silence between us as we waited for her mother to get cleaned up from her gardening. The daughter, in serious trouble for showing up with me unannounced; Meredith Baumbach, mortified by her grimy appearance.

Marcy directed: "Turn off that politics crap. I can't freaking stand it."

I squinted in the direction of the countertop radio, one of those compact component units with a CD player and tape deck—how quaint. It must have been at least twenty years old. "My pleasure."

Marcy and I had barely spoken about politics. Since Sedge Island we'd barely spoken, period, except to discuss Duncan Devereaux, the demos she cut, what it all could mean, and so on. Marcy more or less agreed that politics wasn't worth discussing, and I turned off the radio.

Marcy had much bigger issues on her mind—part of the reason for our visit was that her mother had gone for a new series of CT scans two days before, and had been 'cagey,' in Marcy's words, about revealing the results.

As Marcy had told me, Meredith had been on and off chemo for nearly two years, her body dying from the cancer, her body further ravaged by the chemo. Marcy had hinted at the outrageous costs of the cancer drugs, but that insurance, thank god, was covering most of the bill—nine thousand a month in meds, but Meredith only had to cover two-fifty or so in deductibles, at least after traversing the fabled doughnut hole.

"What are you expecting the results to be?"

Whispering: "As Mick Jagger once said, I got no expectations—you should ask her. It's been the same story forever, now."

Meredith cleared her throat from the narrow hallway in the aged but updated home, with its smaller rooms and higher ceilings and an attic that'd been transformed into a second story with two extra bedrooms. I felt awkward and embarrassed to have been secretly discussing this woman's dire condition in her own kitchen, this person I didn't truly know.

"Now: Mr. Beauchamp." Meredith Baumbach, freshened up, announced herself with good cheer as she joined us in the kitchen. "Let's pretend we didn't talk to one another outside, with me all covered in yard dirt."

"Fine by me—you looked rather lovely, truth be told. A woman of the earth."

"Earth to which I'm about to return." Meredith, holding onto my hand. "But, mercy, forget all that mess. How I do love your books, sir. We're all very proud of you here in Columbia—I hope you realize that."

Humbled and moved, I explained that after not publishing a new novel for so long, I didn't receive such a compliment very often. "Though I once did, from many others like you." I recounted a particularly glowing letter to the editor from a reader about *Bittersweet Serenade's* depiction of modern-day Columbia, how it had felt true but fictionalized enough to allow him to see his city in a new light, from a fresh angle. "I took this to be high praise indeed."

"But, you had a book out not too long ago—wait, I have it right in here." Meredith made to get up.

"Where is it, Mom?" Marcy put a hand on her mother's shoulder, stopped her from fully standing. "I'll go grab it."

"Will you get out of my way?" Marcy's mother shrugged off the restraining hand of her daughter, who continued to protest, fussily following Meredith into the living room. Hushed, heated words.

Meredith and Marcy, all strained smiles, both returned and took their seats, a copy of *The Collapse of Language* procured from the living room. "Here—see, I knew I'd gotten it back when it had first come out. I did that for each of your books."

I asked if she'd like me to sign the copy, and any others she had. "Marcy said that you might enjoy having inscribed editions."

"Oh, that would be grand. I'd feel embarrassed to ask."

"Marcy asked for you. It's my honor."

Marcy, her head tilted and looking at me through her auburn bangs, sighed and reached over for my hand. "He's a terribly sweet man, isn't he?"

"And you're a dutiful and attentive daughter."

Meredith pursed her lips and arched a pair of penciled-in eyebrows—only then did I realize that she was wearing a wig. Before it'd looked like a beauty-shop bob. Her real hair, brittle and thin and gone: chemo.

"Very very thoughtful. Yes. She fusses over me, Mr. Beauchamp—"

"—Cort, *please*, my dear—"

"—but the truth is, I can take just as good care of myself as I ever have, and as such . . . well. If you'd be so kind, yes: I'd like you to sign the other books of yours that I have in there somewhere. I'll go look in a few minutes, after we've finished our coffee and I get the table and the kitchen straight."

"I'll get all that, Mom."

"No, you won't. I take care of myself. My whole life. Myself, this whole family, other duties and obligations. Fifty year's worth."

"I turned fifty last year. Some days I feel every inch of those years."

"Fifty, Mr. Beauchamp? Oh, you're just a baby." She laughed. "Now is the time when I ought to be having a cigarette, you know. May I mime doing so?"

"Mom—"

Meredith did so, fake-lighting an invisible Virginia Slim, toking on it like a joint, exhaling an invisible plume of smoke, a gesture into which I bought like a theatergoer immersed in a performance by a master thespian.

"Marcy's brother, bless his soul, he needed quite a bit of atten-tion beyond the normal parenting duties. He had his problems, but he's done so well now that I can't much fault him for the mistakes he made as a younger man. The dreams he had that weren't realistic." Eyes narrowed at her daughter, who sat looking away. "Once he got his feet on the ground, his life became what it had been intended to be."

"'What it'd been intended to be?' What the hell is that supposed to mean?"

"What he was capable of becoming."

"Horseshit, mother. Seriously."

"Doesn't that make sense to you, Marcy? For goodness sake."

"Capable? Capable of becoming? I know where this is leading."

Now I felt as though I'd wandered into a grand filial melodrama that, from the sound of Marcy's pinched voice, threatened to escalate into a row.

"What on earth do you mean?"

"Mother: I am making a living. I am singing and playing, and making a living."

Pitying. "Darling: what you do is not a job-job. You live hand-to-mouth. You could have taught music—Jesus, you still could. You're barely over forty years old. It's too late for a lot, but not everything."

Marcy, a strangled cry—*Mother!*—that came as an epithet.

"Oh—did she lie to you, Mr. Beauchamp? Was she so brazen and bold?" A smile more playful than cruel. "Did she tell you she was, what? Thirty-five?"

A furious daughter. "You're going too far with this little routine."

Dismissive. "As a girl, she gave me the worst time. Told stories like you would not believe."

Marcy's face in her hands. "I knew you would humiliate me like this."

"I know how old she is," I managed to say. "Either way, Mrs. Baumbach, it doesn't matter."

"Ugh." Marcy leapt up and poured herself more coffee, splashing it out of the cup onto the counter. As though burdened and deflated, she dragged herself out of the room.

"How shall I inscribe these?" I asked, trembling hand resting on my work.

"Meredith, please." The elderly, dying woman sat demure and smiling, as though the vicious air around the table had been cleared by a cool breeze. It'd been terribly hot all day. Marcy was right—her mother shouldn't have been outside. "If you would."

I took the story collection, opened to the frontispiece, and signed:

> *TO MEREDITH — THE DIRT UNDER YOUR*
> *GARDENER'S NAILS IS LIKE THE WORDS*
> *ON THE PAGE: THE RAW MATERIALS OUT*
> *OF WHICH A STORY IS MADE. LONG MAY*
> *YOU GROW!*

I swiftly swirled my C B Beauchamp, with the customary flourish off the 'p.' Closed the book, slid it over to her.

"So, a collection of stories. Lovely. But when will see another one of your wonderful novels? Tell me it won't be too long."

"Some difficulties with all that. For a while now. Midlife foolishness. And such."

"I see."

"But lately I've gotten my mojo back, as they say. I daresay I've been getting better work out of these fingers than in some time ..."

Marcy, who'd taken a spin through the living room and found the other books of mine, returned and put them down on the table heavily, rattling all the coffee cups. "All thanks to me," leaning over and giving me a peck. "Isn't that so?"

I smiled and squeezed my eyes. "Of course."

Meredith scoffed. "What's the real reason?"

"Mom—go eff yourself? Wouldja?"

"Watch your mouth," said with motherly annoyance. She fussed around, picking up objects and putting them down and looking all around—Meredith wanted a cigarette for real.

Perhaps if I told the tragic story of the girl and the fire down the road from the cabin, it would diffuse the tension between the two, give them both a reason to consider another aspect of life than their constant sniping and competition, or whatever the dynamic. In truth I wasn't quite sure what drove the simmering acrimony that played out across their faces, and in small gestures—the mother handing the daughter a napkin to wipe up a spilled drop of coffee, the daughter shooing the mother's hand away with impatience. Eye rolling. Sighing. I could give them something else to think about.

I began to tell my story of twin tragedies, and of what I'd come to understand as the source of my writer's block. It'd taken me a long time to realize the importance of my neighbor's fiery tragedy in all this, but saying it aloud to someone, finally, did more to heal me than merely ruminating on how I believed my writing had allowed a young girl to die.

I explained to Marcy and Meredith that I now realized I'd also been suffering from a terminal illness, of a kind—or perhaps worse: A boy, healed following the horror of his parents' murder-suicide, but afflicted again by a house fire about a half-mile away from where I live. After that day, I hadn't written again for a long, long time. Hadn't wanted to, not for all the Folgers in the world.

The other night, after we'd had the most vigorous and satisfying congress I'd enjoyed perhaps ever in all my life, I'd come close to confessing all this to Marcy to explain what must have seemed like mad behavior: In my state of extreme relaxation and satiety, half-asleep, the phantom smell of the tragic fire had tickled my nostrils, and I'd leapt out of bed and raced through the cabin to make sure I hadn't left the tea kettle or the oven on.

The kitchen had been quiet and dark and safe.

And then I knew what the scent had been; I saw a vision of myself sitting hunched over my laptop in the office that day, my headphones on, listening to Beethoven's glorious Ninth. Remembered how I'd smelled the burning. Ignored it; dismissed it. Kept writing while the neighbor girl had died, choking and coughing as the fire exploded all around her, a teenager with her whole life ahead, as the familiar bromide goes. And I'd continued sitting and writing, working on a short story. A meaningless trifle. A time-wasting endeavor lacking in meaning.

An innocent life I might have saved, lost.

Death, close and rattling its chains.

Not that I noticed.

"The day I misplaced my ability to write, I was sitting at home there in the cabin. I'd already been divorced for a while—that's why I'd moved out there. Before, it'd been a second home, a private writing space for me away from Edgewater County, the rest of my family, my wife's family, and so forth. It's part and parcel of the trade of writing. Loneliness, by necessity."

"I've always thought it must be so terrible. And your back and shoulders, from all that typing."

"Oh, yes." I reached behind my neck and massaged a tight knot of flesh. "Dreadful. Especially, ironically enough, on the best days, when you sit there for hours, lost in that wonderful trance . . . anyway, the day of the fire I'd been in one of those states for an hour. Or two. Or more. Even after I'd begun to smell the smoke, you see. For some time," rapping my knuckles against the Formica of the tabletop, "I sat smelling that acrid stench. It'd been a cold day—not by the standards of somewhere farther north, of course, but for the South Carolina midlands, nippy indeed. Not enough for me to have my own wood stove fired up, though." I like it cold in the house. I told them I believe it makes me write with more urgency. "But woodsmoke, out there in Cypress Creek you smell that all the time. All winter long. Overnight I'd had a fire going, and I supposed at first that the smell in my nostrils lingered from that. So I wrote, typing away."

In truth it wasn't a short story, but rather the prior attempt to write the historical novel in earnest. At the time, I called it THE RISING, which I knew the pop singer Bruce Springsteen had already used for what I'd read was a post-9/11 rah-rah anthem, but I didn't care, it was only a working title. I was getting text written, which is the most important part, though not to this story:

"But the smell grew more persistent, what I'd later ascribe to a kind of spiritual insistence that I notice—notice the smell, idiot!—and get up from the desk. About that time I got stuck on a particularly awkward sentence, which in some cases could be said is my stock-in-trade—I write terrible first drafts that must be wrenched and wrangled into shape. As a young man, I thought this a difficulty I alone suffered, but meeting writers in college and being published led me to discover that I was not alone—that there was no good writing; but, rather, only accomplished and diligent and sedulous rewriting, and rewriting some more, until it all becomes as correct and smooth as your authorial eyes can manage on your own. And most of all, you hope, it also reads in a compelling fashion on some meaningful level. Needless to say. But I digress—"

I cleared my throat. Felt the sense memories of the day wash over me.

"But then, I noticed my eyes beginning to burn. I rubbed them. I looked at the window—a haze in the air. I rushed outside, hesitating— was it my own cabin on fire? What about the laptop, the albums and CDs of all my beloved music, my manuscripts, my memorabilia? Outside, the air stung my nose, and something somewhere nearby was on fire in a big way, but not my own house or property. A woods fire could certainly change all that in a second, however, and I still needed to find out what was going on. Right about then I heard the first of the sirens."

Both women leaned forward, their hands resting lightly on their coffee cups, their bodies and faces so alike. A daughter of her mother's flesh. Waiting.

"I jumped on my bicycle, my knees straining and aching and unpre-pared, and went peddling up the incline of my driveway to the two-lane that led to the main road where my closest neighbor lived. The first fire truck roared by right as I made it to the highway, but a quarter-mile up the road the vehicle slowed. Black smoke was pouring out of the thick trees down that way. My heart leapt into my throat—the handicapped girl, Emily Nicole."

"Handicapped? How so?"

"Cerebral palsy. As she'd aged into adolescence, though, she'd started staying home by herself after school, had become a bit more self-sufficient, if only for a few hours every day." I described how with the sound of another siren coming from behind me, I cycled down the shoulder as furiously as I could manage.

"The scene along the road was chaotic—a sheriff's deputy stopped me from getting in the way." I described the firefighters, who were scrambling and improvising and trying to get enough pressure from the water in the truck. The house, already consumed; raging, angry flames leaping and licking upward at the noonday sun. Hellish.

"I shouted, 'There's a young girl who lives there—she's by herself during the day!' 'Well, sir, there's nothing anyone can do about that, now,' a sad-eyed policeman replied. And there wasn't. No one was coming out of that inferno."

Meredith employed a matronly Southern cattiness like I remember from my grandmother, herein deployed to defuse the melancholy. She went tsk-tsk and said, "You couldn't pay me to live in one of those log cabins like you do. Couldn't pay me to do it."

After a while the fire was extinguished by the first responders, who had been augmented by a better equipped crew. The girl's mother, whom I knew on sight, had come roaring up in a Range Rover. She collapsed, was attended to by the same officer to whom I'd spoken.

A wrenching scene—I'd never experienced parental grief like what I saw.

Haunting, one might say.

Firemen entered the smoldering, hissing remains of the house, and after a while an ambulance arrived. A black bag, carried out by a pair of poker-faced EMTs.

"I'd watched Emily grow up. I'd lived in the cabin off and on for ten years, and would be out riding my bike in the mornings when the school bus came to pick her up. I'd wave and smile to her as she stood with her braces and crutches. She grew into a young woman; the bus still picked her up. I spoke with her a few times. She'd been so excited that

I was Cort Beauchamp—she said she'd seen my picture in the paper, I suppose when *The Collapse of Language* came out. I asked her what she liked to do—write or draw? Anything like that? Emily told me she loved going to church. She loved Jesus."

Marcy, dismissive. "Fat lot of good that did her."

I ignored my cynical girlfriend. "How she must have felt, choking and terrified, as fire exploded all around her. They said wiring in the attic that'd been eaten by nesting squirrels had begun smoldering. The resultant fire consumed the old farmhouse that her father had renovated."

"This is all so very tragic." Meredith, her voice cracking. "But, how did this affect your writing?"

"Because, for weeks and months—and now a few years—I felt a burden. I felt guilt. I pondered the dreaded what-if scenario—what if I'd noticed sooner. I'd been the only one nearby for nearly a half-mile. What if upon first smelling the smoke, I'd acted?"

"Oh, Mr. Beauchamp . . . you mustn't think that way."

"The smell of the smoke, though," my voice finally breaking, causing both women to lean forward with concern. I held up a hand. "And the wind that day." I choked, composing myself by coughing a few times. "You don't understand."

Marcy frowned. "What about the wind?"

"Marcy, the wind—it was *blowing in the opposite direction.* The smell came to me, I believe. Came to me against the wind. So that I'd save her. Or some such literary minded nonsense. The universe sent me the smell. So I would act. But I didn't."

"Mr. Beauchamp—how could you believe such a thing?"

"I would say because I notice everything, but it was the fire captain— he asked if I lived nearby, and I said, yes, up the hill. You don't have anything to worry about from this fire. The wind's going that-a-way— away from my house. It's with you, he said. The wind was with me." I took a thoughtful sip of my Maxwell House. "Afterwards, I found that every time I sat down to write, I'd catch that smell in my nose. The smoke. I could taste it at the back of my teeth."

Marcy smiled, pitying me. "The way you do garlic after a meal at Opal's joint."

"Exactly. And I'd look at my work in the grand scheme of life and find it to be lacking in resonance. Lacking in meaning. What I'd been working on that day had been a trifle, and while I'd produced those useless lines and pages of text, a young woman had died, and for no good reason other than chance . . . and my own inattention to signs and signals that should've been unmistakable and clear. Oh, I know it wasn't my fault. I know it's all sentimental, mystical hooey about the smell. But it happened—I believe all those things I told you both, and I've only recently gotten back to a place where I can let the words flow again. I don't catch the scent of that burning house as often anymore. Only now and then." I smiled. "I think I have it beaten. Finally."

Meredith smoked her phantom cigarette, dabbed at a tear sneaking out of her eye. "Well, that's the silliest thing I ever heard. You're not a comic book hero. Not everyone can be saved. Yes, this terrible thing happened. But it only means what we imagine it to mean. So my advice is to un-imagine this guilt you carry, my author friend. That girl's death 'was what it was,' not to sound like those political nitwits on the TV arguing every afternoon . . . it was her drama. Her sad fate. Not yours."

Meredith Baumbach, wise. She saw how traumatic it'd been for me to tell them about poor Emily Nicole and the fire. She changed the subject by flipping back on the tabletop radio, with its vitriolic right-wing talk show we'd silenced, and for the rest of the visit I faked my way through a discussion of politics.

The conversation continued for a while, the coffee cups were refilled, bless Meredith's shaky old dying heart and body, and then Marcy's sister-in-law arrived with her two children, ages by my estimation around four and seven: a rambunctious and ethereal hellion of a girl, and a reserved and suspicious-eyed boy who, like Cadence, barely looked up from a small tablet computer on which his index finger flicked and traced and played what appeared to be a road-race game.

The noise and activity level now ratcheted up by a hundredfold, Meredith rose and stooped and kissed and hugged and oohed and ahed and procured candy and sodas for the children, who both were as pink and chubby as two children could be—too much so, but not to any egregious degree, not in the age of high fructose corn syrup in every-thing—even 'in children's ice cream,' as General Ripper had cautioned, aghast, in *Dr. Strangelove.* I worry about what's in the food and drink the corporations push us all into consuming. I hadn't had a Co-cola, as people where I came from call soft drinks, in a decade. Certainly no diet sodas, either, which Rick Wragg guzzled like well water.

Marcy's mood, souring: Once the children had arrived a cloud crossed her face, and every word out of her mouth came with a sarcastic edge, one that seemed to grate on Meredith's nerves. A war of narrowed eyes ensued. Marcy began griping at her mother about what the oncologist said on her last visit—Marcy believed that the 'cancer industry' had its meathooks in her mom, and were keeping her strung along and alive only to generate profits for Big Pharma, all of which sounded to me like internet conspiracy nonsense.

Or else, right in line with what I'd been thinking about the safety of our food. This, hardly the time for such a discussion.

While Marcy said her goodbyes to her family, I beat a hasty path down the front walk, where I stood whistling and rocking on my scuffed loafers. I took out the pocket-sized Moleskine and jotted down a few notes and whatnot, bits of the conversation we'd had that could be useful—words and ideas and names. Quickly, too, before it all passed away, like glory-borne dandelion seed blown sidelong to the ground and possibly taking root in some story or scene or book I might one day write. The reality, ephemeral; all a writer could do was depict a version. His own.

Leaning against the car and scribbling, I heard the front door slam. Marcy, pinched and seething, power-walked down the front porch steps and stumbled over a crack in the walk, nearly losing her balance.

"Fuck," she yelled. "I stubbed my fucking goddamn toe."

I rushed over, was soundly rebuffed with a further string of vituperative invective the likes of which this self-respecting author will not here attempt to transcribe. I watched her hobble to the car, asked if she were all right.

"I'm fine. Let's get out of here."

We decamped to go and have dinner, quite pointedly avoiding Opal's restaurant, which I wouldn't have suggested anyway.

Over Asian fusion a few blocks away from Opal's, I cajoled out of Marcy what had happened inside the house.

"The woman's in denial. She's wasting her time with the chemo—Cort, she's still smoking. All that business with the miming . . ." Marcy began to seethe anew. "What is the point of the chemo if you're going to keep smoking? For fuck's sake," causing several disapproving heads to turn. "It's a farce."

"Goodness gracious, you mustn't simply confront her with her own mortality like that. It's—it's—rude," lacking a more precise term.

Marcy, taking umbrage, accused me of butting into matters of which I know nothing.

"What's the issue here? Because it certainly isn't her having an illness."

Marcy's mouth dropped open. "Excuse me?"

I explained that as a writer I knew my fair share of psychology, about motivations and subtext—reading between the lines. I asked her again for the source of the anger.

Marcy Baumbach took a deep slug of her red wine which I coveted but resisted, and told her own tale, not unlike how I'd revealed so much of myself to the two of them: how Meredith had never supported Marcy's music, had never taken it seriously. Had been far too cloying and clingy, but a hundred percent behind whatever Freddie wanted to do, including travel and film school; had been hard on her daughter, but for all the wrong reasons; had nay-said and pooh-poohed all of Marcy's dreams.

In general, or so it seemed to me, the two of them had never progressed beyond that contentious teenager-parent dynamic of simply not agreeing on pretty much anything. Said so.

Marcy spat quiet invective. Wouldn't meet my eyes.

I became annoyed—I'd missed out on growing all the way up accompanied by the people who'd spawned me. "Let go of the past. Be glad you had, and have, a mother to love you. Did she care for you? Feed you? Clothe you? Were you beaten or deprived or abused? I ask seriously," I clarified. "Not rhetorically."

Her chin quivered. "Fuck you."

"No—answer me. Did you have these things? Because I certainly didn't."

"NO," she yelled, this time prompting a bluehair even more prim and proper than I pretended to be to turn and admonish us.

"I'll thank you both to watch your filthy mouths." The elderly diner shook a knobby, old woman's finger. "I've waited all week for this fine meal, and I simply won't have you people ruining it."

"Apologies, m'lady." I tipped an imaginary hat. To Marcy: "Well?"

"Well *what*? Answer your non-rhetorical question?"

I opened my hands and waited.

"Yes, damn you—I had a mother who cared for me." Marcy dabbed at newly wet eyes and took a moment, as they say.

She spoke again, finally. "That house you saw today, that neighborhood—it was a wonderful childhood. It was the greatest damn childhood in the effing history of the world," sounding at first like her typical sarcasm, but ending tinged with grudging recognition of inalienable accuracy.

The sentiment held true of my own childhood as well, at least until all that innocence and plenty here in the grand social experiment called America had been ripped from beneath my teenaged feet by a crime of passion on a hot summer night, with moss hanging from the trees and sweat on brows and blood on the floor. Violently Realistic Southern Gothic, let's call my books about it all. "We came of age during a time of material plenty. No doubt."

"And yet . . . I feel like promises haven't been kept."

I pressed for elaboration on this issue, but she declined.

An anecdote designed to give Marcy's dissatisfaction context: "I got trapped in a storage nook, once. I'd been playing hide and seek with my mother, and when I went to hide in an old, disused closet, my feet plunged through a rotted place in the floor, where an undetected roof leak had dribbled for who knows how long. I hung trapped and immobile. I screamed and screamed for help—for her."

"Until she found you?"

"It took quite a while. I was frightened. The floor, falling away beneath my feet. I'll never forget the sensation. So unexpected."

She put her hand on my arm. "But nothing like what would happen to you later."

I explained how that awful night of the tragedy, I would scream for her again in that same voice, a high horrible childish screech I thought

I'd lost to the adolescent, hormonal change that'd come over me the summer before my parents died. Anyone could understand my shriek: "I found them there, entangled in their death as they had been in life."

"Horrible . . . but you make it sound poetic."

"All perfectly goddamned delightful. To be sure."

Marcy, lost in her own rumination and seemingly unsympathetic to my travails, dramatic as they might have been. "Our grim little childhood scenes. Listen to us."

Missing the point. "Do you communicate in any language but sarcasm?"

Chastened. She reached across, took my hand. "How should I treat my mom?"

"Treat her like you had a decent life. So what if she thinks you're wasting your time with music—if you're making a living doing what you love, then it doesn't matter what anyone thinks, not even your mother. Give her a good last few months, or years, or however long she hangs on. Be glad for every moment."

"Hah. Every blessed moment."

"Now you get it. Every. Moment. Blessed."

Marcy, finally breaking down. "Take me home, please."

As I led her out of the dining room I put my arm around her shoulder. The scolding blue-hair paused with a forkful of rice halfway to her mouth and glared with rank animus, certain I'd done and said reprehensible things to cause this torrent of emotion. And maybe I had.

Since I couldn't very well abandon Marcy in this condition, I asked her in the parking lot if she wanted to come stay the night with me out in Cypress Creek, where we could continue a different conversation: the physical one we'd been so enjoying. In the morning, I promised I'd make her griddle cakes and meatless tempeh sausage, which caused her to wrinkle her cute, freckled nose.

"No pig sausage."

I patted my gut. "No fatty animals will be harmed in the making of the breakfast."

I suppose because of the tense dinner, she begged off.

A frost, descending. Yep. That was the moment.

<h1 style="text-align:center">3.</h1>

At daybreak I crawled out of the lonely bed and percolated the Folgers, went to my desk overlooking the gray-lit woods, silent and eerie in the early light and put on my headphones. I dialed around the iPod until I found a mellow, elegant early morning selection: a full orchestration of Chopin's *Les Sylphides*.

With mug in hand, I sat transported.

The music soon became mere background vibrations: I banged out two thousand words on REVIVAL, a pair of blazing scenes of passion and adventure, young lovers taking what could be their last shot at love together, and then the Confederate troops desperately burning the bridge across the Congaree to hold back Sherman's marauders. Peak scenes—it was a method of working I'd developed akin to writing the ending first. Finding a moment of high drama, and building and layering all around that scene.

The only problem I had with the story was that I didn't truly know the ending, other than somehow trying to shoehorn in the second burning of the Sugeree Factory thirty years after the first incident. I toyed with the idea of interspersing the nominally narrative text with the young journalist's newspaper accounts of the burning and aftermath, and perhaps later, text from a book he's written about the wanton destruction of Columbia. I wanted my journalist not to document the burning as Simms had, but to be so broken by the experience that he *cannot* write about it, at least not right away. Instead, Pansy Meredith, with her diaries, would create the narrative of record.

Settling these matters felt like the crack of a home-run bat.

But wait, more: His PTSD from the fire, then, could perhaps provide an impetus for the young lovers to leave Columbia for a time, and the shattered South as a whole, and make their lives and fortunes elsewhere in the burgeoning young country—out in the wilder, western territories, let's say. To return later, much later, to see what'd become of their former glorious Southern city, as valuable a war target as could be imagined, in its wealth and influence a magnet for the vituperative and vindictive nature of the Union troops and their behavior toward the grand old city. To leave, and to return to see whether their former home had fully come back to life.

Not back to life, no; toward a new future. No going back to the ways of old, despite the best efforts of Tillman and the Klan and so many other hidden mechanisms of oppression. In understanding this, only then would my scribe find the fortitude to pen his own account, which he would begin on the final page of my own book.

An ending. Someplace to land. It's all important in getting underway on a novel: having a destination.

Had the city come back to life, finally? I didn't know.

I also didn't really know what sort of place Columbia was like some thirty years after the war, deep into Reconstruction and Jim Crow times. I knew my Civil War history cold, but I'd have to research that other period.

Perhaps worse, what did this say about our fair capital city, that I didn't know the answer to my own literary question? It wasn't enough to have a satisfying dramatic conclusion—I wanted to say more with this manuscript. I wanted to make a statement about my city and its people and its place in the American firmament. I didn't want my characters to leave Columbia, I wanted to give them a reason to stay. To rebuild the town. To find the strength and courage to do so; not to pull a FEAR, as alkie types can tell you about: Fuck Everything And Run. No. That was never—or maybe rarely, depending on how dire the circumstances—an answer worth pursuing.

I'd need to chew on this material, let the story finish on its own terms. That's how the best drama is written—by the hand of its own characters. Not by me; I'm only transcribing, as someone more talented and famous than me first said. Half the time I get up from the laptop and look at the word count for the day, and stare in disbelief at all that I'd managed. So effortless; so mysterious. Life, good.

The next day, Rick, catching me on the cell: "So, after a solid year of trying to convince him," his voice bright and cheery and untroubled, "Cade here goes and announces he wants to start taking piano lessons. Wants to be in the school band. Has been through every one of those classical albums down there—he's living in my media cave, Bo-champ, eating those records alive. What am I gonna do? This shit is your fault man, and I am super-pissed. You hear me? Last night over dinner he got off on this whole bent of how Dvořák was considered the 'voice' of Czech classical music, but that Semtema, or Samtamna—"

"—Smetana—"

"—yeah yeah, whatever, that this Santana guy's stuff is much more patriotic. Now, look here: if I didn't know much about classical music, I sure as shit don't got a clue about what constitutes patriotism in Czechoslovakia. I need you, Bo-champ. Need ya big time, here—I want Cade to come live with you."

A long beat. "Pardon? You want Cade to—do *what*, now?"

He burst out laughing. "Naw, naw, man, I'm yanking that chain. Naw. Couldn't be happier, the kid. Before he rode down to Sedge with you in the Jeep, my boy never gave a crap about music. Alls I wanted— I just wanted to call. And thank you. But get caught up, too—we got our DDC meeting next week, yeah?"

I had talked Rick into rejoining the DDC, to seeing the process through alongside Darren. Much had happened since the beach trip in which I'd convinced Dev, through my quid-pro act of manuscript-reading, to give the committee his sanction, which had still been difficult to achieve; the idea of him appearing at the unveiling of the piece of sculpture that'd been commissioned—the maquette depicted the licking flames of extreme talent bursting upwards out of the sidewalk and trailing music staff and notes, a visually kinetic piece to match the furious energy behind much of Dev's recorded output, and far and away the best of the lot of four entries solicited from local sculptors and artisans—had been unfortunately squelched. Sanction would have to be enough.

Feebee had been the most disappointed. "You spent the day and night in his house, read his fucking novel, promised you'd help him get it published, and you *still* couldn't talk him into coming here and playing a freaking song or two? *We're renaming a street after him.*"

"The issues," I'd explained to the bug-eyed and ferocious Feebee Elmendorf, along with the rest of the committee sitting expectantly as I delivered my report, "go much deeper than shyness, or humility—he was traumatized by what happened to him. And look, he doesn't want to play music in public, though in his home I heard him perform some of the most sublime acoustic guitar I've ever heard," a revelation met with gasps and disappointment and confusion.

The DJ Doober Dougie, terribly anticipatory: "Tell me you pulled tape on that material. Tell me you made a bootleg."

I chuckled and said, no, unfortunately no bootlegging. Continuing: "The crux of the matter is that, on a moral basis, one simply cannot force someone who suffers from PTSD to accept an honor like this. At least in public. Which is at the root of his PTSD."

"I guess that's true." Gendry, her fandom crushed and ground into the floor by my dreadful news. "But I think I'm gonna cry anyway."

Rick probably had the right take: "Couldn't ya guilt him about Wood-Cobb? Something along those lines."

A chorus of disapproval. Rick withdrew the suggestion, pouted.

"While I appreciate Rick's blunt suggestion, Dev made it clear that he thought our attention and gratitude was misplaced, but also that he felt duly appreciative, and would certainly not stand in the way of our little hometown tribute. In fact, when I told him it would be an original piece of art that didn't necessarily have anything literal to do with his music, he grew exponentially more enthusiastic."

Opal, simmering: "That 'enthusiastic' asshole was supposed to provide the cocksucking music himself."

"I did my best." Which was true. I gave them all a what-can-I-tell-you face.

Instead of being a hero for getting as far as I did, however, I found myself still on the meathook: Feebee took me aside and in her colorful and breathless language said that if I didn't try again to get this man to come back to his hometown and receive a goddamn fucking goddamn statue and street renaming, she'd be so disappointed that she'd just die—she'd simply die if they, or we, or me, rather, couldn't deliver on this most salient and crucial of points.

I said I'd try. Didn't even call her out for the callousness of her threat—we'd lost a DDC member to death. An important one. But I let it pass. High emotions all the way around.

Feebee wasn't really issuing orders—she was asking for help. And when people ask you for help, you should give it.

"I figured with all this DDC work we got, and you and Marcy's connection to the big bad rock star Devereaux, well . . ." Rick, finally getting around to his real-real point for calling and pulling me back into the present conversation. "We could get Cade in good with that guy. DD could maybe give him a lesson or two. Dude's gonna owe us one. Right?"

Another assignment. More pressure. I had a hundred emails from Feebee about the DDC stuff, but then I'd already dispatched the heaviest lifting of my role. I also had one from Dev himself, a lengthy, heartfelt thank you for having read his novel and for liking it, that a few of the remarks I'd given he had taken to heart, and how he planned to spend the summer revising.

I'd written back a four-sentence response, to which he hadn't replied:

> *Revision, yes; but don't over-think it. You mainly need*
> *to revise for style and language. The story is solid, the*
> *characters real. You're almost there.*

And, he was. I thought that he could have an actual commercial book success of what I now understood was an action-packed but metaphoric survey of the addiction and recovery process: I didn't know on what Duncan Devereaux had been hooked to produce his need to go to rehab—did that part matter?—but he seemed to have learned quite a bit along the way, why the process fails for some people and works for others, and the dangers of subscribing to tenets and dogmas to the point that they, then, become the addiction . . . and all of it done via allegory, of the suicide cult storming the mountaintop rich man's dry-out retreat. And, all done in about eighty-thousand words. Duncan, an established brand and celebrity, of course wouldn't have any trouble getting a book published.

Hell—any agent worth her salt would surely stoke a bidding war among the Big Five. DD could count on it. Not that he needs the money . . .

I couldn't bring myself to tell him this truth: that, regardless of the book having any artistic merit, with his name recognition and history he wouldn't have to wait very long to get a book contract. To publisher's row, it didn't matter so much about the quality of the work as the idea that a book written by 'Duncan Devereaux' would move copies—look at the sort of celebrity cash-in memoirs that are put out by the pallet-load. He had more here, though. That was the true gospel. And he should be proud. It's hard to write a good novel of any type. So that's what I told him.

Rick wasn't done with his news, or his requests: after I agreed to try to pitch to DD the idea of tutoring Cadence, he suggested I meet them both downtown. That he had another project going, one on which he also wanted my opinion: his dream of opening a music venue.

I scratched down the address, hung up and opened the Macbook, stared at the cursor, tried to remember where I'd left off on CREATIVE CLASS. I closed my eyes and chanted my mantra a few dozen times, falling into a meditative state of mental quiet. Afterwards I wrote for two hours, blazing through ten decent pages. A different sort of meditation.

The building, tucked away on an ill-used spur of Congress Street near the confluence of the rivers, had an arched roof and ornate brickwork, and had in its past incarnations clearly been some sort of industrial structure, one that had sat in disrepair and disuse for some time.

I greeted Cade, Rick, and a commercial real estate broker named Vince Ellenshaw, who looked like a building himself—a thick-necked, broad-shouldered brickhouse of a building, a structure wearing a slick suit and with a big shiny head and mirror shades, an edifice with feet shod in size fifteen Weejuns. He'd been a Southeastern Redtails football star twenty years before. He had a Blackberry and a tape measure clipped to his belt. His crushing handshake nearly finished me—like a pianist or a brain surgeon, my fingers are my lifeblood.

"Man, is this an honor, or what?" Vince, starry-eyed. "I was playing ball at Southeastern when your first book came out. Everybody was talking about it."

"They *were?*" Skeptical, I imagined the musclebound lot of them sitting around the locker room leafing through *Keys to the Rain* looking for the erotic scenes—those had been the ones people always mentioned anyway, right? "Really?"

"Talk of the town."

"That's thrilling to know. I'm humbled, Vince."

"No," taking off his sunglasses. "It's a greater honor for me, Mr. Bo-champ."

"'Champ'—I don't know why it never occurred to me, but I think we just got ourselves a new nickname for Uncle Cort. Don't we, Cade?"

"Uncle Cort, he doesn't need, doesn't need, doesn't need a new nickname." Cadence, distressed, seemed to break out of a brief paralysis, coming over and giving me a big hug around the waist. "I missed you."

My eyes misted. "I understand we have some music to discuss."

"Do we!"

I asked if Cadence wanted to do so while Rick and Vince looked over the property.

"Hell no," his father interjected. "Champ, I need your advice on this one."

I rued the inauguration of this nickname, associated much more with Vince's world than mine. "Then let's go inside."

On the walkaround, as Vince referred to our visit—"Everybody be careful; this building ain't nowhere close to being up to code, and we ought to have hardhats for this"—Rick laid out his plan, which I had to admit sounded wonderful: a classy 'listening space,' as he kept calling it, that would redefine the small-scale live music experience in Columbia. Not a bar full of smoke and drunk people smashing into one another. Artists. Music.

"This is gonna be an intimate freaking space, bro. Five hundred for standing room, maybe a third of that if it's a seated event. We're gonna have everything from Gillian Welch to hardcore punk in this place. Long as they're serious musicians, they get a shot at playing my room."

Cadence poked his head into an electrical closet and began firing off questions to Vince about wiring codes.

I nudged Rick. Nonchalant: "This project, it'll take a pile of capital. Yes?"

His mouth, downturned. "And what don't?"

"Going to the library."

"Hah—good one. And from a writer. But look: I got resources. I got beaucoup credit. My credit's impeccable."

In that moment I remembered Rick's desire to write, the story about his uncle, how I'd gone one better than critiquing by actually editing it for him. Revising it. "I worked on that piece of yours, by the way. The 'Superfan' story." It was as good a topic as any to use in changing the subject, which I thought to be folly. "I hope that's all right."

Rick reddened. I could have sworn steam began leaking out of his ears. His high, rapid-fire vocal delivery seemed to have slowed a half-step and lowered a full octave. "So, what. I ain't a writer? I need you to rewrite my shit?"

I pled for him to hear me out.

"You're just going to rub it in my face, are you?"

Taken aback. "Rick—I never said the story was bad. I wanted to just show you how it could be improved. What aspects you could stand to work on. Like grammar."

A pregnant pause. Rick, a mask of confusion. "Look—I gotta lot on my mind besides that story." He gestured in a sweeping arc around the dusty old building, sunlight streaming in through filthy, wire-reinforced windows full of broken panels that'd need replacing—in fact, the windows made it look more like a prison machine shop than Rick's proposed listening room. "But. Um. Could I take a look at what you did?"

I hesitated, rued the fact that I'd brought up the fiction. I'd truly rewritten his story, molded it more from my own sensibilities than his. If I sent the manuscript to him, it'd be one more insult. But how could I say no? I supposed I could rush home and make cursory corrections to his original and email that instead, which might assuage Rick's feelings, but it certainly wouldn't help him that much as a writer. Rick had language and characters and incident, but he hadn't mastered many of the other basics like POV, and dialogue, and what to leave out—the action of his story made the mistake of spending too much time getting people to walk across rooms and in and out of vehicles and buildings. You learned to skip that part. You trusted the reader to mentally get the character across the room.

Vince and Cadence came strolling over, kicking up ancient industrial dust clouds with every step. "Dad—this wiring's not even up to 1950s code, much less right now! We need an electrician. Uncle Cortland, who should we get?"

I chuckled. Because I'd written a couple of coming of age novels, Cadence—and other people, apparently—thought I had the answers to most anything, when the only subject about which I felt any sort of competence whatsoever had been the discussion I'd just been having with the boy's father about a simple memoir of a short story. "Haven't a clue, my boy. Vince?"

"Not my speciality. Plenty of electricians out there needing work, though, since this economy of ours—well. You know."

He stopped himself with a nearly imperceptible frown: real estate agents trying to close deals didn't talk about unpleasantness like a continuing soft national economy. Hopeless office space empty for years waiting to be leased. Homes by the tens of thousands foreclosed upon by banks. People squatting in houses they could no longer afford, waiting out the repo men and sheriff's deputies coming to enforce eviction notices. Plenty of that sort of work for people, but so much, ironically, that many people were able to live on in their houses for many months after they ceased making the payments. Times were tough, even for the banks—they didn't have enough foreclosure personnel to keep up with demand for their services. A sad situation; a far cry from the idyllic boomer childhood I'd known, and that Marcy and I had discussed.

Which brought me back to the situation at hand. I promised I'd email Rick the rewritten, and re-titled, short story, with a brief note explaining that my intention with such a complete reworking of someone else's piece merely to edify, not to insult.

As for the club idea, however, I felt a need to be direct, to play devil's advocate, if for no other reason than Cadence: Here was a father, aged forty, with a son who seemed brilliant despite his mild disability, but who had a long road of care and schooling ahead. Was Rick Wragg chasing midlife-crisis chimeras with his desire to write? With his having given up a successful small business to take on a hugely risky venture? With this money-sucking idea?

"Aren't you going to need investors for this?" I asked, feeling squeamish. The Southern gentleman in me hated, hated, hated discussing money, particularly someone else's. "What an undertaking."

"An undertaking? Champ, I ain't opening a funeral parlor here. And, yeah. Sure. Investors—why do you think I brought you out here?"

Vince, conveniently and astutely enough, stepped away to make a call, nodding and mouthing, 'Excuse me.'

"Yeah, Dad—we're gonna need investors." Cadence started doing a little finger dance beside his left eye, a little human calculator. "The wiring alone, I think, I think, I think, is going to take a few hundred man-hours; the facade out front is a wreck, the windows all need replacing . . . yeah. And, and, and, Dad, what about the sound in here? Look at all these hard surfaces. All this, this, this brickwork." Cadence shouted at the top of his lungs, making us all jump. "Listen to that! We're gonna get slap-back like nobody's business!"

"Cade-man, you need to dial it back." But Rick seemed more proud than annoyed. "Listen to this guy, would ya? Little twerp knows his stuff."

Cadence folded his arms. "I pay attention. I ask questions," hard on the Q. "That's what, what, what intellectually curious people do."

"A little sponge. I love it. But hey, don't worry—your Dad's gonna get all that covered. We'll drape cloth. We'll put up eggshell. We'll put in a hardwood floor—a dance floor! We'll get hippie bands in here, and all those barefoot Betties spinning around in their tie-dye skirts. Eh?"

"Sounds delightful. But Rick, why am I really here today? I don't know anything about anything."

Rick shooed his son away by giving him an assignment—"Find the boiler. Give me an estimate on how much the HVAC's gonna set us back."

Cadence raced off, his footfalls echoing hollow across the empty space.

"I asked you to come for my son. He misses you."

"I'm at his disposal. And yours. I'll send you that revised story. Take a look—I think you'll see my point."

"That's awesome, champ. Really. So, what do you think?"

"About the story?"

He shook his head, looked around at his future listening space. "This idea,it's the biggest I ever had, dude."

"To be honest?" Here was the tricky part—I've found that when people use that phrase, they're being anything but honest. "In theory, brilliant; in execution, costly and problematic—but like I said to Cadence, I don't know about all that. I never renovated any old buildings, or opened listening spaces. I never built anything."

"You built stories and whole books. Don't sell yourself short."

"My little masterpieces?"

"Sheesh. You should hear yourself."

I apologized. I didn't know from where that sour attitude had come. Sounded a little like Marcy, maybe, who continually derided herself, had poor self esteem, seemed more embarrassed than excited by the fact that she'd cut demos in Duncan Devereaux's home studio.

What would be enough for her?

Rick went on to say that to really show me what he had in mind, he wanted me to go with him to see a similar place, one that I knew about but had never gone inside, not in all my years growing up in Edgewater County, and never, of course, as a refined adult:

The Dixiana, which anchored a corner of the town green in Tillman Falls, had been a semi-famous nightclub for many years—"a honkytonk," as it'd been characterized to me as a child—that catered to blues, bluegrass and country music, and that had a regional and national reputation as a landmark music venue. To me that sounded no different from its 'honkytonk' designation, which in our household stood as a pejorative: I didn't care for Americana or folk any more than rock music, a piteous sub-genre of rhythm and blues that didn't interest me any more than the others. I didn't understand these idioms. My parents didn't listen to such music—they were classicists, and so, too, am I. All the other children were dunderheads, wasting their time on the trifle that was pop music. I told them all as much. I hadn't had many friends, except my parents. And then, not even them.

I agreed to go back home again. I'd call my uncle, which I'd pledged to do more of back in the spring—how much longer did he have, after all? As is typical for me, since then I've allowed myriad other concerns and considerations stand in the way of furthering my relationship with what little family I still have. I use the excuse of being a writer, but hell, maybe I'm just not that good with people.

4.

The Jeep Liberty again, this time hurtling north out of town along Highway 79 toward the Edgewater County seat, Rick again pummeling me with noodling improvisational rock music. As The Dixiana had a strict 21-and-up policy—excepted, of course, for musical prodigies proficient at roots music instrumentation such as the banjo and mandolin—no Cade this time, no classical music talk, no, no, no questions.

The more Rick filled me in on the history of The Dixiana, the more I felt like an ignorant, oblivious fool—the so-called 'honkytonk' I'd always assumed was but a den of low-rent redneck iniquity in reality stood tall among the bluegrass cognoscenti of the country as a legacy, landmark music venue. Myths and legends both, as Rick put it, had stood upon The Dixiana's storied stage and sung their songs. A piece of real cultural history right around the corner from Hillsborough.

I hadn't a clue. And Rick wasn't even a South Carolinian.

Shame. No wonder I've been told that my work doesn't seem especially Southern.

"And really, it sounds like a dream in there," he further informed. "Cadence is missing out tonight."

I asked who I could expect to see playing tonight.

"It's open mic night, but it's a well-respected one—folks come from all over the state for this."

He went on to say that a local lawyer 'curated' the monthly event, which meant that the host got to sing his own songs, too. An Edgewater County thread came together for me, then, as he invoked the name Jasper Glasscock, our other published book-author from Edgewater County.

I'd always wondered what it'd been like for Jasper to spend so much time face-to-face with Coy Wando, to transcribe the killer's horrid and depraved tale of serial murder, and producing from these sessions a tome that'd been the then-private investigator's one stab at literary accomplishment, as well as the real reason Jasper had never written another book, which—as Coy himself had overheard in the very bar we were about to enter—had been a dream of Jasper's, as it'd been of mine. Nope, Jasper got used up by his one book-writing experiment, but with a monster like Wando, who could blame him? As bad as Coy Wando's actual crimes had been, his descriptions of acts for which he'd never been charged went much further into the territory of the depraved and the damned.

I knew something about having images in the mind. Unpleasant ones. I walked into the bedroom and saw my own parents dead in what'd been a bloody ballet of violence like out of a Sam Peckinpah movie. I know from horror. But Coy Wando, a sick little puppy, as they say. Whether he actually did all the crimes, or otherwise.

Twenty years since I read that book, and forty years since my bloody initiation into adulthood—gracious sakes alive, the way time moves so inexorably and enigmatically in its passing. More than ever, I'm glad my cousin Arthur will be keeping that old house for his own family. Just as soon never set foot in it again.

Smoky, grungy, and filled from the front doors to the back wall and behind the bar and the small wooden stage only a foot off the floor with a sense and tone of its own storied history, The Dixiana oozed character and atmosphere. Sure, on one hand this was the very same low-rent beer hall I'd always assumed it to be, but once I took in the wall of framed and autographed 8x10 glossies—many legends of country music and bluegrass had indeed appeared here at one time or another in their career, working what I presumed could charitably be called the chitlin circuit—I realized that right here under my nose had been a vastly more interesting place that I'd ever imagined.

Trudy, to whom Rick introduced himself, was a lanky, middle-aged beanpole of a woman behind the bar who I'd find out later had managed the place for over twenty years; she turned pink when Rick presented me as 'Edgewater County's own answer to effin' John Grisham, Cort Bo-champ."

"I—I read that book of yourn. That thing catches my eye all the time, sitting on my shelf at home," nervous and twitchy. "You done good by us all here in Tillman Falls."

Beyond self-conscious and wondering which book she meant, I sputtered and stammered and thanked her.

Something about being back in my hometown and finding myself so well known felt unearned. I'd always tried to pretend that whatever ties I had to this place existed as only tenuous, gossamer existential threads that had little to do with the person I'd become as an adult.

Maybe I had to feel that way, though. Maybe that was the only way I could set aside the memories of my parents, and what until that awful night had been a relatively storybook edition of an upper-middle class, late–baby boomer American childhood—and the baby boomer American childhood, above all, loomed large as the greatest of childhoods that had ever been experienced in the long, but cosmologically brief span of recorded, civilized human history. Hell of a party to have disrupted by a surprise murder-suicide. Which I still spend far too much time dwelling upon, whether here in Edgewater County or in Cypress Creek or my classroom at ETC.

I chanted my mantra under my breath for a long moment, tried to flush my mind and open its receptors to the sights and sounds of this open-mic night. When the awful bloody pictures try to come back, I empty my mind. It's not easy.

"You talking to yourself?" Rick asked, bringing over a longneck Bud that Trudy had capped for him—Rick, apparently back on the train full-time with the drinking, but I didn't say a word. I wasn't in any position to criticize. I hadn't gone through rehab and the 12 Steps the way Rick had, as I'd found out from Marcy. In the brief time they'd been together, she'd told me such matters had comprised the bulk of the conversation between them—Marcy, of course, a fan of the vino, and the two a bad fit, I thought, for anyone trying to recover from alcoholism.

Why I didn't see it the same way at that moment, I cannot say.

Because I was smitten? That good enough? It'll have to do.

Oh, how I coveted those glasses of red wine she sipped while performing. As about to become clear, I needn't worry about such temptation for long, though, or anything else about my relationship with Marcy Baumbach.

We took our places at a rickety, uneven wooden table, the edges worn smooth by a thousand-thousand forearms resting upon the ancient, varnished knotty pine—the surface had a tacky sort of appearance, as though Trudy needed to run her barkeep's rag over it, but a fingertip flicked across revealed only the heavy finish rather than a layer of spilled beer.

Beneath the varnish of the tables were 1950s and 60s magazine ads, and newspaper clippings from the *Edgewater Advocate* and the *Columbia Record* documenting various area sports and cultural milestones. On our table, I read a clipping from the local paper about the time in 1970 that Rabbit Pettus put on a well-publicized autumn 'Harvest Moon' bluegrass festival held inside The Dixiana, as well as on an outdoor stage that faced a fenced lawn area abutting Forest Knoll Garden, the town cemetery where, yes, my parents are buried—and another piece recounting the fabled tour bus pulling up and disgorging June Carter, Johnny Cash, and Bob Dylan, who all rolled off and paid the cover charge to watch the bluegrass bands. How the country couple had played and sung a mini-set of music, but that Dylan, 'a very shy performer who did not seem to cotton to the close quarters of the packed floor of Tillman Falls's own legendary Dixiana, had gone back onto the tour bus, bound for an appearance at the South Carolina State Fair later that night.'

The shadow of an ample gut fell across the clipping encased in the varnish of the table; a syrupy, gentle Southern musician's voice: "I don't think Dylan got off the bus at all in Columbia, though. I had my older sister Letty drive me over there. We followed them the whole way."

My uncle's lawyer peered down the neck of his guitar at a small device clipped onto the stock, a red half-circle with an LED readout that flashed the chords that Jasper Glasscock strummed. "I was sixteen years old, and if Bob Dylan wasn't my biggest hero, I don't know who was." He strummed, tuned, strummed. "And just for the record? I was the reason he went back onto the bus before Johnny and June Carter sang."

"What happened?"

"I had to ask him some questions. Questions he didn't wanna answer."

We shook hands, exchanged pleasantries, introduced Rick Wragg to Jasper. "And the questions . . . ?"

Jasper glanced over his glasses, then back at his tuning device. "What the different songs meant."

Rick, his eyes shining. "*What did Dylan freaking say to that?*"

Jasper slipped into a decent, nasal Dylan: 'They're all based on famous short stories and acknowledged classics of world literature.'"

We all burst into laughter. "Really?"

"I shit you not. When I looked at his autobiography, and he got to this one part where he was complaining about the critics saying that *Blood on the Tracks* was inspired by his divorce from Sara, when all the songs on it had been 'based on stories by Chekhov,' I liked to fell off my chair laughing. After reading that, I felt like I really knew Bob Dylan." Jasper, strumming a G chord and fiddling with the tuning. "Felt like I had a connection to him—I knew his schtick. How he could pop somebody's balloon. The world needs balloon-poppers, don't you boys think?"

"Oh, goodness gracious—that's a hell of a story." I drank in every detail of Jasper's voice, the way the stage lights flashed from the round lenses and wire frames of his glasses. He had on a Grateful Dead t-shirt, of all bands—a ridiculously loud tie-dye with a screen print on the front: a rainbow-color row of dancing bears. "A mini-interview with Bob Dylan? That's tremendous, Jasper."

"But anyway, I'll let you two homies get caught up." Rick, fidgeting, wiping his hands on his jeans. "I need to make a call—forgot to tell the sitter to keep an eye on Cade and the Googling and the hotspots and the memes."

In Rick's wake Jasper asked, "You got us another book coming out soon? Sorry to say I'm in arrears these days on my reading."

"Plenty of books waiting to be read. No new ones by me. Maybe one day soon." A less rueful admission, this, than in the recent past: after all, I'd been writing with relative fury for several months now. I simply needed to get through the draft of one of the novels, if for no other reason than as a confidence builder, before I began seeking to again publish in earnest. No rush. You can't force these things. "But that'll change. Maybe next year. The destination's the journey, after all."

"That's a good way to put it." Strumming his guitar, at last he seemed satisfied with its tuning. "It's all kinda right-now anyway."

"Nowhere to get to, nowhere to be."

At the sound of a ringtone, Jasper excused himself. I noted that he had iPhone, a man of retirement age yet clearly dialed in to the right-now; he spoke more like one of the twenty-something musicians I'd watched loading gear in through the stage door of the club, which led to the alley and the back deck area.

A deck from which I could stand, if I wished, and contemplate Forest Knoll Garden alongside the road beyond heading west out of town toward bump-in-the-road towns like Parsons Hollow and Red Mound closer to the Pisgette National Forest.

How during my teenage years I'd go after school to visit their graves.

How I felt so little grief standing there, only bewilderment.

The grief, it would come later. An adult feeling, perhaps.

I chose not to contemplate the cemetery. It's a small miracle, I suppose, that my work isn't more interested in matters of mortality. What do I have to add? Prior to Leora, my closest brush with death has been so utterly unnatural that I couldn't possibly have any wisdom to offer anyone. Suffice to say that matters of death constitute a personal journey for everyone, and leave it at that.

Rick Wragg came back from a visit with Trudy already sipping his second beer and speaking inaudibly, his lips moving and head nodding and fingers snapping. Rick, going on one of his Wragg-rants, ideas comin' at him so brutally fast and amazing and epiphanic that he couldn't keep up even if he had a little digital recorder in his pocket like I carry, a device I told him he ought to get to make the most of times like driving around in the Jeep Liberty. Always get ideas when driving.

Jasper was now saying, "Check-check-check-check," into the phalanx of vocal microphones set up across the stage; a drummer tapped and tested his skins; and a guitarist plugged in to a screech of feedback that tore through my eardrums and gentle soul.

"It's already too loud in here, unfortunately."

Rick, ignoring my whining. "So now, what'd Glasscock write, exactly . . . ?"

Over the cacophony of the tuning and tweaking and setting up the gear I explained to Rick how Jasper had interviewed and transcribed the 'last confession' of the notorious Coy Wando, the exploits and terrors of whom Rick, a transplant from 'up yonder,' had never heard. A killer convicted of murdering four young women, a death row inmate who'd go on to take credit for many more. "So, not a novelist, but a writer, still. And look—I was going to suggest that you try writing record or show reviews, or perhaps an article for one of those hi-fi gear magazines or websites could be a way to get into print."

"Insteada the short story?"

"Well. Sure. Instead of through fiction."

"Ah." Rick, dejected. "Forget all that author stuff. I don't got it in me—I fucking suck." He took a drink. "Don't I."

"Hardly."

Hah, his sour expression read. "You never gave me any notes back on that story."

He seemed to have forgotten our conversation regarding my revision—odd.

"I must have forgotten to send it to you," which was true enough. "But Rick, remember: I only took the liberty, and privilege of doing a polish on it for you. The way any editor would." These were falsehoods of such exquisite exaggeration that I felt a hot patch of guilt form on the back of my head like a tiny hurricane of unsettled mental weather. "I did make quite a few changes overall, mainly as an example of how to do this sort of thing," mumbling. "I'll email it first thing tomorrow."

Rick, now happy as a clam. "That means a lot, champ. That's friendship, there."

I smiled and clasped him on the shoulder. "No question."

About eight o'clock Trudy and a squad of kitchen help came through and shooed all of us sitting at the tables into the bar area. They replaced the four– and two-tops with rows of aluminum folding chairs that the small crew of men and women set out with a studied and graceful methodology that seemed part of the act, the atmosphere. Most of them appeared almost as aged as the club's owner, Rabbit Pettus, a member of the Greatest Generation now well into his eighties.

Rabbit, all barrel-chested six-and-a-half feet of himself, held court with Jasper and a lanky shorthaired elderly woman who could have passed for Trudy's mother in a dim back booth near the swinging kitchen door, all sitting and conferring and laughing together the way old friends do. Musicians, milling around with banjos and acoustic guitars and mandolins, filed over to the bar to get drinks, and then by ones and twos, over to pay respects to the club owner—all of which also had the rich and compelling air of ritual, if not worthy of the term liturgy.

My forearm hairs, stippled. *Someone should write a book about this place.*

My spell, broken by a rumbling stomach. During the day at The Dixiana, one could enjoy all manner of down-home vittles, Southern staples like fried chicken and biscuits and barbecue and greens and taters slopped on the side. But only at lunch, and certainly never on open mic nights. My arteries, surely relieved at this news, but I cursed not grabbing a granola bar.

Rick came up behind me gurgling another Bud Light that looked fresh and cold from the cooler. I tried not to be a mother hen about counting Rick's drinks. I could easily drive his Liberty back to Columbia—would be doing so, now, whether Rick had one more beer, or twenty.

My head pounded. Mercy, do I start to feel puny when I let myself get too peckish, too empty. Headache city—that's death for a writer.

I went and grabbed a bowl of popcorn off the bar. I got a wink from the bartender, sexily bored and weathered and backlit by the neon beer signs; Trudy, leaning with a slender elbow and pouring a foamy pitcher of PBR while making small talk with a good old boy clutching a folded bill; a familiar routine. An instant character, this bartender, described as such in the ever-present notebook. I lusted after her—not sexually, but for her stories, surely more colorful than any I could imagine.

As the light began to fade from the sky, giving over to the reluctant gloaming of the lingering summer twilight, The Dixiana gradually filled with music lovers.

Rabbit Pettus stood outside collecting the cover charge himself. Perhaps his longevity came down to attention to detail. He'd make a good writer.

Rick, sidling up with a fresh beer. "I need to ask you some stuff."

"About your story?"

"About Cade." He gestured toward the front door.

On the way out, we both nodded to Pettus. "Look here—don't wander past the property line with that beer in your hand." Brown tobacco juice, an arc that went splat on a sidewalk that needed pressure washing. The whole town looked as though it could use a good scrubbing. "The gendarmes'll write an open container ticket faster than the pigeons shit on old Pitchfork Ben over yonder."

Rick, saluting. "No worries, sir."

The old man, unimpressed, went back to taking money.

Ambling around the corner, we both examined the peeling and fading paint of the famous Dixiana mural and its Johnny-Reb, Confederate flag-waving fighting cock of an anachronistic sports mascot. Rabbit Pettus, and The Dixiana, obviously felt no need to keep up with the times. You had to give it to him—nowadays it takes guts to stand and be counted as willfully offensive.

"Get a load of that flag." Rick, swigging. "Whoa."

"Quite a relic."

"Man—I'm surprised somebody ain't made them paint over that thing."

A shrug; an explanation. "I always heard the mural had more to do with Redtails sports superstition than institutionalized racism."

"Bullcrud."

"It's been a bone of contention in Tillman Falls for years now . . . and you can see how far complaining's gotten anyone."

"Eff that redneck crap." He drawled his words humorless and hard. "Worst part of living down here with y'all."

Rick, a mean drunk. Or so Marcy had said he'd described his drinking persona.

Great.

We stood in the twilight watching as cars pulled into the slanted spaces around the town green and along the Common Street side leading to the cemetery. Being around all the musicians inside made me think about Duncan Devereaux, the progress on the sculpture as well as the planning of the concert, all of which Dev had approved.

No response yet to my request for a phone convo, to ask again for his participation. He suspects I'll put the screws to him about playing. Smart guy.

Rick expressed disappointment at not truly having a role to play anymore on the DDC. I commiserated, withholding the fact that Darren's Buddha-like girth and demeanor had brought a soothing, can-do, surrender-to-the-flow vibe compared to Rick's cocksure, motormouth, caffeine-fueled persona, which'd always rubbed everyone the wrong way—no one more than Feebee; Feebee, who in Leora's absence had come into her own as a leader of the committee, and as I mentioned to Rick, a good bet to run for city council in the near future. I could see it in her eyes and in the way she carried herself—Feebee always had a tidbit about everyone she talked to, retained from the last time her circle had intersected theirs. Bill Clinton had made a successful campaign for the presidency out of that kind of calculated and accessible retention.

I surveyed the musicians now spilling out onto the sidewalk, the people hanging out on the front of their cars, the monuments and magnolias and benches and old courthouse. From inside the bar, the sound of twangy guitars. "This is a music lover's heaven, right here. It wasn't this way when I was a kid. It really was just a honkytonk back then."

"You know what they say about old whores and ugly buildings."

I did. I asked him if this was what he wanted for his listening room in Columbia.

He belched, cleared his throat. "The attitude—sure. We're going to have the fold-out chairs with the cushie bottoms instead of those rusty old things like Rabbit's got in there." Rick paced back and forth, held his fingers aloft in a two-fingered gesture that made me think of Meredith Baumbach's wistful, wishful fake smoking—Rick had been one, too. If he were going to drink, I wondered why he didn't go ahead and simply pick that deleterious habit back up as well. "But we're going to do more than just have bands come through and try to make the nut back at the door and pay the band outta the bar. We're gonna do this right. They get paid, we get paid. Perfect balance."

"Oh—it's going to be a bar, now, too?"

"Well, yeah. Course. No other model I can come up with, champ. Gotta have alcohol sales."

I figured I might as well go for it: Rick needed someone to point out that he was no longer sneaking a sip of champagne at a wedding—an admitted and once dry drunk was now on his sixth beer, and not to sound like some nattering grandmother, but at barely nine in the evening?

"What's with all the glug-glugging." I tried to replicate the euphemistically humorous manner that Rick often communicated. "Huh?"

"*Pardon moi, mon frere*, but a few brews never—"

"Rick: you said you shouldn't drink anymore. That that was bound up in everything that'd gone wrong for you in life."

"'Bound up?'" Rick scowled, a mask of anger like I'd never before seen. "I don't talk that way."

"A turn of phrase."

"Who you think you are, champ, my dad? Old man's dead. And like I told my brother and my uncle both, I don't need you or nobody else to take his place, pal. So—"

My hands, held in a gesture of supplication. I apologized. Told him I was worried. A niggling old worrywart.

Truthfully, at this point I wanted to be done with Rick Wragg. I know how that must sound. But I wanted to be sober. I'd gotten my mojo back. I had no business, really, in a venue like this, not unless I planned to write about a honkytonk and needed to research the atmosphere the way Rick had wanted to scope out the sound reinforcement. Not to mention our mutual connection over Marcy. All too complicated and internecine.

"Look—I'm done." He poured out the last foamy swallows of his light beer onto the sidewalk by the mural. "You know what American beer's like? How it's like getting it on in a canoe?"

"How's that?"

"Cause it's 'fucking close to water'."

I chuckled; I got it.

Rick, an apology, one duly accepted. "Let's go hear ourselves some bluegrass, get me a cuppa joe, and later we'll make our way on back. Sound good?"

I agreed that it did.

5.

As guests of Jasper we were awarded complimentary wristbands that made Rick stop and hold up the line and make a speech about how awesome the bar was, and too that Rabbit was out here earning his keep. How the best piece of advice anyone ever gave him was never to be an absentee owner, how to really make it, you had to—

"Hurry the fuck up, d-bag," an eager music fan called out from the growing knot of show-goers. "I gotta piss."

"*You better watch the mouth.*" Rabbit's deep old man's voice grew and rumbled across the green, a tornado siren. "I hear one more goddamn word like that out of anybody's mouth and I will shut this show down in a skinny New York minute."

Chastened, the line inched forward.

Rabbit Pettus reminded me of one of my grandfathers, but I'd never gotten to know either of them very well. Perhaps I'd set up an interview with the man, who exuded less decrepitude than the sturdy longevity of the stately old oaks across the street on the town green. Write up The Dixiana for a magazine feature story. I hadn't tried my hand at that form in ages. I made a note to this effect.

Nearly every chair was filled and SRO along the walls; with our wristbands Rick and I were now pointed over to the row of booths where Rabbit's party sat. A server took our drink order; Rick tried to get a coffee, but she said all that they had was some instant that Rabbit liked to drink.

"I think it's—I dunno what. Folgers, maybe?" The server, scratching behind her ear and popping gum. The acne-scarred, chubby young woman wore cut-offs and a skintight, midriff top bearing The Dixiana's rootin'-tootin' old-timey logo replicating the elaborate neon sign out front, with the tag line *50 Years So Far.* "Something like that."

"Excellent—make it a double. One for me, one for my friend."

"Nah, nah, fuck that noise. Diet Coke all the way, baby."

The young woman grunted, and her energy sagged—a couple of teetotalers weren't going to tip out to any significant degree.

As for me, I ignored the music. Instead, I leaned back and tried to listen to the murmuring conversation between Rabbit and the other Dixiana insiders huddled in the booth, but I could only hear rumblings and mumblings. The stories they all could tell. Probably a lot more interesting than anything I could make up.

※

Jasper's country numbers seemed to be his big 'hits' around these here parts. A melancholy ballad he introduced as "Halfway Hopin'" featured lyrics like:

> *She turned wine into water, spun gold into straw*
> *She took a broken promise to mend a broken law*
> *The more I love her, the less I like myself*
> *The more I love her, the less I like myself...*

And

> *So here's my prayer I won't make her cry*
> *And that this time she won't say goodbye*
> *It's why I'm hopin' maybe this time she'll stay*
> *But I'm halfway hopin' maybe she'll stay away...*

All of which held the crowd in rapt and silent attention. His voice, quavering, broke at times with that lonesome, awful high country ache, a feeling and appeal in the music that at last I felt like I understood. A depth of complex emotion on display. Superb artistry.

Which little prepared me, however, for the next tune, a twangy, uptempo showstopper with the abhorrent, skin-crawling moniker "Mama's Pussy."

"This here's a song about a cat," he hollered, "and the woman who loved the creature." The audience, raucous in its demonstrative glee.

> *More than she loves me*
> *I can guarantee*
> *If she had to choose*
> *between that pussy and me*
> *you know which one it'd be*

And the audience all screamed along:

> *Mama loves that pussy!*
> *Mama sure loves that old pussy!*

The lyrics came syrupy and smooth like the steel guitar accompanying Jasper, played by a young man with an enormous mane of dreadlocks that bounced as he ran a small metal tube up and down the strings of his instrument. For such esoteric poetry fraught with evocatively salacious Oedipal content, the song left me no less melancholy for my own mother, a feeling I've often tried to ignore, have wanted to forget. To remember was to grieve. To hurt.

I shoved away the feelings, more than a habit in my case, a seeming lifelong vocation, though one paying only in the most interior and personal of currencies.

We sat listening to Jasper tell his song-stories and introduce different singers and players trying out original tunes and covers. I found myself charmed and entertained, even if some of the warblers taking the mic might have benefited from a more complete course in vocal training.

No matter—the passion, shining through.

Despite Rick guzzling Diet Coke for an hour, in the end I insisted upon being allowed to drive Rick's Jeep Liberty back down the chuckholed highway to Soda City. I knew well the strip of weathered asphalt, one whose pitted surface improved once we crossed over into Richland County.

"Just cause I knocked off a couple beers don't make me a drunk. Again."

"Be that as it may . . ." I held out my hand. "You can drive yourself home from Cypress Creek. But I'm tired, I want to get back quickly, and I'm taking us on a shortcut I know."

He fumed, but shoved the bundle of keys into my hand. "Be gentle. You know this's still a new car."

"It'll be fine."

We motored out of Tillman Falls on the West Side Highway, which took us along the ridge and away from the river. We went through a crossroads with a sign that read PARSONS HOLLOW and CHILTON, with arrows pointing in opposite directions. With the sun roof on the vehicle open to the velvet, impenetrable dark of the moonless sky, the waning evening enveloped us, the deep summer Southern night.

Rick dialed around on his satellite radio until he found the classical channel, which he didn't have programmed into his favorites. We listened to Schubert's Piano Sonata No. 16, a contemplative, at times dramatic piece that accompanied our otherwise silent traverse with a kind of lonely, aching gracefulness that grew in intensity the way making love with Marcy felt. She'd said that compared to sex with Rick, our passionate union came so tenderly and patient. I'd replied that I didn't consider such matters a competition. Or hoped not, anyway.

"This music is depressing."

I tried to argue for Schubert.

"Nah. Nah. Sounds like we're in a freaking funeral home."

Shrugging, I switched over to the other classical channel where we found Mozart's Jupiter Symphony. Robust and busy and uptempo. It carried us through the dark countryside, every now and then the shining eyes of deer flashing from the shoulder alongside the wooded highway.

I climbed out of the Liberty in my gravel driveway, which had been suffering erosion and would need to be refreshed. Rick said, "I'm sorry again about yelling at ya. I know you're trying to do right by me, ain't ya?"

I assured him I was, and offered to have him sleep on the couch if he felt as though he couldn't drive. He demurred, showing me he was sober by walking an imaginary line and touching his nose. I chuckled and we gave one another a brief man-hug.

The last thing Rick said was that he'd invite me to what he called a *charrette*, which I went inside and googled to learn was a term for when a planner brings in a group of experts and end-users to brainstorm and spitball a design problem or project. Another trip to the building on Congress Street would be in my future.

I took a moment to email his story I'd revised, after which I sent Marcy a text that read 'Hello and good night,' to which she replied with a cold and simplistic reply: GN.

6.

The next week, I became more concerned about Rick.

At Marcy's behest we'd gone down to the Old Market to attend a weekly outdoor concert series sponsored by the downtown merchant's association. Naturally, I saw many of the same faces from my committee and other various endeavors through the years of my public writing career, but it would be Rick Wragg who commanded all the attention:

Despite being out of the rigging game, Rick nonetheless hung around the soundboard while his erstwhile business partner, Darren, stayed busy patching and knob-twiddling and preparing for the musicians, a group that as Marcy and I arrived were still unloading their gear. While she hung around and made small talk with the young men wielding their guitars I'd gone to check on Rick, who I know had to have seen me wave at him, but in response had only looked away quickly. Had set down the plastic cup of beer he'd been drinking on the low brick wall by the pop-up tent and the front-of-house rig.

When I came over to speak, however, Rick greeted me with warmth, pumped my hand; and, he and Darren grilled me over my progress in getting Duncan Devereaux to come and play the unveiling ceremony.

Told them I'd done all I could. "At the end of the day, it is what it is."

Rick shook his head. "Damn."

"I tried to warn you all."

"Want to mic-check for me, soundman emeritus?" Darren asked Rick, busy chewing up an Altoids peppermint.

"You got it, man." Rick, glancing over to the portable stage that occupied one end of the commercial strip, closed to vehicular traffic for the duration of the evening concert. "No sweat." He paused long enough to give Marcy a quick hug, then scurried up on stage to begin the ritual 'check-check-1-2-3-4' I'd gotten so used to hearing from hanging out with all my musician-friends and lovers.

But he went further: as Darren fiddled with one particularly wonky mic connection—it sounded muffled and mid-rangy, very different in coloration from the other two mics—Rick began making odd simian-like grunts.

Darren chuckled. "Oh, boy. Not ape-has-killed-ape."

"Ex-cuse me?"

"You'll see."

Rick said into the microphone: "Ape has killed ape." Heads turned. "APE HAS KILLED APE," he shouted, causing the mic to feed back a little. Darren laughed again, knowing and satisfied. He said into his own mic, which Rick could hear through the stage monitors, "Okay, got it, monkey man."

But Rick kept chattering and making odd sounds. He beat his chest. He screamed into the mic, a high, desperate chimp-like war cry. Rick began monkey-walking back and forth across the front of the stage. Everyone standing around on Wateree Avenue there in the heart of the Old Market, cops and bums and musicians and beer vendors, were standing silently watching Rick Wragg.

Darren had stopped laughing. "Wragg always takes a joke too far."

"I'm concerned about his drinking," I blurted.

Darren grunted his own simian click of approbation. "Word to that. But Rick, he's no alcoholic. He just likes to drink too much. Big, big diff."

Well meaning folks had said that about me, too. I knew different.

Onstage, Rick had swung down by one arm, shrieking and beating his chest with his free hand, before dropping to the ground and rejoining us, high-fiving a homeless man who'd been boozily swaying on his feet at the end of the stage, an unheard symphony of inebriation buzzing inside his grizzled head. Rick went over to the beer wagon, bought two Bud Lights, handed one to the guy.

As Rick started back over toward me, I went to the other side of the street, to the Starbucks where I got a 'tall' blazing hot coffee that tasted so burnt and bitter that I poured most of it out into the storm drain. After a few overly loud rock music numbers, I begged Marcy to leave, but she refused, and I went home alone that night, like I had all week now.

I'd been swapping emails with Dev off and on for most of a day when he finally called, but I had to let it go to voicemail—I'd been breathlessly summoned down to the television studio to sit as an expert witness about the arts community's attitude toward the governor's yearly assault on the budget of all such activities, a demand made by her own ideological base more than a true mandate from the populace at large. Or so I would argue.

One more favor to Leora's ghost—I hoped she'd become a member of the grateful dead for all this standing-in I'd consented to do in her honor and memory.

The producer from the station told me what was expected of me: to discuss the arts budget situation live, yadda yadda; sure sure, I said. I put her on speaker and switched over to message mode, where I texted Dev that I'd be on TV later, and would call back after that. I rang off with the news producer, then sent Dev the text. If he were calling, it must have been important.

I felt beleaguered. I'd been drinking coffee and writing all afternoon. Plus, school started back in a week, and I had an extra class this term—Modern American Lit, a snoozer full of disinterested kids satisfying a requirement, and nothing like when my fiction workshops brim with curious, ambitious would-be scribes.

And . . . on top of that rigmarole, the ramp-up to the DDC concert. How fortunate I am.

And I mean that—I feel a part of this community again. A part of life. Maybe one of my students will be inspired by a work of great literature, and become a writer.

Even better: simply become a better human being, no matter what trade they ply.

Twenty harried minutes later I pulled up to the station, WKNO. Getting out of the car I noted two large black SUVs like in those DEA caravans you see with people of color pulled over on I-95. A couple of guys in suits, hanging around.

Security detail? For whom?

I'd barely gotten a hot foot into the lobby when met and grabbed by the arm by the producer, Cassie Kilbourne, a woman of Feebee's generation possessing a pinched, crooked posture; a dangling laminate; and a harried, hollow-eyed look on a face gray with stress.

"Mr. Beauchamp, you are a prince for coming at the last second like this. As I said on the phone, Leora Wood-Cobb had been scheduled to debate the governor's spokesperson. Somebody really dropped the ball on this."

"I'd say so—she's been dead for two months."

"The issue kept getting tabled in the legislature—the vote's coming up this week, however. Hey, that's TV news, right? It's all last minute."

"I can see that written on your face." I said this in a soothing purr. "We'll be fine."

"Aw," Kilbourne replied, relaxing her stiff posture. "You vibed me, there. That was very 'Dude' of you."

"Pardon?"

"*The Big Lebowski?*"

"Sorry?"

"The Coen Brothers movie? The Dude?"

I told her I hadn't seen it; she replied 'never mind' and swept me back toward the studio, where she said the governor was already in makeup.

"Wait wait wait," I sputtered, digging in my heels. "The governor?"

"Yes—you're going to debate Governor Three-Rivers." Sheepish. "It was supposed to be Rudy Hoonigan"—the governor's spokesperson—"but the issue was so important that . . . well. The big gun came out."

"Guns, indeed: I feel ambushed. I'm not sure—"

"You'll be fine."

I'd completely misunderstood—I wasn't merely going on TV to offer pithy opinions on what I thought about the government's role in funding organizations like the arts council. I was here to debate the governor, the figurehead for an entire movement that'd sworn to cut and gut any such lefty quality-of-life nonsense like the arts. To her and her fellow culture warriors, the arts promoted dangerously untenable ideals like providing material support for the purposes of facilitating free expression.

As for me: besides being a writer, I'd grown up around two people, my parents, who hated the Baptists and the small-minded backwoods preachers who perceived books and ideas and art as a threat, who in the modern age had manifested as would-be theocrats pushing a wildly anti-American agenda. I had to temper that kind of thinking. I didn't want to come off as particularly partisan and argumentative. That's how an ideologue debates. I wanted to be a man of ideas.

I took a deep breath. My mind felt sharp. I was glad now it'd been a surprise, this television appearance. I didn't have time to overthink my position.

On the set, I immediately loathed the looming, hot lights. Local TV stations had exceedingly tiny studios, room enough only to build the anchor desk and hang a green screen for the weatherperson. WKNO happened to produce a longtime local daytime talk show, *Midlands Magazine,* from a separate set tucked into the opposite corner, a miniature version of the standard *Tonight Show* format with a host's desk and a couple of chairs for guests.

There, the governor, all red dress and long, bare legs and pearls and bleach-blonde hair. Some Native American. Three-Rivers and the bubble-headed anchor, Cynthia-Anne Goforth, cut from the same cloth. I could see in their sparkling, nonintellectual eyes that they'd already colluded, and likely planned to triangulate and assassinate me on television.

I wouldn't let them. I couldn't. My colleagues were all depending on me to articulate the necessity of funding COPA.

Once the red light of the camera opened and my turn to speak came, I began to expound:

"If," I pondered, "we as a people agree that it's morally correct to find money for all manner of depraved and deadly imperialistic behaviors, by the same token oughtn't the collective we finding within our pocketbooks enough generosity to fund a few community arts grants out of that same, general pot of taxpayer monies? Oughtn't such aesthetic concerns be worth consideration? Indeed, I fear that holding the opposite opinion displays a pernicious shortsightedness, and smacks of an abject failing of government rather than the deft execution of what most of us regard as a primary duty, in this case in the form of the promotion of the general welfare, i.e., happiness of the population over which they hold sway and are hence responsible." I continued, leaning back and bugging my eyes like William F. Buckley, a childhood hero and expert wielder of the rhetorical zinger. "What sort of happiness—um—ought we to pursue with all of our—um—wealth and security? In short, I think it's safe to say that of all the many complex and enriching facets of modern life, conveniences and technologies that give us access to what is essentially the whole of human knowledge, the personal expression afforded us by art-making is—arguably, of course—a large and significant aspect of what makes *life itself worth living*. Indeed, I daresay that some philosophers might agree that making art could possibly represent the entirety of our reason for being on this rock hurtling through the void. The highest expression of our innate divinity."

Silence. Dead air. "And so on," I managed to conclude.

"But this mo-ney thing," Governor Three-Rivers sniped in her annoyingly nasal bleat, with her little uh-huh affectation coloring every possible break in her train of thought, "it simply ain't happening. Nope. There's no there-there. And if there's no there-there, it ain't happening. I don't hate the arts, Mr. Bo-champ. Nuh-uh. But in the face of the other problems our little state suffers, we can't afford them—none of us can."

"What we can't afford is to trample on the arts," I insisted. "What is life supposed to be like? Going to market and buying things and going home and watching television shows about the things we've bought? You know," I leaned forward, "what is money, anyway? How is its worth determined, Governor? *What is money*," I demanded. "What does it mean?"

"Oh, ha ha, nuh-uh." The Governor, smiling and wagging a nail. "Nobody's going over to hippy-dippy la-la-land. We're saying there's no there-there, and that's that. End of story. I urge the legislature to do the right thing by the taxpayers who elected me, and uphold my veto of the arts budget."

Wrenching my body in the uncomfortable chair and taking a breath, I found I had no time to reply:

"Well! That's that, as the Governor says," the host chirped. "We want to thank both Governor Three-Rivers, as well as South Carolina's own Cortland Beauchamp, author and educator. And now, back to the sports desk for the preview of the big game this weekend . . ."

That's that, indeed.

Walking out ahead of me, Three-Rivers leaned over whispering to her aide-de-camp, a young woman in a plaid skirt with thick ankles and glasses who I later found out was the Governor's seventeen year-old niece, working as a 'paid consultant' to the governor of this no-money state. Ah, Shameless Sandy, they called her—there'd been no end to the nepotistic gifts and grants she'd handed out to family and supporters alike. But it was too late, and if I'd brought such hypocrisy up on camera, to what end?

No there-there. Nuh-uh.

Outside on the sidewalk, only half a block from where I'd snubbed her following Leora's funeral, I tried to dance away from the Governor's entourage, but it was too late, and the chubby teenage aide-de-camp came huffing and puffing after me.

"My aunt—I mean, the governor—would like a *wuh*-word with you," she wheezed.

"Would she, now?" Even as much as I loathed the woman and all for which she stood, I couldn't say no. Could I? "Um."

Echoing my thoughts: "Do you really need to think about this? *It's the governor.*"

I ambled over to the black SUV next to which the security detail stood clustered around the chief exec of the state. A black man with a head the size of one of the Mount Rushmore carvings held up a hand to stop me, but was shooed away by the governor, who broke into a grin.

"Come with me, Mr. Bo-champ."

I couldn't hide my animus. "And what, pray tell, are the charges?"

"Now, now," taking my arm. "Don't be like that. Think of this as a date."

"*Pardon?*"

"Hush. Relax."

Her face hardened and she barked orders. "I'm going back to the office at the dome. We're walking."

Bustling commenced and the entourage piled into the SUV, which crept behind us the entire three blocks to the green-glowing capitol building, holding a kind of ghostly, eerie grandeur in the encroaching Carolina nighttime of this ordinary Tuesday.

"I appreciate ya sparring with me back there. Uh-huh. Good stuff."

"You—appreciate it?"

"Sure I do. You can't just have a message, Cortland. You have to have something to oppose. Ya can be for stuff all day long, but you gotta be against something, too. Get it? You understand?"

I told her that I did, more or less. "But, Madam Governor, you can't really believe some of those things you say. About the arts not really mattering." She started to speak, but it was my turn to cut off someone else. "I don't disbelieve you about the money part, and in theory, you're probably right—if we can't pay for it, then maybe we shouldn't do it. But you don't really believe that all we need to do is go and shop and build and buy and consume. Do you? Isn't there a higher ideal that art inspires us to? A higher truth?"

"Sure, sure. Me and my husband, we loved Spoleto this year. Concerts, plays, whole bit. We support the arts. But it's who I am right now that I have to say those things. And I believe 'em—oh, sure I do! But I believe what I believe as a certain means to an end, and if your way of looking at things was the prevailing way to go, then I'd probably be waving a banner around like you people did at the State House over here," gesturing with a manicured index finger and referencing a rally that'd been held last week on the grounds, one I missed because I'd been so caught up in writing. "That was a real good showing."

"Well, that's a terribly predatory and manipulative attitude for an ostensible leader of the people—"

"Please, sir. We aren't children," she admonished with the same long-nailed finger as before. "But in any case, I didn't ask you on this walk to go through all that hoo-haw all over again. Nuh-uh. No, I sure didn't . . ."

An awkward beat. The sounds of light traffic passing us, a siren wailing from far down the long hill to the bridge across the river. "You know we burned our bridges trying to keep Sherman's troops from taking the city. A last ditch effort to forestall what everyone had been hearing: that the general was coming here with one aim in mind—to burn the seat of secession. Burn it to the ground."

"Which they did."

"You a student of history much?"

"I would hope so."

"What do you think about Simms? His legacy?"

A long beat. "I'm embarrassed to say you've got me."

"William Gilmore Simms?"

She snapped her fingers. "The mayor of Columbia. During the Civil War."

I shook my head. "A writer. Like me. He wrote and published the account of the burning, in a newspaper called the *Columbia Phoenix*. Among other accomplishments."

"Right; right. I remember now."

But of course she didn't. Few outside the classroom, or inside, for that matter, would. Poor old unrepentant Southern landowner. All that work, all those words, languishing. Too late to do anything about it now. And certainly not with this airhead. This phony.

I asked her what, then, she wished to discuss, because I certainly hadn't a clue so far.

"Okay, okay. I was the one who asked them to get you to debate me tonight. I felt that you were a worthy person to articulate a usefully opposing viewpoint from my own position, yes; but also because I have a favor to ask of you, one that I hope you'll consider with all due—consideration."

"Lay it on me."

"If you'll take Wood-Cobb's place on the arts council. Run COPA for me."

Flummoxed; panicky. "But . . . aren't you trying to do away with COPA?"

She scoffed and bade me to cross the street onto the capitol grounds. We walked underneath the giant magnolias and around the statue of old Jimmy Burns sitting there in a set of judges' robes, his back to the city and keeping a trained eye on them venal rascals in that State House.

"I don't want to shut COPA down. Didn't you listen to anything I said? 'Something to oppose.' Besides, the legislature, they'll overturn my vetoes. They do every time. It doesn't hurt me—it only makes me the underdog. You really don't know much about politics, do you?"

"Not as such."

"Then you'll be perfect for this."

"There have to be simply scads of people vastly more qualified. And of your same political persuasion."

"Oh, where's the fun in that? And yes, I can think of three or four people here in town, or at Southeastern, or down in Charleston, or in the upstate who'd be much, much better—certainly people who've supported me politically. But listen to you, you old South Carolina smoothie. Lord have mercy," she mocked. Despite claiming heritage here, her accent from a career in broadcast journalism came flatter than the thin hoecake batter my grandmother used to pour onto the sizzling breakfast griddle. "You argue the case well. You not only held your own on TV, you had me for breakfast, lunch, and dinner! I got a haircut live on TV just now—oy! You are fearless. Go for it, Cortland! Be all you can be. You know how to put a good spin on stuff—that's ninety percent of the battle right there. Put a buff and a polish on the words."

"Well . . . it is my training and vocation to do so."

"See? But more importantly and seriously, dude? Time to give something back. I know how you felt about Leora. I heard you talk about her at the funeral, remember?"

I did.

"And it pays well," a confidential whisper. "More than teaching at Edgewater Technical College. I'd bet."

"Really, now. I thought money was tight?"

"It is. No way you'd be starting at Leora's salary. Jesus, she'd been there forever."

Money, eh? Nevertheless, I said in so many words, I don't know 'bout none of this mess. "Seems like this would be a better job for someone like Feebee Elmendorf, with PR experience."

No time for further debate. She checked her phone, got a naughty smile, fired off a text, again found my eyes. "Sleep on it. Don't say no; don't say yes. I'll be in touch."

She shook my hand and strode away toward the copper dome, her security detail appearing out of the shadows and spiriting her inside the old building, which managed to survive the burning back in 1865 only because the damn thing hadn't been finished yet. The boys in blue had gotten their licks in anyway—brass stars marked the spots where the cannonballs had been fired from across the Congaree at the under-construction edifice, ammo lobbed from somewhere nearby Rick Wragg's remodeled old West Columbia saltbox. Simms had been watching over it all, horrified and sick, and not even knowing that his own plantation, Woodlands, had already burned. Also a historian, Simms's library of ten-thousand volumes, gone. Imagine watching Columbia burn, then going home to check on things.

Maybe he couldn't disavow the Confederacy and his way of life because he'd seen it taken away in such a brutal manner, and being unmindful of Eastern concepts like karma might likely have sustained grudges, and this despite being on the clearly wrong side of history. Simms had endured many tragedies, after all, both personal and career related. Many triumphs along the way, but at what cost. He'd lost a few children to disease and accidents. Certainly the loss of the city and his home must have paled compared to losing one of your own progeny.

Certain? How would I know how it felt? I'd sired no children to lose.

Few people may remember Simms these days, but then again, most of them probably don't know about February 17, 1865, either, and none of us know in the way that Simms did. We can't imagine it. I barely can, and I've done some research, yea and verily.

Maybe that's why I had been blocked for so long on my historical novel. Too much distance from the past. A good thing in the case of slavery, and the war, and the burning of Columbia.

Cupping my hands: "Madam Governor? Thanks for the dialogue tonight."

Her voice echoed back across the hallowed grounds of governance. "You betcha. Let's grab lunch. I got an idea for a book I'd love to lay on you ..."

Folks in my circle may have called her the Soda City Saboteur for her stand on arts funding, but in that moment, I knew she wasn't truly a threat. Such an unserious person couldn't possibly change everyone's lives in such a negative manner.

Could she?

Nothing like what William Tecumseh Sherman had pulled. He'd been the real saboteur.

Hadn't he?

Who could really know what happened that night? Simms? Emma LeConte? I supposed their accounts would have to serve.

I didn't know what was more annoying, finding out that the governance of the state was but a game to this vapid child who'd finagled her way into a position of leadership, or that I now had to decide whether to take this actual job and quit teaching and probably put writing projects on hold that were only now beginning to simmer on the creative stovetop. Or maybe the fact that I now had to walk all the way back to my car, on feet that ached, in my oldest and scruffiest pair of Weejuns, soles so worn they'd all but developed holes. No wonder Cynthia-Anne Goforth's eyes kept flitting down, her nose wrinkling with disdain. If I were about to become a politician, I supposed I'd better buy myself a couple of new suits, as well as a new pair of shoes.

7.

The double date—Freddie Baumbach, Feebee, Marcy, and me—came off a disaster, and the beginning of the end of my relationship with my lover. I thought that I'd met Freddie's wife at Marcy's mother's house, but it was whispered to me that with a separation now in effect, in the interim Freddie had begun dating Feebee.

My, how fast things changed.

Marcy had told me her brother had had all sorts of problems, many alcohol related, but felt happy and grateful now, not only to be alive, but to be involved in the arts in Columbia: Freddie, a one-time aspiring filmmaker, now in theatrical exhibition as director of the Main Street Bijou, the city's art house cinema.

The two ex-addicts at the table shared a condensation-dripping, large bottle of Pellegrino; the girls, a bottle of Sauvignon Blanc that held no attraction for this reformed red-wine aficionado.

"Hey," nudging Marcy, her beak buried in the iPhone. "Ground control to Baumbach."

Distracted, not looking up. "Yep?"

"Hey—I'm somewhere over in this direction."

"Oh, sorry. It's just that it's Dev. About the demos."

Freddie and Feebee, neither of whom had been told about Marcy's recording sessions, both started chattering with questions and excitement. Once Marcy filled them in, both her brother and his date had to pick up their jaws from the floor.

"*You're going to make it,*" Feebee fairly screamed. "Duncan Devereaux is producing your album? Oh, my god—you're going to make it."

"He says he thinks so, too." She blinked back tears. "But I'm not making an album, only as a songwriter. Selling the songs to somebody else."

Not certain why Marcy was crying—happiness, yes, but something else was going on. "Songwriting royalties on a hit record are nothing to sneeze at."

Feebee held her hands together, prayerful. "Oh-my-god. This is unbelievable."

Freddie raised his glass of mineral water. "Congrats, sissy."

Right then, our buddy Rick Wragg came reeling across the dining room with a city councilman and a member of the planning commission in tow, all three with noses redder than that of a famous Christmas reindeer. Thanks to their descent upon our table, we didn't get back to Marcy's demos until later, and with a personal plot turn that I already saw coming. A big one.

Marcy confessed to me what else had been going on: not only had Dev offered to produce an eventual record for her, but as she'd discovered in the course of their emails and texting and Facetiming, they possessed a real rapport.

"Dev has tons of musical ideas for me."

"Does he, now." I could see the train a-coming. "Collaborators."

"It's a pretty common method of writing songs."

"I've heard of such endeavors. Gilbert and Sullivan, Bacharach and David, Jagger and Richards . . . and quite unlike novels. More of a solitary endeavor."

"Yeah. More solitary." She chewed her lip. "Dev wants me to come back down to the island."

"That—you should come."

"To work on the demos."

"Not us," I clarified. "You . . . alone."

"Only for a week or so. He's busy with his book, too. Amazing guy, really."

"I don't disagree."

Without turning it all into one of those scenes, blurting out my hurt and jealousy and deep-seated notion that they'd fallen for one another, I instead gave her my blessing, though with one proviso: persuade the damn guy to get over himself and get his traumatized rock-star ass up here for the sodding ceremony. If she wouldn't mind employing their so-called rapport at full strength.

The final meeting of the DDC took place at the familiar library conference room; back where it all began.

In the planning of the concert and unveiling, the CityArt festival tragedy remained close on everyone's mind, especially Rick's ex–rigging partner Darren, who'd been the first to suggest that the show take place there in the street right next to the unveiling of the street art, and this despite the calamity of the prior stage collapse.

Honestly, I was surprised that Glimmer Twins would be doing the sound reinforcement for the concert—could that possibly look good to an outside observer, using the same company whose work had fallen, when people had been injured and so on and so on? And yet the idea of replacing them had never been discussed, not by Feebee, nor Darren, nor any of us. GT had been a part of the DDC from the git-go; they had the gig. Or rather, he, Darren, had the gig.

Rick. I wondered how he was doing. I hoped to holy heck he wasn't slip-sliding down into a worse pattern of drinking than I'd observed, and over which I'd confronted him—at the restaurant with the others he'd been as potted as a houseplant. Kept apprised by the odd email reports from Cadence, I knew that his dad's work on his music club was continuing apace.

As for the placement of the stage, Darren summed up: "I think what we need to do is take back the streets from that bad juju that messed us up last time—we'll have an alternate venue lined up in case of inclement weather, but I still don't see needing McNabb Arena. But if you want it in that atrocious-sounding tin can, I can rig it. The price will be accordingly higher."

Feebee had been the first to come around, nodding and say, yes-yes, of course, of course, the concert should be on Main Street. "But some of us are hoping, still, to have Duncan's participation," she reminded the table, fixing her lovely eyes on me. "That's why I keep bringing up a larger venue."

My mind wandered. I'd been consumed, of course, by the governor's offer, as I had by the recent breakup with Marcy, but I snapped into fully felt embarrassment: I'd let everyone down, now exponentially complicated on a personal level by the cooling Marcy sitch, as Rick might have put it. I hadn't produced our rock star for the committee, though the lovely note he'd emailed about sanctioning the project had lifted everyone's spirits.

It's not my place to further pester him, I explained to the committee members. The man had said he wanted to be left alone to write—how could I work against such a wish? Dev had some chops. His book was a winner. He should be left to his art, which right now doesn't happen to be music. I'd said as much to both bodies—the DDC, as well as Marcy's hot torso, in bed with her before the revelation about going to Sedge Island, when I had advised resisting the urge to bother Dev about her demos.

Our last moments of intimacy. Knew it before I knew it. Call it writer's intuition.

How I will carry with me those bittersweet memories of my summer with Marcy Baumbach, and that last night as I lay whispering against the warm, toned flesh of her abdomen, advising her as I had already to allow moldy, untenably adolescent desires for fame and glory to pass away. To revel in the moment—this moment, every moment. To accept that abundance might just be at hand. And in the meantime, to go on writing more songs, which she hadn't done all year. For herself. Not for posterity—to please herself. That's the true secret source of all successfully creative energy. To see if we can meet our own expectations.

"Express yourself completely, then become quiet," I murmured, semi-quoting the Mitchell translation of the Tao. "Invest in the fullness of now."

She had huffed and muttered and gotten up out of bed, went to get in the shower.

I'd gotten up to go make coffee, smelled woodsmoke, stared out the kitchen window into the deep dim woods, sighed. Like I said, I knew: that had been the last time we'd made love.

The truth was, Marcy herself could now probably talk Dev into coming up here—she'd left for Sedge Island two days before the DDC meeting. She had wept and apologized. Said her heart was full of me, sort of, but that Dev felt real—yeah; it wasn't just about the demos, there was a spark there—and so she had to go.

Okay.

I guess I understood she was breaking up with me, but I didn't at first. Not until she was driving away.

No wave. A goodbye nice and final.

I got it.

Ouch.

OUCH.

"But of course." Feebee, bringing me back down to Earth. "We still might see an appearance onstage by Mr. Devereaux—right, Cort?"

I nodded, sour and sad for myself. "Oh, anything that can be imagined's possible. We just shouldn't *advertise* that it's possible. Nothing worse than promising something you can't deliver—which I try to avoid doing."

The assembled membership seemed to sigh in unison, a pall of disappointment hanging in the air like a blue haze of back-room cigar smoke.

The discussion went on, then, among the live music aficionados and the superfan, Gendry Lizette, about who should perform: other Columbia bands who'd been working the circuit alongside Devereaux back in the 80s? Current local acts? A mix? I hadn't a clue, and sat mute.

Decisions: A talent booker would be consulted; personal calls would be made. Many of those same musicians from the early days, it was reported by Gendry, were still around, some still playing in various guises, others having moved on. Darren mentioned a band called The Prognosticators, a fixture around the city for ages. They sounded to me like a Vegas magic act. My shoulders were aching from shrugging about it all.

Adjournment. Feebee called my name as I exited the library; a final set of marching orders.

"You've taken it this far." Feebee, gripping my arm and grinding her nails into my sport coat the way Marcy used to dig her nails into my back. "Get Duncan Devereaux."

"Sounds like a good title for a spy thriller."

"I'm not joking, and I'm not making up a plot for one of your novels." Desperate, her eyes moist. "I need this to be big. To work. Leora would want it this way."

I snapped. The voice that came out sounded very much like that of an irascible grandmother I had on my mother's side, a Depression-era, no-nonsense woman who rarely suffered fools. "I wish you people would stop invoking her name to get something out of me—don't you realize how important she was to me? How close? Leora is not a symbol for you people to wield like a cudgel every time you want a piece of Cort Beauchamp. Like family: I lost a family member. Damn your selfish asses."

Feebee's mouth dropped open. She held up her small, manicured hands. "Hold on hold on hold on—if you don't want to help, that's fine. But I'm not trying to manipulate you. I'm just asking. But if you weren't going to follow through, you should've quit coming to the meetings."

Chastened and chagrined. My outburst had made heads turn, including the homeless men from the park and across the street who wiled away their days with nothing better to do but hang around the Gospel Mission or the library, bless their hearts. At least they were readers. "I'll see. I'll do my best—and I'm sorry. Feebee, I've let you—"

Feebee put a finger to her lips, gave me a hug. "My big smart sweet writer. Now go and call Duncan Devereaux for me, angel. Pretty please." She kissed me full on the lips, and for a split second there seemed to be heat in the air between us . . . then she darted down the escalator and out the sliding doors, off to another meeting.

As well established, I hate being given assignments, I like setting my own agenda and pace. Why else would I have wanted to become a writer?

Other reasons, certainly. I'd been an only child, ambling around those woods and fallow fields on what'd once been a working, quasi-plantation. I wondered how many slaves my people had owned. I wondered if they'd worked as hard as Feebee had been trying to work me. Not to mention this foolishness from the Governor about my taking Leora's place. Forget it.

But how ridiculous, my hectoring voice of conscience intoned, *this comparison of yourself to a whipped field hand*. From whence this petulance and whining, I ask, within an educated, fifty-year-old white man, who despite some familial drama and personal foibles has had every opportunity handed to him and every dream come true, however modestly realized? Now we were getting down to some true foolishness indeed.

I wandered the stacks downstairs on the ground floor—fiction. I touched spines and read jackets and first and sometimes second pages. These days I read mostly on the iPad, but I will always enjoy walking around the library, pulling volumes from the shelves, smelling them, feeling the weight of them. Will never grow out of the pleasure of cracking open a brand new volume, or a signed, first edition at the Book Expo or an antique mall. And as for those devices, of course innumerable books exist that haven't been converted for e-readers, and may never be, like many more books, films, and recordings that have already been lost to time. Forever.

We need our libraries. We need them more than we need new books written by punters like me, probably.

That evening, I got up enough courage to Facetime with Dev.

After uncomfortable small talk, and feeling guilty over the Marcy deal—or so I believed I could tell—he not only agreed to perform at the unveiling of the monument in the new arts district, but also that this would also be the world premiere of the songs making up the centerpiece of his new album.

"Tremendous news. You're a regular factory outlet of creativity."

"I feel inspired."

"I'm sure."

"So maybe it's time for me to show my face."

Why now? I asked, staring at the iPad's Retina-display image of the angular and thoughtful Duncan. He leaned out of frame, long fingers splayed on top of his shorn head, came back. "Why anybody does anything—feels right. Right time. Right moment."

"Marcy's got some terrific material." Holding his gaze. "Doesn't she?"

"Truly. We'll—we'll be playing some of her songs, if she'll let me."

Her dreams, coming true. No wonder she'd left me with such haste. "How wonderful. I can't thank you enough for everything," forcing the corners of my mouth into some semblance of a smile before ringing off.

A hero I'll be after all, but at a serious personal cost. No one ever need know that juicily little sordid detail, however, except for the participants, whose names and characters will be duly disguised in the fictionalized version, coming soon to a word processor or Moleskine notebook near you.

8.

But then it didn't work out, not at all: the afternoon of the unveiling, a shiny blue DVD that FedEx delivered included, as Dev explained in an email that'd popped up on the iPad about the same time, a heartfelt, personal thank you from him to the people of Columbia, as well as an in-studio performance of material both new and established.

Desperately uncool news: he wouldn't be appearing after all; that he couldn't come up with the right energy, his chakras were blocked, some such nonsense.

I felt ill.

Hope no one's 2 disappointed, he wrote. *But I just can't.*

"No one will be disappointed by any of it," I said aloud, fumbling around and typing out a response on the virtual keypad. "No, Devereaux. Not at all."

Feebee and the rest of them had put together quite the shindig, the whole of Main Street shut down and many thousands of people milling around waiting for the show and the sculpture. Meanwhile, I hung out down the block in an old spot, Opal's bar, but not up to my old tricks: all afternoon I'd been quaffing iced tea and scribbling madly in a fresh Moleskine into which I'd broken to begin the next round of notes on REVIVAL . . . and maybe some actual text.

"What have we here?" Opal, emerging from a confab in her office with Doober Dougie and Mandy Polk-Richardson, who already had on their VIP laminates dangling from lanyards.

I shut the notebook. "Just writing somebody a love letter."

Opal's eyes, sparkling. "Poor Feebee—she's vomiting blood over this stormy weather forecast."

"*Excuse me?*" It felt as though a giant exclamation mark must've appeared over my head—earlier the forecast had been stellar, calm winds and clear. "What weather forecast?"

She punched me in the arm. "Just yanking your chain."

I let out my breath. "Oh—thank god."

Her hand, lingering on my bicep. Everyone laughed. Mandy and Dougie decamped, laminates swinging.

Fingers, tracing the line of my linen sport coat. "Oh—Cort. So sorry about Marcy."

"What's all this, then," I asked in skepticism. "You heard?"

"I heard." The weight of her hand. Lingering. Moving up to touch my face. "You poor brokenhearted writer of mine."

Her eyes, two pools of affection. I knew; I'd seen this before.

I told Opal that if she kept up her caressing, we risked the appearance of a naughty protrusion.

"Maybe that's what I want to happen?" A question; a little frown. "It's been on my mind."

"Since when?"

"Since Marcy stole you. Away from me."

"I didn't know you wanted me."

She shrugged. "I was biding my time."

"*Why didn't you say something?*"

Another shrug. "It's complicated."

Our voices in whispers, our bodies close, we debated the merits of this confession. Our lips, closer.

As she took me by the hand, the debate ended: Opal stood on tiptoes and kissed me behind the ear, on the lobe, and on around to my now damp and quivering lips. The medical condition I'd predicted occurred with a vengeance.

As we grasped one another, a deep, pulsating vibration carried through the floor and into my body, which I realized represented the soundcheck from Darren's massive stage he'd erected around the corner on Main Street. The first band would be playing in just over two hours, after the unveiling, the speeches, and the playing of the DVD on the projection screen stretched across the front of the Netbank building.

None of which I cared about—Opal's tongue had found its sexy way into my mouth.

"I missed you." Slurping, wet kisses more delicious than her food. "So much."

I explained that I had as well, even if I hadn't quite realized it until that moment.

"In my office," breathy and urgent. "Hurry."

I held my Moleskine in front of my protrusion as we hurried through the empty, mid-afternoon bar and into her office behind the rear dining room, probably where the fire chief had shuffled his papers in the days when the building had been a firehouse back in the early part of the twentieth century. Buttons, zippers, clasps. A pulsing warmth inside me, and then me inside her. Objects falling off her desk.

Holding my gaze throughout the lovemaking, furious and intense. A rightness, there between us. I'd felt this the first time around, until we'd both convinced ourselves that it wasn't working, that we were too different, that our musical tastes—Opal had been a punk rock aficionado, after all—were too divergent. But here, as she stroked my face and I kept myself inside the throbbing pocket of her exquisite womanness (he wrote in a contest-worthy instance of purple prose), I felt a union with Opal D'Alessandro that seemed so genuine and nurturing and wholesome that a word and a thought formed, and my erection held itself and even redoubled:

More, came the word.

MORE.

"Oh, my."

Yes, as I explained. Then, I showed her. She gritted her teeth, ground against me.

Opal gripped me with every available body part. A pulsating magnificence. A sublime moment. Building. Our gaze locked, glimmers and reflections from the overhead fluorescent tubes like shimmering starlight in her eyes.

"Opal—how I've missed this. How I—"

"Shut up. Would you?"

"Yes, ma'am."

But interrupted: Trousers in a pile around my ankles, Opal with one delicate tattooed ankle up on my shoulder and biting the back of her hand to stifle cries of slippery, incipient release, the door flew open and slammed against the wall, causing an overloaded bulletin board to clatter to the floor: Feebee, entering in a bustle. "Opal oh my god you're not going to believe what's hap—*AIEEEEEEEEEE!*"

We all froze.

Snapping into motion, Feebee whirled and exited, banging shut the door. But lingering outside, sounding chastened. "Oh, guys, I'm so, so sorry. But I've simply got to tell you the news."

"Five minutes!" I shouted, not caring, refusing to give up the moment. "If you please."

"Yeah, for fuck's sake—can it like goddamn fucking wait, Feebee?" Opal started thrusting up against me, whispering, "Come on, big boy."

"But guys—it's Duncan Devereaux. He just pulled up in a black SUV. He's here. Cort, you did it. He's here. So, hurry up and come. Both of you!" Her high heels clip-clopped away at double time across the hardwoods of the restaurant dining room.

We collapsed against one another in laughter, now, rather than passion. But despite the occasion we weren't done with all that, no. I reached across and locked the door, and afterwards we finished, joyfully and lovingly, in a manner befitting two old friends falling back into lust, if not something more.

9.

The word got out, or perhaps the general public had gotten the inkling from all the press in which the unanswered question of Dev's appearance had come up in virtually every article and TV news story, but downtown Columbia fairly teemed with people, thousands. Because of the 40DD heavy metal career, the crowd possessed a decidedly biker and good old boy edge; but overall, and due to the nature of the other acts on the bill—a hip-hop duo who'd recently broken out on a major label, a pop songstress like a younger Marcy who'd recently gone to Nashville in the hopes of getting a contract, Opal's brother Tony's jamband paying tribute to the hippie element, and the Prognosticators doing their bit with what was described to me as the avant-garde music of its day—the throng seemed as diverse, and surprisingly well behaved, as one could have wanted.

Fresh from a sponge bath in the staff bathroom of the restaurant, Opal and I sat on the VIP dais across from the stage proper, watching as the guys in the Progs, as they introduced themselves, finished up their set with a tune called "Watcher of the Skies," a composition by a 70s rock band with a biblical-sounding name that escapes me.

Dev, with a sheepish Marcy in tow, had come over to the restaurant right as Opal and I were going to meet Feebee in the Netbank command center, the very place and piece of carpet on which poor, dear Leora had breathed her last breath while the storm had raged all around us. Opal bade the manager and chef to spare no flourish for the two guests of honor.

As president of the merchant's association, Opal thanked Dev for coming. Marcy and I took a moment off to the side.

"So—you and Opal back together?"

My cheeks flamed. I hoped Marcy couldn't smell the sex on me.

"That obvious?"

"An ex-girlfriend knows."

"Is that what we are? Exes? You never quite said."

"I suppose so, now."

"I see."

Now it became Marcy's turn to blush. She couldn't meet my eyes. "Dev's the one who admitted he'd fallen for me. All right? What did you want me to do?"

I told her I understood—the music connection was undeniable. "I only want the same thing I wanted before: for you to follow your heart. And to pursue your dreams. Now you've found the perfect way to do both."

"What must you think of me," she asked, glancing up through her long lashes and cute bangs with those eyes that'd so melted my heart. "I must seem like a whore."

"You see a way to realize your lifelong ambition in a way that I could never facilitate—how bad am I supposed to feel?" A coldness came over me—I did judge her. But I kept this to myself. "Truthfully, it wasn't working for me anyway, Marcy."

"Oh. I thought—"

"What?"

"Nothing."

Opal and Dev turned to rejoin the conversation. "Well, I guess we won't be playing the DVD, then?"

"Please do, if you would. Play that first. And then I'll play for you all."

As the Prognosticators exited, the lights dimmed, and Darren's crew reset the stage for the first public appearance by Duncan Devereaux in fifteen years. The crowd, ordered by concert emcee Doober Dougie to turn their attention to the large screen against the Netbank building.

En masse, thousands of people rotated ninety degrees, and the short program began. At the appearance onscreen of the gray-haired DD, the crowd gasped and cheered, thousands of hands fluttering in the air.

"I didn't know what this was about at first, or if I did, I didn't much care for it," he said from his videotaped position behind his home studio mixing board, in the chair where I'd once sat listening to Marcy sing. "But once a few people persuaded me that it wasn't just about me, or my relative fame or the records I sold or any of that bullcrud," to audience titters, "I said okay to this. By now you've seen the sculpture," gesturing somehow in the right direction at the wonderfully flowing, modernist metaphor for the waves and decibels of music that'd emanated from Columbia-based instruments and records and speakers and vocal cords. Words to this effect, uttered by Dev in a heartfelt and eloquent speech, caused even hirsute, fully grown biker types to weep into their beards and bandanas.

And then, Dev made Marcy Baumbach a local celebrity as well, by including footage tagged to his speech: the songbird, alone in his studio, singing one of her original songs, a beautiful and plaintive melody, whose lyrics conjured images of lost love—or what I had thought might be love. Burgeoning love. Maybe.

Marcy, sitting on the other side of Opal, screamed out at the sight of her disheveled appearance on the video. I watched Marcy watching herself, her protests melting into a face frozen not with mortification, but in awe: I could tell from the angle of her gaze that she looked not upon herself, but at the backs of the heads of the crowd all looking at her. A super on the image read:

COLUMBIA'S OWN, SINGER-SONGWRITER MARCY BAUMBACH

After the mellow song finished, the video faded out and the crowd cheered politely, somewhat confused by the sight of this unknown woman. Once Duncan Devereaux appeared from behind the curtained backdrop and announced, "You'll be hearing more from her soon," the crowd convulsed and screamed not for Marcy, but the hero they came to see play.

In this moment, on that wave of adulation, I saw the point of it all, and the DDC's work became complete in a way I could understand: the completion of our task felt not unlike the coming together of a long novel, one on which you'd been working all summer, but only at the moment of ultimate culmination—you've finished a draft!—do you come out of your long dream of creativity, realizing that you've done something with your time and toil to produce a book; a song; a painting; a play; a decent semester of teaching, with any luck inspiring your classroom of students.

And maybe, if you dare, to allow yourself to entertain the thought that someone else will one day appreciate what you've done, feel what you felt, and care about what happens in your story.

Here, the throngs shouted their veneration for Duncan Devereaux, projected their undying love upon him—no question, as Rick would put it. I felt some of that love, a roar and an energy that felt like a sentient, living being there on the street with us. Amazing. I wondered if my own characters, and their stories, had ever made anyone feel like the sound of Duncan's voice and guitar made this crowd. I cared not to dwell too long upon the possibility of such rarified glory. Not with Opal nearby.

Speaking of caring, and stories, and characters, the one who'd been such a part of the whole ball of narrative threads, Rick Wragg, had also been the most noticeably absent from the festivities—oh, he'd been included and invited, but Rick not only seemed to have descended into what I suspected were the relative depths of alcoholism, but paradoxically he'd also pressed ahead with his listening room, which he'd decided to call Congress Street Station.

All this I knew not first hand from Rick, of course, but from Cadence, who'd liked my 'Author' page on Facebook that my student Walid had helped me set up, and had begun sending me messages reporting on his father, about whom he'd become worried, he said. With the end of summer, Cadence had gone back to live with his mom in Virginia. I'd written back to say I'd reach out to Rick and check on him. He didn't call back.

On my way into Columbia to see Opal and attend what Feebee had called the DDC debriefing, I had an inkling that I ought to swing over to the site of Rick's club, that I'd find him there, and glory be, I did.

Pulling up to find him speaking with a grim-faced man in khakis and a plaid, shortsleeved, button-down shirt who wielded a clipboard and an iPhone, Rick shook my hand with his own bony claw, one that quivered. He explained that he'd come to meet with the gent, a city inspector who finished up his business in a quick consultation with Rick while I screwed around with my voice recorder, trying to remember an idea that'd come to me as I'd been making my drive over, but it'd slipped away. Happens.

"He looked like some sort of authority figure."

Rick shook his head. Described all manner of problems the building inspectors were giving him. "I'm in trouble. This's costing— shit. It's getting out of control."

"What's the principal issue?"

"It's a firetrap. Or was, till somebody got happy with the asbestos," an expensive problem to abate, especially for a building that will play host to the public. "I don't think this fucking thing is gonna fly."

"Ah—money. Ever the money issue."

"Don't tell me some story I already heard too many times, author. Money can—" He mimed an obscene gesture better imagined than described. "The other renovations alone—oh hell. Don't want to sound like I'm hitting ya up."

"Another location, maybe?"

Waved around, dismissive. "I don't know. I'm dropping back into Plan B or C mode. Thinking about going in with some guys to buy this joint over in the Old Market. Maybe get my foot in the hospitality door with a good old college beer bar."

"Not a music club?"

"We'll get around to the music. Shit-ton of money to be made from—"

"Selling booze? What about the listening room? What about—?"

"So," he blurted, ignoring the questions. "I heard the rumors going around. Oh, yeah—you're coming out of everything, just everything, stinking like a dang rose. Aren't you. A white rose, clean and pure and blue-ribbon number one winner and all that. The arts commissioner? What does that pay a year, to do nothing? Fuck. But me? Look around," spitting into the clay. "I got nothing, now. Devotion to a dream, devotion to a dream," a bitter mantra. "All a fairy tale."

I told him I was sorry—sorry about the club, as well as how of late I hadn't been a very good friend to him, or Cadence.

"That's the worst part. That kid talks about you all the time." Rick, popping a translucent green Listerine tab onto his tongue. "You got to make that up to him."

"And so I shall."

I asked him if he'd been writing, and he replied that yes, yes, despite being so busy getting this place up and running, he'd been working on some stuff, just as I'd advised him. That he'd looked over what I did to his 'Superfan' story, and liked it.

"You really edited the living Christ outta that. Didn't you."

"Intended not as an insult, Rick. Only a lesson in storytelling. In what to leave out."

"I get it; I feel ya. Appreciate the effort."

I wished him well, hoped that something one day came of the writing. He didn't know what the future held, gesturing to the red brick warehouse that now would continue to lie in crumbling slumber.

Before I pulled away I took a moment to tap out a Facebook message to Cadence that his dad seemed all right.

Cadence replied almost immediately with a sweet and hopeful message thanking me, which I read on my phone during the final, uneventful DDC meeting, one that Rick, a founding member, should have attended as well: all had worked out, no problems, no issues. A huge success, in fact. Duncan's appearance onstage did more than make his diehard fans happy for a news cycle or two: our efforts had put Columbia, South Carolina on the cultural radar screens, as Feebee put it, of the entire world.

Feebee grinned. "In other words, give yourselves a hand. Good job, committee."

We duly applauded ourselves, exchanged handshakes and hugs.

"Feebee, you should run for that open city council seat." Gendry Lizette, still beaming and shiny at having had her brush with stardom, said as we were gaveling ourselves out of existence as a committee. "Think of the bumper stickers."

"Now, don't give me any ideas."

"Feebee, consider me for the post of head speech writer," I offered. "Go for it."

"One Feebee to rule them all." Opal, slinging an arm around her colleague's neck and posing. She thumbed her iPhone to snap a grinning selfie of the two attractive women, both with thousand-watt smiles. "I can get behind this."

On the way out, we all made pledges to stay in touch. To think of other arts projects to benefit the city.

And done.

Like letting out a breath. Release; a cathartic drama drawing to its close.

Now, I thought, walking with Opal through the burgeoning boho arts district buzzing with activity, time to get fully back to my own work, continue my own contribution to letters. A mission, a charge to keep: get back to the writing, as well as a new projects surely to come along. Having projects in the pipeline makes one feel so industrious and useful, doesn't it? I know it does this writer. Feels like being alive.

EPILOGUE: REVIVAL

After almost a year of writing on not one but two novels—including, I'm happy to report, the burning of Columbia epic—I'm shocked one night to run into Marcy under the marquee of the Main Street Bijou, newly reopened following a successful renovation her brother Freddie oversaw during the fall and spring.

Killing time waiting for Opal to finish with her work at the restaurant, I shoved in my earbuds and went for one of my street-strolls, listening tonight to a succession of Chopin's nocturnes, a quiet, contemplative piano accompaniment for a twilight walk through downtown with its twinkling strings of lights in the trees, its museums and galleries and storefronts. Many new businesses. Maybe an investment in the arts pays off in more prosaic dividends than our esteemed governor seemed to believe.

As for the stroll, I needed to walk off the carbs. Now that we're married, Opal feeds me all too well. But 'twas ever thus.

I know, I know, that's all big news, as was running into Marcy, but first, a work update: my new novel called *Creative Class*, a romantic drama built around a rock singer and a poet and their circle of artistic peers, is undergoing a final edit for release next year by a small press eager to work with me. The central conflict of the book, see, is that female poet leaves the rock singer for another man who can further her career, a writer whose book is climbing the bestseller charts; the climax is their reconciliation, and an acknowledgement that true love rules, is more valuable than professional success and artistic validation, yadda yadda, because, if we don't have anyone with whom to stroll down sidewalks and country lanes alike, what do we have? Damn thing got me a new agent, who made a quick deal for essentially no money or PR support, which is how it goes these days. It's coming out this fall from a regional, independent publishing house of some renown and respect.

Back in the game. Not too shabby.

But in the modern, digital, DIY age, can't I be in my own game anytime I wish, rejection slips be damned? Of course I can. Anybody can.

Feels like freedom.

Traditional success, however, has blossomed for debut novelist Duncan Devereaux, whose novel has not only "dropped," as the kids say, to a certain degree of acclaim and wide sales—starred reviews in the trades; a headline notice in the *Review of Books*, as well as an interview—but he's already well into drafting the third episode in his series, and for which he's received a fat advance. So it goes: after the best selling *Retreat*, his prospects as a marquee writer name now seem limitless. Little twerp has the first sequel, *Savior Machine*, already in the hands of his editorial team.

But hey: I was not only warmly thanked in the acknowledgments, but best of all, asked to blurb. It's no joke—more readers have seen my blurb on his back cover than have ever thought about touching one of my own books. Win-win.

"So, it's a trilogy now," on the phone when I'd called about begging a reciprocal blurb for *Creative Class*.

"It's all three-fers nowadays."

"Weren't there eight Harry Potters?"

Duncan, musing. "I think it was eight movies, but only seven books."

"What happened to no sequel?"

He grunted, his soft and affected voice a touch modest. "I got talked into it."

We discussed erotic vampires and dystopian teenage romances and loglines and what publishers wanted; Duncan had finally figured out what I already knew: that he'd had a considerable advantage not because he was the greatest writer in history, but because he'd already been famous.

"If I'd been just some schmoe from Sedge Island—or Columbia—who'd written a rip-snorting good yarn, I doubt they'd have given it a second look."

"You wonder about that. South Carolina doesn't have that kind a reputation outside the region. Or maybe inside the region, either. But we've been at a disadvantage for a long time. Especially Columbia."

"How's that?"

"They burned us to the ground, Dev. They burned us to the ground. Made us pay, or so it sometimes feels, for an entire culture's worth of admittedly indefensible sins against humanity. And sometimes it seems as if they'll never let us forget slavery. But some of that is our own fault, I suppose. Those of us clinging to the old ways of thinking. The old prejudices. The order of secession was signed here in Columbia. We had some blood on our hands. Some responsibility for which we had to answer."

"I didn't enslave anybody. And I don't hold any prejudices—except maybe against myself."

I let his contemplative remark settle.

All we can do, I finally expounded, is to strive to rectify that for which we were burned asunder. Make art that speaks to the positive aspects of our co-created mutual reality, art that one hopes matters. Has something to say. That speaks not only to a notion of Southernness, no; instead, to illuminations of the universal human spirit and condition. Duncan grunted in assent, said that even if he didn't have time to read the novel—just joking, with a chuckle—he'd still be happy to blurb.

As for Marcy, I hadn't seen her since the week before Christmas, when her dear, wise mother had lost her long bout with cancer. The holidays: simply the saddest time to die, certainly, in the life of any American family. But at least she'd passed away peacefully, in her own bed, in her own time, surrounded by her pets. A graceful way to go, which made me happy for her and her family. Gave me peace and solace.

Marcy, exiting the theatre in a small crowd of people and accompanied by what seemed a new beau already, one she described in his introduction as "award-winning," both as a photojournalist as well as an artist. Marcy herself had sold songs, one of which was already on its way to becoming a country music radio hit. "Top twenty, anyway."

"How wonderful. Have you gone to Nashville, then?"

"No—a couple of months ago, I moved to New York."

A longstanding dream of mine, unfulfilled. "Have an office in the Brill Building?"

"Hah—I wish. Maybe if I have another hit or two."

To my delight I find that two of her songs have been recorded by up-and-coming pop vocalists, a new personal peak and triumph—and who knew how much money she could make.

She told me the names of her songs. "Actually, one's a pop tune. A new song. About heartbreak."

"Now there's a subject for a country song. If I ever heard one."

"Still kinda wish it was me I was hearing on the radio. But some money, that'll be a plus."

"No doubt—but you know, you deserve it."

"Do I?"

"You proved that there's something to be said for tenacity."

A look crossed her face—*yeah, sure.*

I shook the hand of the photographer, who seemed keen to compete with Marcy's achievement by detailing for me his relevant, recent artistic triumphs, including a show at a gallery here in town that Marcy had helped arrange to coincide with their visit, a gallery I hadn't heard of—as someone so immersed in the arts one would think I'd know all such places by name, but Columbia's been on the move as an arts hub for some time now. We have so many galleries and writer's groups and music events and theatre productions going all the time that it's difficult to keep up.

I congratulated the gent, Phil, who cut a dashing figure in leather jacket and tight jeans, a hint of wintergreen Altoid on his breath, manly stubble on his cheeks. Sensing body language from Marcy, he twirled his keys, gave me a squint-eyed look of suspicion, said he'd go around and get the car. And how nice to meet me.

In Phil's absence, I asked Marcy what sorts of photographs her new man took.

"He works with shadows—is that how one would describe it?" she asked, pondering. "Phil shoots shadows. Isn't that just the most interesting thing you've ever heard?"

"Marvelous. But—what about—?"

"Duncan?"

"How have you been?" Marcy, deflecting the question and holding her face in a bright, forced smile that I knew withheld much deeper emotions. Or so the narcissist in me hoped. "You and Opal happy?"

"Yes, very much so," but it was her and DD I wanted to discuss. I pressed.

"Eh. If we must." She reported that her romance with Duncan Devereaux had sputtered and faltered. Her index finger, spinning next to the temple. "Dude's got issues."

"Don't all the troubled artists."

"Hey," hands on hips. "Speak for yourself." A softness came over her face. A hint of the old affection between us, bittersweet. "Congratulations, by the way. I'd've been there at the wedding, but I was getting moved in."

"We missed you."

"And I you. Cort, I—" Her eyes became dewy. "I don't know what to say. Except, we had a lovely time together. Didn't we?"

I told her that I thought so. Ephemeral, but one that would always linger in my memory. "It's difficult for me to fully love anyone. After what happened to my parents—"

"You don't have anything to explain. And this didn't have anything to do with you. All me. I screwed us up."

"It wasn't meant to be. From both sides of the coin."

"I suppose not."

"No."

Before the moment could get any more squishy, Marcy's beau pulled up in a Mercedes, tooted the horn. We hugged, tight. A bloom of the old heat, now forever bittersweet.

As she climbed into the car she paused, glancing around at the restaurants and bustle on the sidewalks, her face color-struck in streaks of pastel from the neon of the refurbished movie marquee: "This cow town, it's really turned into something. I'm not sure I ever expected to see Main Street so busy again. So alive."

"Enough of us, you included, imagined it this way again. An aggregation of good will, I think."

Her smile, crooked and skeptical. "Hope and change?"

A jingled the quarters in my pocket. "Took long enough. A hundred and fifty years or so."

"Your writer guy—what was his name?"

I had to search my mind. "William Gilmore Simms?"

Nodding. "He'd be proud, wouldn't he."

Another bloom inside, this one more fulsome than sad. "Most assuredly."

I waved farewell, pledging to see and duly admire Phil's photographic exhibit. In thanks he gave me an appreciative power fist, held aloft as they roared away toward the Confederate memorial on the State House grounds. "You rock, dude," his voice echoing down the canyon of the buildings. Marcy, stealing one last glance back at me. Smiling. I gave her a thumb's up. Wished her well.

Left to continue my stroll along Main Street, I noted the lights and dome of the capitol visible down the corridor of Columbia's main drag, and with it, what was otherwise so apparent: a vibrant, growing arts district there in the heart of the city, progress that would've surely delighted and surprised my dear departed mentor and advocate.

But not without a great and last cost: There, the bank lobby where Leora died, the thought of which caused a gust of a sigh to blow through my soul; here, the corner where Rick's stage fell that same day. An eventful, tumultuous year—enough to inspire a novel.

As for the job offer with COPA to replace my one-time mentor, of course I had to say no—when would I write? As a concession, however, I did offer to judge the next fiction competition, an honor I'd enjoyed in the past. Having just received the blind-copy entries for short story finalist, I was compelled only last night by one particular story, about an autograph and memorabilia hound of a rock music fan, told in a bracing and rat-a-tat prose style that gripped me from first page to last, that has the feel of a winner about it. I can't for the life of me imagine why it all seems so familiar.

Rounding the corner to see the OPEN sign in D'Alessandro's front window go dark, I whistled my way down the shadowy block in time to see the staff and their boss come tumbling out together in a chatty, demonstrative knot. The new arts district had brought much business to the downtown restaurants, but tired or not, these youngsters were off work and ready to hit the watering holes to unwind.

"Well, I'll be darned if it isn't world famous Southern scribe, Cortland Beauchamp." My wife's cheery greeting warmed me anew. "Come give us a squeeze."

"Greetings." The grit of the sidewalk crunched under the hard leather soles of my Weejuns. After kissing Opal, I adjusted my glasses and bounced on the balls of my feet. "How was work, my dearest darling?"

"We'll make it to next week. Robbing Peter to pay Paul. Same as it ever was."

"Sometimes the same-old is a good thing."

Not that our life is that way. We've been married a few months now, and still haven't figured out where to live. For now, we alternate between my cabin and her house in the countryside closer to Edgewater County.

"How was your walk?"

"Distracted. A lot on my mind these days."

Opal held my eyes, her gaze filled with anticipation. "Me too."

I wondered what was going through her mind. "Such as?"

She shrugged, bit her lower lip. Looked fetching, as yummy as her cuisine.

I felt gripped, suddenly, by a compulsion: I wanted bitter, weak, day-old Bunn machine restaurant coffee. I could taste it already. "Feel like having a cup?"

"Cuppa joe? At this hour? Maybe."

"IHOP? Waffle House?"

She shook her head. "Rather go home with my husband. Really tired."

I told her that as hard as she worked, she ought to be tired. "Bless your heart."

"It's more than work, I think."

We'd arrived at the parking lot. I hit the clicker. The car barked a sharp, naysaying, atonal chirp—I'd hit the wrong button. I asked her to elaborate.

"You're not going to believe this fucking shit."

"What?"

"Drumroll."

"What, *what?*"

"Don't kill me. But—" Sheepish, giggling, spinning around and throwing her hands in the air like a lithe, graceful dancer: "Cort, I do believe I'm pregnant."

The end . . .

ACKNOWLEDGEMENTS

These books don't write themselves, nor are they polished and published without an enormous amount of effort and assistance from outside the author's mind. In that spirit, I'm forever indebted to the following literary angels who helped make LTGPA possible: Chris Compton, Steve Armato, Michael Spawn, Travis Bland, Lorna Festa, Jenni Brennison, Carla Damron, Darren Woodlief, Devon Jeremy, Cindi Boiter and Bob Jolley of Muddy Ford Press and The Jasper Project, William Glenn Christopher, Bentz and May Kirby, and Greg Bates for a songwriting lyrics assist; Merritt McNeely, Michael Miller, Belinda Gergel and the rest of my friends and colleagues on the "Hootie and the Blowfish" committee; and fellow merchants, customers, and coffee shop denizens in my neighborhood, Five Points (referred in my fictionalized Columbia as "the Old Market"). Most obviously, I hope, affection and thanks go out to the Columbia arts community of which I'm honored and proud to be a part.

Major placements in literary heaven are also secured for the Mind Harvest Press team, without whose help this volume might not have seen publication at all: Elizabeth Leverton, Marc Cardwell, and Catherine Shuler.

Last, thanks to my dad David McCallister and the rest of my family, especially my late mother, Andria McCallister, to whom all my works are lovingly dedicated in spirit if not letter; and of course my immediate and present family in the form of Jenn McCallister and our eight beloved cats, one of whom, Mickey, left us right as the work on this book was finished—a heartbreak to accompany the pleasure and triumph of seeing a dream come to fruition. Love and gratitude goes out to all—I couldn't have achieved any of this without you.

Return to James D. McCallister's
"EDGEWATER COUNTY, SC"

in

KING'S HIGHWAY
FELLOW TRAVELER

and

DOGS OF PARSONS HOLLOW (2017)
RECONSTRUCTION OF THE FABLES (2018)
DIXIANA (2018)
DOWN IN DIXIANA (2019)
DIXIANA DARLING (2019)
MANSION OF HIGH GHOSTS (2020)

DIXIANA

www.ingramcontent.com/pod-product-compliance
Lightning Source LLC
Chambersburg PA
CBHW071231190726
48292CB00007B/2241